THE
URSULINA

ALSO BY BRIAN FREEMAN

The Deep, Deep Snow

THE FROST EASTON SERIES
The Crooked Street
The Voice Inside
The Night Bird

THE JONATHAN STRIDE SERIES
Funeral for a Friend
*Alter Ego**
Marathon
Goodbye to the Dead
The Cold Nowhere
Turn to Stone (e-novella)
Spitting Devil (e-short story)
The Burying Place
In the Dark
Stalked
Stripped
Immoral

THE CAB BOLTON SERIES
Season of Fear
The Bone House
*Cab Bolton also appears in *Alter Ego*

THE URSULINA

BRIAN FREEMAN

BLACK STONE
PUBLISHING

Printed in the United States of America

First edition: 2022
ISBN 978-1-6651-0969-7
Fiction / Mystery & Detective / Police Procedural

Version 1

CIP data for this book is available
from the Library of Congress

Blackstone Publishing
31 Mistletoe Rd.
Ashland, OR 97520

www.BlackstonePublishing.com

For Marcia

I know you'll never forgive me for what I did.

Believe me, I'm not trying to convince you that I'm a better person than I am, or asking you to find any sympathy for me in your heart. I won't even ask that you not hate me. It's too late for that.

No, I just want you to understand how I came to the place I did and why I felt I had no other choice. I'm sure you've asked yourself that question many times over the years.

Why? Why did I do it?

Well, sweetheart, this is the answer. Now I can finally tell you. But be patient with me, because some secrets are difficult to share and prefer the shadows to the light of day.

I was only twenty-six years old when the monster came back to Black Wolf County. The answers you want begin with the death of a man named Gordon Brink at Christmastime that year. However, if you really want to understand everything that happened—and I'm taking a leap of faith that you do—you have to go even farther back in my life.

Years back, to the night I met the Ursulina face-to-face.

So let's start there.

We'd gone boating in the national forest, just me, my father, and my older brother. I was ten years old then. We spent the days on the lake, them with lines in the water, me with a book in my hands. At night, we'd pitch a tent, and my dad would grill the fish he caught, along with mushrooms he'd picked, showing me which ones were safe and which ones weren't. Then, around the fire, we'd sing Rolling Stones songs. Probably my most vivid memory of my father is him channeling Mick on "Get Off of My Cloud" while chewing on a mouthful of beef jerky.

That camping trip is nostalgic for me. The three of us rarely spent much time together as a family because we were too busy making ends meet. I never really knew my mother; she died of leukemia when I was three. And yes, I know that only adds to the horror of what I did to you. With my father behind the wheel of a truck for weeks at a time, and my brother already taking jobs at sixteen, I had to fend for myself. By the time I was seven, I was biking back and forth to school alone. At ten, I was doing most of the cooking in the house.

It was 1969. The world was going crazy in other places, but in Black Wolf County, life went on without any real unrest. A couple of local boys died in Vietnam, and we mourned them and then went back to work. We had no choice. To this day, the joke in Black Wolf County is that we call it that because the wolf is never far from our door. Jobs have always been few and far between here. We're remote, a county of dirt roads and dense trees, where close neighbors are measured in miles. Back then, tourists hadn't really discovered us, other than a couple of lakeside resorts, so life and work revolved around the local bar, the high school, and the church.

And the copper mine.

Our lives rose and fell with the fortunes of the copper mine. We didn't have much, but one thing we had a lot of was land.

Land was cheap and vast. To a ten-year-old on that camping trip, the whole forest felt as if it belonged to the three of us. I don't recall seeing another soul while we were away. Of course, that didn't mean we were the only creatures to be found there. The wilderness teemed with raccoons, deer, wolves, bears, moose, and cougars. We'd find their tracks and scat wherever we went, and even when we didn't see them, we knew they were out there watching us.

That was why, when I left our tent in the middle of the night, I took my father's gun with me for protection. I'd been shooting for years. If you live here, you know how to shoot. It's not optional.

Our tent was pitched near the shore of a large lake shaped like a sunflower, with inlets sprouting from its round center like petals. I stood by the water for a while, scratching the mosquito bites on my arms and legs. The moon was full, making the night bright. I could see very clearly the quiet dark water and the silhouettes of fir trees crowding the fringe of the lake. Somewhere close to me, an owl hooted. I scanned the night sky to find him, but he was hidden in the trees. I've always felt a special connection to owls. Looking back, I wonder if the owl was giving me a warning about what was waiting for me in the woods. But I didn't listen. I just headed into the forest so I could do my business far from the campsite.

I carried a flashlight in one hand and the loaded Colt revolver in the other. The gun with its extended barrel was almost as long as my forearm. I wore hand-me-down shorts that had belonged to my brother when he was much younger than me, plus a ratty white tank top that swam on my skinny frame. I hadn't developed yet. Not that I ever really would. My black hair was long and as scraggly as a witch in a windstorm. On tiptoes, I didn't clear five feet, which made it easier to walk, because I was shorter than most of the dangling tree branches.

Ahead of me, I found a small clearing. Lightning had felled an old-growth oak, scorching the bark into charcoal and taking down several young birches as it fell. The ground was soft with leaves. I *located a hollow where I could squat and do what I needed to do. I had to put the flashlight and the gun at my feet, so I could balance my hands on my knobby knees. The thick crowns of the trees threw a blanket between me and the moonlit sky, so with the flashlight off, I was literally as blind as if a hood were covering my eyes.*

While I was in that awkward position, I heard a noise.

First came the snuffly snort of a breath, like a huffing sound. It was loud and close. Then snapping and rustling followed, the sound of undergrowth being crushed in the woods just in front of me. And then, worst of all, the noise stopped. The silence meant that whatever was out there could hear and smell me and had paused to investigate.

The most dangerous animals are stealthy hunters who don't like to be heard, so my first thought was: bear. That didn't really bother me very much. Black bears are common around here, and it wasn't cub season, when the mothers get protective. Once he got a whiff of me, I figured he'd be on his way. Even so, I finished up what I was doing as quickly as I could, then felt around the ground and retrieved my flashlight and gun. I hadn't heard anything to tell me that the animal was moving away, which meant that I still had company somewhere close by.

I turned on the flashlight. Slowly, I lit up the trees, first one way, then the other. I sang a song under my breath—"Jumpin' Jack Flash"—partly to make myself feel better, partly to give the shy bear a reason to lumber off to other parts of the forest.

Just to be safe, I also used both thumbs to drag back the hammer on the revolver and cock it.

Huffffff. Another quick, loud, angry snort.

The landscape crackled under the weight of heavy paws.

I swung my flashlight toward the noise. At the end of the beam, I glimpsed something moving between the trees, maybe twenty or thirty feet away. The beast was there and gone in a blink. I saw it for only a second, but I had never seen anything like it. It was most definitely not a bear. It walked on two legs the way people do, more than seven feet tall, with a thick, matted coat of shaggy orange-brown fur. It looked right at me when it saw the light, and I saw the reflection of its eyes like two bloodred suns.

Now I was scared.

I stood alone in the clearing, absolutely frozen in place, unable to move a muscle. I wished I would hear those thunderous footfalls head away, but the beast had stopped again. Another loud growl rumbled out of the darkness, and the sound had a menace to it, like a threat.

I was trying to decide what to do when I heard a familiar shout not far away. It was my father.

"Rebecca?"

He was looking for me, thank God. He would save me. I put my head down and charged back into the woods, making as much noise as I could, my flashlight beam bouncing crazily as I ran. I crashed through brambles that grabbed at my tangled black hair and scraped their woody fingers across my bare arms and legs.

I hoped that the noise would scare the beast away, but it didn't.

There it was. Its giant shadow loomed in front of me and blocked my path. I didn't dare bring up my flashlight to see it clearly. All I could make out was its shape, hunched and huge, twice my size. We were so close that I could smell its stench and feel the heat of its breath. With a swipe of a paw, it could slash off my face. I tried to scream, but there was no sound in my throat. My whole body shook.

I lifted the revolver, struggling to keep it steady. My quivering finger slid over the trigger. I dropped the flashlight to the ground and balanced my wrist with my other hand. At that range, even a scared little girl couldn't miss.

But I couldn't do it. I just couldn't.

I could not kill this thing, which had done nothing to me. Somehow I think it sensed that, as if we had a truce between us. He would not hurt me, and I would not hurt him.

"Rebecca!"

My father shouted again, much closer to us.

At the sound of his voice, the monster stomped past me. The sharp claws on one of its paws scraped my arm as he passed, drawing blood. I held my breath, wondering if he would carry me off with him—but no. The beast vanished into the trees, leaving me behind. When I saw the beam of a flashlight, I called out, and seconds later, my father appeared in the woods. His face dissolved into relief when he saw me.

"Rebecca! What are you doing out here?"

I shrugged, as if it were no big deal. "I had to pee."

"Well, you scared me half to death. Come back to camp."

"Yeah, okay."

"Are you hurt? You're bleeding."

"I scratched myself, that's all."

I followed him back to our tent, where he bandaged the cuts on my arm. After that, I pretended to sleep, but my eyes stayed wide open until morning. The rest of the night, the rest of the trip, was uneventful. I had no more strange encounters. Overnight, I would listen for the hufffffff that told me it was nearby, but all I heard was the hooting owl somewhere in the trees.

I found myself wondering where the beast was, and what it really was, and why it hadn't killed me.

Somehow I knew—I already knew even as a girl—that we would meet again.

I never told my father what I saw. Not him, not my brother, not anyone. That moment in the woods has always been my secret. You're the first person I've ever told, sweetheart, but it's important that you know the truth.

You see, this is what you must remember as I tell you the rest of the story.

The Ursulina is real.

PART ONE
YOUR FATHER

CHAPTER ONE

When you're the only woman deputy in the county sheriff's department, and it's Christmas Eve, who do you think is the lucky one who pulls the overnight shift? Yes, it was me.

The snow fell in huge flakes, promising us a white Christmas at the end of a brown December. Around ten o'clock that Monday evening, I was alone in my cruiser on the back roads of Black Wolf County, singing along to a cassette of Mitch Miller carols that my father had sent me from a truck stop somewhere in Wyoming. My brother was away in the oil fields of Texas. I was lonely and fighting a cold and trying to take my mind off the fact that my life was falling apart.

This was 1984. I'm sure you can do the math. You were still almost a year away from being born.

You might think the holiday would make for a quiet night on patrol, but you'd be wrong. Christmas does weird things to people. My first call was to deal with Darius Stedman, who was moonwalking to Michael Jackson on the boom box, in the parking lot of the 126 Bar. Mr. Stedman was wearing a Santa hat and *only* a Santa hat. The temperature was seven degrees outside, and body parts freeze pretty quickly in that kind of weather. So I turned on the siren and went screaming toward the 126 to make sure that Mr. Stedman's various appendages didn't start snapping off.

It's not like he was a regular in the county drunk tank. We had plenty of those. No, he was forty-three years old, a solid citizen, and my former high school science teacher. I liked him. However, he'd lost his wife to a heart condition over the summer, and the holidays have a way of bringing those things roaring back, particularly when alcohol is involved. When I got to the 126, a crowd of bar-goers was cheering as Mr. Stedman danced to "Billie Jean." Ricky, my husband of four years, was among them, but we ignored each other like strangers. I broke up the party, wrapped Mr. Stedman in a blanket, and took him back to his house to thaw him out and sober him up. He spent the next half hour sobbing to me about his wife over coffee.

It made me think how nice it must be to love someone so deeply that it hurts that much to lose them. I'd never experienced an emotion like that, and I wouldn't until the following year.

Until you, sweetheart.

I left when Mr. Stedman finally fell asleep on his sofa. I had to drive by the 126 on my way back to the station, so I decided to stop to talk to Ricky. I was sure he was still at the bar. He was always there, drinking up my county salary and flirting with the eighteen-year-old waitresses. The 126 was our local dirty dive. It took its name from its location on Highway 126 about ten miles outside the county seat, a town called Random. During the summers, they had strip nights and wet T-shirt contests. Dart games turned into knife fights. Cocaine was snorted in the bathroom. And yet almost everyone in the county, from parents to preachers, came in for pizza and drinks at the 126 several times a week, because there was nowhere else to go.

Sundays were typically movie night at the bar, and that always drew a crowd. Yesterday, they'd shown *Trading Places*, which Ricky didn't want to miss because of Jamie Lee Curtis and her boobs. I'd used my cold as an excuse to skip it, but Ricky and I had also had a big fight before he went off to see the movie. I'd lost my cool and said things I never meant to say out loud. Like using the D word—divorce—for the first time.

It had been almost two years since Ricky got fired from the mine for assaulting his supervisor. With no unemployment, we were barely scraping by, and we'd only made the December mortgage payment because my dad gave me two hundred dollars. January was coming and the mortgage was due again, and Ricky was no closer to finding work. However, the fight was less about him and less about money than it was about me. I was struggling with Big Things. Who I was. The mistakes I'd made. What I needed to do to reclaim my life. More and more, I was thinking about a future without Ricky, but the time to say so wasn't in the midst of an argument while we were both drunk and angry. So that Monday night, with it being Christmas Eve and all, I decided to stop at the bar and see if we could make peace, at least for the holidays.

Despite my good intentions, though, I didn't get a chance to see him. Another call came in before I even made it back to the 126, so I had to change my plans. This time, the call came from Sandra Thoreau.

I usually heard from Sandra a couple of times a month about vandalism at her house. She was the lead plaintiff in a sexual harassment lawsuit that two dozen women had filed against the Langford copper mine, and given that the mine was the largest employer in the county, Sandra wasn't exactly popular. The men around here made sure she knew it. She'd had obscene graffiti scrawled on her house so many times that she didn't even bother to remove it anymore. In fact, she'd been adding to it herself by painting anatomically correct drawings of some of the lesser-endowed mine workers, with their names attached. Her motto was to give as good as she got.

I found Sandra sitting on the open tailgate of her pickup when I got to her house. She wore a long, fraying wool coat over a blue nightgown and had a cigarette between her lips and a can of Old Style in her hand. When she exhaled, steam and smoke mixed together in the frigid air. She wore earmuffs over her greasy brown hair and worn moccasins on her feet. Behind her, I could see that the front and back windows of her truck had been shattered by what was probably a shotgun blast. Broken glass littered the fresh snow, and the bits of glass twinkled thanks to the blinking Christmas lights that decorated her house.

"Merry Christmas, Rebecca," Sandra greeted me. She flicked a chunk of glass off the tailgate like a cat's-eye. "Ho ho ho."

"The elves have been busy," I said. "Did you see who did this?"

"I could give you some guesses, but no, I didn't see them. I was in bed and heard the shot. By the time I got outside, they were gone. I could hear tires screeching up the highway."

"Is Henry okay?"

"Yeah, he slept through it. That kid could sleep through a tornado."

Henry was Sandra's eight-year-old son. Yes, no kidding, Henry Thoreau. I was pretty sure Sandra had never read *Walden* and that she'd picked the name Henry because of Henry Winkler and the Fonz. But it was still funny.

Sandra was a single mother and absolutely devoted to that boy. Nobody around here knew who Henry's father was, and to tell you the truth, I'm not even sure if Sandra did, either. She'd slept her way through most of the men in Black Wolf County, married or not, so there were plenty of suspects. But raising a kid on her own was no picnic, and that was why Sandra had taken a job at the mine seven years earlier. It paid well, and she needed the money. After she blazed the trail there, other women followed. Unfortunately, in the eyes of a lot of people around here, women working at the mine were taking badly needed jobs away from the men.

You can probably guess that they felt the same way about a woman working as a sheriff's deputy. So while Sandra was no angel, the two of us had some things in common. As different as we were, she was one of my favorite people. It took guts to stick it out at the mine and even more guts to complain about how the men treated her. In those days, sexual harassment wasn't something women took to court. The dirty jokes, the daily come-ons, the innuendos about sex lives and periods, the leering looks, the wolf whistles, the little touches and massages, the comments about legs and boobs and asses—that was just the ordinary price of being a woman at work.

"Have you had any threats recently?" I asked her.

Sandra shrugged. "What day is it?"

I walked around her truck but found no useful evidence to tell me who'd done this. I stood near Sandra's modest rambler and put my hands on my hips to survey the long driveway and the highway between the trees. Snow had begun to turn the pines into white soldiers. There were tire tracks where a car had pulled up behind the pickup, but they weren't clear enough to help me. Like Sandra, I could probably name twenty boys around here who might have pulled a stunt like this, but I'd never be able to prove it.

"If you didn't see anybody, I can't really do much except write it up," I admitted.

"I know. I wouldn't have bothered to call you, except Norm says I should report everything. He wants a record of it for the trial."

"Yeah, okay."

Norm Foltz was the local lawyer handling the litigation for Sandra and the other women working at the mine. They were trying to turn their harassment claims into a class action lawsuit, and although the mine had been trying to shut down the case for more than three years, Norm had finally beaten the skeptics by getting the class certified. The betting at that point was whether the mining company would offer a settlement or take its chances at trial. I had my money on a trial. The mine owners hated these women, Sandra in particular, and they were out to win.

I heard the static of the radio in my car. More Yuletide cheer was waiting for me somewhere in the county. "I'll write up a report and send you a copy. You can pass it along to Norm."

"Thanks." Sandra lit another cigarette; she was in a mood to talk. "I heard you and Ricky got into it. Money problems, huh?"

"Good news travels fast."

"Well, everybody was talking about it during the movie last night."

"I don't care about gossip," I replied.

"Well, you can say that now, but I know what it feels like to be on the receiving end. Believe me, honey, the games can get pretty mean."

"I know."

I headed for my car, but Sandra called after me. "Hey, Rebecca? Aren't you going to ask me where I was?"

"What do you mean?"

"I heard Gordon Brink's little blond ice queen got the full *Carrie* treatment. Somebody nailed her with a gallon of pig's blood. I sort of figured I'd be the prime suspect, what with Brink representing the mine. But you never came to see me."

"Did you do it?"

"No. I was in the pit all day."

"Yeah, I checked," I told her. "That's why I didn't bother coming to see you. I don't suppose you know who *did* do it?"

"Absolutely no idea," Sandra replied, snickering through her cigarette smoke. "But I'm just sick about it."

"I can see that."

I started for my cruiser again, my boots crunching in the snow, but Sandra wasn't done.

"Rebecca?" she said, with sharpness in her voice. "Don't feel sorry for Brink or his wife or any of those bastards. They killed my dog. I didn't report it, but that's what they did."

"Are you sure?"

"I let Pogo out two weeks ago when I got home from work. He never came back. We never saw him again. You try explaining that to a sobbing eight-year-old boy. The mine people and their lawyers are sons of bitches. I hope every one of them rots in hell."

Sandra wiped a tear from her face. She liked to pretend that she was hard as nails, because as soon as the men at the mine smelled weakness, they'd be all over her. But I knew that, deep down, much of her toughness was an act. I knew, because I often had to wear the same disguise in the sheriff's department.

"I'm sorry about Pogo," I told her gently, "but you know, we lose a lot of animals around here. This is wild country. It doesn't necessarily mean it was Gordon Brink or the people at the mine."

"The next day at work, I found a bag of doggy treats in my locker," Sandra went on.

I shut my mouth.

She was right. Of course, she was right. The games were mean.

"I'm telling you, Rebecca, these people are evil. They care about money, they care about winning, and they don't care about anything else. I don't give a shit what happens to them. I really don't. They deserve whatever they get."

*

Christmas Eve continued on its strange path from there.

I spent the next several hours following up on other holiday problems around the county. Emily and Kevin Pipewell called in a panic to report that their twin girls were missing. When I got there, I spotted the girls eating graham crackers up on the roof near the chimney, where they were waiting for Santa. We got them down and back in bed.

Four-year-old Denny Bublitz called because his parents were sleeping. He'd flushed his goldfish to see what would happen, but after it disappeared, he wanted me to look for it. I told him that Mr. Jenkins at the pet store was in charge of rescuing flushed fishies, and that Denny's parents would be able to get his goldfish back from Mr. Jenkins after Christmas.

Louisa Shepherd, who was eighty-one and still spry enough to chop her own firewood with an ax, called to let me know that she'd baked Christmas spritz cookies and did I want some? Yes, I did.

And finally, Al Poplar called to say he had a gun and was going to kill himself. He'd made the same call half a dozen times since Thanksgiving, and every time I'd gone over there, I'd discovered that the gun was empty. I stopped by again just after midnight and spent almost an hour talking him out of his holiday depression before he handed me the Smith & Wesson.

This time, the gun was cocked and fully loaded.

It reminded me of what my partner, Darrell, always said was the most important lesson of police work: you never know.

By two in the morning, most of the people in Black Wolf

County were finally asleep, which meant I had my overnight lull. I drove back to the town of Random and parked on the empty street. All the Christmas lights were on, making the town look like a Hollywood movie set in the 1930s. Beyond the two blocks of old brick buildings that made up the town center, the national forest loomed at the outskirts, as dark as it must have been for Jonah inside the whale. I got out of my cruiser and crossed Main Street, and mine were the only tracks in the fresh bed of snow.

Random. This was my hometown. I'd lived here my whole life.

Do you wonder why it's called that? A lot of people do. I think they expect there must have been a Jedediah Random who built the first church here. Or maybe there was some Indian, French, German, or Swedish word that got mangled into Random over the years. The real answer is, we don't know. No one can explain why we're here or why we're called what we are. Historians say the word Random started showing up on maps a couple of centuries ago, but they don't know who first made a settlement here. We have no river and no pioneer crossroads to explain our reason for being. The copper mine keeps the town going, but Random was here long before the mine.

I like to think the name explains itself. Random. I'm convinced there was a settler with a sense of humor who is still laughing at us as we try to puzzle it out. He knew life was simply random. It's random where you're born. It's random who you meet along the way.

It's random what you encounter when you're walking in the woods.

I let myself inside the sheriff's office, which was combined with our city hall and the county courthouse in one somber old building with a clock tower, a cupola, and a huge marble statue of Lady Justice. I actually enjoyed the Christmas shift, because I had the building mostly to myself. Our tiny office smelled like cigarettes and the menthol rub that our department secretary, Mrs. Mannheim, slathered on her knees. I turned on the office lights, which flickered on the water-stained ceiling, and I made my way past the desks of the other deputies.

My desk was the smallest. It was located immediately next to the men's bathroom, with an unobstructed view of the urinals whenever the door opened. The sheriff hadn't put me there by accident. He was sending me a message: See what we have that you don't? You're missing a vital piece of equipment to work here, and it ain't your gun.

I dug in the bottom drawer of my desk for my hidden stash of fudge, which was my weakness. Chocolate, with walnuts and dried cherries. I popped a cassette of *Synchronicity* into my tape recorder and listened to Sting, who was watching me with every breath I took. I lit up a Marlboro and relaxed. I eased back in my chair and thought about calling my father, but I didn't even know where he was staying that night. It was silly, but I wanted him to tell me the poem he'd made up for me, to make me feel better after my mom died. I could still remember it word for word.

Things like that stick with you through the years. The good things and the bad things—I know that, sweetheart.

Because Dad wasn't around, I recited the beginning of the poem out loud to myself:

> *Rebecca Colder, Rebecca Colder*
> *She's a little stronger*
> *She's a little bolder*
> *Rebecca Colder, Rebecca Colder*
> *The world can't stop her*
> *The world can't hold her*

Of course, I wasn't Rebecca Colder anymore. I was Rebecca Todd, married to Ricky Todd. The rhymes of the poem didn't really work for me in my married life. Even so, I recited it a couple more times in the quiet of the office, and I thought for a long, long time about the woman I'd become.

I had finished my third cigarette when the phone rang. When that happens in the middle of the night, it's never good news.

"Deputy Todd," I said when I picked it up.

"Deputy, this is Erica Brink."

I was distracted and didn't say anything immediately. In fact, I was silent for so long that she said it again.

"Deputy? Are you there? It's Erica Brink."

"What can I do for you, Mrs. Brink?" I replied finally.

"I just got back to the house. I've been away ever since— well, since the incident with the pig's blood. I went to visit my parents."

"All right."

"The thing is, I can't find Gordon," she went on. "I couldn't reach him on the phone last night, and he's not in the house. His son, Jay, hasn't seen him either. His car is here, all of his things are here, but he's missing. I'm worried that something has happened to him."

CHAPTER TWO

Erica Brink met me at the highway, where a dirt road led to the house they'd been renting for the last four months. She had a flashlight in her hand to signal me, because it was easy to miss the break in the trees on a snowy, pitch-black night. I pulled onto the shoulder, and Erica climbed into the passenger seat beside me.

"Thank you for coming so quickly," she said.

"Of course."

I drove slowly toward the house. Erica and I didn't speak, but I could feel tension radiating from her. Not that anyone could tell by how she looked. When I shot a quick glance across the seat, I saw that her wheat-field curls looked as fluffy as if she'd just come from the salon. She was nestled inside a fur coat that probably cost what I made in a month. We were the same age, twenty-six years old, but she made me feel much younger and out of her league. Her face had a perfect symmetry, and her cool-blue eyes didn't hide the superiority she felt when she looked at someone like me. I was the girl at the Tanya Tucker concert, and Erica was Symphony Ball all the way.

But don't mistake her for a squeaky-voiced blond toy. Erica was also savvy and tough, which you probably have to be to steal a corporate attorney away from his wife of fifteen years. It's one thing to be the mistress. That's easy work. But to get the ring? That takes a ruthless cunning you can't help but respect.

I'd met Erica once before, a week earlier, when she was dripping with pig's blood swiped from a local butcher. Somebody had jerry-rigged a bucket and rope over the front door and waited in the woods to douse whoever came outside. I assumed that Gordon had been the intended target, but Erica wound up in the wrong place at the wrong time. The fact that she didn't go to pieces told me a lot about her. I'd interviewed both of them together, and Erica didn't freak out or shed a single tear. She sat on the front steps, covered in animal blood that had begun to freeze, and told me the story with a kind of frigid, furious calm.

Gordon was the one who looked ready to throw up the whole time I was there.

"Do you know who assaulted me?" Erica asked, as if she'd guessed that I was thinking about our previous encounter.

"I'm sorry, I don't."

She turned her head, piercing me in the gloom of the car with her blue eyes. "Do you not know, or do you not care?"

"I do care, but the fact is, nobody's talking."

"We both know Sandra Thoreau was behind it," Erica replied.

"Well, if she was, it's not likely that I'll ever be able to prove it. Plenty of people hate this lawsuit, but Sandra has people who are on her side, too. Even the ones who want to see her lose don't want to see the mine win."

Erica offered a thin smile. "Gordon said the same thing. He didn't want to call the police after I was attacked. He said it would just make Sandra's people feel like they'd won some sort of victory. They've been harassing us for months, you know. I was willing to let it slide for other things, but not this time. I called the sheriff myself to report it. No offense, but I wasn't surprised when he sent a junior deputy. And a woman, too. Believe me, I got the message. I should just take a shower and shut up."

I wanted to tell her she was wrong, but in fact, the sheriff had used almost those exact words when he'd sent me out here.

We reached the end of the dirt road, where a large clearing had been carved out of the wilderness. The house that Gordon Brink was renting was four stories high, a log-and-flagstone home that looked like an old national park resort hotel. There were several outbuildings on the property, including a barn and machine shed, a hunting lodge in which to clean the guns and hang the dead animals, and a guest cottage that was larger than my own house. The property was a summer home for the retired president of the mine. While he wintered in Florida, Gordon had taken it over to get ready for the upcoming trial.

Erica and I got out of my cruiser. The door of the nearby garage was open, and I saw matching Mercedes sedans parked inside. His and hers. One was spotless, and the other was covered in snow and road spray.

"So tell me what's going on," I said.

Erica nodded at her car, which was the dirty one. "Like I told you on the phone, I got back here about two hours ago. I spent several days with my parents in Minnesota, but I drove all day to spend Christmas with Gordon and Jay. But Gordon's not here. As you can see, his car is still in the garage, but I've searched the entire house, and I can't find him anywhere."

"It's a little early to push the panic button," I told her. "Isn't it possible he spent Christmas Eve with one of the other lawyers?"

"You mean, is he shacking up with a woman on the team because I was away?" she asked in a chilly voice. "If that's what you're thinking, then no. Most of the other members of the legal team went home for Christmas. I called the ones who stayed in the area. He's not with them. And he has no friends among the locals. Plus, Gordon knew I was coming back tonight. He said he would stay up and work until I got home."

"When did you last talk to him?"

"Sunday afternoon. He didn't have any plans to leave the house over the Christmas weekend. I tried calling again last night, but I didn't reach him. Then I tried again before I left this morning and I stopped to call from the road, too. There was no answer. Trust me, Deputy, this is not like Gordon."

"Did you talk to his son?" I asked.

"Of course. Jay hasn't seen Gordon since breakfast on Sunday."

"Did he say whether his father was home the whole time?"

"That's what he told me. He never saw the car leave."

"He and Gordon have been home together for two days, and Jay didn't see him or talk to him?"

Erica rolled her eyes. "Their relationship is . . . difficult."

"Did you search the entire house? It's a big place."

"I did. I checked in all the usual spaces where we spend time. I also called to him on the intercom, which is wired to every room. When he didn't answer, I got worried, so I checked each room methodically. Every room, closet, bathroom. He's not in the house."

When Erica Brink said she'd done something methodically, I believed her.

"The most likely explanation is still that he's with someone else in town," I said. "If you haven't heard from him by morning—"

She cut me off midsentence. "I *am* concerned, Deputy. I don't want to wait until morning. Gordon is not *with* anyone. Last week, I was the target of a humiliating assault, and now I get back home to find my husband missing. He's the lead defense attorney in a lawsuit that has generated countless threats from people in this area. I want to *find* him right now."

I knew she wasn't going to let me go.

I also knew that if I woke up my partner, Darrell, at three o'clock on Christmas morning, I'd better have more to show him than an angry trophy wife.

"Did you notice anything out of order in the house when you came home?" I asked. "Any sign of intruders or a break-in?"

"No."

"Any footprints in the snow? Tire tracks?"

"No. Other than my own."

"Did you check the outbuildings?"

"Yes, I walked around the entire property. I went inside all the other buildings except the guest cottage. Gordon uses that as his office."

"Why didn't you check the office? I thought you said he was going to work until you got back."

"The office is where he keeps confidential legal files on the litigation. The door is always locked when he's not there. No one else gets inside. I walked down there and checked. The lights were off."

"Still, if that's the one place you didn't go inside, I think we should check it out, don't you?"

Erica frowned with obvious reluctance. "Yes, all right."

We hiked through the snow beside the trees and needed flashlights to guide us. Erica stayed close to me. I could tell that the wilderness made her nervous, but to me, the sounds in the darkness were like old friends. And of course, I did what I always did when I was near the woods. I listened for *him*. I'd been searching the forests of Black Wolf County for years to try to find the beast again. I knew he was out there somewhere, and I had the strange sense that he was looking for me, too.

The one-story A-frame cottage that Gordon had been using as his office was on the far side of a shallow hill. In the snow, I could make out Erica's footprints where she'd come here earlier to look for her husband. The front door was locked, just as Erica had said. I knocked, but there was no answer. I circled the entire cottage and peered through each window, but the curtains were closed, and there were no lights on inside.

"I think we should go in," I said.

"I don't have a key."

"I can break a window, but I need your permission to do that. The alternative is to wait until morning to see if Gordon comes back."

Erica's face tensed with indecision. I could see that the idea of breaching her husband's private work space made her uncomfortable. That was probably one of the cardinal rules of their marriage.

Regardless, her worry won out. "Yes, okay, do it."

I told her to move away, and then I took my baton from my belt and shattered one of the front windows with a quick tap. Punching out the remaining shards, I reached in, unlocked the window, and pushed it up. I squeezed through the frame into the cottage, which was cold and had the ashy smell of a log fire. My boots crunched on broken glass. There was no sound inside, and when I did a quick survey with my flashlight, I saw nothing amiss. I unlocked the front door, and then I turned on the overhead light.

Erica looked nervous about setting foot inside. "Gordon?" she called. "Are you here?"

Her husband didn't answer.

The living space was filled with dark leather furniture and a massive fireplace that took up most of one wall. The kitchen was small, but I found half a pot of cold coffee on the counter.

There were two doors on the back wall, one closed, one open. I checked the open door, with Erica following, and it led me into a sprawling room that served as Gordon Brink's main office. File cabinets lined the rear wall, and curtains covered up a long spread of windows looking out on the forest. On the walnut desk, I found a half-smoked cigarette crushed in the ashtray and an open bottle of whiskey with an empty lowball glass beside it.

The floor was covered in a thick cream-colored carpet. Not far from the desk, I spotted reddish-brown drops dotting the shag. I bent down, rubbed one of the stains between my fingertips, and smelled a coppery odor. I looked up at Erica.

"I need to check the bedroom."

The color had drained from her face. "Okay."

"Maybe you should stay in the outer room."

"No, I want to come with you."

We returned to the living room, and I approached the closed door that led into the cottage's master suite. Weirdly, I knocked, rather than just opening it. In the silence that followed, I pushed the door inward. Barely any light flowed from the other room, but the smell hanging in the cold air told the story.

"Erica," I murmured, my own nerves raw. "Back up. Don't look."

"No, turn on the light."

I did.

Next to me, Gordon Brink's wife screamed. She stared at the abattoir inside and then covered her face to block it out.

I had to look. I had no choice.

Blood spattered every surface in the bedroom. The floors. The walls. The furniture. The curtains. The ceiling. In the middle of it all, tied to the king-size bed, was Gordon Brink, naked, dead, his eyes open in horror, his mouth gagged to keep him from crying out in agony. His entire body from skull to feet hung in ribbons, all his skin flayed with deep cuts made in crimson parallel lines.

Like the sweep of an animal's claws.

Across the pale stretch of white paint above the bed, a message had been scrawled using Gordon's blood.

Four words.

I am the Ursulina

CHAPTER THREE

"Looks like the beast is back," Ajax said, whistling with perverse admiration as he studied the kaleidoscope of blood in the bedroom. "This is some messed-up scene, huh? Man, you really don't want to piss off the Ursulina."

Ajax was the nickname for Arthur Jackson, a deputy like me, but four years older. He was tall and extremely good-looking, which he would be the first to tell you. He had full black hair sprayed neatly in place, a long sharp nose and chiseled jaw, and bedroom-brown eyes that always felt like X-rays seeing you without your clothes. He also had an impressive ability to do two things at once. While he was analyzing the murder scene, he was also cupping my ass. When I went to shoo his hand away, he gave one of my butt cheeks a hard squeeze that made me stifle a yelp of pain.

"Knock it off with talk about the Ursulina," my partner, Darrell, snapped from beside the bed, where he was studying Brink's body. "We don't need another three-ring TV circus in town. Last time we had hundreds of monster hunters combing the woods. I don't want to go through that again."

THE URSULINA   29

Ajax joined Darrell at the bed. I stayed where I was, on the far side of the room, with my arms tightly folded across my chest. I felt queasy, but I didn't dare show it. Gordon Brink lay exactly as Erica and I had found him. His arms were over his head, his wrists tied together with rope. So were his ankles. He had a friar's ring of reddish hair around a prominent bald spot, and he had the plump look of a well-fed lawyer. He'd been wearing a suit and tie before he was stripped and killed. We'd found his clothes in a pile on the other side of the bed.

"I don't know," Ajax commented with a chuckle. "Those sure look like claw marks to me."

Darrell had no patience for jokes when we had a dead body in the room. "An animal didn't do this. A human being did. Focus on the crime scene. This wasn't done with a knife. We're looking for a weapon that makes sharp, deep, even cuts."

I cleared my throat and spoke up. "It could be meat shredders."

"What?"

"Meat shredders. You know, like for pulled pork? My dad used to have a set like that. They were long and sharp, so you could dig them into the flesh. Half a dozen parallel spikes, just like we've got here. The wounds look like somebody dug into the body over and over with a ripping motion."

Ajax shook his head. "Carved up like a Thanksgiving turkey. That does not sound like a fun way to die. This had to be personal, right? Somebody must have really hated this guy to do that to him."

"Or it was set up to make us think that," Darrell replied. "Personal or not, this was a premeditated execution. If the murder weapon was something odd, then the killer came prepared. Plus, this was messy. Whoever did this must have been covered in blood, but other than the spatter Rebecca found in the office, they didn't track any of it outside the bedroom. So they must have brought along a bag to carry away their clothes, and probably a change of clothes, too."

I was impressed that Darrell had figured that all out so quickly. Then again, for a small-town cop, Darrell kept up to speed on criminal investigations the way they were done in the bigger cities. We didn't get many murders in Black Wolf County, but I already told you Darrell's philosophy.

You never know.

"We'll search the grounds when it's light for the murder weapon and anything else the killer may have left behind," Darrell went on, mostly to himself, as if he were making a shopping list in his head. "The snow won't make it easy. I also want a couple of deputies checking dumpsters behind Main Street."

"Why?" I asked.

"In case the killer dumped the bloody clothes and the weapon and hoped it would all get hauled away. The ground's frozen, so they couldn't bury them. It's a long shot, but worth a try."

"Yes, okay."

"Next thing is time of death," Darrell said. "When did you say Brink's wife last talked to him?"

"Sunday afternoon. Erica says she tried to reach her husband later that same night, but he didn't answer the phone. She called first thing Monday morning before she left Minnesota. Still no answer."

"All right, we'll see what the coroner says, but we may be looking at the murder taking place sometime Sunday evening."

"Half the town was at the 126 that night for *Trading Places*," Ajax pointed out. "We're only about ten minutes from the bar. Somebody could have slipped out without being noticed and snuck back in before the flick was over."

"We'll need to talk to everyone who was at the movie," Darrell said. "Rebecca, I also want you to get contact information for Erica Brink's family in Minnesota. See if she was where she says she was, okay? I want to make sure that she didn't come home early. Let's see if she has receipts from gas stations on the road, too."

"Absolutely."

"We need to talk to the son. Jay. According to Brink's wife, Jay said he was home this whole time?"

"That's what she told me."

"Okay. Rebecca, you come with me. We'll interview the boy together. Ajax, get started on fingerprints. I want the whole house dusted, but start with the bedroom and the office and the knobs on both sides of the front door."

I watched Ajax's face screw up with annoyance at the assignment. He wasn't used to getting the grunt work.

"Why should I do the prints?" Ajax protested. "Let me interview the kid with you."

Darrell shook his head. "I've seen you do interviews. You scare the crap out of witnesses, and they clam up. Rebecca has a better touch for these things. She knows how to get people to talk. Plus, maybe doing some real work will convince you to keep your hands off her ass. Got it?"

"Got it," Ajax replied coldly.

Darrell stalked from the bedroom, leaving me alone with Ajax, whose face was beet red.

I already told you that Ajax was the county stud. His looks usually got him whatever he wanted, and that included women. He was married to a pretty redhead named Ruby, but he'd been coming on to me since I joined the sheriff's office, even though he and my husband had been friends since grammar school. I kept telling Ricky that there was nothing between us, but when it came to Ajax, Ricky was toting around a big inferiority complex.

Ajax was as tall as anyone I'd ever met, at least six foot six, with a strong, wiry build. He had hands that were larger than my whole face, and he liked to brag that he was big all over. When CCR sang about the fortunate son, Ajax could have been their model. He'd led a charmed life. The draft ended right before he turned eighteen, so he didn't have to go to Vietnam. He went to state college just as the new Division III opened up, so he became a basketball star. When he got back to Black Wolf County, he had a job waiting despite the tough times, because his uncle, Jerry, was the sheriff. Everyone assumed that whenever Jerry retired, Ajax would be elected to take his place, and that was probably true. It wasn't that Ajax was such a great cop, but he had a way of being in the right place at the right time to make the most of opportunities.

"Must be nice to have your partner fight your battles," Ajax commented sourly.

I didn't take the bait by saying anything. In fact, I was a little annoyed that Darrell had felt it necessary to intervene on my behalf. Whenever he tried to get the other deputies to lay off me, the harassment only got worse as soon as his back was turned. But Darrell had three daughters, and I was the honorary fourth girl in the Curtis family. He felt a need to protect me.

"Darrell's retiring next year," Ajax reminded me. "Then you and me will be partners. I can't wait for that."

I still didn't give him the satisfaction of showing any reaction, but he wasn't telling me anything that I didn't already know. Once Darrell was gone, the sheriff would pair me with Ajax in a heartbeat. I wasn't sure what I would do when that happened. The thought of being trapped in a car all day with Ajax was horrifying, and I knew the only way to make him back off was to give him what he wanted. I had no intention of doing that.

"I have to go," I said.

"Yeah, I'll stay here and look for paw prints."

"Funny."

"So what do you think? Did the Ursulina really do this?"

All I could say was something I knew to be a lie. "The Ursulina is a myth."

"Yeah? Well, the myth says the Ursulina is a man who turns into a monster at night. It's pretty hard to look at this crime scene and not think there's something to it. Remember six years ago? Kip and Racer?"

"I remember."

"Two men cut to ribbons, same message on the wall. I mean, there has to be a connection, right?"

"We don't know that. Not yet."

Ajax wiggled his fingernails at me like claws. "Well, you better be careful, Rebecca. If the Ursulina *is* back, you never know who he might be. And there's a full moon outside."

*

Six years ago. Yes, I remembered.

That summer changed everything, sweetheart. Nothing was ever the same for Black Wolf County after that. And not for me, either.

Until that July, most people thought of the Ursulina as one of those scary stories we whispered around the campfire to make kids scream. The legend told of a pioneer family who invited a starving fur trader into their cabin, only to have their mercy repaid with bloodshed. During the night, under the glow of the monster's moon, the fur trader transformed into a giant beast who'd cut the entire family to pieces with its claws. Ever since then, the story of the Ursulina had been passed down from generation to generation.

Did we actually believe it?

Well, I think a lot of people *wanted* to believe it, but there had never been evidence to convince the skeptics. I couldn't help but wonder if there were others, like me, who knew the truth, but a part of me also hoped I was unique. The girl who'd seen it up close. The girl who'd survived the beast. I didn't really want to share the Ursulina with anyone else.

Then came July six years earlier.

Two local men, Kip Wells and Racer Moritz, had been squatting in a trailer in the woods an hour outside Random. The trailer was owned by our local lawyer Norm Foltz, who was away at a trial in Stanton County on the far side of the state. Kip and Racer probably knew he was gone, which was why they'd felt comfortable trespassing. Based on the evidence found inside Norm's trailer, the two men had spent several days emptying out vodka and whiskey bottles, roasting rabbits over a fire pit, and poaching endangered bald eagles.

And then something happened to them. Nobody knew exactly what it was.

When Norm got back to Random, he discovered the bodies of Kip and Racer in his Airstream. The two men had been hideously slashed to death, and just like the murder of Gordon Brink, the killer had left behind a message painted on the trailer wall in their blood:

I am the Ursulina

Darrell had been the investigating officer on the case. He'd told everyone that the wounds on the bodies had been made by repeated stabs from a common kitchen knife and that there was no mythical beast involved, just two particularly gruesome homicides—but it didn't matter what he said. The fire had been lit. Everyone in town wanted to find the Ursulina.

Maybe the story would have stayed a local novelty, but a

B-list sci-fi actor named Ben Malloy, who'd been born in Random, came home to exploit the crime. He turned the Ursulina killings into a lurid television special, complete with a search by hundreds of volunteers canvassing miles of the national forest for any sign of the beast. I was out there hunting, along with half the county. We didn't find any clues, but Ben got what he wanted. Huge ratings. A profile in *Time*. And, soon after that, a weekly series about mysteries and myths called *Ben Malloy Discovers*.

After that, our area became known as Ursulina Country. People came from around the world to launch quests to find the monster. Hours away in Mittel County, the city fathers scooped us by launching a popular festival called Ursulina Days. It didn't matter that the murders had taken place nowhere near there. They laid claim to the Ursulina by arguing that the pioneer family whose deaths started the legend had lived in Mittel County. Of course, they'd made that up, but there was nothing those of us in Black Wolf County could do about it.

As for Kip and Racer, their murders went unsolved. Darrell was fighting an uphill battle to find evidence and witnesses, because no one really *wanted* the murderer to be caught. A human killer would spoil the myth, and local businesses saw dollar signs in the story of the Ursulina. Plus, nobody missed Kip and Racer. The consensus around town was that the monster had done us a favor by wiping them off the earth. Darrell was pretty much the only person who actually wanted to see the crimes solved. To him, it was a matter of principle. Murder was murder.

That was how the Ursulina legend took off.

That was also how I got a job in the sheriff's office. I'd been on my own that summer. My father was away on the road, and my brother was hauling nets on an Alaskan fishing boat out of Seward. I had a freshly minted associate's degree, but no idea what I wanted to do with my life. I was young and restless. As the media besieged the sheriff's department with Ursulina calls, Darrell needed someone to answer the phones, so I volunteered. Darrell was a neighbor, which meant I'd known him since I was a girl.

Eventually, my part-time role on the phone turned into a paid gig as the office secretary. I probably would have stayed in that job until I retired, but Darrell's partner drowned in a boating accident right around the time that Ricky got fired from the mine. Darrell knew we needed more money, and he told me I had the makings of a great cop. He also had a niece on the county board who'd been riding the sheriff hard about hiring a woman for the force.

So I became Darrell's partner. We'd been partners for almost two years.

I was about as welcome in that role as Sandra Thoreau was when she got her job at the mine. The other deputies made sure I knew it. They began filling my desk drawer with porno magazines and used condoms. When I didn't lose my cool, they switched to dead rats instead.

Sooner or later, they figured I'd quit.

But I didn't. I wasn't going anywhere. I kept my head down, and I took it, and I never said a word. In my heart, I was still Rebecca Colder. A little bit stronger, a little bit bolder.

CHAPTER FOUR

I caught up with Darrell outside Gordon Brink's house.

He was bent over at the waist, his hands on his thighs. Around others, he kept a poker face at the sight of blood, but I knew him better. We dealt with a lot of blood. Together, we'd witnessed severed limbs from mine accidents, shotgun suicides, and shredded faces that had gone through car windshields. None of that compared with the horrors Darrell had seen as a marine in Korea, too. He remained stoic through all of it, but I knew how deeply he felt things, and blood in particular seemed to give him flashbacks of his days in the service.

Given how much my own dad was away, I'd grown up thinking of Darrell as almost a second father to me. He was the most solid, serious man I knew. Religious. Faithful. Humble. He'd told me once that life was a relay race, where you take the baton from your parents and pass it along to your children, and in between, you try to run around the track with as much strength and grace as you can. I liked that philosophy.

You wouldn't really have been impressed to look at him. He wasn't tall, and he'd never been a pretty boy like Ajax. Even in his sixties, he kept his hair military short, jet black, not a gray strand to be found anywhere. His nose had a drooping hook, and his ears looked big and wide under his buzz cut. His cheek had a long scar where a North Korean bullet had sliced him. It would have killed him if it had been another inch to the left. That kind of good fortune made him conscious of the choices he made in living his life, and he was determined to make the right ones.

If there was one quality about Darrell that sometimes made me bite my tongue, it was that he had a black-and-white outlook on the world. Things were good, or things were bad. Things were right, or things were wrong. His own moral compass always pointed due north, so he was quick to pass judgment on people. Even at my young age, I'd figured out that the world was a lot more complicated than that.

"I'm sorry, Rebecca," Darrell said when I joined him. He was still bent over, breathing hard.

"For what?"

"For telling Ajax to keep his hands off you. I know you hate that."

"Don't worry about it." I noticed the pale cast of his face. "Are you okay? That was an ugly scene back there."

"I'll be fine. I've seen worse."

I shoved my hands in my pockets and glanced across the white field of snow. "I know that, but you don't have to pretend with me."

Darrell straightened up, wiping away a little sweat that had gathered on his brow even on a cold night. "Thanks."

"So what do you think?" I asked, because I was very curious to know if Darrell had come to any conclusions yet. "This must be a copycat, right?"

He put on his stolid deputy's face again. "I don't know. Maybe. If it's the same killer, where has he been for six years?

And why come back now? The only thing I do know is that none of these crimes were committed by a mythical beast."

I could have given him a different take on that, but I didn't tell him what I was thinking.

Inside the house, we found Gordon Brink's son, Jay, in a bedroom on the top floor. This was three stories above the main floor master suite that Gordon and Erica shared. The huge house felt oddly empty and quiet—so much space for only three people— and I thought it had to be strange for a boy from the city to be stuck here in the middle of nowhere. The bedroom was large, but clean and uncluttered, which surprised me from a teenager. I assumed that Jay shared his father's organized legal mind. On the other hand, the posters on the log walls—all neatly hung and absolutely level—revealed a rebellious spirit and a bookish intelligence. I saw punk bands like the Flesh Eaters and Dead Kennedys, alongside portraits of Oscar Wilde and D. H. Lawrence. He had half a dozen bookshelves crammed with classics like *Moby Dick* and *Leaves of Grass* that would have put other seventeen-year-old boys to sleep.

Jay lay on top of the carefully made king-size bed when we arrived. He had his hands behind his head and was staring at the ceiling, and he was dressed in a flannel shirt and corduroys, with bare feet. He didn't acknowledge us, although he obviously knew who we were and why we were there. He was a handsome kid, thick reddish-brown hair, a prominent nose and close-shaved face, with intense dark eyes. He was tall but not particularly muscular or athletic. He'd just lost his father, but I didn't see any indication on his face that he'd been crying.

Darrell went to the large bedroom windows, stared outside for a while, and then turned back to Gordon Brink's son. "Jay, I'm Deputy Darrell Curtis. This is Deputy Rebecca Todd. We're very sorry about your father."

The teenager didn't look away from the ceiling. "Thanks."

"You and I met last week," I reminded him. "I came over here when your stepmother called about the bucket of blood."

"Yeah, I remember," Jay replied. "Do you think whoever did that also killed Gordon?"

"It's too early to know."

Darrell was still by the window, and he nodded at me to continue the interview. I pulled a chair next to the bed and sat down. "I know this is a difficult time, but you might be able to help us figure out who did this to your father."

Jay still showed no reaction on his face, and his voice had a flat, numb quality to it. "I have no idea."

"Well, you might have heard or seen something that was important. A lot of times, people know more than they think." I took out a notepad from my pocket and uncapped a pen. "I'd like to go over a little background with you first. Okay?"

"Sure."

"Your stepmother, Erica, says she was away in Minnesota for the past several days. Is that right?"

"Yep."

"Were you and Gordon the only ones staying here while she was gone?"

"Yep. Just him and me. The associates and paralegals stay in a motel. Gordon gets the big house. That's how it works."

I noticed for the second time that Jay called his father "Gordon." Looking at Darrell, I could see that he'd noticed it, too.

"Where does your mother live?" I asked.

"Milwaukee."

"You don't live with her?"

"Normally, I do, but Gordon decided to bring me with him while he worked on the trial. It wasn't up for debate." The teenager rolled his eyes. "He said the Milwaukee schools were giving me all sorts of crazy ideas."

"Like what?"

"Like we value money over people in this country. And lawyers are some of the worst offenders."

"When did you get here?"

"October."

"It must have been hard going into the high school in the middle of the semester. We're pretty cliquish around here. Outsiders have a tough time being accepted."

"Really? I didn't notice."

I heard the sarcasm laid on thick.

"Let's talk about the last few days," I said. "When did you last see your father?"

"Sunday morning at breakfast."

"Have you been home since then?"

"Yep."

"But you hadn't seen your father for two days?"

Jay shrugged. "Gordon usually had lunch in his office. I wasn't allowed inside. Nobody was. He wasn't in the house for dinner on Sunday or Monday, so I had leftovers from the fridge."

"Didn't you think it was odd that he didn't show up for dinner?"

"No. Sometimes he'd work all night. I figured that's what he was doing."

"Even on Christmas Eve?"

"It's not like we were waiting up for Santa," Jay replied.

"Did you hear your father in the house on Sunday or Monday? Do you know if he slept in his bedroom?"

"I have no idea."

"Did anyone come by the house in the last few days? Did you see anyone?"

"Nope."

"Are you sure? This is very important, Jay. You didn't see or hear anybody else around here in the last two days?"

"Nope."

"And you were home, you were in the house, the entire time?"

Jay stuttered a little. "That's what I said."

Darrell noticed the teenager's hesitation. He interrupted from where he was standing by the windows. "You didn't go out at all?"

"No, I was here."

"Did you look outside on Sunday night?"

"I don't remember. If I did, I didn't see anything."

"Your bedroom windows look out on the front yard," Darrell went on, gesturing through the glass. "If somebody drove in here on Sunday, there would have been headlights."

"I didn't see any lights, and I didn't hear anybody outside."

"Were you in your bedroom all evening?"

"No. Not the whole time. I watched some TV. The den's on the other side of the house. Maybe somebody came by while I was doing that. I don't know."

"What did you watch on TV?" Darrell asked.

More hesitation. "I don't remember."

Darrell frowned. I knew he didn't believe what Jay was telling us. I leaned forward and put a hand lightly on the boy's wrist.

"Jay, do you have any idea who killed your father?"

"No."

"Do you have any idea why someone would want to harm him?"

"I assume it's because of the lawsuit."

"Why do you assume that?"

"That's why we're here. What else could it be?"

"Did your father talk about getting threats? Did you hear threats directed at him in town or at school?"

Jay finally turned his head and looked at me. "I can't remember a day when there haven't been threats. Nobody wants us here. They've made that very clear. I've had shit smeared on my locker half a dozen times. People broke our windows and slashed our tires. You saw what happened with Erica."

"Do you know who was involved in any of these incidents?"

"No."

"Was your father worried about them?"

"He said it was the usual harassment that comes with big lawsuits."

I let the silence between us linger while I studied Jay's eyes. He was a smart kid, but with stormy waters underneath the calm. Maybe it was the usual teenage angst, but I got the feeling there was more to it than that.

"Erica says your relationship with your father was difficult," I said quietly.

"You could say that. He didn't like me. I didn't like him."

"Why is that?"

"Mostly, I think he hated the fact that I knew who he really was."

"Oh, yes?" I asked. "Who was he?"

Jay turned away and stared at the ceiling again. "You'll figure it out sooner or later. Gordon was a monster."

*

When Darrell and I were back outside, I lit a cigarette. I didn't like smoking in front of him, because his wife was dealing with lung cancer and he blamed it on her lifelong habit. He'd given it up himself years earlier. Most of the other deputies smoked, and Darrell never said a word to me when I did it, but I felt guilty anyway. Even so, I was exhausted, and my nerves were shattered. The cigarette relaxed me.

"What's your take on Jay?" Darrell asked.

"I think teenage boys hate the idea of growing up like their fathers, and fathers want their teenage boys to grow up just like them."

Darrell responded with a low chuckle. "True enough. On the other hand, calling Gordon a monster? That's an interesting choice of words, given what was on the wall. Almost like he'd seen it for himself."

I shivered in the cold, my fingers trembling as I held my cigarette. The word rattled around in my head. *Monster.*

The snow had stopped, but the wind had come up in its wake, throwing silvery clouds around us. We stood near the dark trees that grew in a ring around the clearing. It was winter, and it still wasn't dawn yet. I did what I always did, what I'd done hundreds of times hiking in the woods since I was ten years old. I listened for the *huffffff* that told me the Ursulina was close by.

"You don't really think Jay killed him, do you?" I asked.

Darrell took a while to reply. "No, I don't. Then again, what's my philosophy of life?"

"You never know."

"Exactly. You never know. Here's a kid who obviously had a terrible relationship with his father. He was at the house the whole time, so he had plenty of opportunity and no alibi."

"Bad relationship or not, I can't see a child doing that to a parent."

Darrell shrugged. "Lizzie Borden took an ax."

"So what's next?"

"Next we talk to Sandra Thoreau. The lawsuit is still the likeliest motive for murdering Brink. We need to find out if anyone on her team has been making noises about going after him. It's mostly been mischief up to now, but that kind of thing can get out of control fast."

"Okay."

I wasn't done with my cigarette, but I threw it in the snow and stamped it down. I stared into the trees, still expecting a rustling in the branches and the noise of heavy breathing. My mind was awhirl. Everything was catching up to me—the night, the sleeplessness, the cold, the blood. Darrell called my name, but I was distracted and didn't answer. He reached out and squeezed my shoulder.

"Are you all right?"

I managed a weak smile. "I'm just tired. And I'm fighting a cold. My head's all congested."

He hesitated before saying more. "I heard you and Ricky had a fight."

"Money problems. We'll get through it."

"Is that all?"

"That's all."

Darrell didn't push. Not right away. He studied the expression on my face, and I felt like one of his daughters again, under the watchful eye of their father. I didn't like lying to him, and I was pretty sure he'd heard the rest of the gossip.

"Listen, it's early," he told me. "We don't need to spoil Sandra's Christmas morning at the crack of dawn. I want to go back to the office and pull the files on Kip and Racer anyway. Why don't you go home and sleep for a couple of hours? I don't need you with me. We can meet up later."

Normally, I would have protested special treatment, but I was glad for an opportunity to get away and clear my head. "Sure. Okay. I'll take a shower and then head back to the office. I won't be long. An hour, tops."

"Take as much time as you need."

I smiled at him. There were days when he felt like my only lifeline around here. "Thanks."

I headed across the snow for my car, hoping he'd let it go, but I knew he wouldn't. He called after me in his soft-spoken voice. "Rebecca? This is your business, not mine. You don't need to tell me anything if you don't want to, but I have to ask. Are you thinking of leaving Ricky?"

My voice was as quiet as his. "I don't know. That's the honest answer, Darrell. I really don't."

"Well, if that's the choice you make, you know I'll support you."

"Thanks," I said again.

He was silent for a long time, but he had a look that said he wasn't done. "Do you mind a word of advice?"

"Go ahead."

"I know the type of man Ricky is. I know that kind of man all too well. I saw them in the military, and I see them around here every day. They're tigers. You can see it in their eyes. They're always waiting for their chance."

"What are you saying, Darrell?"

"I think you know what I'm saying," he told me. "If you go down that road, Ricky's not going to take it well. You need to be very careful, Rebecca. Never turn your back on a tiger."

CHAPTER FIVE

At home, we had no power. The generator had run out of fuel, and the house was an icebox. I hoped the hot water tank had enough heat left to let me take a shower.

Ricky and I owned a little two-story house in what locals jokingly called downtown Random, namely the five or six blocks around Main Street where a few hundred people lived. From our front door, I could walk to the sheriff's department. The house wasn't much—two small bedrooms upstairs; a kitchen, living room, and dining room downstairs; and an unfinished basement where mice took shelter from the winter cold. The yellow paint on the wooden siding was peeling away, the front porch needed repair, and the roof leaked over our bed when the rain got heavy. Even so, it was ours, and I didn't want to lose it.

We'd stretched to buy the house three years earlier, with help from my dad. I didn't know then that Ricky would be fired a year later and our income would be cut in half. But we were a young couple in Black Wolf County, and buying a house was what you did. There were no apartments, so either you lived with your parents or you saved up enough to strike out on your own.

Or you left the area entirely and headed for the city. We'd stayed in my dad's house for two years after we got married, and with him gone all the time, he was fine to have us live there as long as we wanted. But in his house, I was still a kid, and I wanted to be all grown-up. That was how life was supposed to go. You got married, you bought a house, you had kids.

I wanted that whole fairy-tale life more than anything. Believe me when I tell you that, sweetheart. But a fairy tale was not what I got.

When I got home, I kicked off my boots and sat on the living room sofa with my coat on. The Christmas tree in the corner was the only indication of the holiday. The tree was so tall that the top branch bent over at the ceiling, but we'd put it up right after Thanksgiving, so it was already turning brown and dropping needles. The ornaments on the branches were all the same, red and silver glass balls, and one had fallen to the floor and cracked. We couldn't afford gifts, but my dad and brother had sent a few things, which we'd put under the tree. I'd made big plans to cook a roast and potatoes and bake pies in the days before Christmas, so all we'd have to do is heat everything up, but those plans had gotten away from me.

"You're late."

Ricky came into the living room from the kitchen. He gnawed on a pan-fried chicken leg from the refrigerator and sat down in the armchair next to the tree. He wore pajama bottoms, and his chest was bare.

"Yeah. Sorry."

"I figured you'd be in bed when I woke up. You know, I sort of expect my wife to be in my bed in the morning."

"Well, that was the plan."

"What happened?"

"Gordon Brink got murdered."

Ricky arched an eyebrow. "No shit? Who did it?"

"We don't know yet."

"Somebody kills a lawyer, do they get a prize or something?"

"It's not a joke, Ricky."

He wiped the chicken juice from his mouth with his arm. "So are you home for the day now?"

"No. I need to go back."

"It's Christmas."

"Yeah, and this is a murder."

He sighed with a little hiss through his front teeth. I think that was what frustrated me more than anything else, more than the drinking, more than the money he wasted, more than the times he came home smelling of drugstore perfume. It was the blame he directed my way when he didn't get what he wanted. Like everything was my fault. Like we were drifting apart because of me. I was the one going to work, taking the night shifts, coming home and cooking meals and doing laundry. I felt like my life was a matchstick house, and I was holding it together with nothing but little dabs of glue. But to Ricky, it was never enough.

I'd met him at a high school football game six years earlier. This was not long after I'd gone to work at the sheriff's office. At halftime, I was sitting by myself in the bleachers when a man with a cheesy grin under his mustache introduced himself as Ricky Todd. He wasn't tall, but he had a tough, strong, mine-worker's body, with big feathered blond hair and a mustache so thick you could mop the floor with it. Men came up to me all the time, so that wasn't unusual. I was pretty and unattached, which is a rare combination in this town, but I had the reputation of shooting men down like Snoopy in his Sopwith Camel. Ricky didn't let that stop him. He sat down and started talking to me.

What was it about him?

Why did I agree to go out with him when I'd turned down the others?

It wasn't his looks, that's for sure. In high school, he'd been popular and handsome, but then he went fishing with Ajax one summer, and while Ajax was horsing around with the reel, a hook caught Ricky in the face and yanked off a big chunk of his nose. The surgeons did their best to repair it, but it never healed right. Girls lost interest in him after that, in the shallow way that teenagers do. Ricky made jokes like it didn't bother him, but way down deep, he was bitter as hell.

I didn't care how he looked. No, what made him different was that he seemed fascinated by who *I* was. He asked a lot of questions, about my childhood, about growing up on my own, about my mother. It flattered me that he found my story intriguing. I didn't understand then, or maybe I was too young to realize, that men can be like that about things they want to own. That one way to control someone is to learn everything about them, so you always have ammunition to use when you need it.

I married Ricky not long after that. Darrell, my father, my brother, they all told me I was moving too fast, but I was in a rush to feel normal at that point in my life. I wanted to do what other Black Wolf County girls did. I married a mine worker, I worked to make us extra money, I went to the 126 and drank and joked with friends, I cooked and cleaned and had sex with my husband on Wednesday nights and Saturday mornings. Lather, rinse, repeat.

That was how my life went for three years. Maybe that's how the rest of my life would have gone, if Ricky hadn't heard his supervisor making a joke about his damaged nose and thrown the man through a window. The assault got him fired from the mine. Everything changed after that; everything began to spiral downward, for me and for him. I began to see the other side of my husband, as if I were orbiting around the dark side of the moon. His failures as a man somehow became my shortcomings as a wife.

Darrell was right about the danger of living with tigers. Believe me, as a cop, I knew what happened behind closed doors to too many of the women in Black Wolf County. Ricky hadn't touched me, not yet. Even so, I'd grown wary of what he might do. I'd noticed the heat of his temper, like a gas flame on high. When we argued, I saw him clenching his fists. His demands in bed had begun to make me uncomfortable. I felt like he was testing my boundaries, pushing me to see how far he could go before I pushed back. It was almost as if he wanted me to give him an excuse. All along, he had this odd, taunting look in his eyes that said: *I dare you.*

"I'm going to take a shower before the water gets cold," I said. I got off the sofa and slipped out of my winter coat, but Ricky blocked my way.

"Was Ajax there?"

"What?"

"Were you with him this morning?" Ricky asked.

"I wasn't *with* him. He's a cop. He was at the crime scene, too."

"Yeah. Sure he was."

"What's the problem? What are you talking about?"

Ricky's blue eyes looked like ice on a glacier. "I know you're screwing him."

"No, you don't know that, because I'm *not.*"

"He says you are. He threw it in my face at the movie on Sunday."

"Well, Ajax is a liar. He pushes your buttons, and you let him do it."

"He comes on to you," Ricky said. "I've seen him do it."

"Yeah, he comes on to me and every other woman in town, but there's nothing between us."

I was tired of this argument. We'd had it over and over. I was done defending myself, but I still felt the need to be a peacemaker. On that day of all days, I needed a little bit of peace.

"Look, I'm sorry about the argument on Sunday," I went on. "I'm stressed about money. I'll talk to my dad. He'll help us out."

"It's not my fault there are no jobs, Bec."

"I know. And I know it sucks that I have to work on Christmas. I'll make it up to you. But right now, I need to shower and get back."

With that, I dragged my tired body up the stairs to the second floor.

In the bathroom, with a little morning light coming in through the window, I stood in front of the mirror and took off my clothes. I hung up my uniform carefully, as if it were a disguise. I unhooked my flimsy bra and peeled down my underwear, and I stared at my reflection in the gloom. Two dark eyes stared back at me, dark as coal, with thick eyebrows like two black slashes. Underneath them were the bags that makeup couldn't hide. I hadn't slept more than a few minutes in days. My nose was Rudolph-red from the freezing cold temperature and from sniffling and sneezing. My cheeks were flushed, and my entire head felt thick.

I had a V-shaped face and a tiny mouth, but my lower lip bulged in a way that made men think I was puckering at them. I wasn't. My black hair hung to my shoulders. It was messy, with split ends and a few strands going their own way no matter how many times I brushed them down. I was skinny. I've always been skinny. You could see my shoulder bones, my narrow hips, my knobby knees. My arms were as scrawny as the chicken leg Ricky had been eating. My breasts made shallow pyramids that ended in tiny pink points. My skin was pale, my whole body china white. It wasn't just the winter; even in the summer, I never tanned.

I may have seemed fragile on the outside, but this was tough country, and no matter if you were skinny and small, you did what you had to do. I shoveled snow. I cut down dead trees. I cuffed drunks twice my size.

That was me, sweetheart. That was your mom.

I mean, not yet, but soon.

I climbed into the tub and turned on the shower. The brown water wasn't hot anymore. It dribbled from the showerhead, mostly cool. I didn't wash my hair, because I had no way to dry it with the power out, and I couldn't leave it wet. Instead, I tucked as much of it as I could under a plastic shower cap. I soaped up quickly, watching dirt run down the drain, and I rinsed off, freezing.

When I yanked back the shower curtain, I screamed.

Ricky was right in front of me. He looked me up and down, his wife's naked body, me shivering like a soaking-wet cat and wearing my stupid yellow polka-dot shower cap. His chest was still bare. His pajama bottoms and underwear were pooled around his ankles. The pudge of his stomach swelled from his waist, but everything else was muscle. He dangled, already beginning to grow. His hands took hold of my shoulders, and he squeezed with his thick fingers, not enough to hurt me, but definitely enough to remind me of his strength.

I felt the weight of his arms shoving me to my knees and making it very clear what he wanted.

"Ricky, not now," I told him. "Not like this."

I held my breath, wondering if words would be enough to put him off this time. He waited a long, long moment before he let go. Then he laughed, as if this was only a game. As if we hadn't been on the verge of something ugly. He yanked up his pajamas with a shrug, but he gave me a look as he did, and I saw that same strange challenge in his eyes.

I dare you.

CHAPTER SIX

"Where were you on Sunday evening?" Darrell asked Sandra Thoreau when we visited her later that morning. That was his very first question. We hadn't told her about Gordon Brink, but I assumed that phones had been ringing all over town with news of the murder. She didn't look surprised to see us.

Sandra's eyes went from Darrell to me and back to Darrell. We were seated in the living room of her small rambler. When I'd seen her shortly after midnight, she'd been smoking and drinking a can of Old Style, and she still was. In between, she'd tied her hair back and put on jeans and a loose gray sweatshirt. I saw a few toys near the Christmas tree where her son, Henry, had unwrapped them. Henry himself was in the front yard, building a snowman. Sandra had told the boy to go outside when we arrived.

"Well, shit, Darrell," she replied, blowing smoke at us. "Merry Christmas to you, too."

"Believe me, Sandra, I'd much rather be home with my family than here asking you questions. The sooner we get this done, the sooner we're out of here. Now tell me about Sunday evening."

She shrugged. "There's nothing to tell. I was watching the movie at the 126, like most everybody else. Probably fifty people saw me there."

"Did you leave the bar at all during the film?"

"Yeah, I went out to grab a smoke and enjoy a little peace and quiet for a few minutes. I've seen the movie before. Did I hop in my car and go slice and dice Gordon Brink? No, I didn't. I mean, that's what this is all about, right? That's what you want to know?"

"What time did you get home?" Darrell continued, focused on Sandra's alibi. This time, he was asking the questions. I wondered if he thought I'd go too easy on Sandra because we were both women in what the rest of the town considered men's jobs.

"I don't remember. One o'clock. Two. By that point, I was pretty wasted."

"Did anyone see you leave?"

"Ricky," Sandra replied, with a sharp glance at me. "He was still there. He's always there."

"Did you have a babysitter for Henry?"

"Yeah. That cute Davis girl. Kelli. She was asleep on the sofa when I got home. Henry was in bed. I didn't wake either of them up. In the morning, I made breakfast for the three of us, and Kelli went home."

"So Kelli can't confirm what time you actually got back home?" Darrell asked.

Sandra sighed. "No, I guess she can't. You got me, Darrell. Do you want to put the cuffs on me now?"

Darrell softened a little. We were all tired, and nobody wanted to be doing this on Christmas Day. "I'm sorry, Sandra, but we're talking about a murder, and you've got a hell of a reason to dislike the man who was killed."

Sandra stubbed out her cigarette in an ashtray. "Dislike

him? Yeah. That's for damn sure. Kill him? No. That would be stupid. I'm about the last person in town who would want to see Gordon Brink dead. Me and the other girls at the mine have been waiting *years* to get our day in court, and we finally, finally had it in sight. And now this. I know what happens next. The mine asks to have the trial pushed back because their lead attorney croaked, and they need more time to get someone else up to speed. Meanwhile, there goes another year of my life. So do I give a shit about a bastard lawyer like Brink getting killed? No. Good riddance to the scumbag. But believe me, I'd have given him a kidney if it meant keeping my trial date."

She got up from the sofa and went to the window, where she watched Henry rolling in the snow. Her face had a sunken cast to it, which reflected years of hard living. She was in her midthirties but looked a decade older. I knew Sandra drank a lot, smoked a lot, and probably dabbled in harder stuff, too. She could go toe-to-toe with any of the men at the mine when it came to swearing and telling dirty jokes. But something changed in her eyes when she saw her son. When it came to Henry, she was a mama bear with a cub.

"Do I need to get Norm over here?" she asked us, turning away from the window. "If you seriously think I could have done this, maybe I need a lawyer."

"We're just trying to figure out what happened," Darrell replied. "Do you have any idea who could have done this? Did you hear any talk about Brink over at the mine? Any threats?"

"I stopped listening to talk long ago. The only thing I do at the mine is try to get through my shift without someone sticking their hand down my pants. If I do that, it's a good day."

"I know it's not easy for the women over there."

"Not easy? It's been seven years, Darrell. Nothing ever changes. That first year, I was one of four women in the whole place. All I wanted was to do my job. Instead, they grabbed me, harassed me, threatened me, did everything they could to get me to quit. They tried to buy me off to get me to go away. But you know what? You go through that shit, and you decide pretty fast that you're never going to let them win. I would have chewed glass before I gave up my job."

Darrell let her light another cigarette before he continued. "When did you last see Brink?"

"About ten days ago. Norm and I spent four hours in a deposition at Brink's house. The two of us on one side and Brink and his circus parade of lawyers, paralegals, and secretaries on the other."

"How did that go?"

"Oh, great. Lots of fun. Brink asked me everything from how many abortions I've had to how often I diddle myself. He wanted a list of all my sexual partners in the last ten years. I asked if he had a calculator."

"They can *do* that?" I asked.

"They can do whatever they want unless a judge says no. Norm says they're trying to intimidate us. They figure we don't want our dirty laundry aired in court. Me, I don't care if they ask me to show off my Adam & Eve toys for the jury. They can't shame me."

"Did the other women get the same treatment from Brink?" Darrell asked.

"Oh yeah, he went after everybody else, too. Birth control, affairs, porn, you name it. All except Ruby, of course. She's their star witness, so they treat her like Snow White. Ruby thinks all of us girls are blowing everything out of proportion, you know. Boys will be boys."

Sandra shook her head in disgust.

I knew that the bitterness between Sandra and Ruby Jackson

ran deep. Ruby had been a vocal opponent of the lawsuit from the beginning, and having her on the other side undercut the entire case. Unlike Sandra and the others, Ruby had the advantage of being married to Ajax. All the men at the mine knew Ajax and didn't want to get on his bad side. That protected Ruby from the worst of their behavior.

"There's what, two dozen other women who are part of the litigation now?" Darrell continued. "That's a lot of husbands, brothers, and fathers who must have been mad as hell about Brink asking questions like that."

"Yeah. People were pissed. So?"

"Did anyone seem more upset than the others? Did anyone have plans to get even?"

"People blow off steam all the time. They get liquored up and say stupid shit. You know it doesn't mean anything. Sure, we all hated Brink, and there may have been some pranks that went over the line, but that's it. The fact is, we wanted our day in court. Nobody from our side was going to mess that up."

"What about the people on Brink's team? Did you see any friction between them? Arguments, disagreements?"

Sandra shook her head. "No, Brink was the big bad partner. Nobody challenged him. The others barely even opened their mouths. There was one secretary who looked upset by the questions he was asking, though. She gave me this look a few times, like she felt sorry for me."

"What was her name?"

"Hell if I know."

"What did she look like?"

"Kind of an Amy Irving type. Cute."

Darrell rubbed the scar on his face as he tried to decide what to ask next. I knew he didn't really believe that Sandra had killed Gordon Brink. Pig's blood all over Gordon's wife? Sure.

Cutting him into ribbons? No. It takes some serious, blind, soul-deep rage to do that. Like a dormant volcano that wakes up with an explosion. That wasn't Sandra. With her, what you saw was what you got.

"You're tuned in to the gossip around town, right?" Darrell said.

"When it's not about me," Sandra replied with a wink. "Which isn't very often."

"Was there any gossip about Brink? Any stories going around town?"

She pursed her lips and thought about it. "Not a lot. Nobody ever saw him. He hardly ever left that house. Folks around town know his kid, Jay, better than Gordon. Jay goes to the high school. From what I hear, he's had a rough time from the other teens. I felt bad about that. It's not his fault who his father was."

Outside the house, we heard Henry calling for his mother. His snowman was done, and he needed his mom to come out and admire it.

"Is that all?" Sandra asked us. "Are we finished?"

"For now."

"Well, you know where to find me."

The three of us headed to the front yard, where Sandra oohed and aahed about Henry's snowman. Before we left, Darrell signaled to Sandra again and spoke to her under his breath.

"There's one other thing I need to ask you. At any time during the lawsuit, did you get questions about Kip Wells or Racer Moritz? Or did Brink or anyone else mention them?"

Sandra's face furrowed with concern. "Kip and Racer? No, why? They were killed before the lawsuit ever began."

"Do you know if they ever worked at the mine?"

"Not while I've been there."

Darrell nodded. "Okay. Thanks for your time, Sandra. Merry Christmas."

He headed down the driveway. I went to follow him, but Sandra grabbed my elbow before I could walk away. "What's going on, honey? What does any of this have to do with Kip and Racer?"

"I can't say."

"Come on, everyone's going to know sooner or later. Tell me."

I still kept quiet, but Sandra was smart enough to make the connection for herself. Her face bloomed with shock as she put the pieces together, and she exhaled a cloud of steam into the cold air. "Son of a bitch. After all these years. He's back, isn't he? The Ursulina is back."

CHAPTER SEVEN

I got to work early the next morning, but Darrell beat me there. He had the records from his investigation into the murders of Kip Wells and Racer Moritz spread out on the table in the conference room. This wasn't the first time he'd done that. We didn't get many cold cases in Black Wolf County, and Darrell didn't like unfinished business. So whenever things were slow—which happened a lot—he hauled out the file and insisted on going over the details with me.

Every time Darrell brought out the crime scene photos, they sickened me all over again. Nearly every square inch over every surface inside the mobile home was covered in blood, much as it had been in Gordon Brink's bedroom. According to Darrell's theory of the crime, Racer Moritz died first. He was found at the back of the trailer, stabbed so many times that the autopsy couldn't give an accurate count. The postmortem blood test showed that he'd been drunk and high on weed at the time of his death. There were no signs of a struggle, so Darrell suspected that Racer had been asleep or unconscious when the murder occurred.

Kip Wells had been found just inside the trailer door. Darrell speculated that the killer murdered Racer and then waited for Kip to return before attacking him from behind. All the knife wounds—more than a hundred, the coroner said—were in Kip's back. The frenzied attack on his body had continued long after he was actually dead.

Then there was the message from the Ursulina, painted on the trailer wall in Kip's blood.

For as much time as Darrell had spent on the investigation, he didn't have much to show for it. The trailer where the killings occurred belonged to Norm Foltz, who used it as a campsite when he took hiking trips in the forest. He was an amateur photographer and naturalist, so when he wasn't in a courtroom, he was usually in the woods. Sometimes he went alone; sometimes his son, Will, went with him. But because of Norm's extended stay in Stanton for a trial that summer, the trailer had been unused for a few weeks. It was impossible to know exactly when Kip and Racer had begun squatting there.

But why were they dead? And who killed them? Darrell didn't know. Honestly, in Black Wolf County, nobody cared. Kip and Racer had bullied people around here from the time they were teenage dropouts. If there was a break-in or theft in town, deputies usually knocked on their doors first. Even the 126 had banned them, and it took a lot of bad behavior to get thrown out of the 126. Many of their worst crimes went unreported, out of fear of retaliation. One woman had accused them of rape, and a week later, her house burned down. People got the message to keep their mouths shut. So when the Ursulina ended Kip and Racer's reign of terror, pretty much everyone was grateful. If anyone knew anything, they didn't rush to give Darrell evidence to solve the case.

Even the Ursulina hunt, filmed for television by Ben Malloy, turned out to be a bust. Darrell let Ben and his volunteers trample through the forest surrounding the crime scene, because he hoped someone might find evidence of the real murderer while searching the ground for Ursulina tracks and Ursulina poop. But we didn't find a thing. Kip and Racer's killer, like the Ursulina, had disappeared from the woods without leaving a trace.

"Question," Darrell said, as we sat across from each other at the conference table. He liked to use me as his sounding board, as if the process of thinking through the case again would help us unearth something we'd missed.

"Kip, Racer, now Gordon Brink," he continued. "What are the similarities between the cases?"

"Well, the crime scenes obviously," I replied. "The Ursulina message. Plus, the extreme violence in how the victims were killed."

"And the differences?"

"The crimes happened six years apart. The victims back then were two local thugs versus an out-of-town partner at a corporate law firm. There's nothing to connect them. We've got different murder weapons and different locations, one residential, one in the national forest."

"What about possible motives for Kip and Racer?"

"Take your pick. They had their fingers in a lot of pies, everything from drugs and poaching to theft and assault."

"And Brink?"

"Presumably the lawsuit."

Darrell frowned. "So what does your gut tell you? Are we looking at a copycat or at the same killer?"

I reflected on what to say. "Well, everything about the second crime scene feels staged to look like the first. They're the same, but they're also different. That sounds like a copycat, doesn't it?"

I didn't have time to find out if Darrell agreed. Before I

could say anything more, I heard the rustle of paper and the loud crunch of someone eating potato chips. I looked up and saw Ajax in the doorway of the conference room. He listened to us, with his tall body slumped against the doorframe. "You're both forgetting something, you know."

"Oh, yeah?" Darrell asked. "What's that?"

Ajax came into the room and sat down across from me. His long legs stretched out, and I felt him rub my calf with his boot under the table. I pushed my chair sharply backward. He grinned and extended the bag of potato chips to offer me some, but I waved it away.

"There's someone connected to both crimes," Ajax said.

"Who?" Darrell asked.

"Norm Foltz. Kip and Racer were in his trailer. He's the one who found the bodies. And now we've got Gordon Brink, who was on the other side of Norm in the mine lawsuit. He has links to all the victims."

"Norm also has no motive," Darrell pointed out.

Ajax's thick eyebrows teased up and down. "Well, it was a monster's moon. Who knows what happens to Norm after midnight? Maybe he transforms into a werewolf or something."

"Not funny," Darrell said.

Ajax shrugged off the reproach. "Okay, well, Norm has no motive that we know of, but that's different from not actually having one. Like Rebecca says, Kip and Racer were into everything. As for Brink, there could have been something personal between him and Norm that we don't know about. And I'll tell you something else. I didn't see Norm at the movie at the 126 on Sunday night. So where was he?"

Darrell hated to acknowledge that Ajax was right, but in this case, we both knew that somebody needed to ask Norm some questions.

"Okay, go talk to him," Darrell told Ajax. He looked at me. "Take Rebecca with you."

My horror must have shown on my face. "Why not do the interview yourself?"

"Sorry," Darrell replied, shaking his head. "Norm and I are best friends, everybody around here knows that. You guys talk to him first. Find out what he knows."

Ajax practically hummed with satisfaction at the assignment. He crumpled up his empty bag of chips and hopped to his feet, and he pointed his long finger at me like a gun. "Come on, Rebecca. Chop-chop."

I waited until he left the conference room, and then I groaned. "Darrell. Are you kidding? Me and Ajax?"

"You're going to have to learn to live with him sooner or later. You might as well start now."

That was true, but I did a lousy job of hiding my annoyance. In the office, I shrugged on my coat, then followed Ajax out of the courthouse building, trying to keep up with his long strides. The Christmas snow lingered on Main Street and on the roofs of the buildings, but the day was bright and clear. Ajax slipped Foster Grants over his eyes as he slid behind the wheel of his cruiser. I kept a stony silence as I took the passenger seat next to him. He squealed his car into a U-turn and sped out of town like a Ferrari driver at Le Mans. Somehow I think this was supposed to impress me.

Ajax shot a sideways glance across the car and saw my mouth bent into a sour frown. "Jesus, lighten up already."

"Lighten up?" I fired back. "Do you really have the balls to say something like that to me?"

"What's eating you?"

"You know what. What did you say to Ricky? Did you tell him we were sleeping together?"

He chuckled. "Hey, we were just kidding around. Everybody knew it was a joke."

"Everybody?"

"Sure, the whole gang at the movie. That's what we do, you know that. We drink, we shit on each other. Hell, Ruby was right there. She heard everything I said, and she knew I was kidding."

My fists clenched. "Don't do it again. Don't joke about me and you. Not to Ricky, not to anyone. Got that?"

"Got it," he replied with a sarcastic salute. Then he shoved his sunglasses down to the end of his nose like Tom Cruise. "But just so you know, anytime you want more than what Ricky's packing, I'm happy to help out."

"Oh, shut up, Ajax. Just shut the hell up."

"Yes, ma'am."

We didn't speak for several minutes after that. I fumed in the passenger seat. We headed into the nowhere land that occupies most of the county, past miles of white-flocked evergreens hugging both sides of the highway. Eventually, Ajax got to a lonely T-intersection, where the 126 crossed with a dirt road that I knew well. Going left led toward Norm Foltz's house, which was next door to the house where Darrell and his family lived. On the other side of Darrell was the house where I'd grown up with my father and brother. Almost a quarter-mile separated each of the lots, but we were all neighbors.

However, Ajax turned in the opposite direction.

"Where are you going?" I asked.

"I need to stop home first. I forgot my lunch."

"Can't you skip it?"

Ajax shook his head. "Man, are you on the rag, or what? Give me a break. It'll take five minutes."

He drove fast enough to get a little skid on the rear tires. The unplowed road was rutted with tracks in the snow. Three miles from the highway, we got to his house, which was a freshly built two-story big enough for a large family. The yard had been cleared, but there were still a few dozen tree stumps jutting out of the drifts. It was more house than you'd expect from a thirty-year-old deputy, but we all assumed that the sheriff had kicked in cash for his nephew.

"Want to come in?" Ajax asked.

"No, I'll stay out here."

"Suit yourself. I won't be long."

He got out of the car and marched up to his front porch. I saw the door open, and his wife, Ruby, came outside to greet him. He gave her a peck and then slapped her ass as he went inside. She glanced at the cruiser, which was when she spotted me. Her mouth pushed into a thin, unhappy line. I got the feeling that Ruby wasn't convinced that her husband had been kidding around at the 126.

Ruby had a lush shag of deep mahogany hair that hung well below her shoulders. She was bony and small, except for the basketball-sized bump in her stomach. After she'd left the mine, they'd had two kids back to back, and the third was due in the next month or so. Her face was Barbie-doll pretty, in the same Ken-doll way that Ajax was handsome. She had fair skin, a sharp little dimpled chin, and big green eyes that could turn from sweet to ferocious in a blink. The genetic combination of Ruby and Ajax was undeniably impressive. Their kids were gorgeous.

She tramped through the snow. It was cold outside, but she wore no coat, just a holiday sweater and jeans. I knew she was coming to talk to me, so I got out of the car and lit a cigarette as I leaned against the door.

"Hi, Ruby."

"Rebecca."

"How are you? Feeling okay?"

"Fine."

"Number three won't be long now, huh?"

"No, not long."

"Good."

That was all we said, but I heard a different, unspoken conversation going on between us. Ruby knew what her husband was like. She knew that Ajax cheated on her every chance he got, because you couldn't keep that kind of thing quiet in Black Wolf County. But Ruby was also intent on making sure that no matter who Ajax slept with, he always came home to her and her kids. She'd mess up any woman who tried to get in the middle of her marriage, and the look in her green eyes told me that she thought I was exactly the kind of woman who might try to do that. I was trying just as hard to tell her that nothing was going on between me and Ajax.

Finally, Ruby got more pointed.

"So where's Darrell? Don't you usually ride with him?"

"He asked me and Ajax to do an interview."

"Uh-huh."

"Gordon Brink got killed," I added.

"Yeah, I heard."

"So that's all it is," I told her, which was as close as I could get to saying out loud that I wasn't trying to steal her husband.

"I suppose you're talking to Norm," Ruby said.

I covered my surprise that she'd guessed right. "Well, we'll be talking to everyone who knew Brink. That's how these things go."

"You should start with Norm, that's all I'll say."

"Why?"

"Ajax didn't tell you?"

"Tell me what?"

"About Norm and Gordon."

"No, what about them?"

Ruby glanced over her shoulder at their house. Ajax was still inside. I could see her weighing whether to say anything, but I think she loved the idea of lording a secret over me. "I had a deposition with Norm at Brink's house a few days ago. Norm was trying to get me to say the men were harassing Sandra and the others at the mine. He kept pushing hard for X-rated details."

"What did you tell him?"

"I said the worst sexual harasser I ever saw at the mine was Sandra."

"So what does that have to do with Norm and Gordon?"

"We took a break midway through," Ruby explained. "I had to pee. I have to pee like every twenty minutes with this kid sitting on my bladder. When I was done, I passed the back door to the house on my way back. I saw Norm and Gordon out in the yard, and I could hear they were having an argument. It was really hot, like they might go after each other. Gordon was shouting at Norm."

"Was it about the deposition?" I asked.

Ruby shook her head. "No. It didn't have anything to do with the lawsuit. They were arguing about Gordon's son. Jay."

CHAPTER EIGHT

Norm met us at the door before we even had a chance to knock.

I'd been in his house many times over the years, going back to when I was a girl. My father wasn't as close to Norm as Darrell was, but any neighbor quickly becomes a friend around here. Our families had spent a lot of time around the firepit in Norm's backyard, eating homemade Swedish potato sausage, playing Jarts and volleyball, and telling ghost stories. It was Norm who'd first told me the legend of the Ursulina when I was six years old.

"Ajax," Norm welcomed him, with a smart twinkle in his blue eyes. "So Darrell pawned me off on you, hmm? What a smart man."

Then he wrapped me up in a hug. "Hello, Rebecca. How are you doing? Are you okay?"

"I'm fine."

"You sure?"

"Yes, I'm okay. Really."

He whispered in my ear, "If you ever want help with anything, I'm here for you."

News traveled fast around Black Wolf County. I was sure

Norm had heard about the troubles between me and Ricky, and I understood the kind of help he was talking about. Among the DWIs, estate plans, and petty criminal cases that were his bread and butter, Norm also handled the occasional divorce.

"Well, come on back," he told us. "Let's chat."

He led us to a four-season porch overlooking the backyard and the thick forest. Norm's house had started small, but he'd expanded it with a second story, a finished basement, a detached garage and workshop, and a multilevel deck, all of which he'd built himself, with help from his son, Will. In the middle of the snowy lawn, I could see an elaborate swing set Norm had constructed years earlier. I'd pushed Will there when he was just a little boy, but since then, he'd turned seventeen, grown to six foot two, and become a high school running back.

I took a seat on a wicker sofa, but Ajax remained standing, as if he could use his height to intimidate Norm. I knew that wouldn't work. Norm simply eased into a cushioned armchair and took a sip from a glass of orange juice. He wore an L.L.Bean checkered flannel shirt, cream-colored khakis, and heavy wool socks with no shoes. He always looked comfortable in his surroundings, whether it was at home, at the courthouse, or deep in the woods.

Norm was in his midforties, rangy and lean, with thinning blond hair and long sideburns. He was a rarity around here, in that he wasn't a native. He'd been born in Madison but had grown up hunting and fishing in this part of the world thanks to his father. After he graduated from law school and married his wife, Kathy, he'd whisked her away to Black Wolf County, bought this house, and built up a legal practice in an area that didn't trust lawyers. People had mixed feelings about him from the start. He was a Sierra Club Democrat in a region where mine workers thought the environment was code for taking away their jobs. Even so, there was a legal niche to be filled in this area, and he filled it. When you got caught doing ninety with six empty cans of Schlitz in the front seat, you needed someone like Norm.

"Gordon Brink," he said, leaping to the correct assumption about why we were there. "Wow, that's a shock. Just horrible. I talked to the coroner about it, and he filled me in. I wouldn't wish that kind of death on anyone. Not even Gordon."

"The coroner told you about the crime scene?" Ajax asked with surprise.

"Oh, sure. He wouldn't do it with anyone else, but Ross and I go way back. He knows that if you arrest somebody, I'll probably be the one defending him. Anyway, I suppose you want to ask about the argument I had with Gordon last week, right? Ruby told you about that?"

I watched Ajax deflate as Norm took the air out of his big news. "Yeah, what was that about?"

"Well, you've met Gordon's son, right? Jay? Smart kid. Sort of quiet and intense, but a decent boy. He transferred into the high school in October when Gordon arrived in town. The other kids gave him a hard time—some really terrible stuff. Will felt bad about it. You know Will, he likes everybody, everybody likes him. He made a point of reaching out to Jay. The two of them have become friends."

"I'm betting Gordon didn't like that idea," I said.

Norm shook his head. "No, he most certainly did not. I mean, it was obvious that Gordon and Jay had a bad relationship. As a father, I get that. Will and I have always been close, but even with him, the teenage years haven't exactly been Saturday in the park. That's just the age. But Gordon seemed to have no clue how difficult it was for Jay around here. Empathy isn't exactly a job requirement for partners at white-shoe law firms."

"Get to the argument," Ajax said impatiently. "What was it about?"

"In the middle of Ruby's deposition, Gordon pulled me outside. He told me to keep Will away from Jay. He accused me of using my son to goad Jay into spying on the litigation. Needless to say, I didn't take that well. I told him that I would never exploit my son like that, and that if either of the boys tried to give me inside information about the case, I would have shut them down on the spot. I also told him that he should be grateful to Will, because Jay had no other friends around here and was incredibly isolated and unhappy. Gordon told me to mind my own business, and I couldn't really object to that. It wasn't my place to interfere. So I let it go, and that was the end of that. When we went back inside to continue the deposition, Gordon acted as if nothing had happened. He was a master at compartmentalizing things."

"It must have made you mad," Ajax insisted. "Gordon attacking you and your son like that."

"Of course it did. But not mad enough to kill him." Norm's mouth bent into a tiny smile. "Not even during a monster's moon."

"Where were you on Sunday evening?" Ajax asked. "I didn't see you at the 126."

"Kathy wasn't feeling well. We stayed home."

"Can anyone verify that?"

"No. The two of us watched a movie on our new VCR. I got her a copy of *Wuthering Heights*. She loves Olivier."

Ajax sat down next to me and scowled like a chess player who didn't see any winning moves. None of this was going the way he'd expected. When he didn't ask anything more, I leaned forward on the sofa and took over the interview.

"Norm, do you have any idea who could have done this to Gordon?"

"I really don't. It's shocking and completely unexpected. However, if you're looking at anyone on the plaintiff side of the litigation as a suspect, I can tell you, you're barking up the wrong tree. Yes, a lot of people were angry at Brink, but I made it clear to the women and their families that any kind of violence or illegal behavior worked against us. The last thing we need to do is give the judge an excuse to rule against us on key motions."

"That didn't work out too well for Erica Brink," I pointed out. "She got a face full of pig's blood."

"You're right. Except that wasn't us, either."

"No?"

"No. Erica wasn't the target, and neither was Gordon. Jay was. It was kids at school who did it. They simply hit Erica by mistake."

"Are you sure about that?"

"I am. Will told me."

"Do you know who did it?"

"Yes, I do, but I'm not going to tell you. Sorry, but it's not my job to help you do yours. Anyway, Will laid into the kids who did it, and you don't want to mess with my son. They won't do it again."

I shook my head, because Norm had an answer for everything, and his replies left us nowhere to go.

"We talked to Sandra," I told him.

"Yes, I heard about that," he replied smoothly. "Please don't do that again without me present. She's my client, and I don't want her answering any questions without counsel."

"Even if she's innocent?"

"*Because* she's innocent," Norm said.

"Okay. Well." I found myself stumbling, like Ajax. "If it was no one on the plaintiff side—"

"Then was it someone on Gordon's side?" Norm continued

calmly. "I have no idea about that. I didn't see any of his people outside of the deposition proceedings, and hardly any of them said a word to me. They were all eager young associates. None of them struck me as Jack the Ripper, but as Darrell likes to say, you never know."

"Sandra mentioned a secretary who didn't seem too happy with the questions Gordon was asking. She didn't know her name, but said she was sort of an Amy Irving look-alike."

"Penny Ramsey."

"Did you see any tension between her and Gordon?"

"Hard to say. Penny's young, so she may have a few remnants of her soul left. Souls don't last too long at corporate firms, you know. But tension? I didn't notice. Sandra probably has a better eye than me for things like that. If she saw it, it's probably true."

Norm checked his watch, which was the signal for us to move it along.

"Is there anything else?" he went on. "I hate to rush you, but things are pretty busy for me. Gordon's dead, but life goes on. I'm sure the mine will be asking for a continuance, and I need to be ready with a motion to oppose it."

"I think that's all for now."

"Good."

We were about to stand up, but Ajax suddenly interrupted. "Hang on. What about Kip and Racer?"

Norm settled back into his chair with a little sigh. "What about them?"

"If you talked to the coroner, then you know the crime scenes are similar. You're the only person with a connection to all the victims."

"You think I killed Kip and Racer?" Norm asked, chuckling.

"I think you know more than you're telling us."

Norm studied us like a cat debating the physics of a jump

from roof to roof. Strangely, when I looked at Norm's face, I realized that Ajax was right. Norm *was* hiding something. I narrowed my eyes in apprehension of what he might say. What did he know that he'd kept from us for six years?

"Fair enough," he replied finally. "I guess I can share this with you now. Not that it's likely to help you with regard to Gordon's death. Do you remember what was found in my trailer, in addition to the bodies and the blood?"

I knew. "Liquor bottles. A lot of them."

"Yes, exactly. A couple of weeks earlier, there had been an overnight break-in at a liquor store way over in Mittel County. The owner was lazy about cleaning out the cash register at night. The thieves took several hundred dollars and a few cases of beer and spirits. Somebody spotted a car peeling away that matched a stolen vehicle here in Random."

"So what?" Ajax said. "We already suspected that Kip and Racer were behind the robbery. That's why we were looking for them."

"Yes, but what you don't know is that Kip Wells called me. He thought he and Racer were likely to be arrested at any moment and they wanted me as their lawyer. Of course, I was in the middle of the trial in Stanton and couldn't come home. Kip wanted to avoid the two of them being found until I was back in the county."

"Norm, what did you do?" I asked, with a chill in my voice.

He shrugged. "I may have mentioned to Kip during our conversation that I was disappointed at not being able to spend time in my trailer because I was away from home."

"You told them to hide out there to avoid arrest," I said.

"I did nothing of the sort. That would be illegal."

"*You're* the reason they were there," I said again, shaking my head with disgust.

"Rebecca, I made an offhand comment about being unable to visit a secluded property I owned," he told us, still playing lawyer word games. "What they chose to do with that information was up to them. When I got back to Random, naturally I made a stop at my trailer to make sure everything was secure. That's when I found the bodies and called Darrell. However, to be clear, that's *all* I know about the crimes. I have no idea who killed Kip and Racer."

*

Outside, Ajax and I lit up cigarettes next to his cruiser.

We both leaned against the hood. He stood close enough to me that his thigh brushed against mine. I was thinking about Norm and what he'd done, so I didn't bother to move away. Believe me, Ajax noticed. He was smooth, taking his time, not spooking the bronco. After we'd smoked for a while, he slid his arm behind me like a teenager at a movie theater, and soon after that, his fingers began to stroke my hair. Just a casual thing. Harmless. Yes, I should have stopped him, but I didn't. At that particular moment in my life, I liked being wanted. I couldn't remember the last time Ricky had touched me with anything resembling affection.

And I know, I know, sweetheart, that's how it starts. One time you get tired of resisting. One time you let it go, and the next thing you know, your whole life is in ruins. That's how it happened for me.

Finally, I threw my cigarette into the snow and pushed Ajax away. That was only because I heard the whine of a power saw and spotted Will Foltz inside one of the open doors of Norm's workshop. I felt a little embarrassed at the idea that Will might have spotted me standing so close to Ajax. It didn't take much to start rumors around Black Wolf County.

Ajax saw him, too. "We should talk to Will."

I nodded. "Let me do it, okay?"

"Why?"

"I've known Will his whole life. He trusts me. Plus, if Norm sees you talking to his son, he won't like it."

I crossed the driveway and went inside the workshop. Will was in the middle of crafting a miniature gazebo, something you'd put in a flower garden. Like his father, Will loved building things. He'd been designing and crafting everything from rolltop desks to built-in bookshelves since he was about ten years old. Ricky and I had rocking chairs on our back porch that Will had made for us as a wedding present.

He was a handsome kid. His physique was burly, but he was sleek, strong, and fast on the football field. His blond hair was thick, with some curl where it covered his ears. What made him irresistible was his high-wattage smile. Will turned on that smile, and high school girls swooned. All of Darrell's girls were in love with him. A kid with that kind of charm could have become another Ajax if he'd had the wrong personality, but I had never known Will to exploit his good looks. As gregarious as he was, he only dated occasionally. He had too many other things on his plate.

"Hi, Will."

Like a light bulb, that smile flashed to life. "Hi, Rebecca."

"That's a beautiful gazebo."

"Thanks. I'm making it for Mr. Stedman. His wife always wanted one, and I thought he'd like to have it for her, you know?"

"That's sweet." I let him sand and plane for a minute, and then I went on. "Did you hear about Jay's dad?"

He didn't stop what he was doing. "Uh-huh."

"Norm says you and Jay are friends."

"Yeah, we hang out sometimes."

"Have you talked to him?"

"Sure. I called him as soon as I heard."

"How's he doing?"

"It's hard to tell with Jay sometimes," Will replied, eyeing the length of the board. "He keeps things all bottled up."

"I heard Jay and his dad didn't get along too well."

Will rolled his eyes. "That's the understatement of the year."

"It wasn't good?"

"It was terrible. Gordon expected Jay to be just like him, and that was the last thing Jay wanted."

"What did Jay want?" I asked.

"I don't know. I'm not sure he knows. He'll probably be a writer or something. I tried to tell Jay that lawyers weren't so bad. My dad's a lawyer, and he's one of the good guys. I'll probably be one, too."

"When we talked to Jay, he called his father a monster. Do you have any idea why he'd say something like that?"

Will finally stopped his woodworking, and his brow wrinkled unhappily. "Why are you asking me about Jay, Rebecca?"

"We're trying to figure out what happened to his father."

"Well, Jay didn't kill him," Will said.

"I never said that he did."

"Yeah, but you're thinking it, right? Look, Jay and Gordon didn't get along, and he may not show how upset he is about his dad getting killed, but that's just the way he is. It doesn't mean he doesn't feel bad about it."

"Do you think Jay has any idea who murdered Gordon?"

"Not that he said to me."

"He told us he was home the whole time, but he says he didn't see or hear anything. That's a little weird."

"He probably had his music cranked," Will said. "Put on 'Holiday in Cambodia' and you won't hear much of anything else."

"Sure."

"If Jay says he doesn't know anything, then he doesn't."

"Okay. Well, thanks, Will."

The teenager nodded at me and went back to his work. I started out of the garage, but when I'd reached the snow, he called after me.

"Rebecca?"

"Yes? What is it?"

This time there was no magnetic smile. Will had a serious look on his face. "I'm not kidding. You need to believe me. No matter what you think about him, Jay didn't do it. He didn't kill his father."

CHAPTER NINE

Ajax and I tracked down Gordon Brink's secretary before heading back to the sheriff's office. Penny Ramsey was staying at a motel only a mile from the 126, along with the other members of the mine's legal team. She looked extremely nervous talking to us.

"I can't say anything about the litigation," she insisted, when we were together in her small motel room. "That's privileged. If I said a word, I'd be fired."

"We're not looking for legal secrets," Ajax said. "We just want to find out who killed your boss."

"Yeah. Okay." Penny put her ear to the wall of the motel room. When she didn't hear anything, she sat down on the twin bed, which was covered with heavy law books. She closed them one by one, and then she took a stack of yellow pads filled with spidery handwriting and shoved them inside a suitcase on the floor. "One of the associates is staying in the room next to me. He went cross-country skiing, but he could be back at any time. We need to do this fast."

Ajax took a wooden chair and sat in front of her. They were

face-to-face, their knees nearly touching. Sandra had called her an Amy Irving look-alike, and she was right about that. Penny had frizzy brown hair, parted in the middle, and blue eyes that looked a little wild, as if they might go spinning around without warning. She was small, no more than five feet tall, and to me, she didn't look much older than twenty. She had pretty features but went a little heavy on the blush.

"You must still be in shock about Gordon's murder," Ajax said.

"Of course. Yeah."

"Do you need some water? Kleenex or something?"

"No, I'm okay."

"Well, if you need to stop and catch your breath, you just tell me. Okay, Penny? Do you mind if I call you Penny?"

Her nervous mouth broke into a little smile. "No, I don't mind."

"I'm Ajax."

"That's a cool name."

He gave her one of his broad grins. "Thanks."

I stayed in the corner, trying not to groan. I felt a grudging admiration as I watched Ajax work his magic on her. It was strange, seeing him operate on a woman other than me, but I wondered if this performance was partly to let me see how good he was at seducing his prey.

"How did you hear about Gordon's death?" Ajax asked.

"Erica called Hal Barker. He's the senior associate on the team. Hal told the rest of us."

"You must have been surprised."

"Well, sure, but I already knew something was wrong. Erica had called earlier to see if I knew where Gordon was. She said he was missing. Although at the time, I figured that was just an excuse."

"An excuse for what?"

"To see if Gordon was with me. Erica watches me all the time. She thought Gordon and I were having an affair."

"Were you?"

"*No.*"

Her denial was swift and sharp, as if even the idea of an affair with Gordon disgusted her. Ajax heard it, too. He glanced at me for help, and I came over and sat on the bed next to Penny.

"Is there something we should know about Gordon?" I asked.

"Nothing at all." She pretended to be calm, but I saw her chest rise and fall like the rapid breaths of a bird. "Erica was suspicious of all the girls. I guess when you take your husband away from another woman, you're always looking over your shoulder to see if someone is trying to do the same thing to you."

"It doesn't sound as if you like Erica very much," I said.

"I don't like women who turn a blind eye to who their husbands are."

"Who was Gordon?" I asked.

Her wild eyes met mine. Somehow, I knew exactly what she was going to say. "He was a monster."

Ajax and I exchanged a glance.

"Why would you call him that?" he asked.

Penny looked down at her lap. "I shouldn't be telling you any of this. If it gets back to the firm that I've been talking to you, I'm out, and I need this job. I need the paycheck. Look, I've worked for Gordon for two years. This was my first job out of high school. I was lucky to get it, because the firm is very exclusive."

Ajax put a hand on her shoulder. "Anything you tell us doesn't go any further than this room."

He knew that was a lie. Penny should have realized she was being played, but behind those scary eyes, she was a single city girl on her own in a small town, and she was being talked up by a very handsome cop.

"It sounds like you knew Gordon better than almost anyone," Ajax went on, massaging her ego the same way he'd massage her thigh if they were in bed. "So you may know something that would help us catch whoever did this."

"I don't know anything."

"Well, you called him a monster. What does that mean?"

Penny began to backtrack. "I just meant he was ruthless. Hard as nails. Lawyers have to be tough, you know. That's their job. But the things he said to those women, the questions he asked. It was awful."

"Did any of them get angry?"

"Sure. They all did. I couldn't blame them. I wouldn't want someone grilling me about my sex life like that."

"Did you hear anyone make threats?"

"Not specifically. Not in the room. But it got pretty heated sometimes."

I took over the questions again. "Penny, you said Erica suspected you of having an affair with Gordon, but she was wrong about that. Do you know if he was having an affair with anyone else while he was here?"

"I have no idea, but I wouldn't be surprised. All the paralegals are women. So's the other secretary working on the case. We're all young and cute. That's part of the job description if you work for Gordon."

"Did you ever see him with any local women?" I asked.

"No. He worked sixteen hours a day. He hardly ever left the house. Some of us would go hang out at the bar in the evenings and on weekends, but Gordon never did. I mean, back in Milwaukee, he'd usually go out and have a drink and blow off steam with us. Not here. I don't know . . ."

Her voice drifted off.

"What?" I asked.

"Gordon was on edge about something. The whole time he was here, he was angry and restless. He took it out on us. I mean, he's always demanding, but this was worse. This case really seemed to get to him."

"Do you know why?" Ajax asked, frowning.

"No."

"He didn't say anything about it?"

"Nothing. Not to me, anyway."

"You worked with him for two years. What was he like as a lawyer?"

"I told you. Tough. Ambitious. He was the firm's fixer. If a client had a problem, he made it go away. That was why he made partner so fast—two years before any other associate. But there was something different about this case."

"What?"

"Well, for one thing, he tried to hand it off, rather than take it on himself. That was unusual. I heard him say the case was a loser and he wanted some other partner to take the first chair. I figured he was concerned that a big judgment against our client would hurt his reputation. But he couldn't get out of it, because the mine insisted on him."

"How was the case going?"

Ajax asked the question so smoothly that Penny answered without thinking.

"Hal—the senior associate—he's pretty sure we'll win if it goes to trial. He thought the depositions made the women look bad. Not sympathetic. Maybe he was right, but I'm not so sure. I mean, I'm not a lawyer, but their stories sounded pretty convincing to me. But Hal said our witness would offset whatever they claimed and make it sound like the women just wanted money."

"Your witness?"

"A woman named Ruby," Penny said.

Ajax got up from the chair quickly at the mention of his wife's name. "Okay. Thanks. Penny, you've been a big help."

Penny stood up, too. "You won't tell anyone that I talked to you?"

Ajax put a finger over his lips and winked. "You're an anonymous source. Just like Deep Throat. But hey, I could use your help on something else."

"What?"

"People are bound to be talking about Gordon's murder. You might hear things. Stories about Gordon, theories about what happened to him. If anything comes up that you think I should know about, you just call the sheriff's office and ask to talk to Ajax. We can meet somewhere private. No one has to know. Okay?"

Penny nodded, biting her lip. "Yeah. Okay."

Ajax and I left the motel together. We walked across the parking lot, but then I made an excuse to go back. "Hang on, I forgot my notebook."

I jogged back across the parking lot. Penny answered the door, and I pointed at the dresser where I'd left my notepad. I nudged past her to retrieve it, but she didn't move from the doorway. It was clear she wanted me gone.

I came up beside her again and spoke softly. "A monster?"

"It was a poor choice of words, that's all."

"I don't think so, Penny. His son Jay called him the same thing. I was wondering if you talked to Jay one of the times you were in the house."

"No, I didn't."

I waited, a clock ticking in my head. If we took much longer, Ajax would come back, and I didn't think Penny would open up about any of this with a man. "Come on, it's just you and me. What really happened?"

She hesitated. "Jay may have heard me talking to one of the paralegals."

"What did you say?"

"I'm the one who called Gordon a monster," she admitted. "It was me."

"Why?"

Penny bit her lip and said nothing.

"Why did you say that?" I pressed her again.

She glanced at the parking lot, as if confirming that no one from the firm's legal team was nearby. "We were going over deposition transcripts. Everyone else had left for the day. Daphne—she's the paralegal—Daphne and I opened some wine. After a couple of glasses, she asked me about my first job interview with Gordon."

"What about it?"

"She wanted to know if anything had happened between us."

"Like what?"

Penny's face soured. "Let's just say my typing wasn't the only skill he wanted to test."

"He wanted you to sleep with him."

"Yes."

"Did you?"

She nodded unhappily. "It was pretty clear I wasn't getting the job if I didn't, and I really wanted the job."

"What about Daphne? Did the same thing happen to her?"

"Yeah. Her, too. Pretty much everyone, in fact."

"Who knew about this?"

"At the firm? They all knew, but they didn't care. Nobody lifted a finger to stop him. Gordon was a rainmaker. You don't mess with the partner who brings in the business."

"What about Erica?" I asked.

Penny shrugged. "She started out as his secretary, like me. You think her interview was any different? I already told you. Erica knew exactly who her husband was. That's why she didn't trust him."

CHAPTER TEN

Over the course of the next several weeks, information came at us so fast that we could barely keep up with it.

Darrell, Ajax, and I conducted interviews around Black Wolf County. The other members of Gordon Brink's legal team came back from the Christmas holiday, and we talked to all of them. The lawyers. The paralegals. The other legal secretary. They were more discreet than Penny Ramsey, but the picture they painted of Brink largely agreed with everything she'd told us. He was a tough, ambitious lawyer. He was obsessed with winning. And although none of the women used the same word that Penny had, I could see it in their eyes regardless.

He was a monster.

We talked to the plaintiffs, too. Not just the women, but their families and friends. Every interview gave us a new suspect, because they all hated Brink. He'd spent hours digging into the most intimate details of their sex lives. He'd exposed their affairs, abuse, incest, and abortions. He'd called them liars. He'd left them in tears. As far as the plaintiffs were concerned, Gordon

Brink deserved to be cut up into little pieces, and whoever did it deserved a statue in the town square.

But nobody knew who'd actually killed him.

We checked every dumpster behind every business in town. We dug through the garbage in the county landfill, but we didn't find the murder weapon or the killer's bloody clothes. It's not like the murderer could have buried them under the frozen ground or thrown them into an ice-covered lake, but as soon as the spring thaw arrived, they'd be gone forever. There's a lot of land around here where people can make things disappear.

When we'd gathered all the evidence, we still had nothing. We had a body, we had motives, we had dozens of people who would have wanted the victim dead, but we didn't have a single witness who could place anyone at Gordon Brink's house on Sunday night. The only person who'd been there with him was Jay, and he still claimed to have not seen a thing.

It was the same situation Darrell had faced with the murders of Kip and Racer. No one really cared if Brink was dead. No one really cared if we put his killer behind bars. The town was ready to forget about this crime, to plow it under the snowdrifts and move on. Only Darrell still cared, because he was the kind of man who couldn't leave a crossword puzzle unfinished. He had no intention of giving up. But even he knew the case was going nowhere.

By the time a full month had passed after the murder, we'd hit a wall. Evidence dried up. There was nobody left to talk to, no facts left to uncover. It was late January, and as the temperatures sank below zero, the investigation into the death of Gordon Brink turned as cold as the winter.

I assumed the case would stay that way forever. Unsolved.

So I had to face the other side of my life, sweetheart. The side that involved me and Ricky and our future. The beginning of the end for us came on movie night at the 126, and believe me, I've thought long and hard about whether to tell you any of this. But this isn't just my story. It's yours, and you deserve to know everything.

You see, some very bad things happened to me that January, but the best thing happened, too.

You.

You happened.

*

"Is that what you're wearing?" Ricky asked me, making it clear he didn't approve.

I glanced in the bedroom mirror and saw my reflection wearing a bulky striped sweater, jean skirt, and leggings. I'd brushed out my black hair, but that was a losing battle against the tangles. "What's wrong with what I'm wearing?"

His mouth puckered as if he were eating a grapefruit. "You look like a high school virgin. Show a little skin."

"It's five below zero," I reminded him. "Every time the door opens at the 126, it's a refrigerator in there. You want me to shiver through the whole movie?"

"I want my wife to look sexy when we go out. That's not asking a lot."

"What difference does it make?" I protested. "No one will be looking at me. All the girls will be looking at Sean Connery, and all the guys will be looking at Kim Basinger."

"Ajax will be looking at you. He always does. I want him to see what he can't have."

I shook my head, and exasperation crept into my voice. "Will you let it go about Ajax? He's just trying to drive you crazy. He's been doing that since you were kids."

Ricky began unbuttoning his shirt. "Fine. If you're going to be like that, we'll stay home."

I swore under my breath.

Yes, I could have stood my ground, but I wasn't in the mood for a fight. Not that night. I wanted to drown my sorrows and not worry about anything else. I was in the mood to go out, to laugh, to forget, to drink. Definitely to drink. I wasn't looking forward to the week ahead. I'd made up my mind like a New Year's resolution to split up with Ricky for good, and I'd set up an appointment with Norm in a few days to talk about how to do it. But I wasn't ready to tell Ricky yet, and until I did, I was determined to keep the fragile truce between us.

So I went back to our closet and stripped off my clothes. Ricky sat on the bed and watched me. I switched bras, putting on one that pushed up what little I had to push up. I found a flowered sundress that came only halfway down my thighs. It had poofy shoulders and a scoop neckline and would have been perfect for a Fourth of July picnic, not a late January night at the 126. I slipped it over my head and then did a pirouette that fluttered the hem.

"How's this? Satisfied?"

"Hell yeah. Was that so hard?"

I summoned a fake smile at his reaction. I was already freezing.

That was how we went to the bar, with my arms and legs pebbled over with goose bumps and my nipples trying to burst through my dress so they could get back home and nestle inside a sweater. Ricky got what he wanted. I was definitely the sexiest girl there, because everyone else was buried under layers of flannel. I figured I could keep my long wool coat on to stay warm, but Ricky took it away when we sat down, which left me feeling like a Florida flamingo who'd been shipped to an Alaska glacier.

The 126 was a big place, with blond wood and kitschy décor that ranged from big-game animal heads to vintage hubcaps to coconut monkey faces. It had a central room where they put up metal folding chairs on movie night, and they could seat almost two hundred people. Then there was the long bar, with fake Tiffany chandeliers, neon signs for Budweiser and Bartles & Jaymes, a few beer taps, and red upholstered chairs that bore the butt prints of the regulars. Smaller rooms jutted off from the bar area, where you could play pool, foosball, pinball, and video games.

All this, and there was only one toilet stall for the women. The lines got long.

Ricky and I settled in next to each other for the Bond flick *Never Say Never Again*. He put his hand on my bare thigh. The lights went down low, but the noise didn't. Movie night here was mostly a social thing. If you actually wanted to watch the film, you were in the wrong place. People made shadow puppets on the screen and shouted out the dialogue, because we'd all seen the movie before. Neighbors talked and joked, and teenagers made out, and kids ran around screaming, and we all got drunk. Me included. Very drunk. I drank way too much beer. By the time James Bond was sleeping with Fatima Blush, I was tipsy. I was also dancing in my chair because I needed to pee.

So I headed for the bathrooms, which were down a corridor near the back door, where it was as cold as a meat locker. I passed through a cloud of cigarette smoke and added to the cloud by lighting one myself. The hallway smelled of burnt popcorn and urine. Ten women waited for the bathroom, and I swore at the line, because I didn't think I was going to last that long.

Sandra Thoreau stood in front of me. She laughed at my summer dress. "What the hell are you wearing, honey?"

I rolled my eyes. "Ricky's idea."

"Yeah, no shit. You want to borrow my coat for a minute?"

"You're awesome. Could I?"

Sandra slipped off her wool coat, and I stuck my arms inside the sleeves and wrapped it around myself, feeling warm for the first time in two hours.

"How goes the Brink case?" she asked me. "Know who carved him up yet?"

"No."

"Getting close?"

"No, we're nowhere. Darrell's not happy."

"Too bad."

My head spun with the alcohol, and I talked more than I should. "Nobody cares anyway," I said.

"Oh, yeah?"

"Yeah. Kip, Racer, Brink. They were bad men."

"Yes, they were."

"Nobody cares," I said again. "Nobody cares about bad men."

"Hey, Rebecca?" Sandra murmured, her voice going down to a whisper as she put her lips to my ear.

"Yeah?"

"Ricky's a bad man, too."

It was a relief to hear someone else say it out loud. Like I wasn't alone. "Yeah. You're right. He is."

"Honey, you need to get out of that marriage."

"I know."

"You're so much better than he is. I never understood why you married a loser like him. You're pretty, you're smart, you're tough. You're special."

I sighed and closed my eyes, feeling unsteady. "I never wanted to be special. I just wanted to be normal. Around here, normal girls get married."

"Okay, but why Ricky?"

"He said he loved me."

"He was lying," Sandra said.

I didn't understand. I couldn't focus. There was too much noise, too much smoke, too much cold, too much stench wafting out of the toilets. I was going to be sick. "What are you saying?"

"The football game? The first time you met him? He'd been watching you for weeks."

I stared at her, seeing two Sandras, then three, then four, like a mirror in a fun house. "That's not true."

"Honey, he bragged to everybody at the mine that he was going to get you. Ricky was stalking you like a deer in the woods."

I took off Sandra's coat and handed it back to her. "Here."

"I'm sorry. Maybe I shouldn't have said anything. I didn't mean to upset you."

"I'm not upset."

"You're crying, Rebecca."

"I'm not crying. I just really, really, really need to pee. What are those women *doing* in there?"

I was going to lose it. If I didn't do something right then and there, I'd be peeing on the floor. I squeezed my bare legs together. I rubbed my face, which was wet, and I didn't even know why. I saw the bar's back door at the end of the hallway, and I wobbled that way on my heels, practically falling down. The only thing I could do was go outside in the snow. I could pee there. I really had to pee.

Then I met Ajax.

He came out of the men's bathroom. There was never a line there. He was like a foot taller than me, looking all cocky and handsome, like Sean Connery when he was in *Goldfinger* and not older than dirt like in *Never Say Never Again*. Ajax checked out my face, my dress, my arms, my legs, my nipples, pretty much everything I had to offer the world. His mouth bent into a grin. It was a cute grin. He knew where I was going and what I had to do, and he thought it was incredibly funny.

"Gotta pee?" he asked.

"Oh, yeah."

"Go in the men's room. I'll watch the door."

"Thank you, thank you, thank you, *thank you!*"

The men's room was foul, but I didn't care. Nudie photos hung over the urinals, and the floor was wet and yellow where the boys had missed. A machine sold condoms and cigarettes, but someone had broken the glass and taken what was inside. The bathroom had one stall, and I ran in there and shut the door and barely got my underwear down before Niagara flooded over the cliff. I practically screamed with relief. As I sat there, I tried to read the graffiti on the door, but the dirty jokes and limericks made somersaults in front of my eyes.

By the time I was finished, yes, I was definitely crying, and I was trembling with cold so hard that my knees knocked together. I didn't want to go back out there, I didn't want to face everybody looking at me, I didn't want to sit next to my husband again, but all I could do was go to the sink and try to clean myself up. I closed my eyes to make the world stop spinning, but I was riding a Tilt-A-Whirl inside my head.

Then he was there with me. I opened my eyes, and he was right there.

Ajax.

I hadn't heard him come in. He turned me around and nudged me gently against the sink. His hand lifted my chin, and he bent down and kissed me. I won't lie to you, sweetheart, he was a good kisser, and I needed to be kissed. I didn't push him away. I put my arms around him and pulled him close to me. His body pressed against mine, and I could feel his muscles, hard everywhere. His hands were all over me. His fingers snaked under my skirt, pushing aside my panties, going places they shouldn't go.

I finally woke up to what was happening, but I was too late. I shoved him backward and slapped him hard, my wedding ring making a gash across his cheek. That was going to leave a scar. He was going to hate that. But I saw in that same moment that we weren't alone. Ricky stood in the doorway of the bathroom. He'd seen everything; he'd seen Ajax kiss me, seen me kiss him back, seen me do nothing but moan as his worst enemy groped me under the dress I'd put on for my husband.

My cheeks flushed red. I stammered but couldn't get out any words. Ricky grabbed my wrist. He grabbed it hard. As he pulled me out of the bathroom, I saw drunken images popping in my head like flashbulbs: Ajax bleeding profusely; people staring at us; Sandra shouting my name; the back door flying open; and then the moon and stars shining as Ricky carried me kicking and flailing across the snowy parking lot and threw me inside the car.

Nobody did a thing. Nobody tried to stop him.

Ricky didn't say a word as we drove home. His silence felt utterly terrifying, cold and deadly. I sobered up fast. Twenty minutes later, we got to the house, and I didn't want to go inside. Bad things waited inside. So he came around the passenger door, ripped it open, and again he wrapped me up and took me bodily inside as I squirmed and fought and screamed.

The light was off in the hallway. The strap on my dress had torn, and I was half-naked in front of him. He was in shadow, full of primal rage, completely out of control. A tiger. Slowly, I backed away, but he advanced toward me. There was a little lamp from my father on the table near the door, and Ricky picked up the lamp in a rage and threw it to the floor with a crash.

He was going to kill me. I knew that.

He was going to beat me to a pulp, and then he was going to kill me. I turned and ran for my life. He charged after me, yelling the most horrible things, calling me awful names. I ran up the stairs, but he was right behind me, catching my heel and trying to drag me down the steps. I kicked and broke free. I got to our bedroom and slammed the door shut and locked it, but that wasn't going to stop him for long.

I went to my dresser and wrenched open the top drawer and reached for the gun inside. By the time I had my service revolver in my hand, Ricky was kicking open the door. It flew off the frame, and there he was, his eyes black with rage, his fingers curled like claws. I lifted the gun and pointed it at him.

"Stop," I shouted.

He kept coming at me.

"*Stop!*"

This time I fired. Not at him. Over his head. The explosion sounded like a bomb, loud enough that I thought my ears would bleed. Plaster and dust cascaded on him from the ceiling.

"The next one goes in your head," I told him.

Ricky stared at me, and he knew I was serious. He put up his hands, but I could tell that he wanted to put those hands around my throat.

"We're *done!*" I hollered at him. "We're over. We're through. I never want to see your face again. Get out of here, Ricky. I want you out of this house. Leave right now and never come back."

He backed away. I went toward him, my gun leading the way. I kept it level, my arms rock solid. He turned around as he headed down the stairs, and we crunched over broken glass in the hallway. I'd lost a shoe during the chase, and my foot began to bleed.

When Ricky got to the front door, he faced me again. I saw the taunt in his eyes. The threat. "You're making a big mistake. You don't want to do this."

"Get out!"

"I'll be back, and then you'll see what I can do to you."

"If you're not out of this house in five seconds, I'm going to shoot you dead."

He'd lost this round, and he knew it. He turned around and stalked away. Seconds later, the door slammed shut with him on the other side. I kept pointing the revolver at the door, unable to drop my arms. I heard a roar as he gunned the car engine outside, and then I saw the headlights as he sped off toward Main Street.

I slumped against the wall and slid to the floor. Slowly, carefully, I uncocked the revolver and laid it beside me. Then I put my face in my hands and sobbed.

After that night, sweetheart, I knew that nothing would ever be the same. I also knew, because I knew Ricky too well, that this was far from over.

CHAPTER ELEVEN

I was still in the hallway the next morning when I heard a knock on my front door. I knew it wasn't Ricky, because Ricky wouldn't knock. I pushed myself off the floor and went and put the chain on, just to be sure. Half the time, we left our doors open in Black Wolf County, but I didn't think I'd be doing that for a while. I opened the door a crack and saw Darrell on my front step.

His face was grave with worry. He knew.

"Are you hurt?"

"I'm okay," I replied in a low voice.

"Where's Ricky?"

"I don't know. I made him leave."

"Come stay with me and the girls," Darrell said.

"No. This is my house. I'm staying."

"What do you need?"

"Half an hour," I told him. "I need to shower and change, and then I'll be ready to go."

"That's not what I meant. What do you *need*?"

"I need to work."

"Rebecca, you're in no shape for that."

"Yes, I am. Give me half an hour, Darrell. I'm fine."

He shook his head. "Well, in that case, how about I make coffee?"

I worked up a stubborn smile. I undid the chain and backed away, and I had to hold my dress up at the broken strap to keep it from falling. The morning air blew in and made me shiver again. It was still dark out, so I turned on the hallway light. Darrell came in, his eyes taking note of everything: the broken lamp, the blood on my foot, my revolver on the floor.

"Rebecca," he murmured.

"Coffee," I told him.

I went upstairs. I took a long, hot shower, feeling the sting of cuts and bruises, but the soap made me feel clean again. I washed my hair, which always turned it into a bird's nest. When I was done, I brushed my teeth and put on my uniform, and I put my gun back in its holster. Just like that, I was a deputy.

The smell of fresh coffee drew me downstairs. I took it to go, in a Thermos, and brought it with me to Darrell's cruiser outside. We hadn't said anything more to each other. It was early, seven thirty in the morning on Monday, with the pink glow of the horizon struggling to push away the night. I sipped coffee and felt it revive me. Darrell didn't start the engine. He studied me the way a father would.

"Are you going to tell me what happened?" he asked.

"I'm sure the gossip's all over town."

"I don't listen to gossip."

"Too bad. This one's juicy."

"Don't joke, Rebecca. What's going on?"

I could have given him the *Reader's Digest* condensed version. Ajax came on to me, and I let him, and Ricky caught us, and he would have strangled me if I hadn't gotten to my gun. What else was there to say?

"I'm getting a divorce," I said.

"You're sure?"

"Yes."

"Think you'll change your mind?"

"No."

Darrell started the engine. "Well, it's about damn time."

And that was that. That was all he had to say about it.

Of course, that was *not* that. Not even close. I wasn't fool enough to think this was over. But I'd had a hot shower, and I had hot coffee, and for the moment, I didn't want to think about anything else.

"Where are we going?" I asked Darrell, because instead of heading to the sheriff's office, he steered out to the highway. We headed east into the rising sun.

"Norm called. He drove out to his trailer around five this morning. He was planning to get some sunrise photos near Sunflower Lake. But when he got there, he found a car parked outside. Somebody's squatting there again."

"Does he know who?"

"No. Given what's going on, he figured we'd want to check it out. So he came back home and called me."

Darrell kept driving. Ours was the only car on the road at that hour. As the sun got above the trees, we had to squint at the brightness. Norm's trailer was almost an hour outside town, which sounds like a lot, but it really isn't in Black Wolf County. The dirt road that led to where the trailer was parked ran along the border of the national forest land. Skiers, day hikers, fishermen, and photographers all parked along here and followed the trails through hundreds of square miles of woods, rivers, and lakes. I'd done it myself dozens of times. It was in this same stretch of woods where we'd gone camping when I was ten, and I'd come face-to-face with the beast.

We followed the dirt road for another eight or nine miles. The plows didn't come this way often, so we skidded through rutted snow. Darrell knew where he was going. He parked before the trailer was visible, so as not to advertise our arrival. He angled the car so that no one could escape around us. We both got out and hiked between the trees in the morning stillness, and ahead of us, we saw Norm's Airstream.

Just as Norm had said, a car was parked outside the trailer door. It was a yellow Cadillac with California plates.

"What the hell?" Darrell murmured.

We peered in the car windows, but we didn't see anything to give us a clue about who owned it. There was a Rand McNally road atlas on the passenger seat.

I walked completely around the Airstream, which was familiar to me. The campsite was the same; the trees were the same. Norm hadn't moved the trailer in six years. I felt a little queasy, remembering the blood inside that had turned the white walls red. I put my ear to the metal exterior and listened, but I didn't hear anything. I didn't know if that meant the trailer was empty, or if the owner of the Cadillac was asleep.

I made it back to Darrell and shook my head. "Nothing."

He took the lead on the way to the trailer door. His hand was near his gun, close enough that he could unholster it quickly if needed. His other fingers curled into a fist, and he pounded on the door.

"Black Wolf County Sheriff! Open up!"

When there was no response, he repeated the warning. This time, we saw the Airstream shudder and heard heavy footsteps. Darrell and I waited cautiously on either side of the door, and finally, it opened outward.

A pudgy giant of a man in a velvet bathrobe smiled when he saw us.

"Hello, Deputy Curtis," Ben Malloy said to Darrell in a booming voice. "I figured I'd see you around here sooner or later. Looks like it's time for us to go Ursulina hunting again!"

*

I'd never actually talked to Ben Malloy before, but I'd seen him on television and around Black Wolf County, of course. He was our local celebrity, a native of Random who'd gone on to success in Hollywood. Not that he was Tom Selleck or Richard Chamberlain or anyone like that. He'd had a supporting role on a 1970s sci-fi series as an alien fighter pilot who could replicate himself at will. Ben was funny, and the character was popular, even though the show itself only lasted for a couple of seasons. When it ended, he'd spent a year trying to land a new show, but other than minor guest parts on *The Bionic Woman* and *Charlie's Angels*, he didn't have much luck.

Then came the murders of Kip and Racer, which brought the legend of the Ursulina to life right in Ben's hometown. His documentary about the crime and the search for the beast became one of the highest-rated shows of the year on NBC, and shortly thereafter, *Ben Malloy Discovers* premiered in prime time. For the next three years, he explored crop circles, the Bermuda triangle, Amelia Earhart, UFOs, reincarnation, and a variety of other unsolved mysteries every Tuesday night. The Ursulina had made Ben a rich man.

"What are *you* doing here?" Darrell asked him.

Ben trotted down the steps of the trailer. He reached into the pocket of his bathrobe and pulled out a pipe, which he stoked with a match. His pipe was his calling card. He'd ended every episode of his television show by smoking a pipe in a dark, cobwebbed library as he offered a final theory on whatever mystery he'd explored that week.

"Are you kidding?" Ben replied, taking a first puff. "Another Ursulina attack! The beast returns! This is big news, Deputy."

"I meant, what are you doing *here*? This trailer doesn't belong to you, or did you somehow forget that?"

"Oh, yes, yes, I know, but Norm won't mind. He's a good guy. I would have called him, but I didn't get into town until after midnight. I figured the whole county was asleep. It was too late to check in at the Fair Day resort, and honestly, I wanted to spend the night out here with the beast. Back where it all started! Back where he made his first kills! Let him smell me, let him know I was in town again. So I did a little nighttime filming here by the trailer with my Super 8."

Ben had a fast, exaggerated way of talking, as if he was always reading from a script and the camera was never off.

"Filming?" Darrell asked with a sigh.

"Filming, yes, of course! Five minutes after my mother told me about the latest murder, I was on the phone to the bigwigs at NBC. They're jazzed about a follow-up to the original documentary. Couldn't be better timing. I've got a team on the way, and they should be here in a couple of days. I'm already setting up interviews, getting the publicity engine in gear. Actually, I'd love it if I could interview you, Deputy. Get an update on the search for the monster."

"There's no monster," Darrell replied, "and I don't do media interviews."

"Yes, I know, I remember. That's a shame. Still, you were a big help last time. Two hundred volunteers out in the woods day and night for an entire week! What an event that was! The winter makes it harder, but perhaps we can stage a reprise. Hmm? What do you say?"

"That will be up to the sheriff."

"Of course. I'll call Jerry. It's still Jerry, right? Ajax hasn't weaseled his way into the chair yet?"

"It's still Jerry," Darrell said.

"Excellent." Ben's lips clamped around the end of his pipe, and his cheerful brown eyes focused on me. "Now, who's this smoky black-haired beauty, Darrell? Is she your partner? You've traded up! That last man who was with you looked like a dead walleye washed up on the beach."

"I'm Deputy—" I began, but then I hesitated.

Who was I?

Was I still Deputy Todd? Or was I someone else? Where did I go from here?

"I'm Deputy Colder," I went on, making my decision. And once I made a decision, I didn't go back. "Rebecca Colder."

"Colder, Colder, Colder. Your father is Harold Colder, is that right?"

"That's right."

"Truck driver?"

"Yes."

"Solid man, Harold. Seems to me he and I spent some nights together at the 126 in days gone by, when I was just a sprout of twenty-one or so. I don't recall you being much more than a toddler back then. Now look at you and those dark eyes. Doesn't she have amazing eyes, Darrell?"

Darrell looked as if he were chewing on a steak that was mostly gristle. "I've got to call in to the station and let them know everything is clear out here. And tell Norm that you broke into his trailer."

"Oh, yes, yes, do what you have to do. Rebecca and I will hold down the fort."

Darrell headed for the cruiser. Ben Malloy put his hands on his hips and sucked in a loud breath of cold air through his clenched teeth. He was a tough man to dislike, but also an easy man to be annoyed by. He was very tall and heavyset, but he had the cherubic face of a little boy. His short hair was brown and wavy, and he had a nervous habit of constantly pushing it back from his forehead. For a big man, he had quick, graceful movements.

"So, Rebecca Colder," Ben proclaimed. "Are you going to help me find the Ursulina?"

"My job is to help Darrell figure out who killed Gordon Brink," I replied.

"One and the same! One and the same!"

"This is a criminal investigation, Mr. Malloy. Not a television show."

"Ah, I can see Darrell trained you in his image. No nonsense. Always serious. I like that. Well, it may surprise you to know that I'm a serious man, too."

"Oh, yes?"

"Extremely serious," Ben assured me.

"Serious about what? Money?"

Ben took his pipe out of his mouth and reappraised me with a whimsical smirk. "Well, well, well, you're a smart one, aren't you?"

"Darrell's smart. I just work hard."

"Oh, you can pretend all you want, but I can see you've got a lot ticking behind those dark eyes. People shouldn't mess with you, should they? Well, here's the thing, Rebecca Colder. Yes, I've made a lot of money selling tall tales. I won't deny it. Did ancient astronauts visit Earth and leave their technology behind with the Mayans and Egyptians? Between you and me, probably not. Is there really a curse on King Tut's tomb? Doubtful. But the Ursulina story isn't just about ratings or money to me."

"No?"

"No indeed. You see, I grew up in Black Wolf County just like you, and I know a secret."

"What's that?"

Ben winked and lowered his voice. He leaned in close enough that I could smell pipe smoke on his breath. "The Ursulina isn't a myth. It's real. I've seen it."

CHAPTER TWELVE

The return of Ben Malloy reheated the cold investigation into Gordon Brink's murder. That was mostly because Sheriff Jackson began to get dozens of media calls from around the country asking if the Ursulina was back and whether we were any closer to trapping the killer beast.

"We look like idiots!" Jerry shouted at us in his office behind the closed door. "Did you see *60 Minutes* last night? Andy Rooney did his whole piece on the Ursulina. He rattled off all the unsolved crimes we could put to bed now. He had a photo of the Ursulina on the grassy knoll in Dallas. The Ursulina burying Jimmy Hoffa. The Ursulina parachuting out of a 727 with D. B. Cooper's ransom money."

"Ben knows how to get publicity," Darrell replied.

"Well, it was bad enough when he made laughingstocks of us six years ago. I was *in* that documentary, do you remember? The sheriff with the monster in his backyard. I'm not going through that again! Got it? I want to know who killed Gordon Brink, and I want an *arrest*."

"I want that, too."

"Next time *People* magazine calls me, we better have a human being behind bars, and if you can't do that, then you can start sleeping in the woods until you find me a seven-foot-tall ape." Darrell didn't smile. None of this was funny to him.

"The thing is, Jerry, I wish I could tell you we're close to figuring this out, but right now, the investigation is dead in its tracks."

The sheriff got up from behind his desk and paced. Physically, he was an older, grayer version of Ajax, tall, lean, and handsome, but his personality was like a lit fuse, always one spark away from a blowup. Jerry was in his midfifties, which made him several years younger than Darrell. Back when the previous sheriff had retired, a lot of people around the county assumed that Darrell would run for the job. But Darrell had no patience for politics. He let Jerry do the county fair and the Chamber of Commerce dinner and the 4-H picnic. Jerry had charisma, just like his nephew, and he ran unopposed. He'd been sheriff for more than a decade, and he would probably stay in the job until he was buried in the ground.

"There's no such thing as a dead investigation," Jerry snapped. "Just cops who need to get off their butts and get the job done."

"I can't make up evidence out of thin air, Jerry."

"No, but you can shake things up." The sheriff sat down at his desk again. I couldn't help but notice that he hadn't looked at me once since Darrell and I had come into his office. I might as well have been invisible.

"What do you suggest?" Darrell asked.

"You've got one legitimate suspect in this murder, and you've been treating him with kid gloves. Go in there and rattle his cage."

Darrell sighed. "Jay."

"Exactly. Come on, Darrell, a crime like this is *personal.*

You don't carve up somebody like that unless you've got a hell of a motive. More often than not, that means we're looking at a family member. If you ask me, a wife is always the likeliest person to carve up her husband, but you confirmed that Gordon's wife didn't come back from Minnesota until after Gordon was killed. Right? So who does that leave us with? The son. Jay."

"Except there's no evidence the boy was involved."

"No evidence? I've seen your notes, Darrell. Jay and Gordon hated each other. The kid showed no emotion about his father being killed. He called Gordon a monster—I mean, shit, does he have to spell it out for you? Plus, Jay admits he was home Sunday night. His room overlooks the front of the house, but he claims he didn't hear or see anything. What are the odds of that?"

"Slim," Darrell admitted. "If Jay was in his bedroom, he should have seen something."

"So either he *did*, and he's lying to protect someone, or he killed Gordon himself. Either way, you need to find out."

I listened to the back-and-forth between the two men, and then I jumped in. "Bad relationship or not, Jay doesn't strike me as a teenager who'd kill his father, Sheriff. I talked to his friend Will, who said the same thing."

Jerry looked at me for the first time, and his mouth curled with rage. Just like that, I knew he had it in for me. "Do killers wear name tags, Rebecca? Or maybe they have special tattoos? You can read violence in someone's eyes just by looking at them? That's quite a talent. You must have acquired it in your grand total of two years on the job."

I tried to hold my tongue. I was used to being condescended to, and propositioned, and ignored, but I'd had enough. I didn't really care if I had to quit or if Jerry fired me. I opened my mouth to shoot back, but Darrell smoothly interrupted before I could make a job-ending mistake.

"Look, Jerry, you can be as sarcastic as you want to be, but that's not getting us any closer to an answer. For what it's worth, Rebecca's right. I talked to Jay, too. The kid isn't a killer."

"Really?" Jerry asked, putting poison into the word.

"Really."

The sheriff eased back in his chair and put his hands behind his head. He half smiled, half sneered, and when he did that, he looked exactly like Ajax. "Tell me about Gordon Brink's office."

Darrell looked puzzled. "What do you mean? What do you want to know?"

"Who had access to it?"

"Gordon," Darrell replied. "Nobody else."

"Nobody?"

"According to Erica, he kept it locked up tight."

Jerry looked at me again, and the acid in his expression told me that he knew something we didn't. "Is that right, Rebecca? Does Darrell have it right?"

"Yes. Erica told me she never went inside. She was even reluctant to have me go in there when Gordon was missing. That was where he kept all the privileged materials in the lawsuit."

"What about Jay?" Jerry asked.

"He told us the same thing."

"Yes, he did. I read the summary of your interview with him. *I wasn't allowed inside. Nobody was.* It doesn't get much clearer than that, does it?"

"What are you getting at, Sheriff?" Darrell asked.

Jerry reached into a drawer and pulled out a manila envelope, which he slapped on the desk. He jabbed at it with his finger. "Ajax gave me the results of the fingerprint analysis today. He dusted Gordon's whole office, and guess what?"

Darrell and I stared at the envelope. We could guess what was in it.

"Jay Brink's prints are *all over* the office," Jerry went on. "He was there. He *lied*."

I frowned. "Maybe Jay was in there when they first moved in. Before Gordon set up his office."

"In the bedroom?" Jerry asked.

I stared at him. "What?"

"The bedroom. The bed. Right where Gordon was murdered. Jay's prints are there, too."

Darrell stood up, and I knew he was angry. Angry at Jay lying to us. Angry at being embarrassed in front of his boss. "We'll talk to him."

"Do that. But enough of the pussyfooting around, Darrell. Put the fear of God in this kid. Let him know we mean business. Like I said, either he butchered his father or he knows who did. Get him to admit it."

"Yes, sir."

Darrell headed for the office door, but as I stood up to follow him, Jerry held up his hand. "Deputy Todd, stay here a minute. I need to talk to you."

From the doorway, Darrell gave me a look to see if I wanted him to stay. I signaled no, even though I figured my head was on the chopping block. Darrell went outside and closed the door behind him, and I sat down in the chair again. The sheriff's anger had dissolved into a cold, calm formality, and in my experience, that was worse than when he blew up at you.

"Deputy Todd," he said.

"Actually, it's Deputy Colder from now on, sir. Ricky and I are splitting up."

"Rebecca, I don't care if you want to call yourself Deputy Dawg."

"Yes, sir."

"Ajax has filed a complaint against you."

My mouth fell open. "*What?*"

"He says you assaulted him at the 126 on Sunday night. You slapped him and gave him a deep gash on his cheek."

"I—well, I did, but he—"

"He says you needed to use the bathroom facilities after drinking too much beer, and he offered to let you use the men's room because the line for the women's bathroom was too long. After you came out of the stall, you began making sexual advances toward him. When he declined, you persisted. At that time, your husband entered the bathroom, and you covered your inappropriate behavior by striking a fellow deputy."

I shot to my feet. "That is *not* what happened. Ajax came on to *me*. You of all people know what he's like. You know how he's treated me from the day I set foot in this office."

"If you can't handle the working conditions of this department, you never should have gone after the job," Jerry replied. "Let's face facts. You're not cut out for it. You never were."

"Because I'm a woman? Or because I won't sleep with your nephew?"

The sheriff took a sealed number ten envelope from his desk and pushed it toward me. I could see my name where his secretary had typed it in capital letters. DEPUTY REBECCA TODD.

"This is a copy of the complaint," Jerry told me. "It includes Ajax's statement. There will be a formal inquiry. If the complaint is sustained, you'll be subject to punishment up to and including dismissal."

I shook my head. "You're going to fire me because Ajax stuck his hand up my dress?"

"You should know that I discussed the facts of this matter with your husband, too."

"My *husband?*"

"Ricky confirmed Ajax's version of the events."

"He wasn't even there to see it! He's just saying that because I kicked him out. Sheriff, this isn't fair."

Jerry wasn't even listening to me anymore. He shuffled his papers, put on his reading glasses, and glanced at me as if he couldn't understand why I was still in the room. "That'll be all, Rebecca."

CHAPTER THIRTEEN

"He's not going to fire you," Darrell told me as I drove us back to the crime scene at Gordon Brink's house.

I hadn't told him what happened with the sheriff, but he already knew. Everyone in the department knew, because Ajax was already spreading his version of the story. The version where I came on to him, rather than vice versa.

"Jerry's been waiting for an opportunity to fire me for two years," I said. "And this is it."

Darrell shook his head. "Whatever happened with Ajax wasn't your fault."

I glanced across the front seat. I knew he was trying to be nice—he was always nice to me—but this was a day where I didn't want to feel good about myself. I'd made too many mistakes, and I was paying the price.

"What makes you so sure, Darrell? Do you think I'm some kind of angel? How do you know it didn't happen exactly like he said?"

"If you hit Ajax, he gave you a good reason to hit him. I know what he's like. More to the point, I know you, Rebecca."

I made the mistake of saying the first thing that popped into my head. "I'm not one of your daughters, Darrell. Don't treat me like one."

He shut up instantly.

I could see by the expression on his face that I'd wounded him deeply.

I know, sweetheart. You don't have to tell me that I was being a jerk. What a stupid, graceless thing to say to this man who loved me and had helped me since I was a kid.

No, Darrell was not my father, but where was my own father? Off on the road somewhere. If I was lucky, I talked to him a couple of times a month. I'd always promised Dad that I was fine with that. I knew he was busy, but in fact, his long absences made me feel lost and alone. Not having him around made me angry, if you want the truth, so I can only guess how you feel about me. There were times when I'd desperately needed my father, times when I was hurt and crying and alone and in pain, times when I was so far down in a well that I couldn't see blue sky, and he wasn't there for me. I felt abandoned. Bitter. All I had from him was a poem in my head that he'd sung to me when I was a girl. But I needed more, and Darrell, more than anyone, had stood by me when my father didn't. Here I was snappishly telling him to leave me alone.

Did I apologize for being cruel? No. I kept driving.

Finally, Darrell changed the subject, his voice cool. "Snow's coming."

"What?"

He leaned forward, studying the horizon over the trees. "Snow's on the way. Probably a lot."

He was right. Around here, we learned to read the winter sky. In another day, a blizzard would bury us. In another day, my life would take an irrevocable turn, thanks to the deep, deep snow. Of course, I had no way of knowing that, sweetheart, but as I look back, I wouldn't have changed that day even if I could. That's what you need to understand. Despite everything, I have no regrets.

Anyway, the snow hadn't come yet. I just drove.

We reached the house where Gordon Brink had been killed. Erica was moving out. Boxes were packed and being loaded on a van. She oversaw the process, carefully telling the men what to put where. When she saw us, her face screwed up with annoyance, because we were interrupting her schedule. Even so, she smoothed her golden hair and told the moving men to take a break. Then she led us into the house.

"You're leaving?" I asked when we'd taken seats in the living room, where a fire crackled in the fireplace.

"That's right. Out with the old, in with the new. The firm is sending another partner to take over the litigation. Believe me, I can't wait to be out of this place and get back to civilization. No offense. If you want to talk to me, you can call me in Minnesota."

"Not Milwaukee?" I asked.

"No. I'm going back home to stay with my family for a while and decide what to do next. The last thing I want to do is go back and live in Gordon's house again. It was always his house, not mine."

"Of course."

"So what do you want?" Erica asked. "I'm sorry to be brusque, but there's snow in the forecast, and I'd like to be out of Black Wolf County today."

"We have some follow-up questions for you, Mrs. Brink," Darrell said. "And for Jay, too. Is he here?"

"No. He's in school."

I looked at her with surprise. "Isn't he leaving with you?"

"Jay decided he's going to stay in Black Wolf County for the rest of the school year. Who knows why? I assumed he'd jump at the chance to be out of here and back with his mother."

"Will he stay in this house?"

"No. Norm Foltz offered to put him up at his place. He's all packed. The movers will drop off Jay's boxes at Norm's house on their way out of town." Erica glanced at her watch. "As I say, I'm in a hurry. Can we get through this quickly? What do you need from me?"

"We talked to someone who said your husband had a reputation among the women in his firm," I told her.

Erica's pretty jawline hardened. "A reputation?"

I didn't know how to sugarcoat it, and I didn't want to. "For demanding sex during job interviews."

"Who told you that?"

"It doesn't matter."

"Let me guess. Penny Ramsey. Did Penny happen to mention that *her* reputation is for breaking client privilege? There was one particularly egregious example in which she told a friend outside the firm an anecdote involving one of our client's executives. Gordon made sure she kept her job, when she should have been fired. So it's rich to have her accusing him of anything now that he's dead and can't defend himself."

"Was it true about Gordon?" I asked again. "Did he have a pattern of forcing himself on other women?"

"What does that have to do with your investigation?"

Darrell interjected, "Because that kind of behavior can be a motive for murder."

"If you think Penny Ramsey or some other woman murdered Gordon over a fling on an office sofa, then you should talk to them, not me. I don't have anything to say about it. If that's all you have, then you can leave right now."

She began to get up, but Darrell stayed where he was.

"There's something else, Mrs. Brink."

She sat down again, looking impatient. "What?"

"You said no one other than Gordon ever went inside the cottage."

"Yes. So?"

"Was that always true? Or did you or Jay go in there sometimes?"

"Visit the sanctum sanctorum? No. Never."

Darrell frowned. "So can you think of any explanation for how Jay's fingerprints got there?"

Erica stared at us. "Jay was in Gordon's office?"

"Yes."

"I don't see how that's possible. The cottage was always locked if Gordon wasn't there."

"Could Jay have gotten hold of a key?" Darrell asked.

"I suppose he could, but it doesn't make any sense." Erica stood up again and faced the fire. She was in profile, her face flushed as she realized the implications of what Darrell was saying. "My God. You think it was him. You think Jay killed him, don't you?"

"We need some questions answered," Darrell said. "There are things that don't add up here."

Erica spun around. "Jay threatened Gordon."

"What?"

"He threatened his father."

"Why didn't you tell us this before?"

"I didn't know about it. It happened while I was gone."

"How did you find out?"

"I talked to his mother two days ago. She and I don't exactly have a warm relationship, but I needed to know what she wanted me to do about Jay. He's her son, not mine. He told me he wanted to stay here, and I didn't care either way, but I wanted to make sure his mother was okay with it."

"Was she?" Darrell asked.

"Apparently so. Jay told her he was finally making friends, and he didn't want to get shuffled around in the middle of the school year again. She also told me something I didn't know. Jay and Gordon had a huge argument while I was away in Minnesota. Jay called his mother in tears over it."

"What was the argument about?"

"Gordon planned to send Jay back home to his mother after Christmas break."

"And Jay wanted to stay here?"

"Yes. Which was the opposite of how things were when we got here last October. Jay hated leaving Milwaukee and his mother. Now he hated going back. I don't know why. Maybe he simply wanted to do the opposite of whatever Gordon wanted. As I told you, those two were fire and ice. However, according to his mother, Jay got pretty extreme."

"How so?" Darrell asked.

"Jay said if his father tried to send him home, Gordon would be sorry."

"What did he mean by that?"

"I don't know. But his mother was afraid *you'd* think Jay killed him. She didn't want me to say anything about it."

Darrell frowned. "You said Jay's things are in boxes upstairs?"

"That's right."

"We'd like to search them."

Erica waved us toward the stairs. "Be my guest."

*

Jay didn't have much in the way of personal possessions to bring to Norm's house. His music, posters, books, and clothes had been squeezed into two moving boxes. Darrell took the first box and dumped the contents onto the boy's bed.

"What are you looking for?" I asked.

"I don't know, Rebecca." He was acting distant and professional with me, and I didn't blame him after what I'd said. "A diary, maybe? Jay seems like the kind of kid who might keep one."

"Is that really going to help us? I can't see him confessing to his diary. 'Tonight I had pizza for dinner. Also killed Dad.'"

Darrell shrugged. "Stranger things have happened."

"I don't think Jay killed him," I said. "And neither do you."

"That may be true, but the sheriff's right. Jay is our only credible suspect right now, and the more we find out about his relationship with his father, the more everything points to him. Fingerprints where they shouldn't be? Arguments and threats only a few days before Gordon was killed? No alibi? I may not be certain he's guilty, but I'm no longer convinced he's innocent."

Darrell poked through the record albums and rolled-up posters, but there was nothing like a diary to be found. He dumped the next box, which was filled with books.

"Norm said Gordon thought Jay was spying on him," I pointed out. "Maybe he was. If he was digging up dirt about Gordon or the litigation, that would explain why his fingerprints were in the office."

"Yes, I thought about that."

"Spying on his dad may be unethical, but it doesn't make him a killer."

"No," he agreed. "No, it doesn't. But this might."

"What?"

Darrell pointed at a book on Jay's bed, lying among the classics and the poetry collections that had been stacked in the boxes. I knew what the book was, because I had it on my own bookshelf. Everyone in Black Wolf County had read it.

The Ursulina Murders by Ben Malloy.

It was a blow-by-blow account of the deaths of Kip and Racer and what the beast had done to their bodies.

"For a copycat killer," Darrell said, "this is a road map."

CHAPTER FOURTEEN

Jay sat behind one of the desks in an empty classroom at the high school. Norm Foltz sat next to him. I told you that gossip spreads faster than a telegram in Black Wolf County, so everyone already knew by the time we got to the school that Jay had become a suspect in his father's murder. Norm had arrived to act as the boy's lawyer while we talked to him.

I tried to figure out what Jay was hiding from us. Because he was definitely hiding something. He didn't even look up at me or Darrell as we asked our questions. He sat behind the school desk and pushed around a paperback copy of *The Picture of Dorian Gray* with his fingers. That book was an interesting choice, the story of someone presenting an innocent face to the world while a secret portrait grows more and more horrific.

Jay was neatly put together, his red hair clean and combed. His long, lanky legs jutted out under the desk. He wore an argyle winter sweater that looked expensive; it might have been cashmere. For a teenager trying to fit in with the other kids in Black Wolf County, that was the wrong way to do it. Most of us found our clothes in a Main Street thrift shop, and advertising your money was a great way to be hated. But I got the impression that Jay didn't really care what anyone thought of him, and that included his father.

Darrell led the interview. He wore his marine face, which was no less intimidating in his sixties than it would have been when he was a sergeant in Korea thirty years earlier.

"Jay, when we first talked to you, you said you weren't allowed in your father's office," he began.

"Yeah. So?"

"So why did we find your fingerprints there?"

Jay hesitated before answering, which told me he was making up a story. He was smart, but he had the cocky arrogance of a kid who thought he was smarter than everybody else. "I was just playing games with him."

"What kind of games?"

"Sometimes I'd swipe Gordon's key and go down and mess around in his office."

"Mess around?"

"Move stuff. Just enough that he wouldn't be sure if he'd left if that way himself. Gordon was paranoid, so I liked to mess with his head."

"How often did you do that?"

"I don't know. Three or four times. I hadn't done it in a while."

"Did you look at any of your father's private papers when you were in the office?" Darrell asked, with a glance at Norm.

"Yeah, sometimes."

"About the lawsuit?"

"Sure."

"Did you tell anyone what you saw?"

"No."

Norm put a hand on the boy's arm. "Just to reiterate what

I told Rebecca and Ajax, I never asked Jay to spy for me, and I never got any privileged information from him or Will."

"But I would have done it," Jay added, drawing a frown from Norm.

"Did Gordon find out you'd been in his office?" Darrell asked.

"No."

"He never confronted you about it?"

"No."

"Did he know you'd read materials about the litigation?"

"No."

"Then why was Gordon convinced you were spying on him?"

"I told you, he was paranoid. He was looking over his shoulder the whole time he was here, like he expected something to happen." An inappropriate smirk crossed the teenager's face. "It's almost like he knew the Ursulina would come after him."

Darrell stared across the desk with a stony expression. "Your stepmother says you're planning to stay in Black Wolf County to finish out the semester."

"Yeah."

"I thought you didn't like it here."

"I don't. I mean, I'm sorry if I'm offending your little slice of paradise, but this whole county is a backwater piece of shit. The weather sucks. The food sucks. The people suck."

"Then why stay?"

"Because I've already switched schools once this year, and I don't need to have my grades messed up by switching again. I'm applying to colleges in the fall."

"We heard your father planned to send you back to Milwaukee after Christmas," Darrell said. "The two of you argued about it."

"What else is new? We argued about everything."

"Why did your father want to send you back? He's the one who took you out of the Milwaukee schools to start with. You said he thought the schools there were putting ideas in your head."

"That's right."

"So what changed?"

"Who knows? Maybe he got tired of having me around."

"We heard you threatened him," Darrell went on. "You said if he tried to send you back to Milwaukee, he'd be sorry. What did you mean by that?"

"I didn't mean anything. I just said it. I was spouting off."

"Did you threaten to reveal what you'd seen in his files?"

"No. I told you, he didn't even know I'd been in his office."

"Then what did you mean?"

"Nothing. It was a stupid thing to say."

Darrell reached into his coat and removed a paper bag, and he dropped the contents in front of Jay. It was Ben Malloy's book.

"Is this yours?" Darrell asked.

"Yeah."

"Why did you buy it?"

"I heard stories about the beast hanging out in the woods around here. I was curious."

"Did you read it?"

"I did. Gory stuff."

"The circumstances in which we found your father's body were very similar to what's described in the book."

"So what? You think I killed Gordon and used the book to make it look like the Ursulina did it?" When Darrell's face didn't move, Jay's mouth dropped open with a shiver of fear. "Are you kidding? *That's* what you think?"

"You need to be straight with us, Jay. Did you kill your father?"

"No! No way. I didn't do that."

"Your mother didn't want Erica to tell us about the fight. She was afraid we'd think you murdered your father. Why would she be afraid of that?"

"Mom overreacts sometimes. She knows what Gordon was like to me."

"What was he like to you?"

Jay stuttered. He began to flounder. "I mean, she knows we don't get along. Didn't get along."

"You and your father argued all the time."

"Yeah. I already told you that."

"Gordon yelled at you? He verbally abused you?"

"Sure he did."

"Did the arguments get physical?"

"What do you mean?"

"Did your father hit you?"

Jay frowned. "Yeah. Sometimes."

"How often?"

"Well, all the time, in fact. Pretty much every day. He was a violent son of a bitch."

"Did you ever hit back?"

"No."

"But you wanted to."

Jay's hand curled into a tight fist. "Yeah, sure. I wanted to."

"You hated him," Darrell said, stating it matter-of-factly, like it wasn't even a question.

I watched Jay's eyes flash with anger. "Yeah, I did. So what? He was a pig."

"There were days when you wanted him dead."

"You want me to say it? Fine. Okay. I'll say it. Sometimes I wished he was dead. You bet."

Darrell was good at what he did. Admitting you wanted your father dead was a terrible thing, and even if you didn't kill him, nobody was going to believe your denials after that. Norm obviously thought the same thing.

"We're done, Darrell," he interjected firmly. "No more questions."

Jay continued, still not realizing the danger he'd put himself in. "You don't know what Gordon was like. I told you he was a monster, and you wouldn't listen."

"Jay, not another word," Norm murmured. "That's enough."

The boy slammed both fists down on the schoolroom desk. "No, I'm done pretending about him. Yes, I hated that son of a bitch. He beat the shit out of me whenever he wanted. He told me I was nothing. He called me—"

"*Stop*," Norm insisted.

"But it wasn't me!" Jay shouted at us. "I didn't kill him!"

He sounded like a kid with chocolaty hands telling his mom he had no idea who ate the Hershey bar.

I had to do something. I couldn't watch this kid incriminate himself any further, so I threw Jay a lifeline. No matter what the sheriff wanted, no matter what Darrell thought his duty was, I needed to give Jay a chance to tell us the truth.

"Jay, where were you on Sunday night?" I asked sharply.

The boy stared at me, and I thought his eyes were going to pop out of his head. "What?"

"Where were you?"

"At the house. I told you that."

"Yes, but I think you were lying. Where were you?"

"I was in my room the whole night. I didn't hear anything."

"You didn't hear anything, because you weren't there," I insisted.

"*Rebecca*," Darrell hissed at me. "What the hell are you doing?"

I ignored him and grabbed Jay's wrist. "If you have an alibi, you need to tell us what it is. If you weren't home on Sunday night, you couldn't have killed him. Do you understand that? Nothing else you said or did to your father means anything if you were somewhere else on Sunday night. Where were you, Jay?"

Our eyes met.

He knew I wasn't playing a game with him. No tricks. For just a moment, the classroom felt empty, as if Darrell and Norm were gone, and I was alone with Jay. I could feel his desperation in wanting to open up to me, his secret clawing to get out. His eyes looked into mine and said: *You know, don't you?*

Because I did.

I knew what he was hiding. I can't even tell you how I knew, or what it was that gave it away. But knowing that, I also realized there was no way Jay was ever going to admit it. It was never going to happen.

"I'm telling the truth," he told me again. "I was in my room all night."

And then he added pointedly, "Alone."

CHAPTER FIFTEEN

That night, I sat on the floor of my house in complete darkness, no lights on at all. I wanted it to look like I wasn't home. The fireplace was cold, a whistle of icy wind coming down the chimney and making me shiver. I smoked, but I couldn't even see the gray cloud when I exhaled. Every now and then, I got up and looked out the window, but there was no moon, no starlight, just the thick clouds that would be burying us in snow by morning.

I knew he was out there somewhere. Ricky.

I'd changed the locks since I threw him out, so his key wouldn't work. When I got home, the first thing I did was check the windows to make sure he hadn't broken in. I'd heard he was sleeping on the couch of one of his mine worker friends, but I knew he would come after me sooner or later. He was out for blood. Darrell continued to push me to stay with him and his family for a while—a gallant thing to do, since he was furious at me for interfering in his interrogation of Jay—but I told him no. For every night I spent safely, there was another night after that. Ricky would get to me eventually, and I had to be ready.

He'd left messages on my answering machine. First he was sweet, apologetic, trying to get me to change my mind. *Hey, baby, we can work this out. Come on, you know I love you.* And then, the more he drank, the more the belligerent side of him came out. The profanity. The abuse. The names. The threats. He called me things I wouldn't repeat to anyone, sweetheart, least of all you.

I could have had him arrested, but what would that have done? Soon enough, he'd be back on the street, madder than he was before. No, our day was coming. I didn't know when, but that was why I was sitting alone in the darkness, my gun within reach.

My father had left me a message, too. He was on the road somewhere, drunk and feeling bad. He promised me he'd call more, which was the same promise he made every year, but it never worked out that way. I understood. We loved each other, but we led separate lives. For a long time, I'd thought it was because we were all loners, me, him, and my brother. But that was never really true. It was losing my mom that split us apart. We each went off into our separate caves to grieve, and we never came back out.

There was also something in his voice on the answering machine. It was in his tone, not what he actually said, like he was regretting things in his life that he should have changed and never had. It made me wonder if he was ill. Another few months would prove me right about that.

I was half a pack of cigarettes into my night when I saw headlights in the driveway. Just like that, I was on my feet, my gun cocked and in my hand. I knew the engine rumble of Ricky's truck, and this wasn't it, but he'd be sly enough to borrow someone else's vehicle when he came to get me. The headlights went off before I could see who it was. I heard footsteps approaching the front door, and then somebody called my name in a kind of hush.

"Rebecca?"

It was Ajax.

I stood on the other side of the door, not moving, not answering.

"Come on, Rebecca, I know you're in there."

He wasn't going to go away. I turned on the light in the hallway and opened the door wide enough that he could see the gun in my hand. He put his hands in the air and grinned his typical Ajax grin.

"Don't shoot," he said.

"What do you want?"

He was wearing his deputy's uniform, and his squad car was in the driveway. "Seems like you and me need to figure out how to work together."

"Seems like you need to keep your hands off me," I said.

"I didn't hear any complaints until Ricky showed up." Ajax touched the long, reddish scab on his face where my ring had cut him. "That was when you came down with cat scratch fever."

"Go away, Ajax."

"I'm willing to drop the complaint," he told me, as I began to shut the door. "One word to Jerry from me, and the whole thing goes away. I know you need the job."

"What do you want in return?"

"Nothing. You and me start over. That's all. Come on, let me in, and we'll talk. Just talk, I swear."

I opened the door wider. "You lay a hand on me, and I'll kick you where it counts."

"I believe you."

We went into the living room together. Ajax took one end of the sofa, and I took the other. He lit up a cigarette, and so did I. We watched each other warily. We didn't say anything for a long time, which I suppose was his plan. He simply wanted to sit in my house and let me feel the sexual tension between us. And I did. I had experience in realizing that he knew how to kiss and what to do with his hands. The longer we sat there doing nothing but smoke, the more I thought about taking off his clothes. Just to see what it would be like.

"You'll drop the complaint?" I said finally. "Are you serious about that?"

"Actually, it's already done. I told Jerry to yank it. I told him I overreacted. We were at the bar, we'd both had a little too much to drink. Things happen."

"Thank you."

"Sure."

"You know, I don't get you," I told him, shaking my head. "You've got a gorgeous wife and gorgeous kids. Why do you sleep around?"

"Why do you care?"

"I'm just curious."

"Well, I don't get you, either. You're way out of Ricky's league. Why did you marry him?"

"That's what you do around here. You get married."

"You could have done better."

"In Black Wolf County? Not likely. You take what's in front of you."

Ajax slid his cigarette out of his mouth. "Ricky says you're frigid, you know."

"Excuse me?"

"That's what he tells everybody. You don't move when he screws you, like you can't wait for it to be over."

"I don't give a shit what Ricky tells people," I snapped.

"Is it true?"

"Go to hell, Ajax."

"Hey, I don't blame you. I see Ricky as a two-pump chump. Who wants that?"

"So what are you saying? One night with you will change me forever?"

"Maybe."

"Wow, you've got quite the ego."

Ajax chuckled. "Yeah, I plead guilty to that. But what would it hurt to give it a try? I mean, no one has to know."

He didn't hide what he wanted, which I found strangely attractive.

"Why do you want me as a trophy, anyway?" I asked. "Does it turn you on when I say no? There are plenty of other women around here who are happy to get on their backs for you."

"You've got something the other women don't."

"Oh, yeah? What's that?"

Ajax appraised me from the other side of the sofa. "Honestly? I don't know. But Ricky saw it, too. The first time he laid eyes on you, he told me he'd found a girl who was different from everybody else. This fierce little loner with the amazing dark eyes. I thought he was full of it, but then I saw you myself, and damned if he wasn't right. I thought about going after you, too."

"Except you were already married to Ruby."

Ajax shrugged. "Yeah. There's that."

"I'm not special."

"Oh, sure you are. I don't even think you believe that yourself when you say it. You know you're different."

"I think you should go."

"What, don't you trust yourself around me?"

In fact, I didn't entirely trust myself not to make a stupid mistake. I was curious, amused, appalled, but a little aroused, too. Ricky was right that I didn't get that way often. It's just who I am. Sometimes I wondered what it would be like to have sex with someone where it wasn't about power and control. To meet and be physical with a genuinely good man, as if such a thing existed in this world. But one thing was certain. That wasn't Ricky, and it wasn't Ajax, either.

"I appreciate your dropping the complaint," I said, "but you need to leave. I'm not mad, and I don't mind anything you said. In fact, I appreciate that you were honest with me. But nothing's going to happen between us. Not tonight. Not ever."

He took my rejection gracefully. At least for the time being. I had no illusions that he'd suddenly become a Boy Scout around me. But when I got to my feet, he did, too, and he followed me to the front door without any advances. No hand on my ass. No kiss in the hallway.

"See you tomorrow," Ajax said.

"Yeah. See you."

I opened the door, and I screamed.

Someone stood on the porch right in front of me. In the darkness, I thought at first that it was Ricky, but in the next instant, I realized with a stab of relief that I was wrong.

It was Will Foltz. This big, strong teenage football player burst past me and into the house. Oddly, he was crying.

"I told you he didn't do it!" Will screamed at me. "Jay didn't do it! And now Darrell's trying to arrest him!"

CHAPTER SIXTEEN

Will paced frantically across the green shag carpet in my living room. I'd known him his whole life, and I'd never seen him so wildly upset. His easy smile was gone. His nose ran, and he wiped it on his sweatshirt. His breathing came so fast that he looked like he needed a paper bag to stop hyperventilating. The kid who liked everybody, whose approach to life was as mellow as an Eagles song, was melting down in front of us.

"Will, sit," I told him.

He didn't. He kept pacing. After I repeated it twice more, Ajax stopped the boy in the middle of the room and took him by the shoulders. "*Sit*."

Will slumped onto the sofa, with his face in his hands. I sat next to him. As Will tried to catch his breath, I murmured to Ajax, "An arrest warrant for Jay? Did you know anything about this?"

"It must be Jerry. He wants the Brink case closed. I heard about the interview at the school, Jay going ballistic, talking about wanting his father dead. Combine that with everything else, and Jerry probably thinks they can make the charge stick."

"He didn't do it!" Will gasped again.

I took hold of his meaty shoulder. I'd babysat for him when he was a boy, but this kid was practically twice my size. "Will, tell me what's going on. What happened?"

"Darrell came to my dad's house. He was going to arrest Jay for *murder*. That's crazy! I went and listened at the stairs and heard my dad talking to him. He said Darrell was using intimidation to get Jay to confess to something he didn't do. But Darrell said he had no choice, and he had to bring him in. So my dad came upstairs to get Jay. He was already gone."

"Gone?" Ajax asked.

Will looked down at his lap. "I told him to climb out the window. He ran away. I don't know where he is now."

"That was foolish, Will," I said. "Running makes Jay look guilty, and it puts him in danger, too. You should have trusted your dad. He'll figure out how to make this all go away."

Will shook his head frantically. "No. Dad doesn't know what's going on, and Jay refuses to tell him."

"Tell him what?"

"About Sunday night," Will said. "Jay's lying about what happened. I keep telling him to come clean, but he won't do it. He'd rather risk going to prison for killing his dad than tell the truth. Well, I'm done with that. I'm not going to let him protect me anymore."

Ajax finally sat down, too. "Protect *you?* What the hell, Will? Did you have something to do with Gordon's death?"

But I knew Ajax had it all wrong. This had nothing to do with Gordon.

"Jay wasn't home on Sunday night, was he?" I said.

Without looking up, Will shook his head.

"Where was he?" I asked quietly.

"With me."

"Where?"

"My dad's trailer in the woods."

"All night?"

"Yeah. All night."

Ajax still didn't get it. "What were you guys doing, some kind of Ursulina hunt?"

"No," Will murmured. "I mean, yeah, I'd told Jay about the Ursulina. I even got him Ben's book, because he thought the whole thing was wild, like maybe the beast was real or something. That's why we picked my dad's trailer. It was kind of a dare to see if we could stay there all night."

"You could have just said that," I suggested. "You didn't have to admit what was really going on."

"No. People would have guessed the truth. I already see the looks at school. I hear the talk." He looked at me with a silent plea to say it for him.

"The two of you are . . . gay?" I said with a little hesitation, in case I'd guessed wrong. But I didn't think I had.

"Yeah. That's right."

"Is that why Jay's been protecting you? To keep the secret?"

"Yeah."

Ajax's face darkened, first with surprise and then disgust. If I'd given him a thousand guesses, he wouldn't have gotten it himself. He got up, saying something I won't repeat. Regardless, the slur hit Will like a blow to the face, and he knew perfectly well that more were coming. Every day of his life, wherever he went, people around here would know who he was. This wasn't the kind of story that could be contained, not in Black Wolf County.

"Does your father know?" I asked.

"Not yet. I guess I have to tell him now."

"I know Norm. He'll be okay with it."

Will shook his head. "Don't be so sure."

"Jay wanted to keep this hidden?" I asked.

"Yeah, but not for himself. He didn't want to out me. I told him we should come forward and admit it, but he knew what it would be like for me if people knew. He could go back to Milwaukee, and I'd be stuck here. But I'm not going to let him get arrested when I know he's innocent. He was with me Sunday night. All night. He has an alibi. He didn't kill his father."

"Were Gordon's problems with Jay about him being gay?"

"Oh, yeah. Gordon couldn't deal with it. His son being gay made him less of a man. He actually said that, you know? That's why Gordon took him out of school in Milwaukee. He thought it was the school that had turned him gay. He figured, bring him here, he'll meet a nice blond girl." Will gave a sour laugh. "Instead, he met a nice blond boy."

I noticed Ajax standing in the shadows on the far side of my living room. He didn't say another word; he didn't even look at Will. His revulsion ran deep. I'd like to tell you that he was an exception around here, but the truth is, he was the rule. You could be a lot of things in this part of the world and people wouldn't care, but being gay wasn't one of them. This was the end of Will Foltz, popular kid and football star.

"Gordon found out about you and Jay?" I asked.

"Yeah. He caught us together. Honestly, it was stupid. I should have stopped Jay, but he wanted to do it in Gordon's office. I think it was his way of throwing it all in his father's face, you know? That's how his fingerprints got there. Because *we* were there. In bed. Gordon came back while we were in the middle of things, and he practically had a stroke. That's why he was so crazy for my dad to keep me away from Jay. It didn't have anything to do with the lawsuit. He made that up. He wasn't going to admit what was really going on."

Just like that, in the middle of Will's story, Ajax left the room. He didn't say a word to either of us. He didn't look at me or Will, he just left. Seconds later, I heard my front door slam. The whole house shook on its foundation. Outside, Ajax's car squealed away.

"He's going to tell everybody, isn't he?" Will said.

I wanted to say no, but I couldn't do that. Will wouldn't have believed me, anyway. He knew the score. In a few hours, the news would be all over town. His life as he knew it was over.

"I don't care," he insisted, wiping his face. "Let them find out. Let them all find out. Jay's innocent. I don't care what happens to me."

CHAPTER SEVENTEEN

By noon the next day, Will was in the hospital.

It happened between the first and second period classes. Eight other boys jumped him as he was getting books from his locker. It took that many kids to overpower Will, who fought back and landed plenty of blows before they were able to pin him to the ground and begin beating on him. A couple dozen other teens stood and watched and cheered them on. The attack went on for almost ten minutes before two teachers finally intervened and were able to pull the kids away.

By the time Darrell and I reached the school, an ambulance had already taken Will to the neighboring county, which was where the nearest hospital was located. We arrested three teens who bore the bruises and black eyes of Will fighting back. They refused to identify any of the other teens who'd been involved, and none of the kids who'd watched in the hallway would talk to us, either. Even the teachers claimed to have not seen who else had taken part.

I had to leave the interview room rather than listen to the questioning, because I was sickened by what I heard. I knew these teens, and I knew their parents. Before that day, I would have called them good kids, funny, athletic, even a little naive about the ways of the world. These same teens had set upon a boy who'd been one of their heroes, and there was absolutely no regret in their eyes. They thought that they were the real victims, that Will had made fools of them, gulled them into being friends with a pervert. That was actually the mildest of the words they used to describe him.

There would be no legal consequences for what they did. I knew that. We'd arrested them, but the county prosecutor would make it all go away. Even in the unlikely event that the case made it to court, the judge would give them a stern lecture and set them free. There would be nothing on their records. Nothing that would follow them around for the rest of their lives.

I went back to my desk, but I could hear the other deputies talking about it. Laughing, making jokes. Ajax was among them. Ajax, who'd probably gone straight to the 126 from my house and started the rumors flying. He'd known exactly what would happen to Will as soon as the news got out, but he didn't care. I couldn't even look at him. It sickened me to think I'd actually felt a physical attraction to this man. I sat at my desk for a while and tried to block it all out, but I realized I needed to get away from there. I grabbed my coat and left, feeling as if their voices were chasing me out the door.

Outside, the snow we'd been expecting had begun. It fell in a white cloud, heavy and dense, making the world seem quieter. A storm like this came once or twice in a season, gathering inch by inch as the hours passed, making you wonder if it would ever stop. I got in my cruiser and drove, and other than the occasional plow trying to keep up with the snowfall, I had the highway to myself. I struggled to stay in the lane and not slide off into a ditch, and I had to squint to see.

There's something about the enveloping whiteness of a blizzard that makes you hallucinate. I had the strangest visions out there, of snowy owls, of bodies in the road, of my mother floating in the sky like an angel. I felt the beginnings of a deep depression, as if the emptiness of the blizzard had begun to mirror the emptiness in my soul. I'd felt that way only once before, a hollowness that had dogged me for weeks. There were days during that stretch when I didn't get out of bed all day. I remember it had felt like I held a gun in my hand, and one by one, my brain was shooting down the things that mattered to me. I had never experienced a scarier time than that. I realized my only two choices were to die or start living again. I chose life, and after surviving that summer of discontent, I found the will to go on. That same depression had never come back to me, not like that, but I could feel it out there again. I could see it in the snow cloud, coming for me.

Ninety minutes later, I crossed the county line and made it to the hospital where they'd taken Will. He was unconscious. His face was barely recognizable, his black-and-blue eyes swollen shut, his head bandaged, one arm in a cast. This happy, handsome teenager, a boy I'd known since he was a baby, had been sitting next to me in my house the previous night. A day later, here he was, clinging to life. I sat by the bed and took his hand, and all I could do was tell him in a low voice how sorry I was.

"Who did it?"

I looked up and saw Norm standing by the curtain that divided the room. He had a cup of hospital coffee in his hand, and he looked as if he'd aged a decade in a few hours.

"What?"

"Who did it?" he asked me. "Who told everyone about Will? I know it wasn't you, Rebecca."

"Of course not."

"Then who?" He sat down in the chair next to me. "Ajax?"

"Let it go, and focus on Will," I said.

Norm shook his head, as if letting go was an impossible thing. He stared at his son, with his face frozen into a mask of helplessness and hatred. "My whole life has been about the law, you know? How to get things done within the system. And now the system is worthless. Ajax put a target on my son's chest, and there's nothing I can do about it. There's no law. There's nothing. I just want to kill the son of a bitch."

"You shouldn't say things like that," I murmured.

Norm's face twitched. As he sipped his coffee, he began to cry silently. I'd never seen him cry before.

"What do the doctors say?" I asked.

"He has a broken arm, broken nose, broken jaw, and fractured skull. They're afraid of swelling in the brain. We won't know more until he wakes up."

"He'll pull through," I said, fervently hoping that was true. "He's strong. He'll be fine."

Norm didn't answer.

"Where's Kathy?" I asked, because I assumed his wife was here, too.

"They had to give her a sedative. She's in another room."

"I am so sorry, Norm. This is all my fault."

"There's nothing you could have done."

"Will came to see me last night. I—I wasn't alone. Ajax was with me. Will was so upset, and he wanted to talk about Jay. I should have stopped him. I shouldn't have let him tell me anything until it was just the two of us. I knew what he was going to say, and I should have known what the consequences would be."

Norm stared at me. "You knew what he was going to say?"

"I guessed."

"How?"

"I don't know. I just had a feeling. I can't even tell you where it came from."

Norm shook his head. "He was my son, and *I* didn't know. I didn't have a clue. Neither did Kathy. The only way I even found out today was when I saw what they'd written on his locker. That word. I thought, they made a mistake. They nearly killed my son over a mistake. It never even occurred to me that it was true. When I saw Jay, he admitted it to me, and I couldn't believe it."

"You saw Jay?" I asked.

Norm nodded. "He came to the hospital. He was devastated. Just gutted. The way he looked at Will, the only way I can explain it is that he's in love with him. And do you know what's crazy? I don't even know what the hell that means. I really don't even understand it."

I wanted to ask where Jay was, but Norm kept talking.

"You said Will came to see you last night?" he asked me. "He *told* you about him and Jay?"

"Yes."

"And yet he couldn't tell me. I'm his father, and he couldn't tell me."

"He only told me because he was trying to protect Jay. He knew the sheriff was planning to arrest Jay for Gordon's murder."

"But why wouldn't he tell me?" Norm asked with a sad anguish. "What did he think I would say? Did he think we'd disown him? Kick him out?"

"What would you have done?"

Norm took a long time to answer. "Honestly? I don't know. I like to think I'm open-minded, but I have no idea what I would have said. Maybe he sensed that. You know, the last couple of years, Will has been strange with us. Distant. Not sharing with us the way he did when he was a boy. He and I were always so close, but he's been pulling away from me for a while now. I figured it was just the teenage years. I never dreamed he was struggling with something like this."

"It couldn't have been easy for him."

"No." Norm looked at me. "Gordon Brink knew, didn't he? That's why he was trying to keep Will and Jay apart."

"Yes. That's what Will told me. Brink caught them together."

"I suppose you think this gives Jay another motive to kill his father."

"I'm sure the sheriff will think that, but according to Will, Jay has an alibi. They were together that Sunday night."

"That's not going to satisfy Jerry. We both know that."

"No, probably not. I doubt Will can prove that they were in your trailer together. The sheriff is going to say Will is simply covering for Jay, and people around here will be inclined to believe it."

"Because who wants to take the word of a queer, right?"

"I'm not saying it's fair."

"Will wouldn't lie," Norm snapped. "If he says they were together, they were."

"I know that. But regardless, I need to find Jay."

"So you can arrest him?"

"That's up to Darrell and Jerry. Frankly, being in a cell might be the safest place for him right now. You've seen what the kids did to Will. If they catch up with Jay, it's likely to be even worse. I don't want to see anything happen to him. Do you know where he is?"

"I'm his lawyer," Norm said. "I can't say anything about that. And don't try to tell me he'd be safe locked up in a cell, Rebecca. I know the men you work with. I wouldn't trust what they'd do to him. Besides, even if I wanted to negotiate a way for Jay to turn himself in, I can't leave the hospital. I need to stay here with Will."

"Norm, he's in *danger* on his own."

"What do you want me to do, Rebecca?"

"Trust me. Tell me where he is."

Norm rubbed his face with exhaustion and mussed his thinning hair. "Can I talk to the Rebecca Colder I've known since she was a little girl? And not to the sheriff's deputy?"

"Yes. I promise you that."

Norm stared at his son in the hospital bed. In the low light, Will breathed in and out, but he showed no signs of consciousness. Even so, I felt as if Norm were pleading with his son for advice. And for forgiveness.

"Jay is out of control, Rebecca," Norm said. "He blames himself for what happened to Will. He's desperate."

"That's even more reason for me to find him. Where is he?"

"He was driving his dad's car. The Mercedes. I told him to go back to my house and park the car in the garage and make sure the door was closed. I said he should stay in the house with the lights off and *not* answer if anyone came by."

"How do I get in?" I asked.

"I keep a spare key inside the brass light fixture on the porch."

"Thank you, Norm. I'll find him, and I'll keep him safe."

I got out of the chair, but Norm took my arm gently before I could leave. "Rebecca?"

"What is it?"

He hesitated, struggling again, as if the lawyer were doing battle with the father. "There's something else. You need to be very careful if you go in there."

"Why?"

Norm swallowed hard as he tried to get the words out. "Jay has a gun."

CHAPTER EIGHTEEN

On the highway, the plows had given up their fight against the blizzard, and my tires punched and swerved through wet snow on the way back to Norm's house. Drifts blew into terraced mountains that I had to navigate around. The storm showed no sign of letting up. My snow-ghosts—my hallucinations—followed me across the county, twisting my gut with the things I saw. I had visions of the three victims of the Ursulina standing on the shoulder, their skin in ribbons. I saw Ricky hiding behind every tree. Most of all, worst of all, I kept hearing the lonely, plaintive cry of a baby in the screech of the wind.

Call it a premonition. An omen or a sign.

Was it you, sweetheart? Were you telling me you were out there? Were you crying about things to come?

By the time I made it to the forest outside Random, the gray late afternoon sky had begun to darken into night. When I reached Norm's house, I saw that I wasn't the first to arrive. The vandals had already struck. A gay slur had been spray-painted in huge red letters across Norm's garage, and several first-floor windows had been smashed. Splintered debris was everywhere, and ash and smoke floated in the air with the snow. I realized they'd broken into the workshop and thrown Will's woodwork into the yard and burned it like a bonfire. They'd also scattered the contents of Will's high school locker on the front steps and left a message for him painted on the door.

Don't come back.

I didn't bother knocking. I retrieved the key from the light post near the door and let myself inside. The house was cold, with winter air and snow hissing through broken windows. Sharp fragments of glass covered the hardwood floor.

"Jay?" I called. "Jay, it's Rebecca. Are you here?"

There was no answer. I searched the whole house and couldn't find him. His moving boxes had been delivered, but they sat on the floor of one of the upstairs bedrooms, unopened. When I went outside and checked the garage, I saw no sign of Gordon Brink's Mercedes. Either Jay had left when he'd seen the damage, or he'd never come here at all.

The other kids in town were undoubtedly hunting for him. And Jay had a gun. That was a volatile combination. I needed to find him.

I thought about checking the house that Gordon had been renting, but I didn't think Jay would go back there. And he was still a stranger to the area, so I doubted that he would know many of the hideaways that teenagers learned about growing up here. Plus, most of our secret places were summer escapes, and this was winter, and the snow was falling in waves.

Then I knew.

I knew exactly where Jay would go. He'd return to the place where he and Will had spent the night together.

I got back into my car and headed east. Night fell hard not long after I started out, and so I had to deal with the storm and the darkness at the same time. What would normally take me an hour took me two, as I fought the snow and tried to see. I missed the turnoff to the dirt road that led to Norm's trailer, and I had to do a U-turn to go back and find it. The depth of the snow made the road almost impassible, but a couple of cars had obviously traveled this stretch before me, and I was able to use the ruts they'd left to make my way through the forest. After several miles, my headlights reflected on the chassis of a car parked in a turnoff, barely visible among the trees. I could see that it was a Mercedes. I pulled in behind it and got out. The crowns of the trees overhead gave me a little protection from the snow, but the wind in my face was bitter and fierce. I trudged to the car and shined my flashlight inside, but it was empty.

"Jay?" I shouted, barely able to hear my own voice over the howl of the gales. "Jay, are you here?"

No one answered me.

There was no trail to follow, just snow, but I knew where I was going. I headed along a path through the trees, and ahead of me, I saw a faint square of light like a will-o'-the-wisp. It was the glow of windows in Norm's Airstream. Someone was inside. As I neared the trailer, however, I spotted another car parked at the end of the trail. This one was a yellow Cadillac.

Ben Malloy was spending the night in the woods again.

I thumped on the trailer door. Ben answered with a pipe in his mouth, as he always did. He wore an open bubble coat, red corduroys, and moon boots. He had a camera with a flash attachment hanging around his neck.

"Deputy Rebecca," he said with surprise. "What on earth are you doing out here in the middle of the storm?"

"I could say the same to you, Ben."

"Well, I'm Ursulina hunting, of course. I was getting ready to go stalk the beast. Since you're here, I'd be happy to have company on my quest."

"Have you seen Jay Brink?" I asked.

"Who?"

"Teenage boy. Tall, reddish hair, dark eyes."

"I haven't seen him, but I haven't seen anyone out here."

"His car's parked on the road. I need to find him."

"Say no more," Ben replied. He zipped up his coat and trundled down the trailer steps. "I have a compass, a lantern, and peanut shells."

"Peanut shells?" I asked.

"To mark our trail and make sure we can find our way back. We wouldn't want to get lost out here, would we?"

"No."

"Any idea where to look for this boy?"

I shined my flashlight at the snow in the clearing surrounding the Airstream. It didn't take me long to find Jay's trail. Close by, fresh footsteps went up to the trailer windows and then led into the forest. "There. Jay must have realized someone was inside, so he went off by himself."

With my flashlight guiding us, we followed Jay's tracks. Ben stayed behind me, but he was invisible unless I turned the light directly at him. It was a difficult slog, and I could hear him huffing and puffing, but he didn't complain. He crunched on peanuts, eating them and then dropping the shells like Hansel and Gretel leaving bread crumbs. The smell of his pipe followed us through the woods.

As the wind gusted and sprayed wet snow, my skin felt raw. I pushed my way forward, stumbling into branches that slapped my face. The drifts got inside my boots and melted, and soon my feet were cold and wet. Several times, I lost Jay's footprints and had to stop and scan the ground to find them again before we could continue. During one long stretch, when I was afraid I'd lost his trail altogether, we heard movement not far away from us. Ben immediately had his camera up, and the pop of his flashbulb nearly blinded me. As my eyes swam with orange reflections, I spotted a deer bounding away through the trees.

"Next time, give me a little warning about the flash," I said.

"And miss the Ursulina? I'm sorry, Deputy, but no. Strike while the iron is hot!"

I said nothing. I kept scanning the snow for Jay's footprints. My chest felt tight with fear.

"You don't believe me, do you?" Ben murmured, his voice coming out of the darkness. Strangely, in the cathedral of the forest, it felt right to whisper.

"About what?"

"That when I was a boy, I saw the Ursulina."

"I never said I didn't believe you."

"Well, when I told you about it the other day, there was a strange look on your face, which I assume was skepticism. Believe me, I'm used to it. However, even if you think my television show is a fraud, I'm not lying about what I saw."

"No?"

"No, it really happened. Actually, it wasn't all that far from here. I was camping alone on a weekend in September. I think I was eighteen. The woods have never frightened me, you know. Not like other people. I spend hours out here by myself, and I always feel perfectly at home."

I wanted to say: *Me, too.*

"If I have my bearings right, we're not far from Sunflower Lake," Ben went on. "Do you know it?"

"Yes, I know it."

I knew that lake, because this was where we'd camped when I was ten years old. My father, my brother, and me. This was where I'd gone into the woods and seen him, smelled him, heard him. *Huffffff.* I'd come back to this place dozens of times to search for him. Weird, isn't it? On some level, I missed the beast. He belonged to me in an unfathomable way. Not to Ben Malloy. Not to anyone else. Me. Rebecca Colder. I resented the idea that Ben had seen him, too.

"I was day-hiking along the lake," Ben continued. "I was—oh, I don't know—three or four miles from camp, staying close to the lakeshore. It was late, dusk, everything gray and shadowy, and that was when I heard this loud snort. It wasn't like anything I'd ever heard before. I didn't have a camera or anything, and I couldn't see very well. But I ran along the beach, and that was when I saw him. Just a glimpse as he vanished into the trees with a crash. Upright, huge, spiky orangish fur. I ran, and I found the place where he'd disappeared, but it was dry, and there were no footprints. I spent another hour trying to find him, but he was gone. I've never seen him again. Mind you, I've looked and looked, but all I had was that one glimpse, a split second, no more. I'll tell you the truth, though. Once you've spotted him, you grow obsessed with the experience. I won't die a happy man unless I see him again. I suppose that sounds crazy. You probably can't understand it."

"Oh, I understand," I said with a catch in my voice.

Ben pondered my tone. He turned on his own lantern and held it up to see my face, and then he simply stared at me. I tried to hide my emotions, but everything he said about his sighting—and how he'd felt afterward—was the same way I'd felt since I was ten years old.

"Well, I'll be damned," Ben said.

"What?"

"You've seen him, too."

"Don't be ridiculous."

"You search for him, don't you? You listen for him. Just like me. That snort, it's very distinctive, isn't it? Sort of a *huffffff*."

"I have no idea what you're talking about."

Ben shook his head in wonder, as if discovering a long-lost sister. "That strange look you had. It wasn't skepticism. You were *jealous*. It's hard to share him, isn't it? I know what that's like. It makes you feel special to have him to yourself. I've met a lot of people who've claimed that they saw the Ursulina, but honestly, I'm pretty sure most of them were lying. Except for this one old man. His story was almost exactly like mine, and there was this look in his eyes. A look that said he shared my obsession. I was actually depressed for days after I met him. I know how it sounds, but it's like the monster had cheated on me. And yet, eventually, I came to realize that it was a good thing. I was able to put to rest that voice in my head that said I hadn't seen what I did. You know the voice I mean, don't you?"

"No. I really don't."

I turned away from his light, because I didn't want him examining my face anymore. I swung my flashlight back to the ground, and in the snow piled near the trunk of a fat oak, I saw Jay's trail again. It was quickly being erased by the wind. Soon the path would be lost altogether.

"Come on, we need to hurry."

I moved as quickly as I could through the snow. Ben followed behind me. We were very close to the lake. Even in the darkness, I could see the paler light of a clearing not far away. The inlet was there, washing in from the deeper water, the trees ringing the shore. That's where Jay's footsteps led. Years ago, I'd been the one standing there by the lake, scratching my mosquito bites under the monster's moon, listening to the warning of the owl and having no idea what was waiting for me in the woods.

The footsteps headed straight to the shore.

"Jay?" I called. "Jay, are you there? It's Rebecca Colder."

I stumbled forward to where the trees ended, my flashlight

bobbing because I was practically running. The wind, with nothing to slow it down in the open, intensified to a roar, whipping the snow into a hurricane. The soft ground became a rocky beach under my feet. In some places, the snow was two feet deep, and in others, it had been blown clean down to the rough stones. There was no dark water in front of me, just a thick white bed of winter ice.

The cone of my light lit up a tiny piece of the inlet. There was Jay. He stood on the ice, snow swirling around him. A solitary teenager, overwhelmed by the cruelty of the world.

"Jay!" I called to him over the wind. "It's okay. I'm not here to arrest you. I just want you safe."

I motioned for Ben to stay where he was. I drew closer, walking down to the dividing line where the solidness of the land gave way to the solidness of the ice. Jay was about twenty feet away, buffeted by fierce gales. His hands were buried in his pockets, and his body shook. He looked cold. He'd been crying, but the tears had frozen to his cheeks. In the starkness of the light, his face looked haunted, almost like the hollow bones of a skull.

"Come on, Jay. Let me take you away from here."

I took a step onto the ice, but then I stopped in horror. Jay took a hand out of his pocket and put a gun to the side of his head.

"*No!*" I screamed. "Jay, don't! Put it down. You don't want to do this."

The teenager's arm trembled, and so did the barrel of the gun. "Did you see Will? Did you see what they did to him?"

"I did. It's terrible. But Will's strong. He'll get better."

"The doctors say there could be brain damage. He'll never be the same."

"Jay, listen to me. He'll get *better*." I was trying to convince myself as much as him.

"I did this. He's lying in that hospital bed because of me."

"That's not true."

"I told him to stay quiet about us. Why couldn't he stay quiet?"

"Because Will's a decent, honorable kid," I said.

"I love him."

"I know."

"I love him, but I destroyed his whole life. I wish I'd never met him. I wish I could go back and change everything."

"I understand. Really, I do. I know exactly how you feel. But this isn't the answer, Jay. Put down the gun. Put it on the ice, and walk toward me."

Jay didn't do what I said. Instead, he pushed the barrel harder into his head, and I flinched. I put up my hands and took a few more steps. The snow swirled, and the wind roared. I blinked as ice balls gathered on my eyelids. Under my feet, I could hear the thump of the water pushing like a body against the ice, trying to get free. I felt as if we were surrounded by the dead, all the ones who'd come before us. They came and went in the white cloud, ghosts pointing their crooked fingers at me. I felt a sickness in my stomach.

"Gordon hated me," Jay said. He still couldn't call him his father.

"No, he didn't. Maybe he didn't understand you, but fathers don't hate their sons."

"He hated me, and I hated him."

"Don't do this to yourself," I told him. "Let me get you help. Put down the gun, and let's get out of here."

Jay shook his head. "I'm done."

"You're not. No way are you done. You are seventeen years old, and you have the rest of your life ahead of you. You didn't do anything wrong."

"I want to confess. You're a cop, right? I want to confess."

"Confess to what?"

"*I* killed Gordon," Jay said.

"No, you didn't."

"I did. It was me." He jabbed a finger at Ben Malloy, who'd emerged from the trees and was standing by the lakeshore. "You! Do you hear me? Do you hear what I'm saying? I killed him! I killed Gordon Brink! Me and nobody else! I cut the bastard into little pieces. I sliced him up and watched him bleed to death. You're looking for the beast that did it? The monster? That's me!"

"Jay," I begged him. "No! What are you doing?"

"*I am the Ursulina!*" he bellowed.

"Stop it! You're not!"

"Will lied!" he shouted at us. "He wanted to protect me. Will's not gay. I am. We were friends, that's all. Tell everybody! It was a mistake! He lied because he didn't want to see me go to prison. He made up the whole story. He sacrificed himself for a *lie*. We weren't together out here. Nothing happened between us. I came on to him, and he rejected me. Tell them! I was home on Sunday night. I had a huge fight with Gordon, and I went down to the office to confront him. I hit him, and then I cut him up. Do you hear me? I used the book, and I made it look just like the others. It was *me*!"

"Jay, don't." I was crying. I wanted to fall to my knees. "Don't do this!"

His voice grew calm, and the calm was worse than everything else. It was the calm of someone who'd made his decision. "Please tell them. Save Will. Give him his life back."

"*Jay!*"

The boy's finger slid over the trigger. Time stood still. I ran, but I was too far away to do anything. I screamed at him, but in the next instant, he fired. The wind picked that moment to wail like a banshee, and I could barely hear the noise of the gun at all. The only way I knew that Jay was dead was that his body collapsed to the ice right in front of me.

CHAPTER NINETEEN

My fault, sweetheart.

This was my fault. Will was in the hospital, and Jay was dead. Two sweet teenage boys, one life ruined, one life over. I wasn't able to stop it.

All I can tell you is that I had a breakdown. I didn't want to be who I was anymore. Staring at Jay's body on the ice, the red blood from his head already freezing hard against white snow, I realized that I wanted to get away from everything around me. Leave it all behind. The deaths, the abuse, the loneliness, the failures, the specter of the Ursulina. The monster in the woods had obsessed me for too long.

I knew I had duties to perform. I was a sheriff's deputy, and a boy was dead. There were calls to be made, evidence to be gathered, reports to be written, laws and procedures to be followed. I did none of those things. What I did was leave the scene in a kind of daze. Ben Malloy, who was in shock at what had happened in front of him, pestered me with questions, but I said nothing. I was numb, overwhelmed, unable to function. With my flashlight, I followed the trail all the way back to Norm's trailer. I went to my cruiser, and I got inside and drove away, leaving Ben shouting in frustration at me.

That depression I told you about?

It fell down on me from the sky; it enveloped me like the snow. The gun in my brain that blasted away everything I loved, everything I cared about, everything that had any meaning, made a slow, inexorable turn, until its smoking black barrel was pointed at my face. I felt completely and utterly empty, a shell, with nothing to live for, no happiness, no joy. I'd added nothing to this world with my existence. Drop Rebecca Colder in the lake, and her body would sink with no ripples.

There was no question in my mind about what I should do. I was going to end it. That was my plan; that was all I could think about. The only thing I wasn't sure about was where to go. Where to walk in those final moments. Where to draw my gun and place it in my mouth. I wondered what last image my eyes should have, before the whiteness of the snow became the blackness and nothingness of death.

I drove along the snowy highway, studying each crossroad and wondering which one had a sign that read: *This way, Rebecca*. Half a dozen times, I stopped, contemplating whether to turn the wheel. If you're planning to kill yourself, one place really is as good as any other. But each time, I kept going. I guess life takes you where you're supposed to be, for better or worse.

It was an owl that saved me.

An owl is why you're here in this world, sweetheart.

I squinted through the slush on my windshield, and suddenly, there it was, face in front of me, wings spread like Jesus on the cross. The car hit the owl, or the owl hit the car, and then it was gone, rising in the air, going up and down drunkenly as if it was struggling to soar. I screeched to a stop on the shoulder and bolted from the car, scanning the woods for the bird. The owl had vanished, but its cry called to me, guided me. I ran toward the sound and found a break in the trees, near the entrance road to a national forest campground that was closed for the season.

Somewhere down there, the owl beckoned me with its call.

This way, Rebecca.

The snow came up to my knees. I couldn't walk or run; it was as if I swam through it, which left me breathless. The entrance road took me to a clearing near the lake. The same huge lake that made a kind of sunflower in the middle of the forest, with rounded inlets like petals, which was how it got its name. The lake continued past the spot where Ben Malloy had seen the Ursulina; it flowed into deep water at its core where the winter ice was thin; and it extended all the way to the place where I'd stood and watched the monster's moon, and where I'd just seen Jay Brink put a bullet in his head.

Do you believe in signs, sweetheart?

The owl led me to this lake. It led me to what I was destined to find, because when I got there, I discovered that I wasn't alone. There was a pickup truck parked by the shore, practically buried in snow. It wasn't going anywhere. And from the steamed-over windows, I realized that the truck wasn't empty. Someone needed my help.

I had a purpose in life again.

I shouldered my way through the drifts and tapped on the driver's window. When the window rolled down, I found myself staring at a young man only a few years older than me, no more than thirty, who looked ready to freeze to death. He had no coat; he was actually wearing a short-sleeved shirt. In January! He was a strong, strapping man, with a thick mane of slightly curly brown hair and a perfectly trimmed brown beard. His face, like mine, had a sadness about it, but I couldn't help but notice how handsome he was.

Seeing me, this man gave me a smile that warmed my insides like the smoothest of whiskeys. What can I tell you? It was a smile without guile or cynicism or lust, just the earnest smile of a decent man. I liked him at once. In fact, sweetheart, you may or may not believe this, but I fell in love with him right then and there in that single moment. I saw his eyes and his smile, and I melted. Maybe it was the situation I was in. Maybe I needed to see a kind face when my nerves were stretched to the breaking point. But regardless, something about this man's face made my heart soar.

"You must be an angel," he told me, which was exactly what I was thinking about him. "I wasn't sure I would make it through the night."

I found myself at a loss for words, but then I finally recovered and said, "What are you doing out here, sir?"

"I'd tell you if I could, Deputy, but I don't even know where I am."

"Are you all right? Do you need a doctor?"

"No, it's nothing like that. It's been a difficult day. My mother died this morning."

Something about the way he said it wounded me like the sharpest of arrows. I guess that's the way we all are about our mothers. Saying goodbye to the woman who brought us into the world is a loss like no other. And yes, I know, with you and me, it's much more complicated than that.

"I'm very sorry," I told him.

"Thank you. I guess I had a kind of breakdown after it happened. I just got in my car and started driving. I've been driving for hours through the snow, and at some point, I ended up here. Where am I, anyway?"

"This is Sunflower Lake," I told him. "In Black Wolf County."

"It reminds me of one of my favorite lakes back home. Shelby Lake."

"Shelby," I said, rolling it around on my tongue. "That's a pretty name."

"And it's a pretty lake, too. I don't know, maybe that's why I stopped here. Something drew me to this place. Like this was where I was going all along. Do you know what I mean? I guess we all end up where we're supposed to be."

"I do know what you mean," I said.

"Anyway, the snow kept falling. I didn't really pay attention to it, but a little while ago, I realized I couldn't get out. Disaster sort of creeps up on you like that. And as you can see, I'm not exactly dressed for the weather."

He had such an easy way of talking. His voice had a gentleness that seemed unusual for a big man. I enjoyed listening to it the way I'd enjoy someone quietly strumming a guitar. With his beard covering everything but his lips, he seemed to speak with his eyes. They were chocolate-brown eyes, serious but also sweet. I didn't think I'd ever had a man's eyes look at me the way his eyes did. He studied me carefully, but with no demands, no expectation, no ownership, just appreciation. With one look, his eyes told me I was pretty, and then they backed away to give me space. Which, suddenly, I didn't want. I wanted no space from him at all.

We had a kinship, this man and me, both of us arriving here from dark places. That's the only way I can explain it. And as for breakdowns, I knew what that was like, because I was in the midst of one myself. Weird, though, all my plans for what I was going to do somehow vanished from my mind as soon as I met him.

"What's your name?" I asked him.

"Tom," he told me. "Tom Ginn."

*

Tom's pickup truck wouldn't be moving until the plows came. With my radio, I put in a request to have the campground cleared of snow, which normally they wouldn't bother to do in this season. Even so, it would be hours before they got here. Snow continued to blanket the area, and the plows would be busy staying ahead of the drifts on the highways and town streets.

I could have—should have—taken Tom to the sheriff's office. Essentially, I was AWOL from my job. I'd left a dead body on the ice and done nothing about it, but that night, I couldn't face Darrell, or Ajax, or Jerry. As it turned out, Tom didn't want to go to the sheriff's office either. He was AWOL from his own job. I knew his name sounded familiar, and he reminded me that he was the sheriff of Mittel County, our distant neighbors on the eastern side of the state. He didn't want to deal with questions, shoptalk, or false sympathy from the others in our office. This night was about him and his mother, and I totally understood his desire for privacy.

So I took him home with me.

Something about this man made me feel both protective and protected. Being with him gave me a kind of glow, as if I were part-mother, part-wife. He settled naturally into my house, stoking a fire in my fireplace. His clothes were wet, and he was almost blue with cold, so I let him change in my bathroom and take a hot shower. I put his clothes in the washer. He was a much taller, more athletic man than Ricky, so none of my husband's clothes would have fit him. Instead, Tom put on a terry robe that was a little short for him and then modestly wrapped a blanket around himself. He sat down by the fire, and I showered and changed, too.

We both should have been hungry, because neither one of us had eaten in hours, but we weren't. We sat next to each other on the worn carpet, hypnotized by the flames. He looked absorbed by his own thoughts as he stared at the fire, but I snuck glances at him. His skin had a tanned glow, even in winter, that made a contrast with my stark paleness. His brown hair was still wet from the shower. He was lean, maybe a little too skinny for his height, but strong and muscular. I felt small next to him, but a good kind of small.

"Was your mother ill for a long time?" I asked softly when we'd been silent for several minutes.

"Yes. She had early-onset dementia. It's been getting worse for a while now."

"How old was she?"

"Not even sixty."

"Oh, you must be devastated."

"Well, it's hard to lose anyone you love, but I've been losing her day by day for five years. The cruelty of it is hard to fathom, to see someone so very strong and independent lose any sense of who they are. And unfortunately, my father is well on the same road, too. I expect he only has a few more months. He's living with me now. I really should be there with him, but after Mom passed, I couldn't go home. I asked a colleague of mine, Monica, to stay at my place, so at least I know Dad's okay. But I feel guilty. I didn't even call him to say that Mom—his wife—was gone. He wouldn't have understood, and I couldn't handle that. Thirty-five years together, and they didn't know each other anymore. They were strangers. It's such a lonely disease."

"I'm so sorry, Tom."

He smiled at me again. Then he reached out and took my hand. I liked it.

"You know what's utterly terrifying?" he went on, turning back to the fire. "I know my time will come. It will happen to me, too. Sooner or later, I'll be the man who forgets his past, his friends, his entire identity."

"You don't know that for sure."

"Let's just say my family history makes it a pretty safe bet. Genetics spares no one. But it's not all bad, not really. A cloud over my head like that reminds me to live a life that matters. If I lose my own memory, at least I want to believe that others will have good memories of me."

It made me inexpressibly sad to hear him talk like that.

"Are you married, Tom?" I asked.

"No. Between my job and my parents, I haven't had time for anyone else in my life."

"You're very young to be the sheriff."

"I know." He laughed at himself. "Don't think I'm so special. Truly, no one else in Mittel County wanted the job, and I admit, I did. It's what I've always wanted to do. It was my dream ever since I was a boy watching *The Lone Ranger* on television. Some people go through life never knowing what they want, but me, I always did. My dad was still relatively lucid two years ago. He insisted I go after it when the old sheriff died. I thought I should wait until I was older. I also didn't think I could juggle being the sheriff with caring for the two of them, but he told me, you can't ignore opportunity when it comes knocking or it just moves on to somebody else."

"I think I'd like your father," I said.

"You'd like who he was, that's for sure. Everything I am is because of him."

"Well, I like you, too."

Tom turned and focused his brown eyes on me. The fire made his face shine. Or maybe he was blushing. "Listen to me going on about myself. I'm sorry. I'm just the unwanted visitor here. Tell me about you."

"There's not much to tell."

"I doubt that. Everybody has a story." He nodded at my left hand. "I see a ring. So you're married?"

"Not for much longer."

"I'm sorry."

"Don't be. I finally realized he's not a good person."

"Well, there are men like that. You deserve someone better."

"I'm not sure I do."

"You shouldn't talk like that. I just met you, but I can already tell that you have a good heart. It shows in your eyes. Not to mention the fact that you're very pretty."

This time I was the one blushing. "You're sweet."

"Well, how could I not be to the woman who rescued me?"

"I wasn't even supposed to be in that campground tonight," I admitted. "I was running away."

"From what?"

I hesitated, but Tom made me feel safe, so I told him what was going on. About Will, about Jay, about the body on the ice, about being unable to stay there. He was a sheriff in charge of deputies like me, and I thought I'd see judgment in his face. If one of his men did what I'd done, he'd fire him. But Tom let me off the hook.

"Sometimes it's hard to see the higher purpose from where we are," he said. "If you'd stayed and done your duty, you might feel better about yourself, but I'd still be in my truck freezing to death. Remember that."

"I guess you're right."

"I can call your boss and explain if you want. If you're worried about your job."

"You don't need to do that."

"We all make mistakes, Rebecca, but like I said, life has a way of taking us where we're supposed to be. I'm glad you ran away. You saved me."

"Actually, you're the one who saved me," I said, blurting out the truth.

"How did I do that?"

"You stopped me."

"From doing what?"

I shrugged, as if it were nothing. As if it didn't matter in the grand scheme of the universe. "Shooting myself."

He reacted by grabbing my face with his strong hands, cupping my cheeks gently as if holding on to something precious. "*Rebecca*. Is that really true?"

"I don't know. That's what was in my head. Maybe I would have chickened out."

"Why would you even consider something like that?"

I felt my lower lip quivering. Any moment, I would lose it entirely. I was so full of self-pity, weighed down with self-hatred, that I could hardly breathe.

"I don't know what I'm doing in this world," I told him. "I'm all alone. If I disappeared, no one would notice. No one would care. Some days I just want to walk out into the forest and never be seen again."

I assumed I'd get the usual speech that people give when you talk like that. When they know you've been contemplating suicide. The pat on the head. The platitudes. *You're young. You have your whole life ahead of you.* But that's the last thing I wanted to hear. Having my whole life ahead of me was the problem. That was *why* I'd considered ending it. I couldn't bear to think about living the rest of my life feeling the way I did.

But Tom said nothing like that to me. His entire demeanor

changed. He captured me with those dark eyes and held me fixed with his aura of goodness and concern. It was as if hearing my story had given him a mission, and he was bound to see it through. I didn't think I'd ever met someone who had such a fierce, reflexive loyalty. He was like a younger version of Darrell, and yet he had something that Darrell didn't. I sensed no black-and-white morality from him. He'd seen strong people crumble. He was a strong person himself, and he knew someday he'd crumble, too.

I didn't know this man at all. He was a stranger to me. We'd just met. And yet I already knew—*I knew*—that if I were in trouble, I could go to him, and he would suspend everything else in his life to be there for me. There was literally no one else I could say that about.

That's the man Tom Ginn was, sweetheart.

But of course, you know that.

"What can I do?" he asked. "How can I help you?"

"I have no idea. I really don't."

"Talk to me."

"I don't know where to begin."

"Well, I'm not leaving until you tell me everything about yourself."

"Why would you want that?"

He was honest with me. "There's something about you, Rebecca, and I can't even explain what it is. But I want to know the real you."

"I don't show that to anyone."

"Why not?"

"Because I'm scared of her," I said.

"You won't scare me."

I really thought that was true. I thought I'd finally met a man who would believe me and understand me, a man I could share my deepest secrets with. Honestly, that was the one and only moment in my life when I was tempted to tell another soul about the Ursulina.

But no.

I didn't talk. I was done talking. There was time for that later. In that moment, that was not what I wanted from Tom Ginn. That was not how I planned to spend our night together. I wanted something else from him.

CHAPTER TWENTY

At four in the morning, I got a call from a county road crew to let me know that the campground had been plowed. Tom could go home. I drove him out there in the darkness, and we said little along the way. I suppose he expected me to talk about when we would see each other again, but I didn't do that. I knew he had other responsibilities in life and no room for me. He'd given me one night as a woman in the arms of a good man, which was the only thing I'd asked of him. I'd never experienced a pleasure or closeness like that before.

I never would again.

We parted without saying much to each other, but not awkwardly. The situation between us was simply understood. He kissed me, he held me, he got in his pickup truck, and he was gone. I stood there in the empty parking lot for a long time, savoring what I felt inside myself, feeling warm and happy on a cold, black night. The storm had cleared, leaving behind stars. The wind had settled into a perfect stillness. I hummed, I sang. I blew a kiss to the owl, wherever he was.

Then it was time to go home.

I had to rejoin the world, after a night that felt like an intermission from it. I didn't know if Ben Malloy had taken it upon himself to send the sheriff's department out to the lake to find Jay's body, but either way, I needed to change back into my uniform and do everything that I'd failed to do hours earlier. I was ready to take charge of my life and become a deputy again.

It took me an hour to get back to my house. The roads were slippery, but I admit, I was distracted by my thoughts of Tom. I could still smell his presence in the car and taste him on my lips. We'd held hands as I drove. I knew the time we'd spent together would be a jewel I'd remove from a velvet case in my memory for years to come and polish up until it was sparkling and new again.

I got home to a deserted street and darkness. Dawn didn't break in January until much later. The sweet smoke of the fire we'd made lingered in the air, and the driveway was covered with snow, so I parked on the street. As I walked toward the front door, as I let myself into the house, part of me was still floating. I didn't turn on any lights. I hung up my coat. I didn't—and this is important—I didn't have my gun with me. It was upstairs, where I'd left it with my uniform.

I went into the living room. Blindly, without seeing anything, I gathered up the clothes I'd shed there, as well as the robe and the blanket from Tom. I inhaled the scent of the robe as I held it. So many thoughts raced through my mind: thoughts of Tom, thoughts of my body and the things I'd been missing, thoughts of my job, my childhood, my mother, my father, my brother. The one thing I didn't think about was the danger I should have remembered. I didn't think about Ricky. I'd forgotten all about him. At that moment, my husband didn't exist. I hadn't left the lights on or checked the lock on the door or any of the windows.

Of course, that was a terrible, terrible mistake.

He came at me from nowhere, an invisible man bursting from the shadows. One moment I had clothes in my arms, and then the next moment I was literally flying through the air as Ricky threw me across the room. I'm not heavy; he had no trouble launching me off my feet. I hit the wall and smashed into a glass picture frame that broke, spraying shards that sliced open my face and arm. Before I even fell, he grabbed me and threw me again, this time full speed into the brick hearth of the fireplace. My head struck stone. Pain erupted like the burn of a flame behind my eyes. I slumped to the carpet, tasting blood in my mouth.

"You whore! You goddamn whore!"

He bent over me, shouting in my face. I was on my back, but I couldn't focus on the dark shape over me, because I was caught in a tornado of dizziness and hurt. I put up my hands in a feeble effort to push him away, but he twisted my left wrist hard, and I heard the bone snap like a broken pencil. I couldn't help myself; I screamed in agony. He drove his knee into my chest, making me choke, and then he leaned his whole weight into me. Next he used his fists on my face, over and over, and with each blow, my skull slammed into the floor. He broke my jaw. He broke my nose. Blood from my head ran into my eyes.

I wanted to die to make the pain go away. I begged for mercy, pleading with him to stop.

He just hit me harder.

He hit me and hit me and hit me and hit me until I finally lost consciousness there on the floor. That emptiness was a gift. I had no dreams. I had no awareness of what he was doing to me. Thank God.

By the time I awoke again, hours had passed. The sun had risen. Outside, it was a beautiful morning, the snow and clouds forgotten. A winter cardinal trilled at the feeder beyond the window. Bright light streamed through the living room and across my body on the floor.

I was alone. The house was silent. Ricky had gone.

Everything in my world was pain; every movement stabbed me like a sharp knife. I tried to push myself up, but I'd forgotten my broken wrist, and my arm collapsed under me as another shiver of lightning seared through my nerves. I lay on my back.

For a long time, all I could do was cry.

Cold air through the chimney chilled my skin. I managed to sit up, swallowing down nausea as my vision spun. My eyes were practically swollen shut, making me squint. I could see just enough to realize that I was naked. My clothes, ripped and torn, lay around me, along with buttons that lay on the floor like acorns. I was completely covered in bruises that made me into a horrible rainbow. Blood had dried on the floor around me and all over my face and chest.

There was so much pain it was hard to isolate any one area, but one thing I knew was that the hurt was between my legs, too, a hurt that went deep inside me. When I touched myself down there, I winced, and I knew what he'd done. That was the final insult. The final humiliation.

I'm sorry, sweetheart. I'm so, so sorry to lay this burden on you. I didn't want to tell you any of this. I thought I could leave it out, thought I could spare you the ugly details, but you have to know the whole truth of what happened that night. You need to know the horror I faced. Otherwise, how can you understand?

That was the night you were conceived, the night that brought you into this world. That's where your story began.

Were you brought to life in love? Were you the product of those few blissful hours I spent with a man I'd just met?

Or were you born out of a violence that changed me forever?

I don't know. To tell you the truth, I never wanted to know, never wanted to find out. Maybe I couldn't bear to hear the wrong answer. I can't tell you whether your father was Tom Ginn or Ricky Todd. Sadly, you weren't in my life long enough for me to see the answer as you grew up. The only person I ever saw in your eyes was me. When I held you in my arms for the first time, I saw this perfect, beautiful, miniature version of myself looking up at me.

You were my daughter.

I knew that, I felt that, I sensed the connection we had. I loved you with all my heart, a love that seemed impossible to me because it went so deeply into my soul. I loved you more than I've ever loved another human being, then or since. You have to believe that, sweetheart. I loved you.

But I had to send you away.

PART TWO
YOUR MOTHER

CHAPTER TWENTY-ONE

I spent two weeks in the hospital after Ricky's assault and then another three weeks at home recovering. It was mid-March before I was really up and around. I'm right-handed, so even though my broken left wrist was in a cast, it didn't slow me down too much. My cuts healed, and to my relief, they left no noticeable scars. The bruises began to fade. Miraculously, for the blows my head had taken against the floor, I'd escaped having a concussion. As we neared spring, I was feeling healthy and more like myself again.

My brother called several times while I was recovering, but he had a job in New Mexico and couldn't leave. My father took a few weeks off from the road and practically lived with me during that stretch. He was mostly worthless around the house, with absolutely no experience cooking or cleaning, which meant that most of the time I took care of him more than he helped me. But I liked having him with me for a while, even though we had a way of getting on each other's nerves. Eventually, though, he had to get back in his truck and start making money again, and the house felt empty after he left.

Given what would happen soon, I was grateful for that time we spent together.

Others in town helped, too. For all their many shortcomings, people around here come together when someone needs them. Ben Malloy insisted on giving me five hundred dollars to help with my expenses while I was out of work. He gave it anonymously, but I heard through the grapevine that it was him. Darrell, his wife, and daughters were always bringing over meals. Norm shoveled my driveway. Will, who'd mostly recovered from his own injuries, made me a couple of pieces of new furniture to replace ones that had been damaged in the fight. He talked and walked a little slower than he had, but he was alive, and his charming smile was back, if tinged with more sadness.

As for Ricky, he left town. Rather than face criminal charges, he vanished, taking his truck and the clothes he was wearing and nothing else. No one was sure where he'd gone, but I heard a rumor that he was in Pennsylvania under a different name. With Norm's help, I filed for divorce, which went uncontested because Ricky didn't show up in court.

It was the day after Easter in early April when I got the official confirmation of what I'd suspected for weeks. I was pregnant. Missing a period in the wake of what had happened to me didn't necessarily seem unusual, but missing two was something I couldn't ignore. Plus, the truth is, I already knew. I felt you inside me, sweetheart. I was sure you were there. You gave me the strength to get better.

When the doctor called that Monday, I was eating jelly beans and chocolate and playing with the green paper curlicues filling the big Easter basket that Darrell had made for me. As soon as the phone rang, I knew it was the doctor, and I knew what he'd say. Even before I answered, I remember staring at the Easter basket as if it were a bassinet and imagining a baby amid those curlicues, rather than a chocolate bunny. The doctor broke the news to me, and I started to cry. They were tears of pure joy. Knowing that I was going to have a baby was the first happiness I'd had since awakening on the floor.

I suppose I should have been scared at the idea of being a single mother, but I wasn't. You made up for everything else, sweetheart. The things I'd been through in life had led me to that one moment. Of course, I had no idea if I was having a boy or a girl, but in my heart, I knew you were a girl. Rebecca Colder would have a daughter to share her life. I began to talk to you right away, telling you the things we would do together. I sang to you. I wrote poems for you. I know you don't remember any of it, but I like to think that I'm back there somewhere, that my voice is tucked away in a little corner of your brain.

You're probably wondering if I ever called Tom Ginn to tell him what happened to me, or to tell him that I was pregnant. I didn't. Oh, believe me, I was tempted. I can't tell you how many times I picked up the phone and then put it down. I knew if I called, he'd be at my side in an instant, but it didn't seem fair to push my way into his life like that. He had his father to take care of. He had his own responsibilities. And this sounds so vain, but I looked terrible in those weeks after the beating. I didn't want him to see me like that. In his mind, I was pretty. An angel. A perfect little fantasy, the girl who'd saved him. Instead, he would come to me and see a woman who was swollen and cut and bruised and bedridden. He'd stay out of obligation, not desire. I hated that. When the weeks of my recovery had finally passed and I looked like myself again, I felt that too much time had gone by to reach out to him. His life had gone on. I half wondered if he'd even remember me, although my secret heart said he thought of me every day. But I let him go. I never called.

I assumed I would never see him again.

I was wrong.

*

At the end of April, I went back to work. No, not as a deputy. Jerry got his wish. After my behavior on the night of Jay's death, the sheriff could have fired me. Even Darrell wouldn't have defended me for leaving the scene of a suicide and not reporting it. But Jerry didn't like the optics of firing a deputy for dereliction of duty while she was in a hospital bed after being raped and nearly beaten to death by her husband. So I got a reprieve. Jerry was actually very sweet, visiting me a couple of times during my recovery and making sure I had everything I needed. As I say, people can surprise you.

However, I'd be the first to admit that I couldn't do my former job anymore. I was feeling better and getting around pretty well, but that didn't mean I was anywhere close to the physicality needed to be a deputy. Plus, I was pregnant, so even as my body got stronger, I was already suffering from what the sheriff considered a disqualifying disability. He couldn't imagine that I wanted to come back to work at all, but I had bills to pay, and so he agreed to take me back in the role I'd had before. Mrs. Mannheim transferred to a job in the county licensing bureau, and I became the office secretary again.

The rest of the deputies treated me better after that, partly because of what I'd been through and partly because I was back in a woman's job. I missed being out on the road, and working with Darrell, but I didn't miss the abuse. At that point in my life, I'm not sure I could have handled it.

And the murder investigation? The death of Gordon Brink? Jerry closed the case. He did it while I was in the hospital and unable to offer any kind of protest. The sheriff interviewed Ben Malloy, who told him about Jay's confession to the murder before the boy killed himself. Maybe Ben couldn't hear everything that had been said between me and Jay on the ice—the wind had been howling the whole time—or maybe the sheriff had twisted around Ben's statement to suit what he really wanted to do, which was put Gordon Brink's murder to bed. Had anyone asked me, I would have said that Jay made up the story to protect Will, but by the time I was in a condition to say so, nobody cared. Darrell hadn't objected. Neither had Norm and Will. I suspect Norm had a long talk with Will about it, because as a result of Jay's false confession, Will went back in the closet. I'm not sure anyone believed it, but most of the town pretended, and Will was able to live his life again without violence. In another year, he'd go away to college. I doubted he would ever make his home in Black Wolf County after that.

So we'd found the killer. He was dead, and that was that. The thick folder that Darrell and I had gathered about the death of Gordon Brink got put away.

I filed it myself.

*

In the fifth month of my pregnancy, my father died. I told you I'd had a sixth sense about it coming soon, so I wasn't completely surprised to get the call. He was on the road when it happened, in a cheap motel outside Wichita. The check-out time passed without him leaving his room, and the motel owner found him dead in the twin bed. He'd died in his sleep, which was probably a blessing. According to the coroner, he'd been in the advanced stages of stomach cancer, so he must have been hiding extraordinary pain for a long time. He'd shown me no hint of it while he was staying with me. The end could have been much worse, but apparently God and his heart had decided that he'd had enough.

We had his funeral in Random. Most of the town came. My brother was there, and he and I spent a couple of awkward days together before he headed back to his latest job. After New Mexico, he'd gone to Oregon to work in the lumber mills. He was never going to settle down. The itinerant, Bob Dylan lifestyle suited him, going from place to place, making friends, sleeping with women, leaving them all behind. He had no interest in living in Random again, and he seemed to have no idea what to say to his pregnant sister. I loved my brother, but really, I hardly knew him. We'd spent very little time together. That one camping trip when I was ten years old is still the only real memory I have of us as a family.

My brother and I inherited my father's house, but neither one of us was sentimental about keeping it. I wanted to stay where I was. So we sold it, and the deal went through quickly, because homes didn't come up for sale in our area very often. Norm, jack-of-all-trades lawyer that he is, handled the closing and title work for us. Dad had been whittling away the mortgage on the house, so my brother and I came out of the sale with a reasonable amount of equity—enough to put me on solid financial footing for the first time in my life. I paid off my own little house, and I had enough in the bank that I didn't cringe at the thought of my small paycheck.

All that activity took up most of the summer that year. Life settled into a routine, or at least as much routine as I could expect while I waited for you to join me in the fall. I did my job. I lived day to day. For a while, I stayed something of a recluse, but gradually, I let the town see me out and about again. Occasionally, I'd stop by the 126 and chat with Sandra and some of the other girls. Enough time had passed that they saw me not as a victim but as Rebecca Colder again, the girl they'd known their whole lives.

In many ways, that was the happiest summer I'd ever spent. I read a lot, particularly old classics. I did some writing myself, mostly poetry, most of it very bad. I took guitar lessons and found I had a little bit of a knack for it, so I began to write some songs and play them to the trees in the national forest. When I looked in the mirror, I would catch myself smiling. That was a new experience for me.

Most of all, I was excited about you that summer.

I could feel you moving, kicking, shifting, as if you were impatient to be out in the world with me. As the time passed and my due date got closer, I began to allow myself to dream that I had a future. That *we* had a future.

It still makes me sad to realize those hopes were a mirage.

Just as I got to the last month of my pregnancy, everything fell apart. That fragile confidence I had in my life blew away like a spiderweb in the wind. In a single moment, I knew that happiness wasn't in the cards for me.

You see, the Ursulina came back.

CHAPTER TWENTY-TWO

Darrell showed up at my door before dawn on a Sunday morning in early October. That had once been a common experience for me, but it hadn't happened in a long time. I could tell from the strange look of horror on his face that something was wrong. He apologized for getting me out of bed, but he asked me if I could come with him to a crime scene.

Quickly.

At that point in my life, I didn't do anything quickly. Walking anywhere was an effort. Even getting in and out of bed took ten minutes. I had one of those pregnancy bodies where the rest of me stayed skinny, but you presented like a Thanksgiving turkey big enough to serve a family of twenty, and the weight of you meant I had to pee every hour on the hour. I was still a few weeks from my due date, but I had the feeling you would be coming sooner, rather than later. So I wasn't anxious to stray far from home.

"Look at me, Darrell," I said. "Are you kidding?"

"Yes, I understand, but I got a call about a murder, and this is one where I'd like to have you with me."

"Why me? I'm just a secretary. I'm not a deputy anymore. Jerry would flip if he found out you brought me to a crime scene."

"I'll explain when we get there. I wouldn't ask if I didn't need you."

"Why not Ajax? He's your partner now."

Darrell sighed. "Look, Rebecca, you can say no if you want. If you're not up for this in your condition, then I get it, of course. I feel bad even asking, but I really want your help."

I wasn't going to say no, not after Darrell and his family had been a lifeline for me for most of the year. He knew that. It took me a while to get dressed, and then Darrell helped me out to his cruiser. It wasn't even seven in the morning, earlier than any of the churchgoers would be out, so the streets were empty. As we drove, the day brightened, revealing the palette of reds and yellows in the trees. Soon enough, the leaves would be falling, burying us the way the winter snow does.

Darrell didn't say much along the way. I asked him twice more what had happened, but I realized he wasn't going to tell me until we got there. I wasn't sure if he was keeping it a secret for some reason, or if he was simply having trouble processing whatever it was. He had a queasy look I'd seen on his face before.

It was a look that said there would be blood.

Based on the route we took, I thought at first that Darrell was taking me to his own house, which was down the dirt road near Norm's place, and next door to my father's old house.

"Are the girls okay?" I asked with concern.

"The girls are fine."

"Is it Norm? Or Will?"

"No. It's not them."

That gave me a small sense of relief. When we got to the crossroad, Darrell turned the opposite way, driving in the shadows of the forest for several miles. He finally pulled into a driveway at the house belonging to Ajax and Ruby. Several cars had arrived ahead of us. Neighbors. Friends. But ours was the only squad car. I could see Ruby herself at the base of the porch steps, with her nine-month-old son in her arms. Her red hair blew wildly, and her face was a pale mess of tears.

"Oh my God," I murmured, turning to Darrell. "*Ajax?*"

He replied in a clipped voice. "Yes."

"Dead?"

"According to Ruby, yes."

"What on earth happened?"

"I don't know. That's what we need to find out."

As I struggled to get out of the car, Ruby came toward us, screaming. Her shrill panic set her baby crying, too. One of our mutual high school friends emerged from inside the house and rushed to take Ruby's son from her. At that point, Ruby collapsed, wailing as she knelt in the dew-damp grass.

"He's dead! He's dead! Who did this? What am I going to do?"

Darrell helped Ruby back to her feet. I felt terrible for what she was going through, but I also felt awkward, standing there with no real role to play. I still didn't understand why Darrell needed *me*. The pregnant office secretary. If Ajax was the victim, there were other deputies who could have come here with him to start the investigation.

"Ruby, let's go inside," Darrell told her softly. "Tell us where to go."

She had her face buried in his chest, and she was making incoherent whimpering noises. He let her cry for a while longer, and then he took her shoulders gently and held her until she was able to focus.

"Ruby? I know this is hard, but take us inside, okay? You don't have to show us the body. You can stay with your friends and wait for us. Are the other kids here?"

She shook her head. "A friend took them to her house."

"Good. We'll need to talk to you, but we have to see—we have to see what happened first. Okay?"

"It's horrible. It's horrible. It's unbelievable."

"I know."

Then, like a snake's head whipping around, Ruby's gaze shifted to me, and her entire face contorted from grief into simmering hatred. "What the hell is *she* doing here?"

"I wanted her help."

"She's not even a cop anymore. Get her out of here."

"Ruby, please. This isn't the time. Take us inside."

She stalked away from us with quick, angry footsteps. We followed, with me slowing down the pace. I hadn't seen much of Ruby this year, and when I had, she'd been cold and distant, but this reaction was beyond anything she'd shown me before. I didn't think she'd forgotten the incident between me and Ajax months earlier in the bathroom of the 126, but this seemed over the top for something like that.

We entered the house, and without a word, Ruby simply pointed at an oak door that led down to the basement. After that, she went into the living room and took her baby in her arms again. There were three other women inside who gathered around her. I knew all of them, but they shot me looks that mirrored Ruby's disgust.

Darrell opened the basement door, but then he hesitated. He seemed to see me for the first time, baby bump and all, even though we'd been together in the sheriff's office every day for months. "I'm sorry. I shouldn't have pushed you to come with me. I know you're pregnant, and so much has happened to you, but I still think of you like I did before. I wanted your help, but I wasn't thinking about how you might react. Are you up for this?"

"I don't even know what's down there."

"Well, from what Ruby told me, it's gruesome. If you think this will put you or the baby at any risk—"

"Darrell, either tell me the truth, or let's just go downstairs, okay?"

"Yes. Okay."

I took hold of the railings with both hands. Darrell made sure I didn't fall as we headed down the steps to the cool basement. It was large, sprawling under the footprint of the entire house, but unfinished, with a concrete floor and foundation walls and wooden crossbeams overhead. The floor had no carpet, just a few throw rugs in the middle of the room and a minefield of children's toys. The lights were plain bulbs with chain pulls, tucked among layers of insulation.

"Where is he?" I murmured.

"Far back, Ruby told me. Past the washer and dryer."

Darrell led the way. I felt a sense of confusion and dread as I followed behind him, because I truly had no idea what we would find. It was hard for me to imagine Ajax killing himself. His ego wouldn't allow it. I had visions of a sex game with one of his girlfriends gone wrong. If you believed what the women at the 126 were saying, autoerotic asphyxia was all the rage. Or maybe a jealous husband had finally had enough of Ajax sleeping his way through the married women of Black Wolf County.

Whatever was in my mind, I wasn't ready for what we found at the back of the basement.

Ahead of me, Darrell froze in the way he did when he had to swallow down his bloody flashbacks of the war. I heard him hiss under his breath. He turned back to stop me from going inside, but I did anyway. My eyes absorbed the scene in an instant. It was a small, windowless interior room, with nothing but a twin bed inside. No sheets, no blankets, just a mattress and a single pillow.

I couldn't believe what I saw. I simply couldn't believe it. Ajax lay on the bed, naked and very dead. Not suicide. Not a sex game. This was the past come to life again. Just like Kip Wells and Racer Moritz. Just like Gordon Brink. His wrists and ankles had both been tied, and his fixed eyes were wide, filled with a kind of terror I'd never seen on Ajax's face before. His body had been flayed, sliced open head to toe. His organs were on display, some squeezing out like worms where his abdomen had been severed. The entire mattress below him was soaked red, completely red, as if it had been sewn out of burgundy fabric. Blood made a lake on the floor, too, and splatter filled all the concrete walls, where it had dripped into long streaks like pinstripes.

"No," I murmured, grabbing my head and blinking over and over in pure shock. "It can't be. This *can't* be happening."

But it was.

Months had passed, but the monster had returned. There on the wall, we saw the message scrawled in blood taken from Ajax's corpse. Four deaths with the same signature, the way it had been left every time:

I am the Ursulina

CHAPTER TWENTY-THREE

Upstairs, I needed a drink of water. I found Ruby alone in the kitchen. Her deep-red hair was greasy and loose around her shoulders. She gripped the counter with both hands and stared out the window at her expansive backyard. Her tears had dried on her face, and a fierce, almost wild expression had replaced the sadness. Her jaw was clenched so hard I thought she might bite through her tongue. Her survival instincts were kicking in, the mother of three kids left alone. One thing I knew about Ruby. She was hard as nails.

"I'm really sorry about Ajax," I told her.

Her head jerked around on her swanlike neck when she heard me. Her eyes looked ready to light me on fire. "What are you doing here?"

"Darrell needs to ask you some questions."

"That's not what I mean. What are *you* doing here? I can't believe you'd show your face in my house."

I shook my head in complete bafflement. "Ruby, I don't understand. I mean, I know you're a wreck over Ajax, but what exactly did I do to piss you off? Is this still about the thing at the 126? Because I'm sorry, but that wasn't my fault."

She didn't say anything, but her eyes made an eloquent shift from my face to my belly and then back up again. My forehead wrinkled with a moment of confusion before it dawned on me what she thought.

"Are you serious?" I burst out, unable to control my reaction. "Do you think this is *Ajax's* baby?"

"Isn't it?" she snapped.

"No! I hope to hell he never said it was."

"He didn't have to. One of your neighbors saw him going into your place last January. Do you think I can't read a calendar? You're a worthless little slut. Everyone around here knows the truth."

She was out of control, but I let it go. Her husband had just been murdered, and she was lashing out at anyone she could. I happened to be in the firing line. But I struggled not to scream back at her.

"Look, Ruby, I know how horrible this is, and I know how scared you are for the kids. You don't have to believe me about this, but I never slept with Ajax. Never, not once, not ever. It didn't happen. This isn't his baby. I swear."

I saw the look in her eyes. She wasn't convinced.

"Fine," I said, giving up. "Believe whatever you want. Right now, the main thing is, someone killed your husband. Darrell's trying to figure out who it was, and he needs to talk to you." I cupped my belly, where you were kicking for all you were worth, sweetheart. "Unless you somehow think I managed to do *that* in my condition, too."

Ruby inhaled sharply, her nostrils flaring like a thoroughbred on the racecourse. She stormed past me. I followed, crossing through the living room, where several of our high school friends had heard the whole argument. They all shot me looks that said they didn't believe me, either. I guess I'm naive. All year, people around town had apparently been speculating about me and Ajax, and I didn't even know it. None of the stories had gotten back to me, I suppose because people were too nice or too embarrassed to tell me what others were saying. Ajax himself hadn't seemed any different with me when I went back to work as the department secretary. Maybe he was less flirtatious, but I wrote that off to him having no interest in sleeping with me while I was pregnant.

I made my way to the room off the garage that Ajax had used as his beer-drinking rec room, complete with a *Centipede* game machine and full-size pool table. Playboy posters of naked women filled the walls. Ruby sat on a brown leather sofa. Darrell was already at Ajax's rolltop desk, removing papers from a drawer and stuffing them into a box. I sat down on the other end of the sofa, and Ruby's hostility blew at me like a cold wind.

"What are you doing with all that?" Ruby asked Darrell.

"We have to take everything from his desk and review it."

"Why?"

"I need to go through Ajax's papers, in case there's anything that would tell us who killed him. Threats, that kind of thing."

"Well, I need it all back," Ruby said. "I have bills to pay. With Ajax gone, it's up to me."

"Of course. We'll go through it this afternoon, and I'll have someone drop off whatever we don't need back at your house. If we keep anything, I'll get you a list of what it is."

"I don't want *her* going through it," Ruby said with a glance at me. "Whatever's in there is private."

Darrell sighed. Something in his face told me that he knew what Ruby's problem with me was, even though he'd kept me in the dark about it. "Whatever we find stays inside the department, Ruby."

She shot me one more venomous stare. Then she swept strands of her red hair out of her face. "So what do you want to know?"

"I'm sorry that we have to do this now," Darrell said, "but take me through exactly what happened, step by step."

Ruby rolled her wedding ring around her finger. I could see long, perfect nails, none of them broken. "Thursday morning, the kids and I went to see my sister in Marquette for a long weekend."

"Ajax didn't go with you?"

"He hates my sister. The feeling is mutual."

"Did you talk to him while you were gone?" Darrell asked.

"Yes, I called him later that day to say we'd arrived. He was heading out to the 126. We talked again on Friday evening around seven. That was the last time I spoke to him. I tried calling him a couple of times on Saturday, but there was no answer. That was when I packed up the kids and drove home. We got back after dark on Saturday night."

"Did Ajax know you were coming home?"

"No. I was supposed to stay until Sunday."

"Why did you come home early?"

Ruby tugged her T-shirt down. "Because I assumed he was taking advantage of me being gone to stick his cock between some tramp's legs. I thought I'd catch them together."

"But you didn't."

"No."

"What did you do when you got home?"

"I put the kids to bed. I waited up for a while, but then I went to bed myself."

"What time was that?" Darrell asked.

"I don't know. Midnight."

"Did you go down in the basement at all?"

"No. I checked here in the Playboy mansion, and that was it."

"Were you surprised that his car was still in the garage if he wasn't home?"

Ruby shook her head. "We've got an extra detached garage, and Ajax keeps his restored Mustang out there. It's his baby. I assumed he was driving that. It's his chick-mobile."

"But you didn't actually look to see if it was there?"

"No."

"And then what?"

"I told you. I went to bed."

"Did you hear anything overnight? Cars outside? Noises in the house?"

"No. And I didn't sleep well, so if anything was going on, I would have heard it. It was quiet."

"Why didn't you sleep well?"

"Because I was pissed off thinking that my husband was in bed with another woman! Shit, Darrell, do I have to spell it out for you? You worked with him. You knew what he was like."

Darrell didn't answer, but it was true. He did know Ajax. So did I. Every one of us in that room knew the kind of man Ajax was, and neither Darrell nor I had any trouble believing Ruby's story. Of course, it was also true that she had no real alibi. If he'd come home late, smelling of his latest conquest, they might have argued in the basement while the kids were asleep. She could have hit him. Killed him. Done all the rest and then calmly showered away the blood. Ajax liked to joke that Ruby was a redhead, and redheads were crazy. Looking in her scary eyes, I believed it.

However, I didn't think she'd done it. Her nails were too perfect. You couldn't do what had been done to that body without breaking a nail.

But if not her, then *who*?

"What time did you get up?" Darrell asked.

"Early. Maybe five thirty. The kids wouldn't be up for hours, so I made coffee and decided I would get a jump on the laundry. I gathered it up and went down to the basement." She closed her eyes and exhaled sharply. "That's when I found him."

"Did you touch anything in the room?"

"No. I just screamed. I stood there screaming. Then I ran back upstairs and called you."

I sat on the other end of the sofa, listening to the back-and-forth. I wasn't sure what I was supposed to do. Since I wasn't a deputy anymore, I didn't really know if Darrell wanted me asking any questions, but then again, he'd asked for my help because we'd worked on the Gordon Brink case together. So I decided to butt in. There was an uncomfortable question that needed to be asked, and I could probably ask it better than Darrell. Ruby couldn't be any more pissed at me than she already was.

"Do you know who Ajax was sleeping with?" I asked.

Seeing Ruby's reaction, I realized that she had no trouble getting even more pissed at me. In fact, she practically foamed at the mouth. "Shut up, you little—"

"*Ruby.*"

Darrell interrupted, but not before Ruby called me what she wanted to call me.

"This is not helpful," he went on. "I know you're upset, but Rebecca and I are here to figure out what happened. So let's leave the personal stuff out of this. Please, if you know, answer Rebecca's question. Who do you think Ajax was having an affair with?"

"Now or last January?" she spat in reply.

I opened my mouth to protest, but I closed it when Darrell shot me a look. There was no point in denying it all over again.

"Ruby," he said again. "Come on."

She turned her anger down to a simmer. "Fine. If you want

a list of the women he was with, get me a copy of the phone book. Ajax wasn't exactly monogamous, Darrell. I knew that when I married him. I'd made my peace with it."

I hated to interject again. All I would do was make it worse, but Ruby was lying to us, and I wasn't sure if Darrell realized it. It was the kind of lie that was likely to fly over a man's head.

"You came home early to catch him," I murmured. "You waited up to confront him. That doesn't sound to me like you were at peace with it. Had something changed lately?"

This time she didn't lash back at me, but she also didn't answer my question. Her whole body looked stiff and tense, as if she were holding up a wall that was threatening to fall down on top of her.

"Was it someone special this time?" I went on. "Was it somebody who felt like a threat to your marriage?"

Her knee tapped nervously up and down. "I don't know who it was."

"But there was someone in particular?"

"Yes."

"How did you find out?"

She shrugged. "I'm his wife. I knew. He wasn't acting the same. He was gone more, sometimes overnight. He'd make up lame excuses. Plus, a couple of weeks ago, I went shopping in the next county over. I stopped in at the jeweler where Ajax got my wedding ring. He asked if I liked the necklace Ajax had given me. Except he hadn't given me anything like that. I covered, but I think he knew. Ajax didn't get it for me. He got it for *her*. And if he was buying her jewelry, then I assume it was serious."

"But you don't know who it was?" Darrell asked.

"No."

"Could she have been married?"

"I have no idea."

Her voice was clipped, urging us to move on. I was pretty sure that Ruby did know the identity of the other woman—or at least she had a strong suspicion—but she wasn't willing to tell us. Maybe she couldn't bear to say the name out loud, as if doing so made everything real.

"Was Ajax having any problems recently?" Darrell asked.

"He didn't say anything to me, but it's harder to keep things from your wife."

She shrugged. "I don't know. He was edgy. Anxious. I figured it was the affair, but maybe it was something else."

"What about money?"

"It seemed like we were doing fine. Maybe a little tighter this year, but nothing serious."

"You didn't see anything unusual in your bank accounts?"

"No."

"Can you think of anyone who had a grudge against Ajax?"

Ruby ran her slim fingers back through her hair. "Well, there was this thing with Norm."

"You mean last winter? About Will?"

She shook her head. "No. This was more recent. The lawsuit is finally heating up again. The mine ran out of continuances, so it looks like the case should be going to trial before the end of the year. I got called back for more questions a couple of weeks ago."

"What does that have to do with Ajax?"

"He drove me to the deposition. Norm was outside the house when we got there. He and Ajax got into it before I went inside."

"Over what?"

"Ajax made some kind of joke about Will. I mean, you know what he was like. A queer joke. It was pretty ugly, even for Ajax."

"What did Norm do?" Darrell asked.

"He pulled a gun on Ajax," Ruby replied, "and he threatened to kill him."

CHAPTER TWENTY-FOUR

I'd seen Norm many times throughout the year, but I guess I was so caught up in my own issues that I didn't really look at him. When we stopped at his house, I realized that he looked tired. And years older. He'd lost weight. There had always been a cheerful energy about Norm, a belief that nothing could ever defeat him or slow him down, but it was obvious that the crisis with Will last January had taken its toll.

He covered it well, though. He fussed over me, making sure I was comfortable. He talked about camping, photography, and college football with Darrell. But when we sat out on his back porch and Darrell told him about Ajax, I could see his facade drain away. He hadn't shaved, and he scratched his chin with an exhausted look that said: *What next?*

"I suppose you want my gun to test for ballistics," he said, guessing why we were there. "I'm sure Ruby told you about the threat I made."

"Ajax wasn't shot," Darrell replied.

"No? Well, I suppose that's a relief. What happened?" Norm glanced back and forth between the two of us, and then he leaped to the correct conclusion. "The Ursulina again? Seriously?"

"That's confidential for now," Darrell told him, "although I'm sure the story will be around town in no time."

"Yes, of course." Norm got up and leaned against the porch windows. The morning sunlight made his face pale. "I can't say I feel bad about Ajax being dead. I mean, it's terrible for Ruby and the kids, of course. But I never forgave him for spreading the story about Will."

"Tell us about the threat," Darrell said.

Norm looked at the two of us with regret. "I wanted to take it back as soon as I said it. All I can tell you is, I reacted as a father, not as a lawyer. I would never have actually followed through on it."

"You pulled a gun on him?"

"Yes. Ever since what happened to Will, I'm always carrying. I've started to share your philosophy of life, Darrell. You never know. If someone comes after me or my family, I intend to be prepared."

"What was the argument about?"

"I'm sure Ruby told you. Ajax made a crude joke at Will's expense. I won't repeat what it was, but it was foul. It set me off. I've been working fourteen-hour days, seven days a week, as we get closer to trial, and I was strung out. Not that I'd ever laugh off the kind of thing he said, but I overreacted. Mind you, it wasn't just the joke. It was the fact that it was *Ajax*."

"Where were you on Friday and Saturday?" Darrell asked.

"I just told you. Working. Morning to night. I haven't had a weekend off in a couple of months."

"Can anyone verify that?"

Norm shook his head. "I had a couple of meals brought in. I made some phone calls. Otherwise, I was alone in my office in

Random the whole time. I've hardly seen Kathy or Will. They know the drill. This is the critical time in the litigation."

"So you don't have an alibi," Darrell concluded.

"Depending on when exactly Ajax was killed, no, I don't. And yes, I'm obviously familiar with the Ursulina crime scenes. In fact, I'll do your job for you and confirm what you already know. If I wanted to murder Ajax and make it look like the earlier murders, I could easily have done so."

"Norm," Darrell interrupted, because it was obvious that Norm was losing a grip on his emotions. In most circumstances, Darrell wouldn't have tried to stop a suspect from talking, but Norm was also his best friend. The previous December, Darrell had declined to interview Norm for that very reason, but he didn't let it stop him this time. It made me wonder if he had doubts about Norm and wanted to judge for himself what he saw in his friend's face.

Regardless, Norm kept rambling, quickly and loudly.

"And yes, I *was* in a frame of mind to murder that piece of shit," he went on. "Will almost died, and Ajax was as much to blame as the boys who beat him up. Darrell, you have children, so you know what it feels like. And Rebecca, you're going to have a baby, so very soon you'll understand, too. When your child is at risk, you will do anything to save them. You will walk through fire. You will steal, cheat, lie, and yes, kill, without so much as a second thought or a single regret. There is not a sin in this world you won't commit. You're going to love your child the way I love mine, and that means you'll sacrifice anything to protect them. You'll give up your life, your future, everything that matters to you. Which is what I would happily do for Will."

Instinctively, sweetheart, I closed my hands around my stomach. Norm was absolutely right, and it wasn't even a question of waiting until you were in this world. I was already protecting you. You were the one thing in the world for which I would give up everything. I was a little blackbird willing to go up against a hawk to protect my baby in the nest.

I was a mother.

Norm sighed and sat back down in the chair. "But I *didn't* kill him, Darrell. Yes, I had every reason in the world to want him dead, and I had the time and opportunity, but I didn't do it. Search whatever you want. Home, office, car. Look for bloody clothes, or knives, or whatever else you're hoping to find. You've got the wrong guy."

I knew Darrell wasn't inclined to believe that his friend was a murderer. I didn't believe it, either.

Then again, you never know.

"Can you think of anyone else who might have killed Ajax?" I asked.

"Other than Ruby? I mean, you know how badly he treated her."

"Are you talking about abuse?"

"No, just the constant cheating."

"Ruby thought there might be someone special this time," I said. "A woman he was serious about."

"If there was, they must have been discreet. I didn't hear rumors, and it's the kind of thing the plaintiffs and their families would have been gossiping about."

"How is the litigation going?" I asked.

"It's progressing," Norm replied, with a lawyer's caution. "The new partner handling the case for the mine is a cool customer. Have you met her? JoAnne Svitak. She's every bit as ruthless as Brink. Maybe more so."

"Ruby is a key witness for the mine. Could that be a motive?"

"Well, she's important to the case, but I can't see anyone taking it out on her husband."

"Was Ajax involved in the lawsuit himself?"

Norm hesitated. "Not really. Not directly. But I did ask about him in my interviews with some of the mine workers."

"Why?"

Norm took a moment to decide what information he was willing to share with us. "Ruby's experience at the mine was different from most of the other women's. I wanted to know why she *wasn't* getting harassed. I wondered whether her being married to a deputy gave her some kind of protection."

"Did it?" I asked.

"I think so, but I wasn't able to prove it. Nobody admitted anything about Ajax intimidating or threatening them. However, there was one incident that made me curious. It was all hearsay, and I was never able to confirm it. In fact, everyone I talked to denied that it happened, but that only made me more suspicious."

Darrell leaned forward in his chair. "What was it?"

"According to one of the women on our side, Ruby did have something bad happen to her at the mine. This was well before the lawsuit was filed. Probably five or six years ago. My witness insists she saw a mine worker expose himself to Ruby and try to get her to give him a hand job. He was new to the job. An out-of-towner. What makes it interesting is that the mine fired him the next day. He left town and never came back."

"But your witness doesn't know who he was?"

"No. She doesn't remember his name. I asked Ruby about the incident in her deposition, and she told me that nothing like that had ever happened. I couldn't find a single worker who would back up the story, either. The really strange thing is, it's like this guy never existed. I went through the mine's employment records, trying to find anyone who was hired and fired within a short period of time. No luck. They must have scrubbed their records."

"What does that have to do with Ajax?" I asked.

"That I could establish in court? Not a thing. I couldn't tie him to this at all." Norm shook his head. "But in the dozens of harassment incidents we've documented against the women at the mine, this is the only time that the mine ever took action against one of the men. Someone made a move on Ruby, and they immediately shut it down and got rid of him. Now if this had happened later, after the lawsuit got filed, I could see them wanting to protect her, because she was on their side. But back then? It doesn't make sense. Why help Ruby and ignore what was happening to the others? The only answer I could come up with is that Ajax got involved. Either alone or by getting his uncle to intervene as the sheriff. That was speculation on my part, but that's what my gut tells me. And I trust my gut."

"Did you talk to Ajax and Jerry?" Darrell asked.

"I did, and they both denied it," Norm replied. "But I don't think my witness made it up, and I don't think she got it wrong. So if everyone's lying about it, that means they have something big they're trying to hide."

*

Darrell kept talking to Norm, but I had to take a bathroom break.

When I was done, I went outside for a smoke. I'd been trying to quit while I was pregnant, but that morning, I really needed a cigarette. I was uncomfortable, I was sleep-deprived, and I was unsettled by the return of the Ursulina. For the first time in months, I found myself listening to the forest again for the *huffffff* of the beast.

It was a cold October morning. My boots crunched through frost on the grass. I had no hope of zipping my coat over my stomach, so when the wind whistled at me, I shivered. The gray sky had a winter look about it, as if the sun would never shine again. To tell you the truth, sweetheart, I was thinking about running away. I was tempted to get in my car right then and there and go somewhere else and never come back. Maybe that's what I should have done. But wherever I went, I knew the monster would find me eventually.

I've known that since I was ten years old.

"Hi, Rebecca."

The voice behind me made me jump. I turned around and saw Will, seemingly not cold at all in a short-sleeved T-shirt and khakis. "Oh. Hi."

"Are you okay?"

I shrugged as I took a drag on my cigarette. "Sure."

"When's the baby due?"

"End of the month," I said. "But she feels like she's coming early."

"She? Is it a girl?"

"I don't actually know that, but yeah, I think it's a girl."

"You got another cigarette?" Will asked me.

"Will your dad kill me if I give you one?"

"Probably."

I gave him one anyway, and the two of us stood there smoking. We were alone in the big yard, surrounded by soaring evergreens. Will seemed the same as he'd been, charming and strong, but he wasn't the same at all, not really. He'd discovered that the world can be cruel, and once you discover that, you can't look at life the same way again. You carry that anxiety with you forever.

"I heard you guys talking," he said. "I heard about what happened to Ajax."

"Yeah."

"I didn't like him. It sucks that he's dead, but I didn't like him."

"Join the club," I replied.

"Do you think the same person killed both of them? Ajax and Gordon Brink?"

"I don't know."

"I mean, you and me, we both know Jay didn't kill him. My dad made me shut up about it, but the sheriff blaming Jay was bullshit."

I'd never heard Will swear before. "Yes, I know. Jay didn't kill his dad."

The boy was quiet for a while. He blew smoke in the air, and the cloud vanished toward the trees. "Hey, Rebecca? I need to ask. Are we okay? You and me?"

"What do you mean?"

"You've been different with me all year. Is it the gay thing?"

"No. Of course not."

"Then what is it?"

I shrugged. "I blame myself for what happened."

"That's crazy. Jay killing himself wasn't your fault. Neither was what happened to me."

"I appreciate you saying that, Will, but I feel responsible."

"Why? I came to you. I told you what was going on. That's what started everything. If anybody should feel guilty, it's me. I tried to rescue Jay, and instead I got him killed."

"You did *not* do that."

Will brushed away a tear. "Yeah. I guess. All I can do is live with it, right? But I'm glad you and me are okay. I've been worried about that."

"We're fine."

"Thanks for the smoke."

"Sure."

Will turned away, but then he stopped. He looked at the cigarette in his hand as if it had reminded him of something. "Listen, I should probably tell you this. I mean, it may be nothing at all. When the sheriff blamed Jay for Gordon's death, I figured it didn't matter anymore. But now—with Ajax dead, too—"

I tensed. "What is it?"

"Well, it was a dumb thing. Jay and I were having a smoke one day here in the yard. I had a book of matches from the 126, and I used it to light his cigarette. When he saw the matches, he took the book from me. Then he shook his head and said that was really strange."

"I don't understand. What was strange?"

"Jay used to collect matchbooks when he was a kid. His dad would pick them up for him on his business trips. He had ones from all across the country. For a while, he had mason jars filled with them."

"Okay." I was still puzzled.

"The thing is, Jay was sure that he'd had a matchbook from the 126 in his collection. He recognized the design. The only way he could have gotten it was if Gordon had brought it back from a trip. So Jay thought Gordon had been lying about never being in town before last fall. Like it wasn't the first time he'd been to Black Wolf County."

CHAPTER TWENTY-FIVE

When we were back at the sheriff's office, Darrell and I searched Ajax's desk.

The contents were what you'd expect. Underneath the files of active cases in his drawer, he had copies of *Penthouse* and *Hustler*, many with dog-eared pages so he could find the photos he liked the most. He kept a flask-sized bottle of vodka, plus a carton of cigarettes, a tin of breath mints, and a strip of condoms. We found a pocket calendar, but most of the entries were blank, so we weren't able to determine if he'd planned to meet someone while Ruby was gone for the weekend. There was also nothing in the calendar to tell us if he'd been seeing a woman other than his wife.

As we went through the desk, Jerry stopped by. The sheriff looked devastated by the murder of his nephew, and maybe that was why he raised no objections when Darrell said he wanted to deputize me to help on the case. Darrell pointed out that we were short-handed without Ajax and that I'd worked with him on the previous Ursulina murder. I expected an argument, but Jerry simply nodded his approval with barely a glance at me.

We all knew it would be a short-term assignment anyway, given how far along I was.

After Jerry left, Darrell finally raised a topic that we'd avoided between us for months. Given that the Ursulina was back, we couldn't dodge it any longer. "I know you wanted me to push back with Jerry about closing the Brink case," he told me. "You didn't agree with him blaming Jay."

"I never said that."

"No, but you don't think Jay killed him," Darrell said.

"You didn't think so, either. But Jay confessed, so I get it."

"It was better for Will," Darrell admitted with a sigh. "Jay was dead, but Will still has to live in this town."

"I know. You're right."

"Except here we are with another body."

"Yes. Here we are."

"You're right, you know," Darrell went on. "I never thought Jay murdered his father. I was pretty sure that the same person did all three. Brink, Kip, Racer. If Will's right about Brink being in town years ago, that makes it even more plausible that we're only looking at one killer. There must be a connection that we've missed."

He shut the drawer of the desk and shook his head. "There's nothing here. Let's go through the personal papers I brought back from his house."

We went into the office conference room, where Darrell had stashed the box that contained the contents of the rolltop desk from Ajax's rec room. He pulled out stacks of papers and spread them neatly across the table. There was a lot to review. Tax returns. Bank statements. Receipts. Credit card bills. I took one side of the table, and Darrell took the other, and we began to sift through the piles in silence.

It felt odd, going through Ajax's records, as if I were digging

into the private details of his life without his permission. I'd seen
him on Friday morning here in the office, and he still felt alive
to me. He should have walked into the conference room, sat
down with his cocky smile, and asked us what the hell we were
doing. Instead, he was gone. I'd stared at his body, defiled in
a truly horrific way. It seemed impossible. I couldn't say I was
going to miss him, but I didn't understand why he was dead.

Or who could have killed him.

"Is there anything in the credit card bills?" Darrell asked.

"Ruby's right about the jewelry store. Ajax spent almost a
thousand dollars there last month. If it wasn't for her, then who?"

Darrell whistled. "A thousand bucks? That's a lot of money."

I flipped through more of his statements. "He liked his
toys, too. He made a lot of purchases from sports and auto-part
shops."

"Did he have any outstanding balance on the credit card?"

"No, he paid it off each month. In most months that ran
to a few hundred bucks."

Darrell grabbed for the stack of bank records. "Where was
Ajax getting that kind of cash?"

He took the most recent account statements and passed the
others to me. We paged through them, and I flipped through
all the canceled checks that came with each statement.

"His checking and saving balances aren't high," Darrell said.
"His salary wasn't paying for most of the toys, that's for sure."

"Could Jerry have been helping him out?" I asked.

"Jerry doesn't make that kind of money, either."

"Hang on," I said.

"What?"

"There are no checks made out to the credit card company."

"What do you mean?" Darrell asked.

"He's writing checks to places around town, but I don't

see anything made out to Visa. So how's he paying off those balances?"

Darrell examined the papers spread across the conference table again. Then he frowned and reached for a new stack of bank statements. "He has another account."

"What?"

"Look at these records. He has a separate checking account at a bank in the next county. Not joint, like the accounts here in town with Ruby. This one is just in his name." Darrell went through the pages quickly. "The Visa checks came from that bank. Up until late last year, he was depositing five hundred dollars into that account every month."

"Every *month*? From where? A second job?"

Darrell shook his head. "He couldn't possibly have had another job without me knowing about it. There's no info on where the money came from. He was simply cashing checks every month."

"From who?"

"That's the question." Darrell ran through the bank statements again. "The last deposit was made in December of last year. After that, nothing. He's been working down the balance since then, but he's still got a few thousand dollars built up in the account. He must have been getting those payments for a while."

"December? That's when they stopped?"

"Right."

"That's the month Brink was killed," I said.

*

Later, Darrell and I drove back to the house that Gordon Brink had rented.

I didn't like the feeling of déjà vu or the ugly memories in this place. But in the time since I'd been here, the law firm had made a clean sweep. The retired mine president had decided to stay in Florida permanently, and the house had been repainted and refurnished from top to bottom. There was almost nothing left to remind me that Brink and his wife and son had ever lived here.

The partner who'd taken over the lawsuit, JoAnne Svitak, was exactly as Norm had advertised her. She had an edge that could make you bleed. Her face looked molded into a wax shell of overly white makeup, and the only thing that moved was her eyes, which were blue and severe. Her hair was brown and flowed around her head like an ocean wave caught in an ice storm. She was probably in her midforties. We'd looked her up in a legal directory at the courthouse, and we'd learned that she was the only female partner at Gordon Brink's Milwaukee law firm. I had no doubt that she'd followed a tough road to get there.

When we sat down, she made it clear that she didn't have much time for us. Her clipped answers rushed the interview along.

"Do you know a sheriff's deputy here in town named Arthur Jackson?" Darrell asked her.

"No, I don't."

"He went by the nickname Ajax."

"I still don't know him."

"He was murdered over the weekend."

The news of a homicide elicited no reaction at all. She simply tapped a pencil on the desk and waited silently for Darrell to continue.

"The nature of the murder was very similar to the murder of Gordon Brink, your predecessor," he went on.

"How similar?"

"Almost identical. The same wounds. The same message left on the wall."

"Didn't your department conclude that Brink was murdered by his son?" she asked us.

"That was the sheriff's conclusion, yes, but—"

"So what does this crime have to do with me or my firm?"

"That's what we're trying to find out," Darrell said.

I leaned forward in my chair, which wasn't an easy thing to do. "Ajax's wife, Ruby, is a key witness for the mine in the litigation. It's hard to believe you don't know who Ajax is."

Her eyes had the patient cruelty of a snake. "Anything and anyone related to the mine or this litigation is privileged."

"Your opposing counsel, Norm Foltz, believes the mine covered up an incident of harassment involving Ruby," Darrell went on. "It's unlikely they could have done that without Ajax knowing about it."

"Again, anything related to the mine or this litigation is privileged," she said.

"Even if it involves murder?"

"Murder is your concern, not mine."

"I would think you'd be nervous, given that someone killed the previous lawyer working on the case."

"I'm not, but thank you for your concern."

Darrell and I exchanged a glance. We were both thinking we should have brought along an ice pick to chip through her frozen exterior.

"Do you know if Gordon Brink had any kind of relationship with Ajax?" Darrell asked.

"I'm unaware of who this man is or was. Obviously, I have no idea whether Gordon knew him."

"Ajax was receiving monthly payments of five hundred dollars from an unidentified source. Those payments stopped the same month that Mr. Brink was killed. Was your firm making payments to Ajax? Or was Mr. Brink?"

"I have no idea."

"Can you find out?"

"I have no access to Mr. Brink's personal finances, and anything related to payments made by the firm would be privileged."

"How long did Mr. Brink represent the mine?" Darrell asked.

"Anything about our client relationship is privileged."

"Even how long you've represented them?"

"That's right."

"We have reason to believe Mr. Brink visited Black Wolf County prior to his arrival last fall," Darrell went on. "Is that true?"

"I can't say."

"Because you don't know, or because you won't tell us?"

"I can't say."

"Was he here in connection with your representation of the mine?"

"Anything about our client relationship is privileged. I believe I've made that very clear."

Across the table, Darrell shook his head in frustration. "Well, you've been a big help, Ms. Svitak."

"It's not my job to help you, Deputy."

"Even if it means solving the murder of your colleague?" Darrell asked.

"Gordon is dead. That's not going to change. Right now, my only concern is serving the interests of my client. Are we done?"

"Yes, we are. For now."

"Then please show yourselves out."

Darrell stood up from the table. So did I, with more difficulty. We both shook hands with the lawyer. Her grip was cool and limp. By the time we left the room, she'd already gone back to the paperwork in front of her, as if the time she'd spent with us was a nuisance that she'd already forgotten.

On our way out of the house, I had to pee again. Darrell headed outside, and I tried to locate a bathroom. As I checked the doors, I collided with Penny Ramsey, who was coming out of a room that had been set up as a law library. I hadn't seen Penny since Ajax and I interviewed her the previous December, so I hadn't even realized that she was still in Black Wolf County.

Seeing me, her eyes widened. Quickly, she glanced both ways down the hallway to make sure we were alone, and then she took hold of me by the elbows. "Oh my God! Is it true about Ajax? He's *dead*?"

"Yes, he is."

"What happened?"

"We don't know yet."

Penny covered her mouth with a trembling hand and backed away from me. "I can't believe it."

"Do you know something about his death?"

"No. Nothing!"

"It looks to me like you know something."

I saw her eyes welling with tears, and her fingers nervously caressed the necklace she was wearing. Without saying more, she ran down the hallway, and I saw her disappear into one of the other rooms. The door slammed shut behind her.

I'd only had a moment to look at her, but she'd upgraded her wardrobe, her hair, and her makeup since we met. The Amy Irving innocence I'd first seen at the motel had been replaced by a more polished style. If I'd had to guess, she'd found a boyfriend who was buying her gifts.

Like the expensive gold-and-emerald necklace she'd been fondling.

I was pretty sure I knew who'd bought it for her.

CHAPTER TWENTY-SIX

Darrell dropped me back home after dark. I was exhausted, and although I hadn't told him, I was having sharp pains in my belly as well as a constant dull ache in my lower back. I didn't know if I was experiencing premature labor pains or if it was something else. Maybe it was just the stress of the day. I went inside and turned on the lights, and then I kicked off my shoes and settled into the living room sofa to see if the pains went away. In a few minutes, they did. I began to feel better.

I thought about putting on a record, or playing my guitar, but at that moment, I didn't want to do anything that involved getting off the sofa. I was able to reach the phone, and I wondered for the thousandth time about calling Tom Ginn to tell him about my pregnancy. But no. If I heard his voice, I'd want to see him again. I'd probably fall in love with him again. As tempting as that was, there were too many complications to let it happen.

The house was warm. Or maybe it just felt that way to me, because my metabolism was out of whack. The heat and the tiredness of the day made my eyes blink shut. My head fell back against the sofa cushions, and I slept. I had disturbing dreams of being ten years old again, of running through the woods with an invisible monster in the darkness behind me. I kept calling for help, from my father, from my brother, from Darrell, from Tom. No one came to rescue me. I woke up with a start just as I felt the beast's claws on my skin.

The house was definitely not warm anymore. My unreliable furnace had gone out while I slept. I sat on the sofa, trembling with chill. I checked my watch and saw that I'd missed the whole evening. It was just after midnight.

Around me, something felt wrong. I didn't know what it was. Call it an instinct. A sensation of dread, as if my nightmare had followed me into real life. Except when I studied the room, I saw nothing to explain it. Everything looked the same.

But something was different.

What?

I struggled my way off the sofa and stood up. Outside, the street was dark. My neighbors were asleep. A fall rain had begun, and the wind blew wet leaves from the big oak tree onto the windows. I checked to make sure that the windows were locked, which they were. I still did that every day, part-habit, part-precaution. I always kept the front door locked, too.

Or had I forgotten tonight?

I returned to the foyer and checked. The door was locked, as it should have been. I opened it and stepped onto the covered porch in my stockinged feet. The rain made a gentle, steady music on the overhang and in the street beyond. The rain on fall nights could last for hours. I listened. I eyed the shadows. I smelled the air for something other than peaty dampness, like a cigarette, or car exhaust, or gasoline. But the entire neighborhood felt normal, a night like any other.

Inside, I locked the door again, but my nervousness refused

to go away. If anything, it grew worse. I went to each of the downstairs rooms and checked the other windows, but they were locked, too. So was the door to the backyard. The basement had a dead bolt that was undisturbed, and when I put my ear to the door, I heard nothing. It seemed impossible that anyone could have gotten inside without me being aware of it. And yet that was what I felt.

A presence.

I switched off the downstairs lights and went upstairs. There were only two bedrooms. The smaller room was where I put everything that didn't fit in the rest of the house, so it was a mess. Eventually, I had plans to make it into your room, but for the time being, you were going to stay in the master bedroom with me. I already had a crib in the corner, and people had been giving me clothes and supplies for weeks.

Outside, the branches of the oak tree in my front yard brushed up against the small bedroom window. If someone wanted to do so, they could readily climb the tree and enter the house that way. But that window, too, was locked. I had learned my lesson that I only had to be careless once.

And then there was the master bedroom.

I stood in the doorway, hesitating to go inside. When I turned on the overhead light, it flickered, then popped and went out. I swore. I'd need to get Darrell to replace the bulb for me. With no light, I couldn't see into the shadows. I could cross the carpet to the bathroom and turn on the light there, but the distance across the bedroom felt like miles. A prickling chill of fear went up my back. Darkness was behind me, darkness in front of me.

"Hello?"

I said it out loud, softly, tentatively. There was no answer. Of course not. But what I did hear made me clench my fists until my nails bit into my skin. The wind screeched, wailing like a skeleton trapped in a grave.

It was wind through the crack of an open window.

My legs wouldn't move. I was frozen where I was. I could have stayed in that doorway forever.

You're imagining things. You *left the window open.*

That was what I told myself. I liked cold air at night, and I liked waking up to the chill of the house in the fall. No one could get in there without a lot of trouble. The second-floor window looked out on the backyard, and there were no trees nearby. The only thing on the house wall was a drainpipe, and it would have taken an itsy-bitsy spider to climb up that water spout.

I went to the window. Yes, it was open, just by an inch or two. I threw it wide open and stuck my head out into the breeze, which carried nothing but quiet rain. The yard itself was dark, backing up to the woods. I couldn't see anything. I closed the window again, but this time I made sure it was shut, and I locked it.

I'd opened it myself last night. I'd simply forgotten to shut it when Darrell woke me up in the early morning. That was the answer.

Wasn't it?

I went to the bathroom. Brushed my teeth. With the light on, I checked the bedroom closet, to be sure no monsters were hiding there. I didn't look under the bed, because once I was down on my hands and knees, I didn't think I could stand up again. However, just to be sure, I found an old tennis ball in my nightstand drawer and rolled it under the bed frame. It came out the other side and bounced against the wall.

No one was there.

I knew what was wrong with me. It was Ajax. The body.

The murder. The Ursulina. That was what had me alarmed. That was the bad moon rising.

Even so, I took no chances. When I closed the bedroom door, I took a chair from my makeup table and dragged it across the carpet and wedged it under the doorknob. No one could get in without making a hell of a noise. I also found my handgun on the closet shelf. I always kept the gun loaded and ready. Just in case. For months in the winter and spring, I'd slept with it under my pillow, but sometime during the hot summer, I'd felt confident enough to let it stay in the closet.

Not tonight.

I put it under my pillow again. With that protection in place, some of my anxiety began to ease. I felt a little foolish for letting my imagination run wild.

I began to get undressed. I took off my maternity blouse and bra and threw them into the laundry basket, and I let my oversize jeans fall to the floor, where I stepped out of them. In the closet, I found one of my nightshirts, sized like a bedsheet, and draped it over my body. The flannel was cool and loose.

All that was left were my socks, which always presented the biggest challenge, both on and off. I sat down on the bed and reached for my trusty yardstick, which I slid between my ankle and my left sock. I peeled it off and flicked it in the general direction of the laundry basket. I did the same with my right sock, but it stuck to the end of the yardstick and refused to be flicked. So I retrieved it with my hand.

That was when I noticed something odd.

The bottom of the sock was wet. I hadn't realized it before, hadn't noticed the dampness on my foot.

Why was my sock wet?

Yes, I'd gone outside, but the covered porch was dry.

I stared at the bedroom window again.

The rain had been blowing in while I was asleep in the living room. I'd stepped on the wet carpet while I was looking out at the backyard. I pushed myself off the bed and went to the window, and I let out a tiny sigh of relief when I confirmed that the carpet below the sash was damp.

I could even trace the path of my wet footsteps leading to the bathroom and then to the bedroom door, where I'd secured it with the chair.

My footsteps. No one else's.

I should have left it at that, but I was curious like a cat. I went to the bedroom door and pushed the chair aside, and I opened the door to stare into the cold black maw of the rest of the house. The wooden frame groaned. That was the effect of the wind rattling the walls.

Wasn't it?

No one was here. I was alone.

I made sure my bare foot was dry. Then I stretched out my toes and slid them along the carpet in front of the bedroom door. To my horror, they came away wet. The carpet *outside* the room was wet. Damp the way it would be if someone had tracked wet shoes from inside the bedroom.

I closed the door and put the chair back in place under the doorknob.

I got into bed and left the bathroom light on. That night, I kept the gun not under the pillow but in my hand.

I didn't sleep at all.

CHAPTER TWENTY-SEVEN

Two nights later, I had dinner with Darrell and his family at the 126. It was all-you-can-eat fried chicken night, and hot, greasy chicken legs were one of the more normal things I'd been craving lately.

Ever since my father died, Darrell had sort of adopted me. He'd always treated me like a daughter, but he seemed to make it official at that point. His oldest was just a few years younger than me—she was twenty-four—and he had two younger girls, one who was eighteen, one who was sixteen. I felt honored that they included me as part of their family, since I didn't really have a family myself. But I also felt guilty, because Darrell had other things to worry about. His wife, Marilyn, was in her early fifties, but it only took one look to realize she wasn't doing well. She'd been battling lung cancer for two years, and the disease was winning. She was rail thin and pale, and her curly black hair had been replaced by a wig. I could see in Darrell's face, in his forced smile, that he knew what the future held. He was a strong man, but losing a spouse could bring the strongest of men to their knees.

I didn't want to add to their burden with any worries of my own, so I pretended as if nothing was wrong with me. We ate chicken, and we laughed. The 126 was a madhouse, as it usually was, raucous and rough. Here, even the best of friends were one bad joke away from a fistfight. *The A-Team* played on the television over the bar, but no one could hear it, because the jukebox blasted "A View to a Kill" so loudly that you had to shout at the person next to you. There was new artwork on the wall, a huge painting of *The Last Supper* with Jesus and the Apostles smoking cigarettes and drinking pitchers of beer. Some of the local churchgoers had complained, but at the 126, nobody cared.

I knew everyone there. Norm and Will played rotation at one of the pool tables. Ruby sat at a corner table with her high school friends, her face hard and drawn. Ben Malloy was back in town, going from table to table to talk up his new Ursulina special. The show was scheduled for a prime time debut on the Saturday after Halloween, and Ben had a big party planned at the 126 for the whole town to watch. Everyone was invited. He'd announced a cash prize for the best Ursulina costume, which meant the event was going to be a monster mash.

Sandra Thoreau sat at the bar, nursing a beer and a Merit. She raised her mug at me in a toast. She wore a fraying sky-blue turtleneck, faded jeans, and American flag cowboy boots. She faced outward on the stool, making eye contact with the men around her, assessing who she was going to bring home tonight.

I excused myself from Darrell's table and brought my basket of chicken to the bar.

"Hey," I said to Sandra as I squirmed onto the stool next to her.

"Hey, yourself," she replied with a sympathetic chuckle at my condition. "Looks like you're getting close."

"I'm a couple of weeks away, but it feels like it could be any day now."

"You ready?"

"As ready as I'm going to be."

"Got names picked out?"

"Actually, I was thinking about Shelby," I told her.

"Shelby. That's cool. It's different, I like it. Works for a boy, works for a girl."

"It's a girl."

Sandra smiled. "Well, you say that now, but prepare to be surprised. I was sure Henry was a girl, until the doc held him up in the hospital and showed me his little dick."

"It's a girl," I said again.

Sandra shrugged and puffed on her Merit. On one level, I knew she was right, because everyone had been telling me the same thing for months. Feelings don't matter, and God doesn't care what you think you're having. But you were you, Shelby. You were always going to be a girl. I never had the slightest doubt.

"So, Ajax," Sandra commented. "That's awful, huh?"

"Yeah."

"That makes four now. The Ursulina's been busy. Not that I have a problem with his taste in victims."

"You shouldn't make jokes like that," I advised her. Then I added in a hushed voice, "I do need to ask you something. Have you heard any rumors at the mine about Gordon Brink paying Ajax?"

"Paying him?"

"Five hundred dollars a month."

She whistled. "Wow, nice gig."

"We're not absolutely sure it was Brink, but the payments stopped after Brink was killed."

Sandra took a long swallow of her beer. "Norm told you about Ruby getting harassed at the mine, didn't he?"

"Yes. He also said she denied that it ever happened."

"Exactly. There you go. The little liar. Brink and the mine bought her off. There's your five hundred a month."

"You think?"

"Sure. They tried it with me, but I told them to stick it."

I didn't offer any opinion on Sandra's theory, but it had a plausible ring to it. I had no trouble imagining Ajax trying to squeeze the law firm for cash. On the other hand, if they'd been paying Ruby to stay quiet about the harassment, I didn't know why Ajax would have been keeping the money in a separate account that Ruby didn't seem to know anything about.

"Speaking of Ajax," Sandra murmured.

"What?"

She gestured at the entrance to the bar, where I noticed Penny Ramsey standing underneath a big moose head mounted above the door. The legal secretary looked around for an empty table with an awkward, uncomfortable smile on her face. Even after a year in Black Wolf County, she looked out of place, a city girl in Reagan country.

"You know about the two of them?" I asked.

"Well, that's the hot gossip."

"Do you think Ruby knows?"

Sandra shrugged. "I can't believe she doesn't."

I watched Penny. She was alone, but women who came to the 126 alone didn't stay that way for long. I wondered if that was her plan. Drown her sorrows over Ajax. Pick up a boy. When she took off her coat, I saw that she was spilling out of a seriously low-cut blouse and push-up bra. If she wanted attention from men, that outfit would get her plenty.

She was wearing the necklace, too.

Not a good idea.

I thought about going over and telling her to take it off. Anyone who looked at that necklace knew it was expensive, and there were people in the bar who would happily swipe it and hock it. But that wasn't the real problem. If Ruby knew about Penny and Ajax, she was going to spot that necklace in a heartbeat.

"I don't get it," Sandra went on. "Ruby's way hotter than her. I mean, I could see Ajax getting hung up on you, but why horn around with Little Swiss Miss over there?"

I was flattered by Sandra's comment, but it reminded me that rumors had been flying about me and Ajax all year. "Penny had a thing for Ajax. I doubt he had to ask her twice."

"Well, to screw, sure, but not to spend money on."

I frowned, because Sandra was right. Penny would have been fine for a no-strings-fling, but she didn't look like the kind of woman who would pull Ajax away from his wife. And yet he was buying her expensive gifts.

"Think she did it?" Sandra asked. "Sometimes it's the quiet ones, you know."

"Actually, I think she loved him," I said. "Ajax probably let her think he loved her, too. She was naive enough to believe it."

Sandra sucked on her Merit. "Men. If I didn't like what they had between their legs, I'd give them up for good."

I laughed. "Not likely."

"No. Not likely at all." She gave me a penetrating stare. "What about you? You got your eyes on anybody?"

"Yeah, because I'm a real catch looking like this."

"Don't sell yourself short. You're a catch in any condition, honey. I just mean, you're going to be a single mom like me. I wouldn't encourage anybody to join the club. Life's a lot easier with a man around."

"Not always."

Sandra frowned. "Well, I mean the right man. If there is such a thing. You got the wrong one, that's for sure. At least he's long gone. Good riddance to that son of a bitch."

I glanced around to make sure no one was listening to us, not that they could have heard us over the noise of the bar. "Actually, Sandra, that's something else I wanted to ask you. Have you heard any talk about Ricky lately?"

"What kind of talk?"

"About him being back."

"*Ricky?*" Sandra hissed, with genuine concern in her voice. "Are you serious? Is he in town again? Have you seen him?"

"No, I haven't seen him. I could be completely wrong. I don't know, it's just a feeling. On Sunday night, I could swear someone had been in my house."

"Jesus."

"Nobody's said anything to you?" I asked.

"Not a word, and that would be a tough secret to keep. If he came back, he'd have to be bunking with a friend, right? I think the boys at the mine would know, and I'd hear about it fast."

"Well, keep an ear to the ground, okay?"

"I will. Have you told Darrell?"

I shook my head. "He'd want me to come live with them, but he's got enough to worry about with Marilyn."

"If Ricky's back, you've got shit to worry about, too," Sandra replied. "This isn't the time to be proud, honey. You've got a baby to think about."

"I know."

"That little prick should be in jail for what he did to you."

"Yeah."

"Do you need a gun? Are you packing?"

I patted the purse that was slung over my shoulder. "Always."

"Well, good." Sandra smiled at me, but then her face darkened. I saw her staring over my shoulder. "Uh-oh. Here comes trouble."

"What?"

I turned around. Penny Ramsey had found a cocktail table by herself. She sipped from a glass of white wine in front of her, and she primped her hair and smiled nervously as the men in the bar whistled at the display of her cleavage. But unbeknownst to Penny, Ruby had spotted her, too. Like the black clouds of a storm front coming, Ruby stalked toward Penny across the 126, and silence fell over the bar, table by table, as Ajax's widow zeroed in on Ajax's mistress.

Penny didn't notice Ruby until the two women were eye to eye. By then, it was too late to leave. When Penny tried to back away, Ruby grabbed her wrist and held it while Penny struggled. Ruby twisted the chain of Penny's necklace around one of her fingers.

"He gave this to *you*?" she asked, tightening the necklace like a knot around Penny's throat.

"That's none of your business," she retorted. "Let go of me."

"You were sleeping with my husband. That makes it my business."

"He didn't love you anymore."

"And you think he loved you? You're a fool."

"He did love me. He *told* me. You're just jealous."

"Jealous of a nothing little wallflower like you? The only thing that makes me jealous is this necklace. I want it, and you're going to give it to me."

Ruby bunched her fist together and yanked the necklace off Penny's neck. Penny tried to grab it from her, but Ruby held it out of her reach, letting the chain dangle from her hand.

"Give that back," Penny snapped.

"If my husband bought it, then it's mine. Now be a good tramp and go away."

"Give it *back!*"

"I said, stuff your boobs back in your coat and get the hell out of here."

"No, I won't. I want my necklace."

"It's mine now, so you can just go. Understand?"

Penny leaned into Ruby's face as she swiped at the necklace again. "Ajax said it was over between the two of you. He was going to leave you."

Ruby growled from deep in her chest, an animal cry of rage. "You. Little. *Liar!*"

Her face flushed deep red, practically matching the fire of her hair. With a scream, she flung the necklace into the crowd. Then she grabbed Penny's wineglass and smashed it down on the table, making jagged edges like teeth. With a swish of her arm, she scored Penny's cheek with the broken glass, cutting deep, bloody gashes into her skin.

"See how many men you get with that face, you home-wrecking bitch," Ruby sneered.

Penny stared in silent shock as blood flooded onto her hands.

Then, with a wild scream, she toppled the table, and the two women attacked each other.

CHAPTER TWENTY-EIGHT

"Why are you talking to *me*?" Penny shouted at us in the sheriff's office. "You should be talking to her! She's the one who started it. She's the one who did this. Look at me! I mean, look at me!"

Penny touched the gauze pad covering the stitches on her face and began to sob. Darrell and I waited before we tried to say anything more. Despite the late hour, the office buzzed with activity behind us. We'd had to wake up Jerry, who wasn't happy about the fight, and the sheriff's wife had gone to Ruby's house to pick up her kids from the babysitter. Ruby herself was in a holding cell in the basement.

"We *are* talking to her," Darrell said quietly. "She's under arrest."

"Good!"

"We'll charge her for the assault on you," Darrell added. "If that's what you want."

Penny looked up from the box of tissues we'd given her. "If that's what I want? Of course that's what I want!"

"I thought we might be able to deal with this some other way."

"Look what she did to me!" Penny screamed again. "The doctor says there could be nerve damage. I'll have huge scars!"

"I understand. What Ruby did to you was awful. But Ruby's a mom with three kids, Penny. Ajax was just killed, so she's on her own to take care of those kids now. And you need to remember—"

I knew he was going to add: *You were sleeping with her husband.*

But he held back from saying that. He didn't need to. I watched Penny bite her lip and finish the sentence in her head. Her hands were folded in front of her on the table, and she rubbed her thumbs nervously together.

"Just think about it," Darrell added. "Okay?"

Penny shrugged but didn't answer.

"We'd also like to talk to you about Ajax," I interjected.

"What about him?"

"Given your relationship, you might be able to help us figure out what happened to him."

"I have no idea. I can't believe he's dead."

"When did you start seeing him?"

Penny sniffled. "About six months ago. It was right after Ms. Svitak came to town to take over the case. I thought I was going to lose my job, but she said she wanted people with history working on the lawsuit. So she kept me on. I decided to take a night out to celebrate, and I went to the 126. That's where I bumped into Ajax."

"Did you talk to him, or did he talk to you?"

"He saw me and came over to the bar." She shook her head with awe. "I mean, he was *so* handsome. I thought that the first time I met him, but I didn't think he'd ever be interested in me. But we talked, and we had a few drinks, and then he took me back to my motel. Honestly, I figured that would be the end, you know, a one-night stand. I really didn't care. But he called and said he wanted to see me again. We began to meet up whenever we could."

"Did it bother you that he was married?"

"That was between him and Ruby, not me. Plus, I was all by myself in this place. I liked having somebody to be with."

"When did you last see him?"

"Thursday. We had drinks together at the 126."

"Wasn't Ajax concerned about people seeing you together?"

"We pretended it was an accident that we sat next to each other at the bar. I mean, I'm sure people knew, but we played it cool. Afterward, I met him at his house. Ruby was away with the kids, so we were able to stay there and use his bed. I liked that. I stayed with him all night."

"What time did you leave?"

"About seven in the morning. He had to go to work, and so did I. That was the last time I saw him."

Darrell leaned forward with a curious expression. "Did you see him on Friday night? Or on Saturday?"

Penny's brow wrinkled unhappily. "No. He had to work."

Darrell shook his head. "He didn't. He wasn't on the schedule this weekend."

"Well, that's what he told me."

"Even if he was working, why wouldn't you have seen him after his shift was done?" I asked.

"I called, but he wasn't home."

"When did you call?"

"Both nights. Friday and Saturday. There was no answer."

"Did that concern you?"

"No. I figured he had to work late. And it's not like I could leave a message or anything. He told me never to do that, in case Ruby picked it up."

"Did you go to his house?" I asked.

"No."

"Why not? Did you think you'd find him with somebody else?"

"There was no one else. He loved *me*."

I could see her trying to convince herself. "Penny, Ajax is dead. You need to tell us the truth. You thought he wasn't alone, right? He wasn't answering the phone, because he had somebody else with him."

She lowered her eyes and gave the smallest of nods. "Sometimes, even when I knew Ruby wasn't around, he didn't call me. So I wondered."

"Do you have any names of other women he was seeing?"

"No."

"*Did* you go over there this weekend?"

"No!" she insisted. "I didn't go to his house. You're trying to make it out like I killed him, and I would *never* do that. Never! You should ask Ruby about it. You saw what she did tonight. She's crazy!"

"Other than Ruby, can you think of anyone else who might have killed him?"

She shook her head. "Nobody."

"Did he talk about having problems with anyone? Did he say if anything was bothering him?"

"No. I mean, not really."

I heard hesitation in her voice.

"It sounds like there was something," I said.

"Well, he talked about the lawsuit a lot. He asked me lots of questions about it. He was always pushing me for information. He wanted to know what I'd heard, what I knew, what Ms. Svitak was saying about the case."

"Why was he so interested?"

"I don't know. I figured it was because Ruby was a witness."

"Did he ever talk about money?"

"What do you mean?"

"Well, did he ever mention getting monthly payments from the law firm?"

Her brow wrinkled. "Why would Ajax be getting money from the firm?"

"He never told you about it?"

"No."

"Did he talk about getting money from anyone else?"

"No."

"What about the lawsuit? Did you give him information like he wanted?"

Penny hesitated. "I don't want to get fired."

"Well, you say you loved Ajax. Don't you want to find out what happened to him?"

It took her a long time to answer. "Okay, I probably told him more than I should. I wanted him to like me, and I didn't really see the harm. Ruby was a witness for the mine, so it's not like I was helping the plaintiffs. Besides, he wasn't asking about the harassment or anything like that."

"What did he want to know about?"

"He asked a lot about Gordon."

"Gordon Brink? What about him?"

"He asked if the firm was hiding anything about him. Did Ms. Svitak know things that might come out at trial? Or did she have any idea who killed him? I thought that was weird, because everybody said Gordon was killed by his son. I asked Ajax why he wanted to know, and he told me his partner still had questions about the case. That you were pushing him to find out more."

Darrell frowned. "He said *I* wanted the information?"

"Yes."

I glanced at Darrell, who shook his head.

"What did you tell him?" I asked Penny.

"Well, I told him about a tape recording I'd heard. It seemed to upset him."

"What was this tape?"

"Not long after Ms. Svitak arrived, she was going over archival records of our client relationship with the mine. I was there to take notes. She was listening to a cassette recording of a phone conversation between Gordon and the senior partner of the firm in Milwaukee."

"What were they talking about?"

"Gordon said he'd tried to get Sandra Thoreau to quit the mine. He'd offered her a payout to leave, but she'd turned him down. After that, Ms. Svitak switched off the tape and told me to leave."

"Did you ever hear more of the tape?"

"No. Later, Ms. Svitak told me to destroy my notes about it. That's very unusual. I asked why, and she snapped at me and said not to ask any questions. My guess is, she didn't want anything on paper that might accidentally show up in discovery. The firm doesn't want the plaintiffs to hear what's on that tape."

"You told Ajax about it?"

"Yes, and he freaked out. I don't know why."

Darrell interjected. "Do you know *when* the call was taped?"

"Years ago."

"How many years?"

Penny blinked as she tried to recall. "Seven, I think? I always label my notes with the date of the conversation, and I've got a good memory for that kind of thing. I'm pretty sure it was summer seven years ago."

"Where was Gordon when he made the call?"

Penny shrugged. "Here."

"Here in Black Wolf County?" Darrell asked.

"Yes. He said he'd met Sandra Thoreau that day, so he must have been here."

Darrell eased back in his chair with a heavy sigh. Then he turned to me. "We need to pull the murder file again."

"On Brink?" I asked.

He nodded. "Yes, but not just him. Summer seven years ago is when Kip and Racer were killed."

*

We kept our files in the basement of the building. It was a dank, windowless room, not the best place to store documents, but we didn't have a lot of extra space. Boxes of d-CON kept the mice from devouring our papers. The files were all in bankers boxes organized by date on a series of rusty metal shelves. The archives went back for decades, so if someone wanted to see their grandfather's arrest record for skinny-dipping in the 1940s, it was probably still there.

Darrell didn't say anything as we traversed the narrow aisles, with me squeezing sideways because of my belly, so I was the one who brought it up.

"What was Ajax doing?" I asked. "Trying to solve the murders?"

"Maybe. But that doesn't explain the monthly payments."

"At least now we know why Ajax was buying Penny gifts. He wanted information from her."

Darrell nodded. "Ajax is caught up in all of this somehow. I have to assume that's why he's dead."

We reached the area in the basement where the boxes were kept for the months of July and August seven years earlier.

Everything Darrell had gathered in his investigation into the murders of Kip and Racer was crammed into three heavy boxes, typically filed on the top shelf. I wasn't able to reach the boxes myself, or to lift them, not in my condition. But I didn't need to. The boxes were gone. The other records from that time frame had been squeezed together to make the gap less noticeable, but the murder files were gone.

"Somebody took them," I said.

Darrell grabbed the log sheet that we used to record who removed materials and when. As he reviewed the top sheet, I could see Darrell's own name from the last time he'd pulled the files, shortly after Gordon Brink's murder. He'd noted the date and time in and the date and time out.

That was the last time the records had been touched, according to the log. No one had checked them out. But they'd vanished anyway.

"We need to check Brink's file, too," he said urgently.

Quickly, we made our way to the shelf that held the records from last December and then January of the current year. It took me only one glance to see that the box of materials we'd gathered on Gordon Brink's death had disappeared, too.

"It was here," I told Darrell. "I put it here myself."

Darrell shook his head. "It had to be one of us. A cop took it. Nobody else has keys to get in here."

"Ajax?"

"That's my guess."

"But why? He was part of the investigations. He already knew what we'd found."

"I don't know," Darrell replied, "but we're back to square one. Everything we know about the Ursulina murders, all our evidence, is gone."

CHAPTER TWENTY-NINE

The next morning, we met Sandra Thoreau at the mine. She arrived in the work site trailer from deep down in the terraced layers of the copper mine, wearing a hard hat and yellow reflective suit. She was dirty over every inch of exposed skin, the kind of dirt from which you probably never felt completely clean. She didn't look happy to see us, and I was conscious of the fact that the mine was going to dock her for every minute she wasn't on the clock.

She glanced at Norm, who'd come to the mine with us. The three of us sat in flimsy chairs inside the trailer, but Sandra ignored the chair we'd set aside for her and stayed standing. Outside, a constant rumble of machines made the trailer walls rattle, and we heard the shouts of men trying to be heard over the engines.

"What now?" she asked Norm with a weary sigh. "What do they think I did?"

"It's nothing to worry about," he told her. "I'll let you know what to answer and not answer. Just be truthful."

Sandra shrugged. "Let's make this fast."

Darrell nodded at me to lead the questioning. I found that I liked doing my old job again, even if it was just for a little while. "Sandra, you mentioned a couple of times that the mine tried to buy you off to get you to quit."

"Yeah. So what? I told them to shove it, but if you want proof, I can't give it to you. They didn't put any of this in writing. Their offer was cash on the table, take it or leave it."

"When was this?"

She hesitated. "A few years ago."

"Five, six, seven?"

"I don't remember. I know it was summer, because it was hot."

"Before the lawsuit was filed?"

"Yeah."

"How did this offer come about?" I asked.

I saw a glimmer of understanding cross her dirty face. She knew why we were here. She rolled the answer around on her tongue for a while before saying anything more.

"A guy called me at home," she told us. "An out-of-towner. A lawyer. He wanted to talk to me on behalf of the mine. When we met, he said they were willing to pay me a nice chunk of change if I'd voluntarily leave my job and sign some kind of release. He was willing to give me two thousand bucks right then and there. He even showed me the roll of bills."

"You said no?"

"Two thousand bucks but then I've got no job? Yeah, I said no. The recession was hell back then. I didn't know if I'd ever get another job around here. I was going to hang on to what I had."

"Who was it, Sandra?" I asked. "Who was the lawyer?"

She wiped her nose with the back of her hand. "If you're asking me about it, I assume you already know. It was Gordon Brink."

"You met Brink years before his murder. Here in Black Wolf County."

"That's right. Although it wasn't much of a meeting. I didn't spend more than half an hour with him before I got up and left. It was just enough time for him to bribe me and me to tell him where to go. Honestly, I wouldn't have been able to tell you what his name was or what he looked like, not until he came back here last fall."

"Did you have any other communication with him in the interim? Letters? Phone calls?"

"No."

Darrell, who was sitting on a rickety card-table chair, put his hands on his knees and leaned forward. "After Brink was killed, why didn't you tell us that you knew him before the lawsuit? That he'd been here before?"

"You didn't ask." She gave us a not-very-sweet smile. "If I've learned one thing from Norm during the lawsuit, it's not to volunteer information unless someone asks me about it."

"Were you afraid you'd be a suspect in Brink's murder?"

"I already was, wasn't I? From day one. You made that pretty clear, Darrell. I didn't need to give you any more ammunition."

"Did you kill him?"

"No."

"Where did you meet Brink?" I asked. "Where were you when he offered you the money?"

"He was staying at the Fair Day resort. I went to his cabin, we talked, and I left."

"Do you know how long he was in town?"

"I have no idea. I turned down his offer, and that was that."

"Who else knew about your meeting with him?"

"Back then? Nobody. If anybody else knew, it came from Brink, not me. I didn't talk about it at the mine. I didn't want the other women finding out. The last thing I needed was to put the idea in their heads that they could grab a quick payout and quit. I wanted us to stick together. If one of us left, they'd work that much harder to get rid of the rest of us."

"Do you know if Brink tried to bribe the others?"

"If he did, they didn't say anything about it to me. But the mine saw me as the ringleader. I was the one they really wanted out."

"What about Ruby?"

"I have no idea. Maybe. Who knows, she might have taken the cash. I'm sure she'd deny it, but it would explain a lot."

Darrell glanced at Norm. "Did you know about Brink being in town?"

Norm phrased his answer carefully. "When Sandra came to me about the lawsuit a couple of years later, we discussed the bribe. I had to have a complete history of what the mine had done to try to push Sandra out. I knew they'd offered her money, but not that Brink was the one who'd done it. I didn't know that until he came back, and Sandra confirmed he was the one. I'm sorry for keeping you in the dark about it last winter, but any information I had about Brink was privileged."

Sandra pushed up her sleeve and checked her watch. She glanced out one of the small windows toward the dirt road leading down into the bowels of the mine. "Let's move this along, okay? I'm losing money here. You might as well get to the shit you really want to know about."

"What do you think we want to know?" Darrell asked.

"Come on, this is about Kip and Racer, right? You think Brink talked to me around the time the two of them got chopped up in Norm's trailer."

"That seems pretty likely, doesn't it? Given the similarities between the crimes."

"Well, I don't know what to tell you. I can't even be sure it was the same summer. But if they got killed after I met Brink, I wouldn't have given it a second thought back then. Kip and Racer had nothing to do with me or the mine. I had no reason to think there was any connection between them and Brink."

"What about when you heard how Gordon Brink was killed?" Darrell asked.

Again Sandra glanced at Norm, but he nodded his approval. "Sure, it made me wonder, but I figured Brink was killed by a copycat. When the sheriff said it was Jay, I assumed that was the end of the story."

"Except now there's Ajax, too," Darrell went on. "Was he in the mix on any of this?"

"If he was, I never heard about it."

Darrell shook his head in frustration. "Sandra, we've got four murders, four brutal crimes committed in very similar ways. When Brink was killed, we didn't find any evidence to link his death to the murders of Kip and Racer. There was nothing to tie the three of them together. But now we find out that Brink was in town once before, which you knew but kept from us. Our next stop is going to be at the Fair Day resort. When we check their records, I think we're going to find out that Brink was staying at the resort right around the time Kip and Racer got killed. There's no way that's a coincidence. All these crimes are connected somehow, and right now, the only connection I'm seeing is *you*."

"Well, I didn't kill them, Darrell. I don't know who did."

"Brink came to town to see you. He tried to bribe you. Your lawsuit is at the center of all of this."

"Maybe. But I'm not the Ursulina."

"Where were you on Friday night? And on Saturday night?"

"Home with Henry."

"You're not exactly known to stay in on weekend nights. Why didn't you go out?"

"I wasn't feeling well. Stomach flu."

"So you have no alibi," Darrell concluded.

"I guess not."

"As I recall, your alibi was soft for Brink's murder, too."

Norm stood up and put himself between Darrell and Sandra. "I think we're done for now, Darrell. Sandra has to get back to work, and wild speculation isn't going to get us anywhere."

Sandra walked away to the trailer door, but I called after her. "Hey, Sandra? One more thing."

Norm tried to shut me down, but Sandra waved at him to say it was okay. "What is it?"

"You turned down the bribe and told Brink to shove it. Then what?"

"I left."

"No, I mean what did Brink say when you turned him down?"

Sandra scratched her cheek with black fingernails as she tried to remember. "He was pissed. Brink was a bully, you know that. He was the kind of guy who was used to getting what he wanted, and he thought he could intimidate me. He told me if I was holding out for more money, there wasn't going to be any. And he said if I didn't take the offer and quit the mine, I'd regret it."

CHAPTER THIRTY

The labor pains came back while we were driving to the Fair Day resort. This time, Darrell heard me inhale with a sharp breath and noticed my fists clenching and my whole body squirming in the passenger seat. He was immediately concerned.

"Are you okay?"

"Not really."

"Do you need to go to the hospital?"

"Last time the pains went away after a few minutes. Let's wait and see."

"I'd rather not have to deliver your baby, Rebecca."

"That makes two of us," I replied.

He pulled onto the shoulder of the highway and studied my face, which was taut with discomfort.

"Is this too much for you?" Darrell asked. "If being part of this investigation is putting you at any risk, I'll drive you back home right now."

"No, I want to be part of it. Really."

I breathed steadily and tried to clear my head, which wasn't easy. Fortunately, the pain settled down in a few minutes, as it had before, and my body relaxed. Even so, I knew you were coming, Shelby. You were getting ready to be part of this world. The clock was ticking, and I didn't have much time to get answers to all my questions.

"I'm okay now," I said, and I motioned to Darrell to keep driving. He looked relieved.

We arrived at the Fair Day resort half an hour later. It was situated on the far western edge of the county, built on the shore of one of our largest, prettiest lakes. Color had begun to dot the trees, and the sun was shining, making it a gorgeous October day. A few fishing boats trolled the water. The resort had been around since the 1930s, and a lot of us joked that the towels in the rooms dated back to that era, too. For its time, the place had been elegant, but decades later, it was just a collection of lakeside cabins with outhouses and a communal shower. It was seasonal, and the resort would be closing up for the winter in a few more weeks. I had a hard time imagining Gordon Brink staying here, but seven years earlier, he wouldn't have had many options.

The owner of the resort was a man in his early fifties named Marvin Faraday, who was the son of the original owners. The Faraday clan went so far back in this area that some of us wondered if there was a Random Faraday centuries ago who gave the town its name. He was a rounded Paul Bunyan of a man, the sixth of six children, and he had seven kids of his own. Marvin was also the town mayor, which wasn't a job that took a lot of time around here. He knew everyone, so when Darrell and I came inside the lobby cabin that doubled as his home, he was right there to put both hands on my belly to feel you kick. You must have liked him, sweetheart, because you kicked up a storm to say hello.

He poured coffee for himself from an aging Mr. Coffee machine in the corner of the office, and he held up the pot to the two of us, but we declined.

"Awful news about Ajax," Marvin told us when we were all sitting down. "Awful, awful, awful. You know what happened?"

"We're working on it," Darrell replied.

"Ajax came here a lot, you know."

"Did he?"

"Oh, sure. He had a cabin he liked, probably rented it out once or twice a month. Never came alone. For me, it was hear no evil, see no evil, know what I'm saying? He brought girls here, but I made a point of not noticing who. Man's gotta do what a man's gotta do, and it wasn't any of my business. As long as there weren't any awkward scenes, jealous husbands showing up, that kind of thing, I didn't care. I wish I could be more help."

"Actually, we're not here about Ajax," Darrell told him.

"No?"

"We'd like to ask you about Gordon Brink."

"You mean the lawyer who got killed last winter? What about him?"

"Did you know him?"

Marvin rubbed his beard and thought about it. "I'm trying to think if I ever met him. I don't recall that I did. None of them stayed out here. There was a city council meeting about some of the vandalism the lawyers were complaining about, but as I recall, the mine sent some young associate. The only time I heard Brink's name was after he got killed. Wasn't it his son that did it?"

"We're not so sure about that anymore," Darrell replied. "The thing is, we think Brink may have stayed at the resort several years ago."

"Oh, yeah? I guess it's possible, but I don't remember."

"We'd like to look through your guest records from back then. Specifically from July seven years ago."

Marvin shrugged. "Knock yourself out."

He retreated into a back room and returned a couple of minutes later with a shoebox in his hand. The box was labeled with a black marker for the months of June and July seven years earlier. Inside, hundreds of white index cards were squeezed together in no particular order that we could see. Each card listed little more than the basic information, including a name, cabin number, check-in date, check-out date, total bill, and method of payment. Back then, most of the guests had paid in cash.

Darrell took half the cards, and I took the other. The slowest part of the process was interpreting the handwriting, but when we were both done, we hadn't found a card labeled with a name that even resembled Gordon Brink.

"Penny and Sandra weren't one hundred percent sure it was seven years ago," I pointed out. "Maybe we're wrong about the timing."

"I don't think we're wrong." Darrell glanced at Marvin, who was reading a paperback Louis L'Amour novel. "Marvin? Do you typically ask for ID when people check in?"

The resort owner didn't look up from the book. "Now I do. Seven years ago? I was pretty loose about things back then. As long as people had cash, I didn't really care who they were."

Darrell looked at me. "So Brink could have used a false name."

"If he did, then we'll never find him."

But we went through the index cards again anyway. It took longer this time, hunting for the kind of fake name a Milwaukee corporate lawyer might use. The clue I spotted in the stack of cards turned out not to be a name, but a correction in the check-out date and the total bill. The guest had paid in advance for a two-week stay, but then the date had been crossed out and replaced with a new date that was only five days after arrival.

The name on the card was Jay Smith.

Jay. That felt like more than a coincidence.

I showed the card to Darrell, who spotted the significance of the new check-out date immediately.

"Norm found Kip and Racer's bodies a few days later," he said. "The bodies had been in the trailer a while. I think this is Brink, don't you?"

We showed the card to Marvin, but not surprisingly, he didn't recall one summer guest leaving the resort early seven years ago. If it was Brink, he'd come and gone without leaving footprints, which was no doubt exactly what he wanted. Darrell wandered out of the office with the card in hand, and I followed. A grassy slope surrounded the resort and led down to the lake and the guest cabins. Sunlight reflected on the water like orange stars, and dense forestland ringed the shore. The October air was cool.

"Brink comes to town, checks in under a fake name, and pays cash," Darrell mused out loud, flapping the card as if it would offer up more secrets. "He pays for two weeks, but a few days later, he leaves early. Why? Because Sandra said no to the bribe? There's got to be more to it than that."

I shook my head and didn't say anything. There was nothing I could add.

"Kip and Racer were on the run after robbing that liquor store in Mittel County," Darrell went on. "They were hiding out in Norm's trailer. And yet somehow the three of them are connected. That's the only thing that makes sense."

"The trailer is two hours away from here in the middle of nowhere," I pointed out. "How would Brink have found them? And why?"

"I don't know, but we're missing something important," Darrell insisted. "Brink left the resort early, and based on the timing, he must have left right around the time of the murders. We have nothing to connect him to Kip and Racer, but there *has* to be a connection."

"You think Brink killed them?"

"I don't know, but something happened out there. Either Brink saw it, or he was part of it, or he knew who did it. I think he was *running*."

There was no point in asking what Brink was running from. The answer was right there between us, but we left it unspoken.

The Ursulina.

*

Darrell wanted to see the cabin where Jay Smith, a.k.a. Gordon Brink, had stayed seven years earlier. I wasn't crazy about hiking down the slope to the lake and then having to hike back again, so I let him go by himself while I waited in the car with the passenger door open and my puffy legs dangling outside.

I hadn't been sitting there five minutes when a yellow Cadillac, as long as a land yacht, pulled up next to me.

"Deputy Rebecca!" Ben Malloy announced happily, rolling down the driver's window.

"Hello, Ben."

I felt awkward seeing him again. I hadn't actually talked to Ben since we were together at the frozen lake during the winter. In truth, I'd avoided him whenever he'd been in town for that very reason. I didn't want to be reminded of the night when Jay killed himself. The night when I'd had my own emotional breakdown. The night when I'd seen the best and worst of men.

Ben clambered out of the Cadillac like an oversize leprechaun on the hunt for a pot of gold. His forelock drooped, and he pushed it back with a swipe of his hand. He dug into his pocket for his pipe and chomped down on it, but he left it unlit. "Looks like the big day is fast approaching," he said to me.

"It is."

"Well, I hope you don't miss my Halloween party. I want you to see the new show. It's fantastic."

"That won't be up to me," I said, cupping my belly. "That will be up to Shelby."

"Shelby? Is that the name you picked? I like it."

"Thank you."

"Boy or girl?"

"Officially, I don't know, but I think she's a girl."

"Well, I'm sure she'll be as lovely as you are, Deputy."

"That's sweet, Ben." Then I added, "But you know, I'm only a deputy again for a little while, because of what happened to Ajax. Otherwise, I'm the department secretary. My job changed after last winter."

His face fell, and he looked genuinely upset. "Seriously? Is that true? I'm disappointed. I hope our adventure in the woods didn't contribute to your taking a different role. If I'd thought that, I never would have said a word about what happened."

"Nothing that happened was your fault, Ben," I told him. "I screwed up, and I'm lucky to have a job at all. You did the right thing by telling them about Jay's confession."

"Except we both know it wasn't really the truth," he replied with a sharp eye. "For what it's worth, I emphasized to Darrell and Jerry that I thought the boy was lying when he said what he did. They seemed more interested in putting the case to bed than getting to the truth."

"I guess sometimes the truth is overrated."

Ben winked. "You're preaching to the choir about that. I'm

in television, which means I never let the truth get in the way of a good story. Except when it comes to our mutual friend, of course."

I cocked an eyebrow with a question.

"The Ursulina!" he explained, as if that was obvious. "I haven't forgotten our conversation, you know. Or the look on your face back then. Deny it if you want, but I'm convinced we're both members of the club. We both know he's real. One of these days, I hope to prove it."

I said nothing to verify what he suspected about me.

Ben squatted down and put a pudgy hand on my shoulder. His eyes were serious. "Also, as long as we're talking about that night, I wanted to say that I heard what happened to you later with your ex-husband. I was desperately sorry to find out what you went through."

"Thanks. It was months ago, and I'm much better now. And *you* can deny it if you want, but I know you helped me with your anonymous gift, Ben. I really appreciate it. The money you gave me got me through some tough times."

"I have no idea what you're talking about!" he replied graciously, getting back to his feet. He finally lit his pipe and primed it with several breaths. Then he gestured at the resort around us, which was showing its age. "So what brings you to the Fair Day? I stay here out of nostalgia, but with all due respect to Marvin, the place could use a serious sprucing up. Of course, it's still better than staying with my mother."

"I'm helping Darrell," I replied vaguely.

"Ah, something to do with the latest killing, no doubt. Well, at least Darrell and Jerry are smart enough to keep you involved. That's good. I couldn't believe it when I heard what happened to Ajax. It's tragic for poor Ruby, but a new Ursulina murder only a couple of weeks before my special airs? That's ratings gold.

I called the network as soon as I heard about his death. We're filming a new ending to the documentary while I'm in town."

"That's not in very good taste, Ben."

He shrugged. "Words that will appear on my tombstone! Would you like to be interviewed for the show? I know Darrell would say no, but what about you? The network would fall in love with your pretty face."

"No, thanks."

"Are you sure? We don't have to talk about Ajax or the murder investigation." His eyes twinkled. "We could talk about whatever it was you saw in the forest that you're hiding from me."

"No," I repeated firmly. "No interview."

"All right. If you say so. That's a shame. Anyway, I hope I'll see you at the party."

Ben headed for the hotel lobby.

"Hey, can I ask you something?" I called after him.

He stopped and gave me a quizzical look. "Why, of course."

I maneuvered my way out of the cruiser and stood up, with Ben giving me a little help. My voice was low, although there was no one around. Darrell hadn't returned yet. "Seven years ago, you and all your volunteers did a lot of searching in the woods near where Kip and Racer were killed. I was wondering—did you find anything out there that you didn't share with the sheriff's department?"

Ben stroked his chin thoughtfully. "What did you have in mind?"

"Evidence of murder, rather than a monster."

"Why would I hide anything like that?"

"Because it's hard to sell a myth on TV when you've got a human being in jail for the crimes."

"You think I'd let a killer go free just to get ratings?"

"Actually, I think you might."

"Actually, I think you're right," he told me with a sly grin. "People don't really want the truth, you know. They like the mystery. But in this case, the truth is, I didn't find anything. I wasn't able to prove the Ursulina did it, but I didn't find evidence to suggest someone else did, either. Everything the volunteers gathered and brought in during the search, I turned over to Darrell. He told me he didn't find anything useful to the case."

I nodded. "Okay. Well, I had to ask."

"However, I do have many hours of raw footage from the search stored away in my mother's attic," Ben went on. "Only a few minutes actually wound up on air. If you really believe a human being was responsible for these murders, rather than a monster, you're welcome to go through the footage anytime you want."

My brow furrowed. "Why would I do that? What do you think I'd find?"

"Well, whoever killed those men must have been pretty nervous about that search," Ben replied. "If I were the killer, I would have wanted to be there to make sure nothing turned up that pointed a finger at me. So it's just possible that somewhere in all those hours of footage, we got the murderer on film."

CHAPTER THIRTY-ONE

That night, I dreamed about you, Shelby.

It was the first of many dreams I would have where we were together. As strange as it sounds, you've always been with me. I've felt your closeness all these years. I've never stopped talking to you and wishing things had happened differently.

In my dream, you weren't a baby or even a child. You were all grown up, a beautiful young woman around my age, with dark hair like mine, but straighter and parted in the middle. I could see so much of myself in your face, in those dreaming brown eyes, in the milky pale skin, in the inquisitive little smile on your mouth when you looked at the world and tried to understand it. Those are all things I gave you, even if you don't realize it. It made me sad, though, to see you without the years in between, because it meant I'd missed your growing up. I hadn't been there.

That night, though, the dream brought us together. Rebecca and Shelby. Mother and daughter. We held hands. We didn't talk, but we felt no need to talk. There was this instant, intimate familiarity between us, of knowing each other, of connectedness.

Being with you made me happy. You filled me with a glow of contentment, because you were smart and fearless and beautiful. We were in the forest. Whenever I sleep, I go to the forest. It wasn't night, but the crowding of the trees created a gloomy grayness around us. Birds flitted through the shadows, but oddly, they didn't sing. The world was as still as a painting, no wind, no warmth, no chill. We followed a well-walked path side by side, but the dirt at our feet was dry as dust, and we left no footprints. When I looked back, it seemed as if we hadn't been there at all.

I had so many questions for you. About your life. About your past. Are you married? Do you have children? Do you have friends? Do you laugh?

But I asked none of those things. I simply walked with you through the magical forest, and the farther we went, the more the grayness turned to dark. The birds went away. Night began to fall like a great shadow. A feeling of foreboding crept over me, and I knew what was coming next. It happened this way in all my dreams. In my waking hours, I hunted for the beast, but in my dreams, the beast hunted me.

I heard the noise that had haunted my life, that had become my secret obsession. It was the sound of the monster, drawing near, coming back for me. The reunion that I'd sought since I was ten years old happened every night when I closed my eyes. But this dream was different, because this time, I realized that the beast wasn't here for me. No, this was much worse.

The Ursulina was coming for *you*.

A black shape crashed through the underbrush, its breath loud and heavy. In the darkness, suddenly, I had a flashlight in my hand, the way I did years ago. As the monster stormed toward us, my light shined on shaggy fur and the curves of sharp, huge claws. And I heard crying at my feet. When I looked down, I saw that you weren't a woman anymore, Shelby. You were a baby again, nestled in my Easter basket among green paper curlicues.

Crying. Cold. Scared. Alone.

The beast was coming, and I had to protect you from him. I felt fear like nothing I'd ever known, but also a determined, furious, vengeful rage at the idea that anything would threaten my child. I would never let him hurt you. The beast could have me, it could take me, it could kill me, but you would live. You would be safe. I saw the monster looming in front of me. Tall, hunched, huge. Its great paws raised high, its rancid snorts hot on my face. I saw the claws that would rip me to shreds, open up my body, spill my blood. The teeth that would tear and gnaw at my flesh and consume me until I was completely inside him.

But it would never, never take my baby.

I stepped in front of the basket, shielding you.

"It's me you want!" I screamed at the beast. "It's me you've always wanted. Here I am!"

*

My eyes flew open. I awakened from one nightmare into another.

I lay on the sofa in my cold living room, where I'd fallen asleep, as I usually did these days. The fire I'd built had died to embers, just enough to cast a faint orange glow. One of my kitchen chairs had been pulled into the middle of the room, and a man sat on it, watching me.

Ricky.

He was back.

For an instant, I wondered if I was still dreaming, but I wasn't. Immediately, I grabbed for my purse, which was where I kept my gun, but Ricky gave a low chuckle and waved my revolver in the air.

Next I reached for the phone to call for help, but when I picked up the handset, I saw that he'd sliced the cord.

"What do you want, Ricky?" I asked, trying to cover my terror with the ice in my voice. "Why are you here?"

"Very nice, Bec. I haven't seen you in what? Almost nine months, judging by the basketball you've got down there. And that's how you greet your husband?"

"We're not married. I divorced you after you beat the shit out of me."

Ricky shook his head. His lips smacked as he chewed a stick of gum. "I don't care what a piece of paper says. You're my wife, and you always will be. We went to church. You swore before God to love, honor, and *obey* me. Until death do us part. Remember? There's nothing a court can do to change that."

"Get the hell out of my house."

"*Our* house," Ricky fired back at me.

He stood up from the chair. When he walked toward me, I cringed. I put my hands over my belly, as if I could cover your eyes, Shelby. I didn't want you to see this man, to hear him speak, to have him be any part of your life. Maybe he was your father, maybe not, but he was dead to both of us.

"What do you want?" I asked again. "Money?"

"No, I don't need money. I've got money now. I wanted to see *you*. I've missed you."

Ricky caressed my face with the long barrel of the revolver. I didn't wince or turn away. Not from him. The thought of grabbing the gun flashed through my mind. If it had just been the two of us, I would have done it. I wouldn't have cared who lived or died. But I wasn't alone. I had you, Shelby.

"You look good, Bec," Ricky told me. "I'd forgotten how pretty that face of yours is. Glowing. Isn't that what they call it?"

I swore at him in a loud voice. My eyes burned with defiance as I stared back at him, but he just laughed, because he was the one with the gun.

Physically, he'd changed since he'd been away. He'd shaved his bushy mustache, which only made his damaged nose more prominent. His blond hair was shorter. He'd lost the lazy flab he'd put on while he was unemployed, and he looked tough and muscled again. His stomach was taut, his forearms rippling, his fingers thick and strong. But the menace radiating from him hadn't changed at all.

"I heard you were in Pennsylvania," I said.

He shrugged. "I was, but only for a month or two. Then I moved on. I figured I'd try the desert for a while. I've been working construction in Nevada. There's good money out there if you don't pour it all into the slots."

"So why come back?"

He dragged the barrel of the gun down my neck to my breast. "You and me. We have unfinished business, Bec."

"What are you talking about?"

"I called a friend in town," Ricky said. "Just to see what was up. Just to get all the news. Naturally, I asked about you. I wanted to know what was going on with my wife. He told me about *that*."

Ricky moved the gun lower, until it pointed into the swell of my abdomen. He pushed the barrel in hard, making you kick. I felt my breathing coming harder and faster, terror and fury rolling together like the swirl of ocean waves. He slid the hammer back, cocking it. I didn't doubt for a second that he would pull the trigger. Shooting me, shooting my daughter, would mean nothing to him.

"Who will it look like?" Ricky asked me.

It. Like you were an alien. Like you weren't a person at all.

"Who will the kid look like?" he asked again. "Like I don't already know."

"Me," I spat at him, while I squirmed on the sofa. "*She* will look exactly like me. Not you. Definitely not you."

"Are you saying the kid's not mine?" he asked, poking at my stomach with the gun again. "Is that what you're telling me? Then why don't you just admit that you're a whore? You had it coming, Bec. I gave you what you deserved."

"Get out, Ricky. Get out of here, and go back to the desert. As soon as Darrell sees you, he'll put you in prison where you belong."

"Yeah? You think I'd be convicted of anything because I slapped you around a little? A wife cheats on her husband, he's entitled to payback. Put any man on the jury, and he'll see things my way."

"*Get. Out!*"

Ricky removed the gun from my belly. He undid the hammer and slipped the revolver inside his belt. Then, reaching out with the swiftness of a snake, he pinched my face until I had to cry from the pain.

"I'm not going anywhere. I'm here to stay, Bec. This is my house. You're *my* wife, and you're carrying *my* baby. You may as well get used to the idea. You're going to get the charges dropped. That's the first thing. I don't care what you tell Darrell, but you let him know that if he sees me, all he's going to do is smile and say 'Welcome home, Ricky.' And then you and me are going back to church. You're going to apologize to God for your sins and make a new vow to obey me. Got it? I'm going to move back in here, and I'm going to sleep in our bed again, and you're going to spread those pretty legs of yours for me every single night."

He let go of my face. "Understand? Tell me you understand."

I worked the stiffness out of my jaw and snarled at him. "I'll never take you back. It's never going to happen."

He sat down heavily in the chair again. "Oh, yes, it will. Soon enough, you'll beg to take me back. Do you think I can't hurt you? You're wrong. I'm the one with all the power here. Look at me, Rebecca. I can take everything away from you whenever I want. I can take away your life. I can take away your baby. And there's nothing you can do to stop me."

My hands curled into fists. My aching jaw clenched down, my teeth biting together. My nostrils flared as air pumped in and out of my nose. I wished I could spring off that sofa, fly across the room, and wrap my fingers around his neck. But all I could do was sit there, not moving. He snickered at my weakness and then got up and headed to the hallway that led out of the house.

When he got to the doorway, he looked back.

"Remember what I said," he warned me. "You're mine, Bec. You always will be. The sooner you accept that, the easier it will go for you. I *own* you. I've owned you from the very beginning."

CHAPTER THIRTY-TWO

"I'll find him," Darrell said, trying to reassure me. "There's no way that son of a bitch can hide from me."

Darrell rarely swore, which told me how upset he was. I was pretty sure he'd made Richard Petty time driving to my place after I called him on the phone in my bedroom. He searched the house top to bottom and soon found the window in the basement that Ricky had broken to make his way inside. He nailed it shut with a few pieces of plywood, but we both knew that all Ricky had to do was break a different window next time. Or kick in one of the doors.

I realized that Ricky was right. If he chose to, he could take away my life anytime he wanted, and there was nothing I could do to stop him.

"I've alerted everyone to be on the lookout," Darrell went on. "Every deputy on our team, plus state patrol and cops in the neighboring counties, too. Anyone spots Ricky, they haul him in. I've let them know he's armed and dangerous."

We sat in the living room of my house. It was midmorning on what was going to be a cold, bright day. I huddled on the sofa with coffee, and while I kept a calm smile on my face for Darrell's sake, I felt stress stabbing through my whole body. Plus, a couple of times, a labor pain.

"I've got people reaching out to every mine worker to see if he's been in touch with them," he continued. "Plus high school friends, drinking buddies, whoever—anyone who knew Ricky when he lived here. He's got to be staying nearby. Someone knows where he is, or someone has seen him around town. It won't take us long to track him down."

I wanted to share Darrell's confidence, but I knew Ricky. He knew this area inside and out, and he knew every hiding place around the county. If he didn't want us to find him, we wouldn't. Not until it was too late.

"Until we lock him up, you'll stay with me," Darrell said. I shook my head. "No. No way."

"It's not up for debate. You aren't staying in this house."

"All I need is a new gun."

"I can get you a gun, but I want you out of this place."

"So I let him chase me out of my own home?" I asked. "He threatens me, and I run away scared? That's what he wants, Darrell. He's trying to terrorize me, and I won't give him the satisfaction."

"It's just until we arrest him."

"I appreciate the offer, but the last thing I'm going to do is put your family at risk. You've got Marilyn and the girls to think about."

"Then you'll go to a motel," Darrell said. "You can stay there for a few days while we look for him. No one will know where you are. If there are other people around, it's less likely that Ricky will want any trouble."

I sighed. "I can take care of myself."

"In most circumstances, yes. But right now, I'm sorry, you can't."

I couldn't really fight him about that. So I finally gave in. I packed a bag so that I could be away for several days. Darrell put the suitcase in my trunk, and I followed him to a motel not far from the 126, where he got me a room and insisted on paying for it. I had to admit, it did make me feel better to see other cars in the parking lot and realize that there would be people in the rooms on either side of me. I liked knowing I could get help if I needed it just by shouting.

After I was checked in, I told Darrell I would go back to the sheriff's office with him, but he refused to let me do that. He told me he'd bring me a takeout lunch a little later, and until then, I should relax. Sleep. Read. Take a bath. Whatever. I tried to do all of that, but I couldn't get Ricky and his threats out of my head. I knew I was playing his game, but I didn't have a choice.

I own you.

Locked inside the motel room, with the chain done, I also felt the black hole of depression opening up again. I slipped into its dark cavern, the way I had that night in January. And this time there was no charming stranger stranded in a pickup truck to rescue me. For a few brief months, Shelby, I'd been happy. *You* made me happy. I'd allowed myself to think I could escape my past. But I could see the end of everything coming soon. I just didn't know what the end would look like.

An hour or so later, there was a knock on the motel door. Automatically, I tensed with fear. Was it him? But Ricky wouldn't bother knocking; he'd put his foot to the door and kick it in. Then I wondered if it was Darrell, but it was too early for him to be back here with a hamburger from the 126.

I got up from the bed and went to the door and asked quietly, "Who is it?"

"Rebecca?" a woman said.

"Yes."

"It's Penny Ramsey."

I frowned, then undid the chain and opened the door. Penny stood outside, her face still heavily bandaged from the cuts she'd received in the fight with Ruby. On the other side of the parking lot, I spotted a car with a trunk open and luggage inside. Penny glanced over her shoulder, following my stare. "Yes, I'm leaving town. Ms. Svitak fired me. I'm going back to Milwaukee."

"I'm sorry."

"She says employees of her firm don't get into bar fights. I told her it wasn't my fault, that Ruby started it. She didn't care. She told me I'd compromised the lawsuit with my behavior, that I'd interfered with one of her key witnesses. I don't know, I guess she's right. But that wasn't what I was trying to do. All I did was fall in love with Ajax, you know?"

"Yes, I know."

She shook her head sadly. "He was using me, wasn't he? It was never real. He was stringing me along to find out what was going on with the lawsuit."

"That was Ajax," I said. "He manipulated people. You weren't the only one."

Penny scowled as she looked at her feet. "I got a call from the county attorney this morning. He told me that Ruby pled guilty to a misdemeanor and they turned her loose. Unbelievable. She pays like a hundred bucks to the court and promises to be a good girl. That's justice, huh? I'll never be able to look in a mirror again without crying for the rest of my life, and she goes home to her kids like it was nothing."

"The scars may not be permanent," I told her. "My ex-husband attacked me in January. I was cut like you. But the cuts healed, and now you can't tell. Don't assume it'll be forever. Go see a doctor when you're back home."

"I appreciate your trying to make me feel better, but I'm not in the mood for that, okay? I'm in a mood where I just want to hate everybody and everything."

"Believe me, I know how you feel."

Penny fidgeted in the doorway, as if she were trying to make up her mind about something.

"Do you want to come inside?" I asked her.

"No, I should probably get in my car and go."

"It seems like you came over here for a reason, not just to say goodbye."

"Well, I was going to stop by your house before I left town, but I couldn't make up my mind. And then I saw you checking in here earlier. I figured it must be fate telling me what to do."

"So let's talk," I said.

Penny lingered outside the motel room. "Why are you here, anyway?"

"My ex-husband is back in town. He threatened me."

"Jesus. While you're pregnant?"

"Yes, that's Ricky."

She shook her head. "This place is poison."

"Penny, what did you want to tell me?"

"Hang on. I need to get something."

She walked across the motel parking lot. I saw her bend over at the trunk of the car and remove a paper grocery bag from the local market. Then she shut the trunk and returned to my door. The whole way, she walked furtively, casting her eyes in every direction. She motioned me back inside, and then she followed and quickly closed the motel door behind her. We both sat on the bed.

"There are still a lot of people from the firm staying here," she said. "I didn't want them to see me going inside your room."

"You've already been fired. What more can they do to you?"

"Sue me. Bankrupt me. Make sure I never get another job."

"Over what?"

"Giving you what I'm about to give you."

Penny reached inside the grocery bag. The first thing she pulled out was a cassette recorder and an electrical cord. She looked around the room for an outlet and plugged in the machine. Then she dug into the bag again and removed a cassette tape in a plastic case.

"Ms. Svitak accused me of compromising the lawsuit. Okay, well, I really am doing that now. If she's going to fire me, what loyalty do I owe her or the firm? The fact is, the mine deserves to lose this case. They deserve to be slapped down and hit with millions in damages. They made life hell for those women, and the execs sat in our depositions and lied their asses off. But it's not just that. It's not just the harassment. They're criminals."

"What do you mean?"

"Gordon Brink didn't just come to town to buy off Sandra Thoreau. When she said no, he was planning to do other things."

"Like what?"

"Take your pick. Assault. Rape. Maybe even murder. They wanted her out, and they were going to do whatever it took to make sure it happened. If Sandra wound up dead, you don't think every woman in this county would have gotten the message? Stay away from the mine."

I felt a wave of nausea and another sharp pain. I closed my eyes briefly and tried to focus. "Penny, what's on that tape?"

"You remember the conversation I heard with Ms. Svitak? The one that freaked out Ajax? I found the tape, and I listened to the rest of it. I heard what else Brink said. I heard the shit that Ms. Svitak didn't want me to know about."

"You took the tape from the law firm?" I asked.

"Yeah. And now I'm giving it to you."

I hesitated. What she was giving me was stolen evidence, and I didn't know whether to take it or tell her to go. But then again, I had to hear what it said.

"Play it," I told her.

Penny took the tape out of the case and popped it into the cassette player. She obviously knew the place she was looking for, because she watched the counter as she rewound and stopped at a specific location. She pushed the play button, and the first voice I heard was one I remembered very well.

Gordon Brink.

"It's me. I met with Sandra Thoreau today. She's the primary agitator at the mine."

"How did it go?"

Penny paused the playback. "That second voice? That's the managing partner at the law firm."

"And this was seven years ago?"

"Yes."

"If it's incriminating, why would they record it? Why would they keep it?"

"They're lawyers," Penny replied. "They keep secret records of everything. You never know when you're going to need leverage over somebody."

She started the tape again.

"It didn't go well. This Thoreau is a stubborn little—"

He used the word I expected Gordon to use. I'd heard him use it before, heard the naked contempt with which it came out of his mouth. I won't say it out loud for you, Shelby, but you need to understand that this is how these men saw women. All women.

"I offered her two thousand bucks to quit. She turned it down."

"Would more money change her mind?"

"I don't care. I'm not crawling back to her with another cent. I told her to take it or leave it."

"Do we have other ways of influencing her?"

"Maybe. She has a kid. No idea who the father is. I talked to the mine managers about whether we should work up a court action to get the boy taken away. Get someone from child services to pay her a visit. She's a slut and a drunk, so with the right judge, we could probably get her declared an unfit parent. But the mine is concerned that the process would take too long, and in the end, we might lose. Plus, it could backfire and win her sympathy if our involvement comes out."

"What do you suggest?"

"I think we need to look at a backup plan."

There was a long pause where the managing partner said nothing at all. It made me think that the phrase *backup plan* had a particular meaning within the firm, and everybody knew what it was. Finally, the other lawyer spoke again.

"Is that absolutely necessary?"

"Well, if it were just a question of getting rid of this Thoreau bitch, I might say no. But it won't end with her. If we don't shut this down, the problem's only going to get worse. Sooner or later, this will wind up in litigation, and the client could be looking at substantial liability."

"Can it be done without risk of blowback to the firm or the mine?"

"I'm confident it can."

"How do you propose to do it?"

"I've identified local assets. I'm meeting with them tomorrow."

"Isn't that a risk?"

"If necessary, I can deal with them. They won't be missed."

"All right. I'll expect a report soon."

"Leave it in my hands," Gordon told the managing partner. *"I'll take care of everything."*

CHAPTER THIRTY-THREE

"A backup plan," Darrell murmured. He took a bite of his hamburger and stared out the motel room window. "Did Penny know what that phrase means inside the firm? Has she heard anyone use it before?"

I joined Darrell at the window. Across the parking lot, I noticed that Penny's car was gone. She was already on the road away from Black Wolf County on her way back to civilization.

"No, but she says the firm has represented clients in labor unrest and disputes for decades. The rumor is, they have a long history of using violent tactics for getting their way."

"Except rumor won't get us anywhere," Darrell said. "No judge will let us use a stolen tape from a fired employee to get a warrant. The firm will hide behind privilege. Plus, whatever implications we read into that call, you know they'll give us an innocent explanation for what they mean by *backup plan*."

"Yeah. You're right."

"It also doesn't help that Gordon Brink is dead and can't answer any questions about it," Darrell added.

I picked up my own hamburger and put it down. I ate part

of a french fry but threw it back in the box. I had no appetite. The nausea that had begun earlier was getting worse. When I looked in the mirror, I saw that my skin had turned a ghostly shade of pale. Darrell didn't seem to notice.

Instead, he went to the tape recorder and played the tape of the phone call again. He'd already listened to it six times, and the voices had been burned into my brain.

"'Local assets,'" Darrell murmured. "He must be talking about Kip and Racer. If you were looking for muscle in this area for a job like that, they'd be the ones to call."

I nodded. He was right.

"But that still leaves us with unanswered questions," Darrell went on. "How did Brink know about Kip and Racer? And how did he even find them? They were hiding out because of the liquor store heist in Mittel County."

"Norm knew they were in his trailer," I pointed out.

"True, but I can't see Norm helping Gordon Brink. Plus, Norm was already skirting obstruction of justice by hiding them at all. I don't see him broadcasting the fact that he had two felons in his Airstream. And of course, none of this gets us any closer to the real question."

I knew the question he meant. "What really happened to them?"

"That's right. Brink tells the managing partner that he's hoping to meet with local assets, which we assume to be Kip and Racer. Within a couple of days after that, Kip and Racer are *dead*, and Brink is checking out of the resort early and running back to Milwaukee. He doesn't set foot in town for another six years, and when he does, he gets carved up like the other two. Then a few months later, so does Ajax. Four murders, presumably all connected. Presumably with one killer."

"So how do you want to proceed?" I asked.

"Brink didn't find Kip and Racer on his own. He had help. If not Norm, then who? I can only think of one person, can't you?"

I frowned, but then one of the pieces in the puzzle I was wrestling with fell into place. "Ajax."

"Right. Deputies were looking for Kip and Racer back then, and Ajax was part of the hunt. What if *Ajax* found them?"

"But how would Ajax get hooked up with Brink?" I asked. Then I answered my own question. "Ruby."

Darrell nodded. "And remember, when Brink was killed, Ajax tried to steer us toward Norm and away from any connections that involved the mine or the lawsuit. He didn't want anything pointing at him."

"Except we're just guessing. We can't prove any of it."

"I'm not so sure," Darrell said. He went to the phone in the motel room and accessed an outside line.

"Who are you calling?" I asked.

"The sheriff of Mittel County."

Those words sucked the air out of my chest. I hoped that Darrell didn't notice. My face flushed. I sweated. I felt a roaring in my ears. Tom Ginn. The young, handsome sheriff of Mittel County. The man whose face I could easily picture, as if it had been only yesterday that I'd met him, not almost nine months earlier. The man whose arms I could feel around me, his body wrapped up in mine. The man who had saved me in the space of the few hours we'd spent together.

"Why call him?" I gasped, choking on my words, hating myself for being so obvious, even though Darrell had no idea what was happening to me.

"He can look up the file on the liquor store robbery seven years ago."

"Yes. Sure. Of course."

I wanted to rip the phone out of his hands. And at the same

time, I wanted to make that call myself and talk to Tom and
thank him for being there and tell him all my secrets. But too
much time had gone by. I was part of his past.

"Are you all right?" Darrell asked, because I couldn't hide
the emotions flooding across my face.

"Fine."

"Do you need a doctor? Is it time?"

"No." But it *was* almost time. You were almost here, Shelby.
I could feel it. Was it a sign that on that day of all days, Tom
Ginn would become a part of my life again?

"Are you sure?" Darrell asked.

"I'm fine," I said again.

"Okay."

Darrell dialed our office and asked for the name and phone
number for the sheriff of Mittel County. He announced the number out loud as he wrote it down, but I knew it by heart, because
I'd dialed that number dozens of times from my home this year
before putting the phone done without even letting it ring.

When Darrell made his next call, I sat right beside him,
listening.

"Sheriff Ginn, please," Darrell said to the woman who answered.

Seconds later, in the dead silence of the motel room, I heard
that voice. Two words on the phone, barely louder than static
on the line, but they were like a broadcast from a loudspeaker
in my mind. "Tom Ginn."

Could Darrell see my reaction? Could he see my whole body
tremble and my heart stop beating?

"Sheriff, this is Deputy Darrell Curtis over in Black Wolf
County. I've got a question about an old Mittel County case. I
was wondering if someone there might be able to pull the file
and answer some questions for me."

No!

I didn't want Tom handing off the call to another deputy. I wanted to hear him talking. I wanted to *remember*. I wanted to lose myself all over again in the mellow calm of his voice.

"What's the case?" Tom asked.

Yes—the voice, the voice, the voice. It couldn't have affected me more if it were Frank Sinatra serenading me over the phone. *Tom, I'm here. It's me. Rebecca. From that night in the snow? I just wanted to say—there are so many things to say—*

But I said nothing at all.

"You probably wouldn't remember it," Darrell went on. "It was a liquor store heist. Garden-variety smash and grab. This was back in July, seven years ago. The suspects were two Black Wolf County thugs in a stolen car. Kip Wells. Racer Moritz."

I heard Tom chuckle. I remembered that sweet laugh. The laugh of a good man. "In fact, I remember that robbery very well, Deputy. Mostly because it was my case. I answered the call."

"Is the file still in your archives? Would someone be able to pull it?"

"Well, I pride myself on remembering details, Deputy. If I need the file, I can always grab it, but what is it you wanted to know?"

Tom. It's me. I'm here.

Tom, let me tell you about everything. Let me tell you about Shelby.

"We had a manhunt going for Kip and Racer after the heist," Darrell said. "Later, we found out they'd been holed up in a trailer outside Random."

"Yes, I remember they were dead when you found them," Tom said. "These were the Ursulina murders, isn't that right?"

"That's right."

"Has there been a break in the case?"

"Maybe. We have reason to believe that someone found Kip and Racer while they were hiding out. It may have been one of our own people. I'm sure you were in close contact with the department here in Black Wolf during the investigation, so I was wondering if there was anything you remember that could help us."

There was a long pause.

Tom, are you there? Tom, talk to me, keep talking, I just need to hear you.

"Actually, you're right, I did get a tip about their location," Tom said. "I passed it along myself."

"You did?"

"Yes, one of my colleagues was testifying at a trial in Stanton that week. He was on a break and heard the defense attorney in the case talking on a pay phone in the courthouse. He was sure he heard the attorney mention the names Kip and Racer and something about a trailer. He mentioned it to me when he got back to Mittel County, because he thought maybe the perps in the liquor store robbery were trying to round up a lawyer. I called your office to pass along the tip. I thought it might give your team some clue of where the two of them could be hiding out."

"Do you remember who you talked to?"

"Well, my main contact on the case was a deputy named Arthur Jackson. I remember him because we were both young cops about the same age. I'm sure I would have talked to him about it."

"Ajax," Darrell said, shaking his head.

"That's him."

"Do you happen to have any documentation of the call?"

"I'm sure I do in the file. I'm a stickler for that sort of thing. I'll track it down and send you a copy."

"I really appreciate your help, Sheriff."

"Not at all. You'll have to fill me in about this case when you wrap it up."

"I will. Goodbye, Sheriff."

I saw Darrell begin to put down the phone, but then—*oh my God!*—Tom said something more.

"Actually, Deputy, as long as we're talking, can you answer a question for me?"

"Of course."

"Is there still a woman named Rebecca Colder working for the sheriff's department?"

Darrell stared at me with surprise and curiosity, and I couldn't hide my own shock. He was about to say what any normal person would say in that situation—yes, actually, she's sitting right beside me—when I frantically waved my arms and mouthed a single word at him.

No!

I couldn't do it. I couldn't talk to him. I couldn't make small talk in front of Darrell. If I was going to talk to Tom, it had to be private and profound. I couldn't pretend my relationship with him was nothing when it was everything.

"Y-yes, there is," Darrell replied, with a faint stutter in his voice. "I know Rebecca very well. In fact, she—"

He stopped again, watching my face, trying to decide what to say.

"She was my partner for a while," he went on.

"But not now?"

"No."

I heard Tom's hesitation. Would he ask about me? Would he ask why I wasn't still Darrell's partner? Would he ask where I was and what I was doing and how I was and when it was that my whole life had changed?

But Tom spoke again, more slowly, as if somehow he could

see me in the room. As if he could read my mind through the phone. "Well, when you see her next, please tell her that Tom Ginn says hello. Can you do that for me?"

"Yes, I will."

"Goodbye, Deputy."

"Goodbye, Sheriff."

Darrell hung up the phone and looked at me. He wanted answers, and I had none to give him. "Rebecca?"

I was still without words. Without breath. I had to stop myself from crying. My emotions crested like a wave. *Your emotions, Shelby. I could feel you kicking. You knew him, too.*

Did that mean what I wanted it to mean?

Was Tom your father?

"I met him," I replied blandly. "I met Tom once."

Darrell looked as if he wanted to ask me more questions, but he had the grace to let it be.

I simply sat on the bed and thought: *He remembers me.*

CHAPTER THIRTY-FOUR

Darrell and I found Ruby sitting in her kitchen, with her youngest asleep in a little swing beside her. She stared blankly into a mug of tea. Ruby was a woman whose emotions often ran hot—I'd seen it for myself when I was on the receiving end, and I'd seen it at the 126 when she attacked Penny Ramsey—but that morning, she couldn't summon any fire to her face. A kind of nothingness had overtaken her. As we sat down across from her at the kitchen table, she barely looked up from her tea. Her cheeks were red, her eyes were red, both set against her dirty red hair.

"It's time you told us the truth, Ruby," Darrell said. He had a calm seriousness in his voice that made you hate to keep secrets from him.

Ruby still didn't look up. "The truth about what?"

"Everything. Ajax. The lawsuit. Gordon Brink." Darrell paused before dropping the guillotine. "Kip and Racer, too."

There it was. She finally looked at us, with a little flinch that gave it all away. At the mention of Kip and Racer, fear flitted across Ruby's pretty face like wind through the tall grass. We'd been right about everything. She knew. All this time, she'd been covering up a guilty secret, along with her husband.

"What are you talking about?" Ruby asked lightly, still pretending to be in the dark.

Darrell put the tape recorder on the table and pushed play. I heard it again, the conversation between Gordon Brink and his managing partner. I listened to Brink discussing in a cold, horrifying way his intent to arrange for payback against Sandra Thoreau. Ruby listened, too. There was no mistaking on her face that she knew exactly what these two men were discussing.

"That's Gordon Brink," Darrell said, "but I think you know that."

"Yes. I recognize his voice."

"This was recorded seven years ago. You don't have to read too far between the lines to know what he's talking about."

"I don't know what you mean," Ruby replied. But she did.

"Gordon Brink tried to bribe Sandra Thoreau to quit the mine," Darrell continued, with a snake's patience. "When that didn't work, he had a backup plan. In other words, he was going to make sure something bad happened to Sandra. And the men who were going to carry it out for him were Kip Wells and Racer Moritz."

Ruby's lips puckered nervously. "What does that have to do with me?"

"Brink wasn't local. He didn't find Kip and Racer on his own. He needed someone who knew the area, who could make an introduction. We both know that the person who helped him was Ajax."

Ruby didn't deny it. Or confirm it. She did what guilty people do and tried to wriggle out from the truth. "I don't see how you expect to prove that after all this time. Not with Ajax gone."

"I talked to the sheriff of Mittel County today," Darrell retorted. "Seven years ago, he called Ajax to tell him that Kip and Racer had reached out to Norm. So Ajax knew. He checked Norm's trailer. He found the two of them hunkered down in the forest. Ajax could have brought a team of deputies out there and arrested them, but he had other plans for Kip and Racer, right? Those plans involved Gordon Brink."

Listening to Darrell made me think about how things might have been different. Fate hinges on the smallest of accidents.

If a deputy hadn't overheard Norm talking to Kip and Racer on the courthouse pay phone, there would have been no hint of where they were hiding. Ajax never would have checked Norm's trailer, and Gordon Brink never would have met Kip and Racer. The rest of the dominoes wouldn't have fallen. There would have been no Ursulina murders.

All the other ripples, the ones that came later, never would have happened, either. I wouldn't have joined the sheriff's department or visited that lake where Tom Ginn was stranded. There would be no you, Shelby.

So maybe some things are simply meant to be.

Maybe we can't escape fate. One way or another, it has its way with us.

Ruby reflected on what to say. Really, she shouldn't have said anything at all. What we had was nothing but suspicion and conjecture, but I could see that with Ajax gone, Ruby was tired of concealing her husband's crimes. She wanted the weight lifted from her shoulders.

"Am I at risk myself?" she asked. "Are you going to arrest me for the murders?"

"Were you involved in any of them?"

"No."

"Was Ajax?"

"No."

"Do you know who killed them?"

"No." Then she added, "But someone knows what happened. Brink, Kip, Racer. Someone was there."

Darrell's forehead wrinkled with confusion. "What do you mean?"

But Ruby didn't answer us right away. Instead, she went back to the earliest part of the story.

"You're right, you know," she admitted wearily. "Seven years ago, Brink came to town to try to get Sandra out of the mine. They figured if she quit, the rest of the women would go, too."

"How did you find out? Sandra says nobody knew."

"Ajax was visiting me at the mine. He spotted two of the senior managers talking with an out-of-towner. I didn't know who he was, but Ajax had been out at the Fair Day that morning, and he'd seen the same man talking to Sandra. He put two and two together. You know Ajax. He could smell a dirty deal a mile away. Whatever was going on, he figured there was money to be made from it. So he followed Brink to the 126 and offered to help with whatever Brink was doing. He had his uncle call one of the execs at the mine and tell him they could trust Ajax with anything they needed. Jerry's been in the mine's pocket for years."

"Jerry knew?"

Ruby nodded. "Jerry knew."

"What did Ajax and Brink talk about?"

"How to get rid of Sandra."

"They talked about *killing* her?"

Ruby shook her head, and her eyes widened. "No, no, they were just going to scare her, maybe rough her up a little. Not murder. Ajax wouldn't have gone for that."

"Did you know this was going on?" Darrell asked.

"No! I swear I didn't. I would have told him to stop it. But he didn't tell me until later. Until after Kip and Racer were murdered. At that point, there was no going back."

"So what was the plan?"

"Brink wanted locals who could do the dirty work on Sandra," Ruby went on. "He was looking for a couple of men who had nothing to do with the mine and who couldn't be traced back to him. Ajax said he'd put out some feelers. But the next day, he got a call about Kip and Racer, and he figured out where they were hiding. They were perfect. He talked to them and said he could either turn them in, or he could look the other way if they did a job for a friend. He offered to get them off the hook on the liquor store heist, too. They jumped at it. Ajax told Brink where they were hiding and set up a meeting."

"Did Ajax go, too?"

"No. He made the intro, that's all. Brink gave him a thousand bucks cash for setting it up, but Ajax made Brink go by himself. I don't know . . ."

"What?"

"Ajax didn't say so, but I wondered if he knew what Brink was really doing. Maybe he thought the plan was to kill her, and he didn't want to be there when they talked about that."

"So what went wrong?" Darrell asked.

Ruby shrugged, as if she'd asked herself the same thing many times. "I have no idea. Neither did Ajax."

"Now's not the time to hold anything back, Ruby."

"I'm not. I swear. Ajax went to the Fair Day to talk to Brink a couple of days later, but Brink was already gone. He'd left town. So Ajax went out to the trailer. Jesus. He saw the bodies, and he ran. He didn't want to be anywhere near that scene. He didn't go back until Norm found Kip and Racer and called you."

"Did Ajax try to contact Brink?" Darrell asked.

"Sure he did. He called him at the law firm, but Brink denied knowing anything about the murders. Ajax said Brink sounded stunned to hear what had happened. Brink said Kip and Racer were alive when he left. The deal was done, and he wanted to be long gone when Kip and Racer went after Sandra. He had no idea who'd killed them."

We heard hesitation in her voice.

"But?" Darrell asked.

"But Ajax thought Brink was hiding something."

"Like what?"

"Ajax didn't know."

"Is that when Brink started paying Ajax? To keep him quiet?"

Ruby's eyes narrowed. Her nostrils flared with some of the anger I was used to seeing from her. "Paying him? What are you talking about?"

"Ajax had a separate bank account. He was getting five hundred dollars a month from somewhere. We suspect Brink was the one behind it, because the payments stopped after Brink died. And that makes sense if Brink wanted to stay clear of a murder investigation."

"Five *hundred* dollars? A *month*? That little—"

Ruby hurled an obscenity at her dead husband.

"You didn't know?" I murmured.

"No. He never told me. Sometimes I was surprised that he could afford the things he did. I had no idea he had that kind of money coming in on the side. He never let me near the bills. He said he would take care of everything."

"Did Ajax have any contact with Brink after that summer?"

"Once," Ruby replied, nodding. "When some new guy at the mine tried to feel me up, he called Brink and said the mine better get rid of the guy. They did."

"What about when Brink was murdered?" Darrell asked.

"Ajax had to be worried that Brink's death was connected to Kip and Racer."

"Yeah, he was scared about that. He was concerned that you'd figure out that he was connected to all of it, too. Or that—"

I stared at her. "What?"

"Or that the killer would figure it out and come after him next."

"Did he have any idea who the killer was?" I asked.

Ruby focused on me with her wild eyes. "We both figured it had to be Sandra. I mean, you know what she's like. You hit her, she hits back twice as hard. Ajax assumed Kip and Racer took her to the trailer to whack her, and she managed to take them out instead. And when Brink came back to town, she finished the job. But Ajax and I weren't going to say anything about it."

Darrell leaned across the table. "You said that someone else was there. What did you mean?"

Ruby drummed her painted fingernails nervously on the table, and then she pushed back the chair and got up. We heard her go to another room, and when she came back, she had a white number ten envelope in her hand. She pushed it across the table to us, and Darrell picked it up.

"I found this taped to my front door this morning," Ruby told us. "I don't know who did it, but to me, it felt like a threat. When I saw it, I figured I couldn't keep any of this secret anymore. I've got my kids to think about. I was going to call you, but then you showed up before I had the chance."

Darrell opened the envelope.

Inside was a black-and-white photograph. I leaned close to Darrell to examine it, and when I did, I couldn't help the stunned gasp that escaped my lips. I don't know what I expected, but the sight of that photograph felt like Mount St. Helens leveling forests in its path.

The picture had been taken among the dense trees, but I saw a glint of sunshine reflecting off a silver bullet. It was Norm's Airstream trailer. There were three men standing near it, arranged close to each other in a half circle, and although the shot was slightly out of focus, I knew each of those faces well.

Kip Wells. Racer Moritz. Gordon Brink.

Together, seven years earlier. Together, before the murders happened.

"There was a witness," Darrell murmured with a kind of wonder. "Someone saw them at the trailer."

Yes. And that changed everything.

CHAPTER THIRTY-FIVE

You'll have to forgive me, Shelby, if the next few hours of that day are foggy in my memory. I was struggling to focus, and I've blocked out many of the details. I recall only bits and pieces, and the rest is just driftwood on a sea of pain and joy. But I'll tell you what I can.

Darrell and I returned to his cruiser, but we didn't go anywhere, not at first. We sat in the driveway outside Ruby's house, and he stared at the photograph in his hand with a fixed concentration.

"Who took this picture?" he murmured, more to himself than to me.

That was the first question he was struggling with. Who saw Brink, Kip, and Racer together while their murder plot was unfolding? Because let's be honest about their intentions. No matter what Ruby said, this was not an effort to scare Sandra into quitting. When you enter into this kind of plot, you don't leave witnesses behind. They were going to do terrible things to her, and then they were going to bury her in the forest.

"It must have been Ajax," Darrell speculated aloud. "He

knew they were meeting. He hid out there with a camera in order to blackmail Brink later. That would explain why Brink was paying him."

"That makes sense," I said, through my own haze of confusion.

But Darrell wasn't satisfied with his own explanation. "Except Ajax is *dead*. He didn't tape the envelope to Ruby's door. Whoever did that had to assume Ruby would give the photo to the sheriff's department. This person wanted us to have it. Why?"

That was the other question. The burning question. Not who took the picture, but where did it come from?

"There's nothing incriminating in the photo itself," Darrell went on, still wrapping his head around the puzzle. "The three men are all dead. It doesn't help us figure out who killed them. And yet Ruby's right. It feels like some kind of threat, showing up now. Like someone's taunting us. But about what? What does the picture tell us?"

I felt it, too.

Even as my head swirled—even as I sweated and my heartbeat accelerated and I felt the first embers of what would become a ring of fire circling my middle—I sensed the malevolence behind the appearance of that photograph. An evil spirit, like a cold mist coming in from the sea.

Look what I know.

Look what I found.

"Someone had a key piece of the puzzle in their hands for seven years and deliberately kept quiet about it until today," Darrell continued. "*Who?*"

I shook my head silently. I had no answers to give him.

Instead, I focused on what was happening to my body. Pain clamped onto my insides like a vise, knots of pain that came and went in intervals. My throat was choked with fear, and my brain whirled with uncertainty. What was happening to me? Was it you, Shelby? Were you coming soon? Or was I simply engulfed in the shock of seeing that photograph?

Darrell turned on the engine and said with his usual decisiveness, "Let's go talk to Sandra."

I should have told him no.

I should have been honest that my body was hoisting a flag of warning, but I found myself paralyzed, at a loss for what to do or say or think. I kept making excuses for what I felt. It was gas. It was nausea. It was pressure. It was stress. Anything but what it really was.

"Take me to the hospital," I should have said. Not even home. I was already beyond going home.

But all I said was, "Yes, okay, let's talk to her."

We drove to the mine. That was about the worst place for me at that moment, filled with men and machines and dust and tumult, a dizzying chaos of noise reverberating in my head. I was trying so hard not to let everyone see the tornado of sensations whipping around me. Even Darrell was oblivious. I had to lean on him to make it to the work trailer, and he was so caught up in his questions and his mysteries that he didn't realize—why couldn't I just say it?—*I was having a baby.*

We sat inside while the foreman went to collect Sandra. He didn't look happy about pulling her off the job again. Darrell and I said nothing, and I could tell that his mind was distracted, because he never even looked at me. Anyone who looked at me would have seen the truth.

Sandra did.

A few minutes later, she came into the trailer in her dirty work clothes, saw my face, and immediately did a double take. "Jesus Christ, Rebecca, are you in labor?"

That was the first time Darrell saw me—really saw me—and

realized that something was very wrong. But I shrugged off her comment with a forced smile. "I'm just a little uncomfortable."

Sandra gaped at me as if to say, *Honey, do you want your baby born on the floor?* But when I didn't say anything more, she sat down and wiped her brow. "I don't know what you want, Darrell, but if Norm's not here, I'm not answering questions."

"Then how about you just listen?" he said.

She grabbed a cigarette from her pocket but didn't light it. She waved it in the air and fiddled it with her fingers. "Whatever. Go ahead."

"We confirmed what we suspected," he informed her. "Brink met with Kip and Racer. Ajax was the one who introduced them."

Sandra made a little spitting noise between her teeth. "Ajax, huh? Nice."

"Now all four of them are dead."

"Well, that's a big loss," she commented with heavy sarcasm, ignoring her intention to stay quiet.

Darrell passed her the photograph. "Someone left this picture on Ruby's door. It shows Brink, Kip, and Racer together outside Norm's trailer. Sometime not long after this picture was taken, Kip and Racer were murdered."

Sandra studied the men in the picture. Her face bore no expression, no anger, no disgust, no sadness, no regret. Silently, she passed the photograph back to Darrell. "So what?"

"Did you take the picture? Did you leave it for Ruby to find?"

"No."

"Did you kill Kip and Racer? And Brink? And Ajax?"

"No, I didn't."

Darrell ignored her denial.

"We received this tape, too," he said.

He produced the cassette recorder and again played the conversation with Brink and his partner in Milwaukee. This time, strain overtook Sandra's eyes as she understood the meaning behind what the men were saying. The lines of her hard life deepened on her face. Like me, she knew this conversation was not about scaring her off or roughing her up. This was about men who were planning to kill her, to treat her like a helpless animal, abused and then thrown away. They wanted to send a message to any woman who might follow in her footsteps by working at the mine: *Don't even think about it.*

When the tape ended, Sandra nervously peeled the wrapper away from the cigarette and let the tobacco fall to the floor.

"Remember what I told you?" she said, eyeing me. "These people are evil."

"I remember."

"Did Ruby know?" she asked me.

I didn't answer, but she read the truth in my silence. She curled her lip with disgust as if she were chewing on something foul. "Ruby may be the worst of all, you know. The others were men. I expect that shit from them. But Ruby lied to protect them, even knowing what they did. She threw me and all the other women to the wolves."

Darrell put his hands on his knees and adopted a fatherly tone. "Sandra, it's clear that Brink intended to do you harm. He said you would regret turning down the money. In light of this tape, that was obviously a threat. Did he tell you that your life was in danger if you didn't quit the mine?"

"No. He didn't say anything like that. I just figured the harassment would get worse, and the mine wouldn't do shit to stop it. I was right."

Darrell eased back in the chair and stared at her, letting the silence draw out in the trailer. Although there was really no silence around us. The ground vibrated. The metal walls shook. Men shouted. Engines rumbled. I squeezed my eyes tightly shut, as if my brain could block everything out. It was cold in here, but sweat poured down my face. A spike drove through my back, or at least, that was what it felt like to me.

"You know what I think?" Darrell asked.

He used that calm voice I'd heard many times, the voice that lulled a suspect into confessing everything. Tell them a story. Use a few little bits of evidence to tie everything together, and hope they didn't realize that he couldn't prove anything he was saying.

Sandra shrugged. "Tell me. I can't wait."

"I think Brink underestimated you," Darrell said. "Everyone underestimated you, didn't they? They figured you'd fold. Quit. Run away. But you were tougher than they thought. A lot tougher. You had your kid to think about. So you stuck it out, no matter what the men did to you. After everything you'd been through at the mine, you weren't going to let some lawyer scare you out of your job."

In my head, their conversation began to go in and out, like poor reception on a television set. My breathing got ragged. I opened my mouth wide to suck in more air. I clutched the sides of the chair.

"See, I think you turned the tables on Brink," Darrell went on. "You followed him from the resort. You saw him meeting with Kip and Racer, and you knew what *that* meant, didn't you? The three of them were planning how to get rid of you. Right? Is that how it happened? You knew they'd come after you sooner or later, and you figured you'd better strike first. It was kill or be killed. It was self-defense."

The pain inside me nearly lifted me out of my seat, shot me through the roof, sent me into space.

"How did it go down, Sandra? Did Brink leave? Once the

plan was done, he wasn't going to hang around in Black Wolf County. He'd want to be long gone when Kip and Racer grabbed you. Did you stay in the woods and wait for your chance? I studied the crime scene, so I know Racer was killed first. That makes sense. You wouldn't have wanted to take them both on at the same time. Did you wait until Kip left, and you had an opportunity to confront Racer one on one? He was probably drunk. Easy prey. Easy to kill. And when that was done, you hung around until Kip came back, and you did the same thing to him."

Sandra didn't say anything. I'm not sure she was even paying attention to Darrell anymore. She was staring at me in horror.

"I don't blame you," Darrell went on. "I really don't. Believe me, I know the kind of men Kip and Racer were. If they'd managed to get hold of you, they weren't going to make it quick. Brink probably told them to enjoy themselves. Did you hear him talking about what they should do to you? Did they laugh about it? There just comes a time when you snap, Sandra. I get it. A time when you've taken all the abuse you're going to take. Is that what happened? Is that why you killed them?"

I couldn't stay quiet anymore.

The pain between my legs crashed toward shore like a tidal wave, and when it cascaded over me, I screamed. With my face beet red, I screamed. I lurched to my feet and screamed.

That's the last thing I remember, Shelby. Everything else is black, until much later that night, when I was in the hospital and you were in my arms.

CHAPTER THIRTY-SIX

Two weeks.

We had two weeks together, Shelby. The wonder of that time is emblazoned on my brain. When I'm lonely, when I'm bereft, when I'm crying, I go back to those days and replay the scenes of that movie. It's like God gave me a consolation prize of perfect recall for the brief moments we had.

I spent three days in the hospital. Everyone visited. Darrell. His girls. Ben. Norm. Will. Sandra. They brought flowers, gifts, stuffed animals, and my favorite cherry-nut fudge. They marveled over you, and you didn't cry at all when they held you. Nothing about this new world seemed to frighten you, which I loved. I hoped you would stay that way your whole life. Fearless.

The nurses told me you were the calmest baby they'd ever seen, angelic but so earnest. Life was serious business to you. You had this strangely intense curiosity about all the things you were seeing and experiencing for the first time. Including me. You seemed to know me from the beginning. We lay on the hospital bed, with you on my chest, and we stared at each other for hours. Me memorizing you, this tiny girl with dark hair like mine, this fragile being I'd created. And you trying to understand who this woman was, the mother who'd carried you, the person who would love you forever and do anything to keep you safe.

I treasured our time the way you treasure summer sunshine, with the knowledge that it doesn't last. Yes, I could dream, plan, fantasize, and imagine all the landmarks we would share as you grew up. First steps. First words. School. Games. Books. Christmases and birthdays. But I'm not the kind of woman who can pretend to herself for very long. Deep down, I already knew the truth. You would experience those things without me.

On the fourth day, I brought you home.

Darrell wanted me to go back to the motel, but I was having none of that. I had my own house and my own bedroom in which to sleep, and your crib was there for you to sleep near me. We were a family. The first night, Darrell pitched a fit until I agreed to have his oldest daughter stay with me, but the next day, I told her to go home. I said I was fine. And I was. I've known women who talk about the baby blues, but that wasn't my experience. Despite what my body had been through, I felt strong. I could deal with all of this myself. The feedings. The waking up. The diaper changings. I knew the exhaustion would hit me eventually, but during those days, I was Rebecca Colder, a little bit stronger, a little bit bolder.

After I sent Darrell's daughter home, he came back to lecture me. I told him that I loved him, but I was determined to live my life. What I didn't tell him was that if it came down to protecting my daughter or his, I would choose my own. That was harsh but true. If someone was staying in my house, that was the choice I would have to make sooner or later. So it was better that I stay in the house alone.

We made the most of our time, you and me. Friends and

neighbors stocked my fridge and freezer while I was in the hospital, so we had plenty of food. You took to my breasts with ease, much to my relief. You slept better than I had any reason to expect from a newborn, but during those times when we were up together overnight, I would talk to you, just the way I'd been doing for months. I told you my stories. My childhood. My girlhood. My womanhood. The good and the bad. The pain and the loss and the happiness and the mistakes. When you were days old, you already knew things about me that I'd never told another soul.

I read to you. If you were awake, I read to you all the time. Children's books like Dr. Seuss and Winnie the Pooh and Shel Silverstein. And poetry. Some of it from the Little Golden Book I had as a kid. Some of it just silly poems I made up myself. *Where were you when the firefly flew? Were you a firefly too?* And classics. I read you classics whether you were awake or asleep. If you find yourself with a strange affinity for *Dracula*, well, blame that on me.

I sang to you, too. I played my guitar and did my own off-key versions of "Careless Whisper" and "Making Love Out of Nothing at All." When I did "Radio Ga Ga," I would poke you in the tummy with every "goo goo" and "ga ga."

Oh, Shelby.

The love of those days. I crammed so much into those two short weeks. I barely slept, carried along on this strange river of adrenaline, but I didn't want to sleep. I didn't want to miss a thing. Not a single expression on your face, not a coo as you dreamed. I filed every second away, carefully wrapped up in my memories.

And then we came to Thursday night, ten days after we'd come home.

Halloween night.

I'd always loved Halloween. I carved up a pumpkin with a scary face, and I put a candle inside, and I set it out on the front porch to flicker and grin at the trick-or-treaters. I got a lot of them. I always did. They would ring my doorbell in their costumes, dressed like monsters, faeries, witches, and clowns. No store-bought costumes in Random; everyone made their own. Same with treats. If you handed out Hershey bars, you were lazy, so people made brownies, cookies, Rice Krispies squares, popcorn balls, coconut candies, and seven-layer bars. Me, I was known for mixing up Chex and M&M's and nuts and chocolate chips and any other sweet things I had in the pantry. I poured it all into paper lunch bags to hand out.

Of course, some of the kids came with their parents, and they wanted to see you, Shelby. From five o'clock to eight o'clock, the parade came and went, hardly ever stopping for more than a minute or two. Knocks and doorbells, and screams of "Trick or Treat!" and mothers lightly stepping into the living room to tell me how beautiful you were. Which you were, Shelby. Absolutely beautiful.

By the time the candle in the pumpkin had melted down and gone out, and the kids had returned to their homes, I was exhausted with the efforts of the night. It was midevening. I ate a Wonder Bread, Buddig ham sandwich, and I fed you, and we both decided it was time for a nap. You fell asleep in a hand-me-down onesie with pink stripes, in the Easter basket I still kept from the day the doctor had told me I was pregnant. I held your hand, and you grabbed my finger, and I drifted off to sleep on the sofa next to you.

I was twenty-six years old, soon to be turning twenty-seven. That was the single best moment of my entire life.

*

Then it was over.

I awoke, and you were gone.

I still had the dizziness of sleep, and my eyes landed first on the clock on the mantel, which told me that it was nearly eleven o'clock. Then I looked down at the little Easter basket with the blissful anticipation of seeing your face, only to find that you weren't there.

Instantly awake, instantly panicked, I bolted to my feet.

"*Shelby! Shelby!*"

I tore at my black hair. I wept; my nose ran. I shouted, "Who's there? Hello! Where are you?"

No one answered me.

I called Darrell's name, praying it was him. Or one of his girls. They'd come in and found me sleeping, and they were with you somewhere else in the house. That was it, right?

But no. I knew that was not it.

Like a madwoman, I ran to the front door, which was still bolted shut. I wrenched it open and ran out to the yard, but the street was empty and dark, and there were no cars nearby. Crazy with fear, I ran back inside and slammed the door so hard the walls trembled.

"*Shelby!*"

At that instant, I heard you crying. Wailing for me. The noise was muffled; you were upstairs in my bedroom. I sprinted for the stairs, and if I'd been running next to Jesse Owens, I would have beaten him. I took them two at a time and skidded breathlessly into the bedroom, which was lit only by the glow of the moonlight outside. But that was enough for me to see. There was a rocking chair by the window, where we'd spent hours together.

The Ursulina sat in the chair.

The beast had you in its lap, as you shrieked for your mother. No, I wasn't dreaming. This was real. The beast had furry legs, golden brown. The fur on its torso didn't match; instead, it was shorter and more chocolate in color. The hands were wrapped in brown leather gloves. The beast had a strangely elongated neck, and above it, a large head made out of papier-mâché. Where the fur ended at its ankles, I saw dirty black combat boots.

A Halloween costume.

One of the gloved hands tugged at the cardboard neck. A little door opened below the false head, and I saw Ricky's evil face.

"Boo," he said.

I ran to get you back, but he put his hands around your little throat and warned me away. "Uh-uh-uh-uh-uh. Stay away, Bec."

"Ricky, stop it. Give her back to me."

"We'll see. I don't know, maybe I'll keep her."

"*Give her back!*" I shouted, adding in a long list of obscenities that I'd rarely used in my life.

Ricky laughed as I swore at him. He held you in the air, letting your tiny legs dangle. "She's cute. That mop of dark hair. Just like you. The eyes, the nose. So small, too. Hard to believe we ever grow up when we start out as these puny little creatures. Any little mistake, any little accident, and that's the end."

"Don't you hurt her," I hissed. "Don't you dare hurt her. If you do anything at all to her, I swear to God I—"

"What?" he retorted. "What will you do to me, Bec?"

I closed my eyes for a moment to get hold of myself. I wiped the tears from my face. "Just don't hurt her, Ricky. She's innocent. She never did anything to you. I'm the one you hate."

"I don't hate you. You're my wife."

I'm not, I wanted to scream, but I held my tongue.

"Besides, I would never hurt my daughter," he went on casually. He caressed your face with false compassion, his fat fingers on your neck, making me twitch with fear. "I mean, she is mine, isn't she? My baby. My little girl. She couldn't be anyone else's. Right, Bec?" Suddenly, he bellowed at me. *"Right?"*

I refused to answer him. Even if I knew for sure who your father was, I would never, ever say the words: *She's yours.* No. Because you were not his. You would never be his. I would never allow it.

"What do you want?" I asked him, laboring to be calm. "Tell me what you want."

"You already know what I want. I want my wife back. I want my *life* back."

I shook my head in despair. "Why? Why do you want what we had? We were both miserable and unhappy."

"That was because you didn't know your place," he said. His voice rumbled out of his throat like the growl of a mean dog. "Do you know your place now, Bec? Have you finally figured it out? Do you understand why you've always been *mine?*"

"Ricky, please. Just let me have my baby."

His eyes hardened into ice. "Beg."

"What?"

"Beg me."

"Ricky, for God's sake."

"Did you not hear what I said? Do you still not get it? I'm in charge. From now on, you do *whatever* I tell you to do. And what I want you to do is *beg.*"

I swallowed down my hatred. I felt the horrible years of my marriage rising up in my memory like bile in my throat. All the degradation. Every humiliation I'd endured to keep the peace. I couldn't go back to that. I wouldn't. And yet my life was no longer my own. It belonged to you, Shelby. Not him—you.

"Let me have her back," I whispered. Then I choked out the next words. "I'm begging you."

"Louder."

"I'm begging you."

"Get on your knees." He added with a snicker, "You were always best on your knees."

"Ricky, please—"

"*On your knees.* If I say something, you do it! Do you *understand* me?"

I was crying, furious, desperate, helpless. Rage welled up inside me like an animal consuming my soul, but I did what he wanted. I had no choice. Slowly, I slid to my knees. I put my hands together, as if I were praying. "Give me my little girl. I'll do whatever you say. Just give her back to me."

"That's more like it. That's the wife I remember."

He extended his arms, which were robed in fake mink fur, and offered you up like a gift from the king. I scrambled to my feet and swept you away from him. I folded you up in my chest and held you and kissed you and cried with relief. With you back in my arms, all was right with the world again.

Ricky stood up from the rocking chair. He snapped the little door shut in his costume, closing off his face, leaving only his eyes barely visible through dark mesh. What was left was a bizarre caricature of the monster, seven feet tall, with mismatched fur top and bottom, and red eyes and sharp teeth painted onto the papier-mâché head. It was so false, so fake. And yet the whole effect of it was terrifying enough to make me feel as if I were ten years old again.

"Be at the party at the 126 on Saturday," he said.

"What?"

"I want everyone to see we're together again."

"I can't go. I have Shelby."

"Find someone to watch her."

"I'm *not* going—" I insisted, prepared to shut him down,

but then I stopped. I didn't dare set him off again, not when he was acting like—like a monster. "All right. Fine. If that's what you want, I'll be there."

"Good."

He towered over me in the corner. His gloved hand reached out like a paw to stroke under your chin. I shrank back, trying to shield you, but I was up against the wall and had nowhere to go. You began to cry again, afraid of his touch. He drew his hand back and curled it into a fist, and for a moment, I thought he might strike me. Or do something worse.

"He bragged about it, you know," Ricky snarled.

"Who?"

"Ajax."

My stomach churned with fear. "Ajax? What about him? What are you talking about?"

"I called him. He bragged about you carrying his baby."

I stared back at Ricky, and I couldn't believe what I was hearing. Except yes, I really could.

"*Ajax?* Are you crazy? Are you out of your mind? I never slept with Ajax! How many times do I have to tell you that?"

"It's too late to lie, Bec. Ajax found that out."

"Oh my God! Oh shit! Ricky, what did you do?"

"I warned him," he replied. Even though I couldn't see it behind the mask, I heard the sadistic grin in his voice. "I warned him, but he didn't believe I was serious. I told him the Ursulina was coming to get him."

"Jesus Christ, Ricky. You *idiot.*"

"It's better this way. We have a clean slate without him. I'm willing to forgive you, despite everything. You broke your vow, but with Ajax gone, we can start over. You, me, and our baby girl."

"You killed him! You killed him for *nothing*! It was you!"

Ricky shook his head. His eyes gleamed with a strange, unshakable confidence. "But you're not going to say anything, are you? Everyone knows who really killed Ajax. It was written on the wall. Just like all the others. It wasn't me. It was a terrible, vicious, savage *beast*."

Nausea made my stomach lurch. "You don't know what you're saying."

"Oh, I know exactly what I'm saying. Believe me." Ricky raised his arms high over his head and curled his fingers like claws. He bent down, and he shoved that horrible monster face into my own. I heard the noise of his breath. *Hufffffff.*

"You, see, I have what the whole world has been looking for," he went on. "Bigfoot, Yeti, Sasquatch. I have what all the monster hunters are dying to see. And the sheriff, too. I have a *picture* of the Ursulina."

CHAPTER THIRTY-SEVEN

When dawn came, I bundled you up in a little coat and put the tiniest hat on your head. I wrapped you in a blanket to keep you warm. Then I put you in your car seat, and the two of us drove to the Fair Day resort. The early morning was crisp and cold, the kind of chill you can feel like needles inside your nose. It was below freezing. Out on the lake, a gray film of ice waited to melt with the sun.

I saw the yellow Cadillac in the parking lot, so I knew Ben Malloy was still there. I didn't know which cabin was his, but I nestled you inside my jacket, and I crunched across the frosty grass from door to door until I found one that had a smell of pipe tobacco wafting from inside. I knocked.

Ben answered the door in sky-blue pajamas. His cherubic face lit up through a cloud of smoke when he saw me. "Deputy Rebecca! This is an unexpected pleasure. And little deputy Shelby with you, too! I'm honored."

"I'm sorry to come so early, Ben."

"Oh, I'm typically up at five, so this really isn't early to me. I still have lots of publicity details to deal with for tomorrow's broadcast. Are you going to be at the party, by the way?"

"Yes, it looks that way."

"I hope so. Put Shelby in a costume. An Ursulittle to go along with all the Ursulinas."

I tried to smile, but I couldn't. To Ben, this was a big joke, a carnival like Ursulina Days in Mittel County. To me, this was my life falling apart, crumbling down. I could already see the future, and it made me want to rip my heart out. Ben must have noticed the distress on my face, because he unclamped his lips from around his pipe, and his eyebrows knitted together with concern.

"Are you all right, Rebecca?"

I couldn't tell him. I couldn't tell anyone.

"I need a favor, Ben."

"Of course. What is it?"

"You said you had raw footage from seven years ago stored in your mother's attic. All the film you took during the Ursulina hunt near Sunflower Lake, the parts that didn't make it into the documentary. Is that true?"

"Yes, absolutely."

"I need to see it. Can you arrange that?"

Ben shrugged. "Sure, that isn't a problem. When would you like to do it?"

"Now."

"Now? You mean today?"

"Yes. This minute. I'd like to go over there right now. I'm sorry, but it's urgent. Is that possible?"

He looked thoughtful as he drew out his words. "It is."

"I know this is an imposition. You're very busy. I wouldn't ask if it wasn't important."

"Well, okay then, let's go. I have an old projector in the attic, so it's not hard to set up. My mother will keep you supplied with coffee and muffins, too, as long as you don't mind banana-nut-cat-hair. You do realize, though, that we're talking about hours of unedited film? If you're looking for something specific, it may take a while to find. There's no rhyme or reason to it, no order, no dates, no labels."

"I understand."

He sucked on his pipe again. "You're being very mysterious."

"Yes, I know. I'm sorry."

"Are you sure you can't tell me what's wrong? You may not believe it, but I can be discreet when necessary. I also have a weakness for pretty young women in trouble. Can I help you?"

My face was dark. "No one can help me."

For a moment, my remark left him speechless. "Well, give me five minutes to change, and then we'll be on our way."

"Thank you, Ben."

While he changed, I took you down to the lakeshore. I watched the morning glow on the water and listened to the honking of the geese. My breath made little puffs of steam. I held you close to me and kissed your head and your pink cheeks and murmured over and over how much I loved you. I didn't even realize it until I wiped my face, but I was crying.

Ben was true to his word. Five minutes later, he opened the door with a flourish, dressed in a white turtleneck and plaid sport coat, with pleated tan slacks and penny loafers. He marched across the grass to the resort parking lot and hopped inside the yellow Cadillac. You and I followed him in my car. We drove all the way across Black Wolf County to one of the other small towns tucked among the trees. He parked outside a century-old Victorian house, neatly painted in red and white.

I'd never met Mrs. Malloy. She was tall and heavy and looked a lot like her son, but she was as dour as Ben was cheerful. Her expression didn't change as he said hello, and her eyes traveled over me with grim disapproval. Even you didn't lighten her mood, Shelby. However, she poured hot coffee for me, and after I fished out a cat hair, I was glad to have the caffeine.

Ben and I took the stairs to the second floor. Then he led me to what felt like a secret staircase climbing into one of the house's turrets. The tower had a circular wall and windows looking out in every direction, with a roof that rose to a conical point above us. The wooden floor was dusty, littered by a few dead bugs. Spiderwebs dangled in the shadows. There was nothing much up here but cardboard boxes. Ben seemed to know exactly where to look, and he dug among the boxes and found one in particular, which he carried over to me.

Inside was a Super 8 projector and a stack of more than two dozen silver film canisters. He dragged over another box and propped the projector on top of it and plugged the cord into what seemed to be the only electrical outlet up here. He took the first of the film cans and showed me how to feed it through the machine. Then he retreated to the wall of boxes and located a white screen, which he unfolded and set up. The windows had heavy curtains, and he shut them, leaving the room mostly dark.

"There, you're good to go," he told me. "When you're done with one, you can move on to the next. These are all four-hundred-foot reels, so each one lasts about twenty minutes. Stay as long as you want."

"Are you heading back to the resort?" I asked.

"No, I'll stick around for a while. I haven't been to see Mom in a few days, so I owe her a visit. I can make phone calls while I'm here."

"Don't stay on my account."

"Well, I'll check on you in a bit, and I'll let you know if I need to leave."

"Thank you again, Ben. I really appreciate it."

"In the end, will you tell me what this is all about?" he asked. I hesitated and told him what I believed to be the truth. "In the end, you'll know."

He frowned as he left, and I heard him descending the stairs with heavy footsteps. I was alone with hours of film. I looked around for a chair and saw one near the back wall, so I pulled it across the floor. It was a recliner that had seen better days, but it was comfortable. I'd brought the old Easter basket with me, so I situated you in the basket beside the chair. You were already asleep, and you didn't wake up.

I turned on the projector, listening to its clickety-clack as I watched empty white frames click through the screen. Then, with a rush of color, I was back in the past. Seven years of life melted away. I saw the beach near Sunflower Lake, the pines, the flaky birches, the summer light glinting on the water. Dozens of volunteers in shorts, T-shirts, and bathing suits tramped through the woods at the fringe of the beach, wearing orange baseball hats that Ben had produced, which read: URSULINA HUNTER. Some wore backpacks; some carried buckets. Most were in their teens or twenties.

Seven years earlier. More than a quarter of my life.

Ben had operated the camera himself. He turned the camera around, showing his face in close-up. He looked younger, too, less gray hair, a little thinner, but still with the pipe between his lips. He gave the camera a dramatic stare, rattled off the early August date, and announced in crackling sound, *"This is Ben Malloy in Black Wolf County. It has been two weeks since the Ursulina committed these horrific murders. This is our third day of searching the woods for any evidence that the beast left behind. Will today be the day that we find proof of the monster's existence?"*

From there, the film passed from one choppy scene to the next. Ben interviewed searchers about the horror stories they'd heard of the Ursulina growing up, and they recited some of the tall tales I remembered from when I was a girl. He asked people if they'd ever seen the Ursulina themselves. No one had, but they told stories of noises and grunts in the darkness, of a friend of a friend of a friend who'd seen a strange beast walking upright, of men who went out to hunt in the forest and were never seen again. A couple of the scenes—five seconds here, ten seconds there—had shown up in the original documentary on television. I remembered them.

Some of the searchers called Ben over to view what they'd found. The camera zoomed in on paw prints (they were bears'), giant scat (bears again), and a bloody scene of bones and fur that looked like a wolf kill. With every find, Ben offered breathless commentary that suggested they were on the brink of tracking down the Ursulina's lair. He was a showman at heart.

I finished off one reel and switched to another. Then another. I emptied my coffee and went downstairs to get another cup. I tried one of the cat-hair muffins. When you woke up and cried, I changed you. At one point, because I was exhausted, my eyes drifted shut while the film was playing, and I had to rewind and watch it again. The whole morning passed that way, reel after reel. I knew I was looking for a needle in a haystack, without even knowing whether the needle was there at all. And yet I kept going.

Along the way, I spotted a few people I recognized. High school friends. Mine workers. A lot of beer got drunk; a lot of practical jokes got pulled. You could see the Ursulina myth taking on a life of its own the longer the search went on. The stories got more lurid; the claims got wilder and harder to believe.

During what was probably the ninth or tenth reel, I saw myself. It was just for a few seconds. We weren't far from Norm's Airstream, because I could see its silver frame through the trees.

Ben was interviewing an old man who said his grandfather had told him of seeing the Ursulina come down to the beach under a monster's moon, while he was in a fishing boat in the middle of the inlet. According to the man's grandfather, he and the beast had stared at each other for almost an entire minute before the Ursulina turned around and stomped back into the woods and vanished.

In the midst of this story, I passed behind the old man. I didn't look at the camera, but it was me, with my scraggly black hair and pale face. I was dressed in jeans and a long-sleeved flannel shirt that I'd left untucked. My eyes were glued to the ground as I used a cross-country ski pole to push through the undergrowth and find whatever might be hidden there. I went across the screen from left to right in a few seconds, and then I was gone. I'd been on the search the first day, and I'd come back on the second and third days, too. Like everybody else, I'd found nothing.

Sometime after noon, Ben came upstairs to check on me. He carried a whiff of his pipe smell with him.

"Are you hungry?" he asked. "Mom's got leftover hotdish in the oven. It's better on the second day."

"I'm fine. Thanks."

"Are you warm enough? I can get you a blanket."

"No, I'm okay."

Ben glanced at the screen. This was a nighttime reel, black trees dotted by lanterns, the camera whipping around at every sound. The interviews were conducted in hushed voices.

"You know, if you gave me a clue of what you were looking for, I might be able to help you find it," Ben told me. "I've been through these reels dozens of times over the years. I always think maybe I missed something important. By now, I think I've memorized most of them."

"I appreciate the offer, but I need to do this myself."

"Well, whatever you say. Anyway, I came up here to say I need to leave. I'm going to drop by the 126 and make sure everything's ready for the party tomorrow. Are you okay to stay here on your own? Mom will leave you alone."

"Yes—thanks."

"Okay then. Bye for now."

He returned to the doorway, but then he stopped. "Rebecca, you don't have to tell me if you don't want to, but I'm still convinced you've seen the Ursulina."

I didn't answer.

He gave me a curious smile, and then he disappeared again. I stopped the playback, and I went to one of the windows that looked down on the street, and pushed aside the curtain. Not long after, I saw Ben go outside. He went to his Cadillac, but before he opened the door, he glanced up at the turret, as if he knew I'd be watching him. He put his finger to his forehead in a little salute. I put up a hand. No smile, just a wave.

I sat down in the recliner again. You'd begun to get restless, so I picked you up and rocked you in my arms. I turned on the projector again, and I finished the nighttime reel and went on to the next one. The stack of canisters in the box shrank as the day wore on, and I was beginning to believe that I wouldn't find what I was looking for. I knew it was a shot in the dark anyway.

But with only four reels left, there he was.

I found him at the beginning of a reel from the first day. Ben was giving his introduction about the date and time of the hunt, and a man passed behind him, grinning over Ben's shoulder. He was there and gone in a blink. If you didn't look fast, you'd miss it.

Ricky.

I had to rewind the film to make sure what I'd seen. Then I rewound again. And then again. I must have watched that scene two dozen times before I turned off the projector, and each time felt like a lightning bolt searing my brain.

I wanted to see if he was carrying it, and he was.

Of course he was.

Ricky held a leather strap, swinging it as he walked. At the end of the strap was a camera.

CHAPTER THIRTY-EIGHT

That was my darkest day, Shelby.

When I saw the camera in Ricky's hands, I knew he was the one who'd put the photograph on Ruby's door. I knew he wasn't lying about the Ursulina. Or about what he'd done to Ajax. I realized at that moment that there was no safe place for us in Black Wolf County. You were in mortal danger from him, and you always would be. That was when I made my decision. The thought of it suffocated me with grief, but I was a mother, and I did what a mother had to do.

I sacrificed myself to save you.

That afternoon, I drove to Sunflower Lake. I sat in the parking lot where I'd found Tom Ginn in January and thought back to that night. I remembered what it was like to be in his arms. I thought about hearing his voice on the phone again when Darrell called him. I felt a surge of emotion about what might have been. In my life I've known very few good men, but Tom was one. He is yours, and you are his, Shelby. I don't care what genetics may or may not say.

You have only one father.

I spent hours by the lake that afternoon with you. I prayed for time to stand still, because I didn't want it to end. I didn't want to let go. I talked to you and sang to you. I pointed out the birds when I saw them and the rabbits and squirrels when they crept onto the beach. I plucked the colored leaves from the autumn trees and tickled your face with them. I told you how much I loved you, how much I would always love you, how every single moment of every single day, you would still be in my life, even if I wasn't in yours.

The whole time, I held you, and I sobbed. I cried for everything I was going to miss, and I cried for the things I couldn't give you. I cursed all the events that had led me to that moment and wished I could change them, but finally, I realized I was wrong to think that way. If fate had gone differently, you wouldn't be in my life at all, and I wouldn't have traded you for anything. So I had to make peace with how I'd gotten there. I had to tell myself that the end, the point of it all, the meaning behind the suffering, was you.

You made it worthwhile.

It was a beautiful, blissful afternoon, Shelby, but all good things must end. As the sun set, as darkness crept across the lake, I put you back in the car seat, and I began to drive. You know where I went. I drove and drove in a kind of perfect peace and stillness. We had a long way to go, the two of us, along empty highways, past empty forestland, with the monster's moon shining overhead. But I knew where to go and what I had to do.

*

And when it was done, I returned home the next day. My plan of action was clear. There was no going back. I went to my house for what I knew would be the last time. I slept on the sofa for a while, to get my strength back, but I really didn't sleep much at all. When I did, I had my usual nightmares.

Night had already fallen when I awoke. It was time for the party at the 126.

Time to meet Ricky.

It took me a while, digging in the closet, to find the hat Ben had given me seven years earlier, along with all the other volunteers who were searching in the forest. I still had it.

URSULINA HUNTER.

I wanted to send Ricky a message by wearing it, and I was sure he'd understand.

I know.

Then I drove to the 126.

Everyone was there, seemingly the whole county crammed shoulder to shoulder. There were half a dozen televisions mounted around the bar, all of them tuned to NBC. The documentary would be starting in half an hour, but I saw commercials for it. *Ben Malloy Discovers: The Return of the Ursulina.* The promos featured quick clips of Ben using words like *murder, monster,* and *blood,* plus fake footage of a beast's hairy legs tramping through the forest.

Some people wore recycled Halloween costumes from Thursday evening, but most had come as Ursulinas, short and tall, thin and fat, silly and scary. The 126 had been transformed into a bizarre, drunken zoo, filled with people letting out beastly growls. Ben himself stood on a makeshift stage with a microphone in hand, clapping and egging them on as he paced restlessly back and forth.

I looked for Ricky among the monsters. With his papier-mâché head and long, thick neck, he'd be easy to find, but I didn't see him yet. Instead, I found Sandra, who was obviously going after the prize for sexiest Ursulina, because she wore a fur bikini, along with fur boots and a shaggy wig. She was drinking hard stuff that night, whiskey on the rocks, and she had a pack of cigarettes jutting out of her bikini top.

"Hey, you," she said to me. I heard a looseness in her voice, and I suspected the whiskey wasn't her first.

"Hey."

"Two weeks after you deliver, and you look like that. It kills me."

"Thanks."

"Where's Shelby?"

I'd been prepared for that question. I had a lie ready. "One of my neighbors offered to babysit."

"I'm impressed that you were able to leave her so soon."

I didn't answer. Instead, I changed the subject, because if I didn't, I was going to cry all over again.

"Hey, Sandra? I want you to know I'm sorry."

"About what?"

"All the things Darrell said to you."

She laughed. "Don't worry about that. Ever since, rumors have been getting around that I'm the killer. Now the men at the mine are afraid of me. I love it."

"Still, I feel bad."

Sandra cocked her head as she looked at me. "You okay, honey?"

"I'm fine," I said, lying again.

"The early weeks are tough. I know."

"Yeah, that must be it."

She drained her whiskey and then patted my cheek and left me alone. Around me, everyone else was having a good time. Drinking. Laughing. Growling. My own dark eyes kept probing the bar, going from monster to monster. I wondered if Darrell was here somewhere, but I knew this wasn't his scene. It was better that way. There would only be trouble if he came.

Then I felt a paw on my shoulder.

When I turned around, I saw the cartoonish face painted on the head, the fake mismatched fur top and bottom.

"You're here," Ricky said, with a little surprise.

"You told me to be here," I replied evenly. "I do what you tell me now. Isn't that our deal?"

"Good girl. Where's the kid?"

"She's safe."

That answer made him pause, as if my dull voice were broadcasting a kind of alarm. But Ricky was Ricky, and he didn't let it trouble him for long. "This is good, you know. You and me back together. I've missed you, Bec."

"Sure you have."

"We should celebrate later," he said. "Celebrate like man and wife."

"Sure we will."

I couldn't muster any false emotion on my face to reinforce the lie. I was beyond anger, beyond regret, beyond humiliation. I'd already done the worst thing I could possibly do in my life, so what was left?

"Let's surprise them," Ricky suggested. "Come on, I can't wait to see their faces."

His gloved hands went to his neck, where he peeled away the tape that held the cardboard neck in place. He reached up and removed the balloon-shaped head and pried off the cardboard tube at the same time. With the mask gone, his face was revealed. My ex-husband stood in front of me.

Everyone in the bar saw him. He was right about the reaction. An uncomfortable quiet spread through the 126 like the ripples of a wave in the water. Then the low murmurs began all around us.

Ricky.

People headed our way immediately, zeroing in on us. Sandra got there first. I had to insert myself between them, because she was on the verge of launching a drunken assault. She shoved her face over my shoulder and bellowed her disgust at Ricky.

"You! What do you think you're doing here? I can't believe you'd have the balls to show your face in this town again. Get the hell out before the cops throw your sorry ass in jail."

Ricky just smiled, using that smile that was more like a sneer. He'd used it on me that very first day at the high school football game when we met. Back then, I'd had no idea what it really meant. All those years since then, and I'd never guessed the truth, never guessed what he was concealing from me.

"Didn't you hear the good news, Sandra?" Ricky told her. "Bec and I have reconciled."

She unleashed a curse of disbelief. "Bullshit. That's bullshit."

"It's true."

Sandra turned her attention to me with her face just inches from mine. "Say the word, honey, and ten men will toss this asshole out to the street."

Ricky draped a paw around my shoulder. "Don't be like that, Sandra. Be happy for us. I've apologized, and Bec's forgiven me. We were both wrong. We both did things we regret. The main thing is, we have a child now, and we have to put her first."

Sandra stared at me with a mix of anger and horror. "Honey, you can't be serious. You *cannot* take him back."

I took a deep breath. "It's okay, Sandra."

"Okay? Are you kidding? What's wrong with you?"

"Leave it. Please."

But Sandra wasn't the only one in the bar trying to rescue me. Norm came up to me, too. "Rebecca? What's going on? Are you all right?"

"I'm fine."

"Has Ricky hurt you in any way?"

I shook my head. "No. He hasn't."

"Ricky, you need to leave," Norm told him in a firm voice. "You're not welcome here. Not after what you did."

"I think that's up to Rebecca, don't you?" Ricky replied confidently, not intimidated by the crowd gathered around us, half of whom were dressed like monsters. "What do you say, Bec? Should I stay or go?"

My face must have looked like the rigid papier-mâché mask that he'd worn. "You can stay."

Sandra swore again, more loudly than before, and Norm's eyes narrowed with shocked surprise. He stared at me as if I must be a robot operated by remote control, with Ricky pushing the buttons and telling me what to say.

"Rebecca, did Ricky threaten you in any way? Or did he threaten Shelby?"

"No."

His face darkened with a new thought. "Where is Shelby?"

"Safe," I said.

"Safe *where?*"

"She's safe," I repeated.

Sandra looked ready to spit. "That's it. I'm calling Darrell."

"*No.*" I grabbed hold of her wrist. "No, don't do that. It's fine. Really."

"It's not fine. *You're* not fine."

"This is my choice."

"She just told you she's fine, Sandra," Ricky interjected. "It's time for you to mind your own business for once in your life and leave my wife alone."

"Rebecca is not your wife anymore," Norm pointed out.

"That's up to her, not some piece-of-shit lawyer like you."

Norm shook his head. His eyes pleaded with me to take a

different road. "Rebecca, this man has no control over you. You owe him nothing. He's not your husband. All you have to do is say the word, and Darrell will take him to jail."

"That's not what I want."

"Rebecca!" Norm went on, his frustration boiling over. I hadn't seen him lose control like that very often. "Have you forgotten what this man did to you?"

Just for an instant, my eyes smoldered. "I haven't forgotten."

"Then why are you doing this?"

I wanted to say: *For Shelby*. That was the reason. That was the one and only reason. Everything in my whole life was about you. But there was no way for me to explain.

Instead, I looked at Ricky and said, "Let's get out of here. I don't care about the show. Take me away from here."

"You heard her," Ricky announced to the crowd. "My wife says we're leaving."

He took my hand in a tight grip. As we headed for the door of the 126, a path parted slowly, just wide enough for the two of us to get through. Sandra, Norm, and others followed right behind. When we reached the door and Ricky opened it, Sandra called after me.

"Rebecca, do *not* leave with him. Honey, please. Stay here."

I froze in the doorway and looked over my shoulder at her. My face was stricken. A part of me wanted to stay, but it was too late for that. A part of me wanted to explain, but I couldn't do that, either. I opened my mouth to say goodbye, but I didn't have a chance to say anything at all.

Someone screamed. Not in the bar. On the television. The introduction to Ben's new documentary began with the sound of a woman screaming, making my flesh ripple. Then we heard Ben's dramatic voice filling the silence of the room.

"I'm Ben Malloy. Seven years ago, I brought you to a remote

place called Black Wolf County, where a murderous beast known as the Ursulina had ripped apart the flesh of two men in a savage attack. Ever since that awful day, the people in this area have lived their lives in terror, wondering when the monster would return. Well, last December, they got their answer. The Ursulina came back . . . to kill again."

I didn't need to hear any more.

Ricky and I left the bar together.

CHAPTER THIRTY-NINE

"Where are we going?" I asked Ricky as we drove.

He stayed on the arrow-straight highway, leaving Random far behind us. We continued under the moon's glow, and snow flurries fell from the cold night sky. After a while, I guessed what our destination was, and I said nothing more. Honestly, it felt right to go there, like the end and the beginning of my story coming together in the same place.

It took us an hour to reach Norm's trailer. I could sense my stress rising as we got closer. My heart always felt it, like a shadow coming over my soul. We traveled first on the highway, then on the rutted dirt road through the national forest. Eventually, I saw the familiar glint of the silver frame through the headlights. Ricky pulled off the road onto a bed of fallen leaves and stopped. I could see in the tire tracks that he'd been coming and going for several weeks.

"You've been staying here?" I asked.

"Yeah. Ironic, huh?"

"Weren't you afraid Norm would find out?"

"A buddy of mine rented it from Norm for a couple of

months. Told him he was having trouble with the wife, and they needed time apart. So we have our privacy here, don't worry. It's just you and me."

I got out of the car. Ricky headed straight for the trailer, but I lingered by the woods. Somewhere nearby, I heard the hoot of an owl, like a sign, like a warning. When I'd been ten years old, an owl had tried to alert me that the Ursulina was close by. That I was in danger. I inhaled, to see if I could smell the beast. I listened for the *huffffff.* There was nothing. But I could feel its presence looming over me, the way I had that night near Sunflower Lake. If I plunged into the darkness, I was sure I would find it, or it would find me. We would be reunited, the monster and the girl. In my heart, we'd been inseparable ever since that moment. The two of us joined together by blood.

I followed Ricky inside the trailer. My chest convulsed with terror when I closed the trailer door, as if no time had passed. It was seven years ago again. I was right back where everything had started.

Ricky sat on the bed. He didn't turn on the lights, so he was nothing but a dim shadow. He still wore the fur coat, the fur pants; he still looked like the beast, waiting for me. The trailer floor creaked under my feet as I walked toward him. He patted the bed, which was unmade, and I sat down beside him.

This was my moment of truth.

I'm sorry, Shelby. I wish I could keep this from you forever. I've held back my secret from you, and maybe that was wrong of me. Maybe I should have told you at the beginning—told you who I am and what I did—but then what? I couldn't expect you to understand it until you knew me. Until you knew my whole story.

But now?

Now I have to tell you who your mother really is. You can

decide for yourself if there is any salvation possible for someone like me.

I stared at Ricky. It was obvious what he wanted to hear, and there was no point in holding it back anymore. It was time to say out loud what we'd both known and both kept from each other.

"So you knew all along that I killed them," I said. "You knew when you met me that I was the one who murdered Kip and Racer."

There was enough moonlight through the window for me to see his white teeth.

"Yeah. That was part of the thrill."

I stood up from the bed. I had to swallow down the urge to vomit, hearing my own confession. For seven years, I'd hidden my sins from the world. I'd lied to Darrell. I'd lied to everyone. I'd lived in terror of being discovered. And all along, the whole time, Ricky knew.

He'd found my camera.

"Where are the rest of the photographs?" I asked, with a kind of clinical curiosity. "I want to see them."

"They're in the cabinet over the sink."

I went and turned on the small light there, and then I opened the cabinet door. There was a small envelope of pictures on the lowest shelf, next to a dated thirty-five-millimeter camera. I grazed my fingers across its familiar frame.

It was the camera that I'd seen in Ricky's hand in the film I'd watched at Ben Malloy's house.

The same camera I'd used to take the photograph of Gordon Brink, Kip Wells, and Racer Moritz seven years earlier.

The same camera I'd dropped that day when I was running for my life.

My camera.

I'd dreaded for years that someone would find it. I'd searched for it after I escaped from the trailer, and I'd come back during Ben's Ursulina hunt to search for it again. But I never found it. I'd assumed, hoped, prayed that the camera—and the roll of film inside it—had long since decomposed with the rain and snow.

But I was wrong.

Ricky had found it. He'd found the camera and developed the film inside. And then he'd set about finding the girl who'd taken the pictures.

I opened up the envelope and removed the photographs. I picked up the one on top. It was of me. I'd taken it in the woods that July day. My eyes so dark and serious, my black hair a mess, as it usually was. Sunflower Lake was behind me, shining in the morning light.

I was still an innocent girl in that picture, with no idea of the horror that lay ahead of me.

"I bought the camera that summer," I murmured. "I was still getting used to the features. I remembered using the self-timer a couple of times, so I knew there were pictures of me on the roll. Me, and then a few frames later, them. Brink, Kip, Racer. I was in a panic when I couldn't find the camera. I knew if anyone else found it . . ."

My voice trailed off.

"Why didn't you tell me that you knew what I'd done?" I asked him. "All you've ever wanted to do was control me. Own me. Why not lord it over me that you could expose my secret?"

Ricky's voice oozed with triumph. "I liked you not knowing. I was a cat with a mouse. I had all the power. Anytime I wanted, all I had to do was swipe my paw to take you down. There were so many times when I wanted to say it. Tell you what I knew. See your face when you found out. Sometimes I'd see a look in your eyes, that little fire when you were ready to fight back, and I'd think: Just try it, Bec. See what happens if you push me too far. But I was in no hurry. When you hold all the aces, you can relax and enjoy the game. So I waited. I waited for the perfect moment. And now it's here. It's payback time. You think you can get rid of me? Not a chance. You belong to me, and you always will."

God, I hated the boasting in his voice. The shallow, arrogant ego. I hated that I'd been a fool for him all those years. I wasn't going to live with it anymore, not with the fear, not with the abuse. The time had come. I could feel the electricity sizzling in my blood.

"I need a drink," I said, my voice cool and casual. Like he'd won. Like he'd defeated me. "Do you need one?"

"Sure."

"Beer?"

"There's some in the fridge."

I opened the door of the small refrigerator, which temporarily blocked me from Ricky's view. That was the opportunity I needed. I found two bottles of Budweiser, and I saw that there was an opener next to the sink. When I had the bottles open, I closed the fridge and brought them over to the bed.

I handed one to Ricky, and as I sat down next to him again, he took my wrist and twisted it hard enough to make me wince.

"I want you to say it," he told me.

"What?" I asked, but I knew. I knew exactly what he wanted me to say.

"I want to hear the words from that pretty mouth of yours," he went on. "I've been waiting years for that. Tell me who you are."

He let go of my wrist. I stared at him, working hard to keep the hatred off my face. I couldn't let him see it yet.

Did he really think I'd take him back into my life? Did he really believe I would allow him anywhere near you, Shelby?

After what he'd done to me, after the evil I'd seen in his eyes when he was holding you? I knew what would happen to us. Oh, I knew. Sooner or later, on a day when the cat got tired of playing with the mice, he'd kill us both.

I watched him take a long swallow from his bottle of Budweiser, and he never tasted the powder of the four Xanax pills I'd dropped inside.

"Say it," Ricky told me again.

So I did. The truth is, I *wanted* to say it. I felt a surge of power running through me, a power I knew only too well, a power that had come over me twice before in my life. When I transformed. When the beast and I became one. When I evolved into what I really was.

I told you that the monster was real, Shelby.

I told you that from the very beginning.

I leaned into Ricky's face, and then I whispered the words. The same words I'd painted on the wall in that trailer seven years earlier. The same words I'd painted above Gordon Brink's bed.

The words I couldn't run away from. The words that had defined my life.

"*I . . . am . . . the Ursulina.*"

*

I was twenty years old that July.

I was on my own, my father and brother both working jobs far away. I had no job myself, and I didn't know when I'd get one, because the economy was terrible. Yes, I'd just completed a two-year degree program, but that wouldn't do me much good when no one was hiring. I had no job, no money, no one in my life, and I felt the kind of loneliness that becomes like a friend after a while.

I did only two things that whole summer. I stayed home reading books. And I hunted for the Ursulina.

The legend of Bigfoot was all the rage back then. You'd see him everywhere—in books, on television, in magazines and newspapers. The beast in the woods that walked upright like a man. Was he real or a myth? Were there actual photos of him, or were they hoaxes? Of course, I *knew* he existed, or something like him did. I knew there was one of those beasts haunting the forest near Sunflower Lake. We had a special connection, him and me. I was sure that if anyone could find him, if anyone could draw him out, I could.

That's why I bought the camera. It was a luxury I could barely afford, but if I found the Ursulina again, if I could get a picture of him, then my whole life would change. So day after day, with nothing else to do, I searched the national forest. Sometimes I arrived before dawn and left as the sun went down. Other times I brought a backpack and camped. I'd hike for miles, watching for movement in the trees or tracks on the ground, inhaling the air for a whiff of his breath, listening for that unmistakable *hufffffff.*

I thought he'd come back when he knew it was me. He'd show himself.

It's Rebecca. Don't you remember? Where are you?

But as the days passed, I saw no sign of him. All I did was take pictures. Sometimes of the woods, the lake, the flowers, the animals, the birds. Sometimes of myself, when I would put the camera on a rock and take a self-portrait in the shadows.

That was my summer seven years earlier, sweetheart. The lazy summer of a young woman trying to figure out her future. Until that one terrible afternoon, when I saw sunlight glinting on silver.

Norm's trailer.

I knew where I was. I'd been here before with Norm and Will. I heard voices, and I assumed it was them, so I headed that way to say hello. As I got closer, I also brought the camera to my eyes to take a picture. The light off the trailer reflected like a kind of rainbow, as if I were staring at a spaceship, and I thought that was cool. There were people in the foreground, like aliens. It was only when I stared through the viewfinder and snapped the shutter that I realized the men standing there were strangers. Not Norm and Will.

Three of them. Three men.

Their conversation froze into silence when they saw me. Six eyes locked on me at once; they locked on me and on my camera. I knew at once that I'd just made the worst mistake of my life. Every woman knows hard men of evil purpose at a glance, and I saw it in those men. Two were dressed in ratty clothes; one wore a suit and looked oddly out of place in the wilderness. That man focused on me, as coldly cruel as a reptile. I had no idea who he was, but I was never going to forget his face, and he was never going to forget mine.

He glanced at the other two men and said simply, "Get her."

I ran.

I screamed for help, but no one was around to hear me, not out there. I beat my way through the woods, the branches drawing blood, the vines tripping me up. Behind me, I heard their footsteps trampling through the underbrush like beasts, like monsters. I ran even faster, to get away, to lose them. Somewhere, I don't know where, the limb of a tree ripped my camera away from my neck. It dropped; I just kept running. I zigzagged, changing directions when I heard them getting closer. Desperation drove me on. Maybe I would have gotten away, because I was young and fast, but my foot hit the bulge of a tree root, which flipped me into the air. I landed hard, twisting my ankle, and when I got up again, I couldn't run anymore. I limped for a while until it got too painful to move, and then I squatted down and tried to hide, but they found me.

The men came at me from two sides, and they had me trapped. They tied me up with belts around my wrists and ankles. Gagged me with one of their shirts. Hit me in the face, the first of many blows. And then they carried me, struggling and fighting, on their shoulders like trophy game. The other man was waiting at the trailer.

"Kill her," he directed them, with a hard, casual glance at my face. "Bury her where no one will find the body."

But the one holding my legs—later, I'd find out that was Kip—laughed at him. I remember his exact words. "Just like that? Juicy Fruit like this one? No way, man. First we play."

First we play.

That was what they did, Shelby.

For the next thirty-six hours, they played with me. A day and a half. They played. More than two thousand minutes, each minute making me wish I were dead. They played. I was Juicy Fruit, and they chewed me up. They tied me to the bed, moving me when they wanted to change the game. Faceup. Facedown. On all fours. On my knees. They took turns. Kip. Racer. And the third man. Gordon Brink. He played, too.

I was a virgin when they carried me inside. Soon I wasn't a virgin or a girl or a woman or even a human being anymore. I became an animal, and I did what animals do. I survived. I distanced myself from the body on the bed. She was not me. She was weak, a victim. I dug a hole for my emotions, and I buried them and shoveled dirt over their grave. The only thing still alive inside me was my brain. The brain of Rebecca Colder, stronger and bolder.

Rebecca Colder, who would watch them, study them, learn

from them, find their vulnerabilities. Rebecca Colder, who would figure out how to stay alive.

Racer was the weak link. I realized that quickly. Brink was intelligent, Kip was sly, but Racer was stupid. He drank and drank from the dozens of liquor bottles in the trailer. He smoked weed until the cloud made me choke. He had a hundred pounds on me, so I couldn't overpower him, but he was impatient and careless. When he was the one who tied me up, he didn't get the knots right. That didn't matter if all of them were in the trailer to watch me, but if I had a time when Racer was alone with me, then I had a chance.

Thirty-six hours later, Kip and Brink got ready to leave. Brink was done with me, done with the game. I'd seen something on his face the last time he raped me that made me realize he'd begun to hate himself for what was happening. He wanted *out*. He wanted to erase me and this whole experience from his memory. Whenever Kip got back, that would be the end. If Rebecca Colder was going to get away, it would have to be while they were gone.

So in the darkness, after they left, it was just me and Racer.

He had his way with me again. I no longer even cared, because I knew that when he was done, he would drink. He always did. He drank and drank and drank and drank, and I waited for him to pass out. But the minutes ticked by in agonized frustration, and somehow he stayed conscious. I was terrified that Kip would return, and my opportunity would be gone for good. If Racer stayed awake much longer, I'd have to slip my wrists out of the loose rope and hope that he was clumsy enough that I could evade him. But the trailer was small, and he was huge. I didn't like my chances.

Then, at last, his head tilted back, his eyes blinked shut, and he was out cold.

I freed myself quickly. It took only seconds, because Racer had barely even tightened the knots this time. Silently, I got up from the bed, feeling torture in my body from everything they'd done to me. The trailer groaned with each step I made, so I went slowly, trying not to awaken Racer. I didn't have to worry. I slipped right past him, and he never moved at all. His snores were like blasts from a trumpet.

Ahead of me was the trailer door. Beyond the door was the forest, the night, and my freedom. All I had to do was gather up my clothes and go through it, and I would be gone.

But I didn't leave.

I'm not sure if I can even explain what happened to me next. There were dirty plates in the sink from their dinner, and among the plates I saw a long, sharp kitchen knife. I took it in my hand. I wanted a weapon, because as soon as they discovered I was gone, they'd lay chase. Or at least, that was what I told myself. But as I held the knife, a sensation came over me that was like nothing I'd ever experienced before. A murderous fury bubbled out of that hole in which I'd buried my soul, like a hot spring. I was not weak. I was not a victim. I would not run away from this man, tail between my legs. Standing there in the trailer, I felt myself grow bigger. Taller. Stronger. My breaths came hot and deep from my chest, and when I exhaled, I recognized the smell of the beast from when I was a girl. When I looked at my fingers, I didn't see my own tiny hands anymore. I saw giant paws.

And when I looked at Racer, I saw prey.

You may not believe any of this. I don't know if I believe it myself, except it happened to me, and I know it's true. I was not Rebecca Colder anymore. I had transformed into a monster, just like the legend said. I had become the Ursulina. And with a fierce growl, I leaped upon Racer with the knife, stabbing and stabbing, his blood spurting and flying, soaking me, covering the walls. He awoke in agony after the first blow and tried to push me away, but this huge man was helpless beneath my body. My paws went up and down, up and down, burying the knife over and over until there wasn't enough blood left for his heart to beat anymore.

When I was done, I stood over him, drenched in his blood, and I unleashed a savage, primal, aroused scream of joy.

I could have left the trailer then.

I could have escaped.

But there was more prey to be killed. More vengeance to be done. I stood motionless in the darkness behind the trailer door, and I waited patiently. How long did I stand there? An hour? Two? I could have waited for days if I'd needed to. Then, finally, I heard footsteps crunching in the dirt outside. The door opened, and Kip was back. He had only a split second to see the gory scene that was waiting for him before I struck. My knife rained down on him like a hailstorm, and the more blood that drained out of him, the wilder I became. Until he was dead, too. Until all that was left to do was sign my name on the wall.

To let everyone know who I was.

To make them tremble in fear.

Outside, afterward, I marched into the woods. I made my way to the lake and purified myself in the cold water. When I emerged naked onto the shore, I was Rebecca Colder again. The beast had left me. I barely even remembered what I'd done. I found my way back to the place where I'd parked my car, and I drove home. I had no guilt. No regret. There was nothing to tie me to the murder scene. No one had known where I was going. No one had known I was gone.

It was only when I awoke from a dreamless sleep that I remembered my camera.

The thought of it panicked me. If someone found the camera, the pictures I'd taken would show the world who the Ursulina really was. So I went back to the killing ground to search. Norm hadn't found the bodies yet, and when I saw the trailer again, I felt a wave of horror knowing what was inside, as if the ghosts of the corpses would rise up and surround me. I wasted no time. I looked everywhere, I spent hours, but I had no idea where I'd dropped the camera. There was simply too much ground to cover.

So I sweated out the next few weeks, terrified that someone else would find it and that my secret would be revealed. But no. The knock on my door never came. Even after deputies went through the woods. Even after Ben's Ursulina hunt with all his volunteers. No one showed up to arrest me. As the time went by, I began to believe I was safe.

I never dreamed when I met Ricky that *he'd* already found the camera, developed the film, and decided to collect me like a rare breed of carnivorous butterfly. He found me at a time when I needed to pretend that I was still an ordinary woman, not a killer, not a beast. I needed to punish myself for what I'd done. So no matter what Ricky did or said to me, I kept the Ursulina locked away as the sentence for my crime.

That was my life for six years. A gray, loveless life that probably would have gone on forever.

Until Gordon Brink came back to town.

Until the Ursulina came back.

At that point, sweetheart, I had no idea who Brink was. My mind had a face, but no name. And obviously, Brink was terrified of running into *me*. I can only imagine the horror he'd felt when Ajax told him about the murders. He'd assumed that Kip and Racer had buried me in the forest along with his sins. Instead, he knew there was a woman in Black Wolf

County burning for vengeance, a woman who would *never forget his face.*

Maybe, if not for the pig's blood dousing his wife, he and I never would have met again. She called the sheriff's department without telling Gordon, and I was the one Jerry sent to investigate. Fate. When we saw each other, he didn't miss the surge of violence on my face, the shock that became blinding rage. He knew I'd be back for him. He knew. That Sunday before Christmas, while the town and my husband were at the 126 watching Jamie Lee Curtis take off her shirt, I was knocking on Gordon Brink's office door out in the woods.

He was no fool. He had a gun, because he assumed I was there to do to him what I'd done to Kip and Racer. It was kill or be killed. But I tried to put him at ease. I told him that too much time had gone by, that neither one of us wanted the truth to come out. I said I was there so we could come to some kind of arrangement. Money. A lot of money. I suggested we drink on it.

As he poured the whiskey, I hit him in the back of the head.

When he was unconscious, I dragged him to the bed. I could feel the beast in my bloodstream, putting me into a kind of fugue where I wasn't even aware of what I was doing. When I awoke from my transformation, I was soaked in blood, the meat shredders in my hands. Gordon Brink lay on the bed with the look of someone who'd seen the face of hell before dying.

The message from the beast was already painted on the wall.

In that moment, Shelby, I thought—I swear I thought—I was free. It was over. Done. I'd purged the beast. The past was the past, and it had given up its grip on me. But of course, no evil deed comes without consequences.

There was a horrific price to be paid for my revenge, a bloody trail of grief, loss, and death that followed in my footsteps. Will paid the price. Jay paid the price. Even Ajax did, though that one was by Ricky's hands, not mine. And in a way, Ruby, Penny, and so many others, they all paid for what I did, too.

So did you, Shelby.

You most of all.

In the end, the Ursulina claimed us both.

CHAPTER FORTY

I waited until the Xanax did its work.

Ricky didn't understand at first what was happening to him. Right to the end, he was a fool. His mind spun like a merry-go-round; his muscles grew thick and heavy; his words slurred. When he finally realized what I'd done to him, he came at me in a clumsy charge and wrapped his hands around my throat. Despite my plans, he nearly won. I kicked and fought him, but even drugged, he had the steel-strong grip of a mine worker. I was already blacking out when his fingers finally loosened from my windpipe, and he fell backward.

I stood over him, coughing and choking, as he lay unconscious on the floor. In his ridiculous costume, he was more beast than man. A bully. A brute. I felt no mercy toward him. I thought about him holding you by the neck, Shelby, and my heart turned ice cold.

I didn't hesitate. I took my gun, and with two shots to his head, I made sure he would never hurt you again.

Afterward, I burned the photographs and negatives from

seven years earlier. I brought my old camera to the lake and threw it out into the water as far as I could. There would be no evidence to tie me to the Ursulina murders. No headlines about the girl who became the monster, no publicity, no magazine covers with my face, no new Ben Malloy documentary on NBC. Actually, Ricky did me a favor by taking out his revenge on Ajax using my own disguise. No one would believe that Rebecca Colder, not even a month away from giving birth, had vivisected Ajax. So no one would believe I'd committed the other murders, either. They would remain unsolved. Four victims of a monster whose legend would only grow with time.

That was what everyone wanted. They wanted the myth.

Of course, that didn't mean I was free. I knew that. I was still a killer.

When I got back to the trailer, I took a chair outside to wait for Darrell. I was calm at that moment. Serene. It was the middle of a bitter fall night, with snow swirling around me, but I didn't feel cold. I breathed crisp air into my lungs and listened for the Ursulina, but the beast had gone away. I was my own woman again, ready for what came next.

Darrell arrived at dawn.

I could see his headlights approaching on the dirt road through the dusting of snow. He got out of the car, and when he saw me, a huge grin broke across his face, and he exclaimed in relief, "Rebecca, thank God! I've been looking everywhere. Are you okay?"

He rushed toward me, but he stopped when he saw the revolver at my feet. His smile vanished.

"You'll want to bag that," I told him. "It's evidence."

His eyes took on a stricken look. His face turned ashen. Without saying a word, without picking up the gun, he ripped open the trailer door and ran inside, and a moment later, I heard his howl of despair. The entire Airstream shuddered as Darrell pounded his fists on the walls.

When he came back outside to confront me, tears were rolling down his cheeks. He shook his head over and over. "Rebecca, *why?*"

"You know why. He was going to kill me. He was going to kill Shelby. Nothing you did would ever keep him away from us."

"I would have put him in jail."

"For how long, Darrell? Six months? A year? Then he would have gotten out and come back."

"Rebecca, I can't hide this. This is murder. I can't protect you from it."

"I would never ask you to. I knew what I was doing. I made a plan and carried it out. I drugged my ex-husband and shot him in the head. I'm guilty. I accept the consequences."

With another awful groan, Darrell fell to his knees in front of my chair. He reached out and hugged me tightly, and I hugged him back. I felt miserable, seeing his disappointment in me. This was my sin, my crime, but he felt responsible, like a father who'd failed his child. Somehow, he should have been able to save me. Keep me from harm.

I understood how he felt. I understood only too well.

He kept his hands on my shoulders, with his wretched face right in front of mine. I watched dread spread across his features, a horror of things unknown and unsaid. Then he asked me the question I knew was coming.

"Rebecca, *where is Shelby?*"

"She's safe, Darrell," I told him, my voice cracking, my heart breaking. "My baby is safe."

"Where is she? I have to know where she is."

"She was in danger. I needed to protect her."

"How? How did you do that?"

"I took her away from here."

"*Where?* You need to tell me where you took her."

"To a place where no one can ever hurt her again."

Darrell put his hands on both sides of my head. He leaned his forehead against mine. "Oh my God. Oh my God, Rebecca, please don't say that. You can't tell me that. Rebecca, *what did you do?*"

*

What did I do?

I did the only thing I could do, Shelby. I saw only one way to save you. And to save myself.

I wasn't going to be free to raise you. I was going to prison for murder, for years at least, maybe for the rest of my life. Even if someone from Black Wolf County agreed to take you in, that wasn't the childhood I wanted for you. Do you think I could live with you seeing me once a month and putting your little hand against mine on the other side of a sheet of glass?

No.

My other choice was to let the state take you away. Except I couldn't pretend or fool myself. I wasn't going to have a choice. Murderers don't get to pick the family to adopt their baby. That's not how it works. The state was going to take my little girl away and give you to total strangers in some other part of the country, and *I would never even know who they were.* I would sit in jail, and for the rest of my life, I would have no idea where my daughter was, or what your name was, or whose family you'd joined, or whether they were good to you, or whether you were happy and safe. You were going to disappear from me as completely as if you'd never existed at all. I couldn't bear that thought.

So I put you in my car, and I drove you far away from here.

I drove for hours to the other side of the state. That drive is still so vivid to me, Shelby. That long, long drive. The road was ours, nothing but the glow of my headlights and the immense black forest and the stars overhead. You slept peacefully, with no idea that your little life was about to change forever.

I drove to Mittel County. I drove to Tom Ginn.

I arrived after midnight at his house in the middle of nowhere. I wasn't sure I was in the right place, because the house looked like a church, glowing with stained glass, with high walls and a steeple rising over the white roof. But when I got out and checked the mailbox, I saw that this was where Tom lived. I took you out of your car seat and secured you in that silly little Easter basket among the paper curlicues. I couldn't bear to go back home and see the basket sitting there, like a reminder that you were gone.

I put the basket—I put *you*—at Tom's doorstep. And I rang the bell.

Part of me wanted to run. Drive away. I thought about leaving you there in his care anonymously, like a gift from God. I wasn't sure I could bear to see his face again when he answered the door. What would he say? What would I say? I was terrified that he would reject me, that he would reject *you*. As I stood there in the cold, it all seemed suddenly absurd, that I could ask this man with whom I'd spent a single night nine months earlier to *take my baby*. To accept a child into his life from a woman who was about to confess to him that she'd killed three men and was planning to kill a fourth. By all rights, he should arrest me, not help me.

But I remembered how I'd felt in January—that if I were in trouble, I could go to Tom, and he would suspend everything else in his life to be there for me. I still believed that. I hoped I was right.

Except of all things, he didn't answer the door. I rang the bell again and again before I had to accept the fact that he wasn't home. I'd driven all this way, and Tom wasn't there. I had no idea if he was on patrol, gone for the night, looking after his father, or on vacation somewhere thousands of miles away. I didn't know what to do. I sat down on the doorstep next to you, listening to the wind, watching the night, wondering what I could possibly do next when I had nowhere else to turn.

How long did I sit there? I don't know. It felt like hours. I took off my coat because you were cold, and I wrapped you up in it, and I shivered. Then I cried. And I prayed. God had no reason at all to listen to the prayers of someone like me, but I hoped that maybe, maybe, maybe, he would answer my prayers for you, Shelby. You had done nothing wrong. You were innocent, pure, and perfect.

To this day, I believe God listened, because it was in the midst of my prayers that Tom came home. Down the road, I saw a truck coming at high speed. He didn't even pull into his own driveway. He stopped the truck in the middle of the road, got out, and saw me. I'll never forget the look on his face. He ran—*he ran!*—up the steps, and in the next moment, we were holding each other, kissing like lost lovers. If you ever wonder whether one night can change your life, Shelby, I swear to you it can. I'd spent one night with this man nine months earlier, and I was still madly in love with him. I'd been in love with him ever since that night.

Do I dare say it out loud?

He loved me, too. I saw it in his eyes. I felt it in how he kissed me.

When we breathlessly broke apart, he said in a rush: "I was at the lake. I was in my boat out on the water, and—this sounds crazy, crazy!—an owl flew down and sat on the end of the boat.

It was like a sign that I had to go home. Someone was waiting for me. And here you are. God, here you are! What's going on, Rebecca? Tell me how I can help you."

I bent down to that little Easter basket and lifted you up and cradled you against my breast. "Meet Shelby," I said.

Tom stared into your eyes, and you stared into his. Just like him and me, it was love at first sight for the two of you. He didn't ask why I'd brought you there. He didn't ask if you were his. He beamed at you with a sweetness I didn't think was possible in this cruel world. He reached out in that moment and took you from me and pressed your cheek against his soft brown beard.

"*Shelby*," he murmured, with a kind of reverence in his voice.

And I knew. There was still so much to explain, so much to tell him, so much I had to ask, so many questions and answers. We had hours ahead of us to talk, but I knew right then and there when I saw you in his arms.

Everything was going to be all right.

*

So you see, Shelby, by the time Darrell found me at the trailer, I was already at peace. I'd made peace with my past, with my crimes, with my choices. You had a father who would love you and care for you, and no matter where *I* was, I would know that you were safe with him.

That's why I was able to tell the terrible lie I did.

Because I had to lie. We both did. Tom and I made a sacred vow between us, a promise sealed with a kiss and blessed by God, an oath to keep you safe. It was also a crime. He knew what I'd done, because I told him. I confessed, holding nothing back. By letting me go, he was risking his career and his future. If anyone found out about us, he would have been ruined. They would have put him in prison like me. They would have taken you away, too, and everything we'd planned would have been lost.

So he lied. He had to erase me from your story. There was no Rebecca Colder, no night of love in a blizzard last January. The woman who left the baby at his doorstep was a mystery. She put that sweet child there, thinking she'd left you at a church, and then she drove off into the night and disappeared. All that remained was the owl. The sign from God that brought Tom home to find you. The little girl who would become his daughter.

And I lied, too. I told the worst lie of all.

Rebecca, what did you do?

I lied to Darrell when he asked me that.

I lied again to Norm when he asked me the same question later that day. *Rebecca, what did you do?*

I lied to the judge when I pled guilty and accepted my punishment.

If I hadn't lied, they never would have stopped looking for you. Rumors would have spread across the state. Questions would have been asked. Sooner or later, they would have found Tom, and they would have found you.

You wouldn't have the wonderful life he gave you, Shelby.

So I had to lie.

Rebecca, what did you do?

I lied. No matter what it did to me to say those words, I lied.

I told them that I'd buried my little girl in the woods and that they would never, ever find her.

CHAPTER FORTY-ONE

And now you know the truth, Shelby. That's how your story began. The rest of it, everything that followed, belonged to you and Tom, not to me. Life passes so quickly, doesn't it? Yours did. Mine did, too.

I spent twenty years in prison for the murders of my ex-husband and my baby daughter. Don't feel bad for me about that. I did terrible things, and regardless of what had been done to me, I had no illusions that I should have escaped punishment. I also won't give you any illusions that it was anything but hard. For months, I did nothing but cry every day, drowning myself in self-pity. For months after that, I became angry and combative with the guards and the other prisoners, and none of that went well for me. And then more months—years—passed in a dreary endlessness of boredom and routines, every day exactly like every other to the point of numbing my brain into a kind of dead despair. The only things that would break up the routine were not the things you wanted. Fights. Bullies. Threats. Twice, there were riots. When that happens, you find yourself craving boredom again.

I spent most of my time alone, but people came to see me from Black Wolf County. They had to drive a couple of hours to get to the state facility where I was housed, but many of them made the trip. Sandra saw me almost every month in the early years, until she moved to the Florida Keys to live on a yacht. After the revelations about Brink, Kip, and Racer came out, the mine settled the lawsuit and paid her and the other women several million dollars. That's right. Millions. Sandra stuck it out in the cold for a while, but then she decided that she'd had enough of winters. I still get postcards from her. It looks nice down there.

Ben Malloy visited whenever he was home to see his mother. We talked a lot about the Ursulina. I never admitted to him what had happened when I was ten years old, but he remained convinced that I was one of the chosen few who'd seen the beast. I also think—I don't know, it was just a glint in his eyes—but I think he was the only person who genuinely suspected that *I* was the Ursulina. That I'd been the one to commit the murders. Not as a woman, mind you, but as the monster I became. He never said it out loud, but I think he would have loved to do a documentary about me.

Norm was my lawyer, so he came to see me, too. Not that there was really much law to be handled after I pled guilty. He reminded me regularly that we had attorney-client privilege between us and that I could tell him anything without fear that he would pass the information along. I knew what he was driving at. You see, Norm never believed that I had harmed you, Shelby. Not for one little minute. He was sure I'd figured out a way to set you free; he just didn't know how or who'd taken you in. He wanted to help, but I wasn't going to take that risk. After a while, he realized that I was determined to leave things the way they were.

Will accompanied Norm to the jail a few times, but just as I'd expected, Will left Black Wolf County after college and moved to New York. He only made occasional visits home after that. He became a lawyer like his father and signed on as counsel for a human rights organization. I was proud of him, and I've written to tell him that more than once.

There was only one person who didn't visit me, one man from my hometown that I really missed. Darrell never came. Not once. His daughters all did, and they apologized on his behalf, but I just don't think he was able to face me. I told you, Darrell saw life and people as black and white, evil and good. Somehow this girl who'd been like a daughter to him had proved to be both, and he simply couldn't deal with it.

Two years after I went inside, Darrell's wife passed away of cancer. I wrote him a long note of condolence, but he never replied.

And so it went for me.

Twenty years is a long time. You don't dare think about the end, because thinking about it only makes it seem farther away. Instead, you live each day, expecting nothing. Eventually, you give up obsessing about what you can't have and resign yourself to the few things you can have. I decided that I still had a life, even behind bars. I read hundreds of books. I taught myself Spanish. I got a four-year degree in English Literature and then a master's degree. And I wrote you letters, Shelby. Letter after letter, pouring out my thoughts, hopes, and dreams for you. I never mailed them, of course, but I wrote several times a week throughout those twenty years. If you'd like to see them, I still have them.

Tom wrote to me, too. He had to use a kind of code, of course, because there is no privacy for prisoners. He never mentioned your name; he simply told me about his daughter. It was like keeping you in my life. I was so grateful to him for that. He shared all your landmarks, all your special occasions. Every now and then, he dared to send a photo, too, and you grew up just the way I thought you would.

You looked just like me.

*

At the age of forty-seven, I rejoined the world and had to figure out how to live in it again.

The first thing I did was take a bus to Mittel County. You were twenty years old then, already working with Tom in the sheriff's office. I saw Tom in secret on that trip, and he pleaded with me, begged me, to introduce myself to you, but I didn't think it was safe. There were too many ways for my presence to open up Pandora's box, even after twenty years, and I wasn't going to risk upending the life you had. Or his.

But I can remember sitting in a booth at a restaurant called the Nowhere Café, across the street from City Hall. You were in another booth with Tom, whose hair had gone prematurely silver, making him look even more handsome and distinguished, if that was possible. Yes, seeing him made me fall in love with him all over again, and I flatter myself that he still had feelings for me, too. He'd never married. His whole life, he told me, was you—and obviously, the feeling was mutual. I could see that in how the two of you looked at each other. You idolized him, Shelby. You would have done anything for him. That was as it should be.

Being free again, I had decisions to make. Tom said I should move to Mittel County and adopt a false name if necessary. He even hinted at the idea of our being together. I thought about it. Oh, yes, I thought about it. But there are some realities in life. I wouldn't have been able to be so close to both of you day after day and still keep my secret. Sooner or later, it would have come out. I told myself that I was protecting the two of you, but I guess the truth is, I was also protecting myself.

I was scared, Shelby.

Scared of you. Scared of what you'd say to me, how you'd feel about me, if you knew who I was. I've said I would understand if you hated me, and I mean that. But I couldn't bear to actually hear those words from your mouth. It was easier to keep you as a sweet little dream and not have to deal with the ugly reality of making amends for my past.

But I couldn't move far away, either. I couldn't simply leave you behind. So I moved to the little resort town of Martin's Point on the far side of the county, and I got a job at an ice cream shop. My claim to fame was suggesting a flavor called Ursulina Poop—chocolate-hazelnut ice cream swirled with fudge and studded with nuts and malted milk balls—which became their biggest seller. It was part-time seasonal work, but I still had some money in the bank, enough to live a frugal life in a little apartment. I was an independent soul growing up, and I still am. I didn't really need people, and after years behind bars, I found it hard to be around others for any length of time. I spent my days quietly. I had the library, and I had the national forest.

Yes, I still hiked whenever I could.

I still listened.

But in all these years, I've never heard it again. *Huffffff.*

Every now and then, I found an update about you, a bit of news to make my heart sing. I saw you in the newspaper from time to time. A couple of times, you even came into the ice cream shop, but I deliberately stayed in the back and didn't talk to you. You had your life, Shelby, and you didn't need me in it. I simply watched you quietly and enjoyed what I saw. You looked beautiful and strong. A little lonely like me, maybe, but no one has a perfect life. Still, you looked happy.

That was all I needed to know.

*

It was fifteen years later when I saw the news about you becoming sheriff of Mittel County. I couldn't have been prouder. But not even another year after that, my heart broke when I read in the paper that Tom had passed away. I remembered his fears from years earlier that he would suffer early dementia, the way his parents had, and tragically, those fears were realized. He was only sixty-six, just four years older than I was. I'd lost the love of my life.

I couldn't stay away from his funeral. I had to be there. I drove to the little church on that Saturday afternoon, but I had to struggle to find a seat, because the church was packed with mourners and friends. People came from miles away. Everyone knew Tom. Everyone loved and respected him. And they felt that way about you, too, Shelby. I could see that. There were so many tears, so many people who stood up and talked about what Tom had done for them, what Tom had meant to them.

The eulogy you gave him made me sob, Shelby. You talked about him finding you on his doorstep. You talked about the life he'd given you. You cried, smiled, laughed, and joked. You stood up there with my dark hair and my dark eyes, and you got through that awful day in a way that would have made Tom proud. You were just what I'd always wanted you to be. Fearless.

I wished I had the courage myself to go up to you and tell you my story. To tell you *our* story. To explain, to help you understand, to answer the questions you had. I already knew what I would say when it came to that, when we were finally together, because I'd had those first words in my head for years.

I know you'll never forgive me for what I did.

But it was too late for ancient history.

So I waited until the very end, until everyone else was gone, and then I had to go to the front of the church and look at that wonderful man in his coffin, with his silver hair and a face that had a sweetness and grace even in death. I put a finger on my lips, and then I put that finger on his lips, and I whispered through my tears, "Thank you, Tom."

And when I turned to go, there you were in front of me. Shelby. My little baby, now thirty-five years old. The sheriff of this county in your crisp, pressed uniform. Courageous, lovely, even when you were heartsick with grief. You'd just lost your father, and I was the woman who'd given you away.

"Hello," you said to me.

It was the first time my daughter had ever spoken to me, and I had to choke out my own reply. "Hello."

"I'm Shelby. Tom's child."

"Yes, I know."

"Have we met before? You look familiar to me."

"No, I'm sure we haven't. My name's Rebecca. Rebecca Colder."

"How did you know my father?"

I tried to figure out what to say. How do you say anything, when your heart is so full and so broken at the same time?

"A long time ago, he saved my life," I said.

"How did he do that?"

I wanted to tell you the truth, Shelby, because the truth was simple. *By saving you.* But nothing about my life was simple.

"I was in trouble a long time ago, and he got me out of it," I said.

"I'm glad."

"He was a wonderful man."

"Yes, he was." Then you added, "I was very lucky to have him."

"I'm sure he felt the same way about you," I said, wishing I could reach out and take your hand. Hug you. Put my hands on your cheeks. Tell you about that day in the snow with Tom and the little Easter basket and the hundreds of letters to you that are still in a box under my bed.

"I'm so sorry for your loss," I went on.

"Thank you."

That really should have been all. That should have been the end. I wasn't about to ask you or God for anything more. I'd already been blessed far more than I deserved in life. So I took a last glance at Tom's peaceful face, I smiled into my daughter's lovely dark eyes, and I walked away down the aisle of the church to live the rest of my life alone.

That was when you called after me, Shelby.

It was just the two of us in the church, and you called after me with a strange, hopeful certainty in your voice. I heard you walking down the aisle behind me, your steps getting faster as if you didn't want me to leave. Then you said the one word I'd wanted to hear from your lips since I first held you in my arms.

"Mom?"